GOD'S END

BLIZZARD OF SOULS

MICHAEL MCBRIDE

snowbooks

Proudly Published by Snowbooks in 2008

Copyright © 2008 Michael McBride

Snowbooks Ltd.
120 Pentonville Road
London
N1 9JN
Tel: 0207 837 6482
Fax: 0207 837 6348
email: info@snowbooks.com
www.snowbooks.com

British Library Cataloguing in Publication Data
A catalogue record for this book is available from the British Library.

ISBN 13 978-1-905005-76-5

Printed and bound by J. H. Haynes & Co. Ltd., Sparkford

For my Mom

BOOK TWO:

BLIZZARD OF SOULS

"And pray ye that your flight be not in winter."

"For in those days shall be affliction,
such as was not from thae beginning of the creation
which God created unto this time, neither shall be."

"And except that the Lord had shortened those days,
no flesh should be saved: but for the elect's sake,
whom He hath chosen, He hath shortened the days."

"And then if any man shall say to you, Lo, here is Christ;
or, lo, he is there; believe him not:"

"For false Christs and false prophets shall rise,
and shall shew signs and wonders, to seduce,
if it were possible, even the elect."

"But take ye heed: behold, I have foretold you all things."

"But in those days, after that tribulation,
the sun shall be darkened,
and the moon shall not give her light,"

"And the stars of heaven shall fall,
and the powers that are in heaven shall be shaken."

— Mark 13: 18–25

CHAPTER 1

I

MORMON TEARS

Phoenix stood on the white sand, staring out across the Great Salt Lake, Mormon Tears, as the sun rose somewhere behind the black clouds. Though it appeared as only a muted stain of gray against the distant horizon, he could feel its radiating warmth on his face. Closing his eyes, he reveled in the sensation, its gentle caress on the soft skin of his eyelids chasing away the bitter cold that sliced into him like hooks of ice. He sighed and the wind stole the cloud of exhaust from his lips, carrying it back over his shoulder. Deep inside he could feel a sense of contentment, of peace, for the first time in his entire life. The theater of the sky stretched infinitely in all directions, though a lone spotlight of sunshine permeated the ceaseless nuclear stormheads to shine upon him on his stage of sand, the foamy ivory brine lapping at his chafed, red toes. He knew he needed to enjoy moments like these, for they would be fleeting. The dark power was building beyond where the sky met with the seemingly eternal black water and the spotted islands of smooth stone rising from it. Even from such a great distance, he could feel the enemy's swelling ranks gathering their awesome strength for the battle to come. His adversary's evil power emanated across the hundreds of miles like an earthquake, issuing aftershocks of impending bloodshed that caused the earth itself to shiver.

In his mind, the ebony waters continued rolling toward the shore, the waves bringing with them a thickening slush of ice. Lightning crashed from roiling thunderclouds, an ultraviolet blue against their black hearts, turning the waves crashing into the beach to a deep crimson.

They were coming.

The time had come to begin preparations.

"It's beautiful, isn't it?" Missy said from behind him, causing him to open his eyes.

Phoenix turned to face her, a smile forming on his lips as it always did when he saw her. After living so long in the darkness, unable to see her face even in his mind, he tried to commit every expression to memory, the sound of her voice more comforting even than the beat of his own heart.

"Yeah," Phoenix whispered, though he'd already forgotten all about the lake behind him.

Missy blushed, but didn't appear self-conscious in the least. She had a quiet confidence about her that belied a hidden strength she had only begun to tap. He worried that she didn't see him as he saw her, but it didn't matter. The only thing that was truly important was being close to her.

She walked past him to the edge of the water and imagined the sunrise.

"We aren't safe here, are we?" she asked without turning to face him. She didn't have to try to read his expression as she knew that he would tell her the truth.

"We're safer here than anywhere else."

"That wasn't my question."

"No," he whispered. "They will find us here."

"What are we supposed to do then? Where can we possibly go?"

"They'll find us wherever we go. This is where we are supposed to be. This is where we will make our stand."

"And will we win?"

Phoenix remained silent.

"That's what I thought," she said, turning back to him with a wan smile.

"I didn't say we wouldn't."

"You didn't say anything at all."

"The truth is that I just don't know."

"How much time do we have?"

"I'm not sure. All I know is that the time is at hand to ready ourselves for war."

"Against whom? Those black lizard men?"

"Against God," he whispered.

A shiver crept up her spine, erupting as goosebumps from the backs of her arms.

"Come on," she said, forging a weak grin and trying to force the implications of his words from her mind. "The others are making breakfast. I'm sure we could both use something to eat."

Phoenix matched her smile and turned his back to the inland sea. More people had arrived during the night, their vehicles parked at odd angles all across the beach, the sounds of life only now beginning to filter out of the system of caves in the stone hillside. There was an old pickup with a camper shell in the bed off to the left, shades drawn tightly over the windows. A ring of motorized dirt bikes surrounded a canvas tent, the tarp covering it flapping on the breeze. Mountain bikes and ten-speeds leaned against the rock fortress, which they had only begun to explore. There were a half dozen cars parked off to the side as a windbreak, all of them older models from a dirty white Ford truck with California plates to an ancient Buick now more rust than metal. Nothing with integrated computer components survived the blackout trailing on the heels of the atomic wind. Phoenix had heard someone speculate in the darkness about an electromagnetic pulse created by the nuclear detonations, but that meant nothing to him.

The mutated equines that he and his friends had ridden in upon appeared as comfortable in the water as they did in the air, their crested seahorse heads rising from the lake behind him as they splashed toward the shore from wherever they had gone during the night, summoned by the aroma following the thick black smoke out of the mouth of the widest cave. Phoenix didn't recognize the scent, but his mouth was already beginning to water.

"What is that?" he asked, his voice dripping with wonder.

"Baked beans," she said with a chuckle.

"They smell wonderful."

"Are you telling me you've never had baked beans?"

He grinned, his eyes alight. There was something charming about his naïveté.

Faces he only vaguely recognized from during the night began to emerge from where they'd bedded down at a comfortable distance from one another, drawn by the intoxicating scent. Soon they would have to reach out to one another or they would be butchered like so many sheep.

They needed to steel themselves against the coming winter.

II

THE RUINS OF DENVER, COLORADO

Death leaned back into his throne of bones, built from the remains of those migrating westward and unable to find suitable shelter before the Swarm overcame them. Their skins were stretched from ceiling to floor, stitched together to form a tent-like partition in the middle of the top floor of that leaning black tower. Everything else had been shoveled out the shattered windows to create the feeling of isolation that he demanded. The only light inside his chamber was produced by the illumination from his golden eyes, though he would still have been easily able to see without. Even in complete darkness, he could clearly discern the outline of every long bone forming the structure of his throne and the flayed skin stretched between. Broken ribs and the crushed skulls created a small mound beneath to raise him above his subjects.

Closing his eyes, he focused his concentration, the ragged dewlap of crimson scales stretching beneath his chin like a cape, shivering. In a heartbeat, he was seeing through the eyes of Famine, their collective consciousness allowing him unflinching access to their minds. He was crouched atop the roof, poised at the edge like a gargoyle. The white horseman, his polished opal skin reflecting the blue lightning tearing the sky, stared thirty stories down to the charcoaled ground. Enormous vats of molten metal burned in a ring around the base of the building, billowing clouds of smoke and flame into the grumbling sky. The Swarm seethed beneath, their glowing eyes like so many fireflies. His gaze rose from the masses at the foot of the monolithic fortress to the horizon, where a flood of their minions still poured in from the eastern plains, following the trail of devastation. Torches blazed from the skulls staked to the line of poles leading to the skyline, burning the oily mess of fatty fuel sucked from the dead. Formerly placid fields of wild grasses were now rife with briars and brambles, covered with thorns sharp enough to carve through a buffalo's hide.

Famine opened his mouth in a soundless scream, releasing a flume of locusts that expanded into a whirlwind, swirling around the massive tower of darkness before funneling through the open windows and into the bowels of the construct.

With a flick of clear eyelids over his reptilian irises, Death was transported into another section of the fortress, somewhere in the bleak shadows beneath his feet. The sounds of screams pierced his ears, an exquisite choir of agony. Pestilence used her fingertips like scalpels, opening the bodies of the damned to grant access to the legions of mosquitoes crawling out of every orifice of her mummified form, her parchment skin ripping away to birth the large insects. Death watched through her lifeless eyes as the mosquitoes squirmed around in the open wounds of the bodies nailed to the conference tables in front of her. Men and women alike cried out in their divine pain, raging against the spikes pounded through their wrists and ankles to secure them to the wood. Their abdominal contents shifted sickeningly beneath the shimmering skein of the peritoneum that contained them like a layer of plastic wrap, beneath which the mosquito larvae could be seen wriggling through the blood and tissue.

The ceiling of the subterranean room slanted under the weight of the canting building, the residual radiation still emanating from ground zero filling the claustrophobic air with the smell of burning hair and skin. Torches flickered from the walls where they burned a seemingly exhaustless supply of human grease, highlighting a medieval torture chamber crossed with a modern day conference room. The juxtaposition lent a surreal feel to the intense suffering as though the pain stretched through even the barrier of the ages. With a roar of wings and a buzzing that vibrated the floor beneath Pestilence's dainty feet, the cloud of locusts filled the room, descending upon the bodies nailed to the tables, crawling all over them. They burrowed into the lacerations inflicted by the former surgeon's touch, fertilizing the larvae with mutagenic DNA in their tobacco-spit spew, before scurrying back out from the flesh and buzzing contentedly back toward the roof, leaving in their wake an absolute silence bereft of the screams of the now recently deceased.

Pestilence observed with clinical detachment as the miniature mosquitoes metamorphosed into elongated flagellates like wingless dragonflies and lanced into the various organs. Even God, it seemed, could not always predict the outcome of His experiments. The crossing of the insects' chromosomes, wound into helices in the burbling cauldron of creation itself, created an encephalitic swelling in the human spinal column that produced the reptilian armada of the Swarm. She needed to discover what other mutations could be caused by attacking other areas of the anatomy. Would alterations to the pituitary gland produce dramatic changes in growth patterns? Would parathyroid interactions significantly alter bone density? What other modifications could be made to produce creatures of limitless potential?

Death smiled twin rows of razors as the changes began to manifest in those formerly dead bodies, savoring the surprising physical mutations arising from Pestilence's Mengele-inspired experiments.

His consciousness shifted slightly and his vision was narrowed by the ragged tears in the mask over War's eyes. He sat high atop his monstrous steed Thunder, surrounded by rubble. A traffic light leaned away from the corner over which it had once lorded, half-buried beneath a wall fallen from the façade of what had once been an ornate church. The scorched outlines of the people who'd been vaporized near the epicenter scarred the few structures that remained upright, spectral visions of their last terror-filled moments the only testimony to their existence as their ashes had long since blown away. Now all that remained was the Swarm, their reptilian bodies crammed shoulder to shoulder in the intersection, phosphorescent eyes glowing like crackling embers from burning logs. The air was alive with hissing, tatters of scales flaring from beneath wide chins resplendent with the rich colors of autumn leaves as they scuffled to establish their hierarchy. The weakest of the species lined the sidewalks, their bones picked clean by the more ferocious.

War raised his right fist, sharp spikes standing from his knuckles, and all movement as far as he could see ceased abruptly. The hissing dwindled to silence. Surveying the throng of his minions, all eyes focused upon him, he finally lowered his arm and gave a single nod. His gaze turned to the enormous smelting pots suspended over the massive bonfires encircling the fortress. Deep black smoke gushed from the burbling fluid like volcanic lava, firing spatters of molten metal above the rim.

The crowd came to life around him, scrabbling up the fallen telephone poles and girders and plunging into the fiery metal. Hissing escalated to a deafening reptilian scream as bodies floundered in the scalding magma, rolling nearly unconsciously over the lip and falling twenty feet to the ground. Barely alive, they crawled away from the fire before another could fall down atop them, the metal taking on the appearance of liquid silver on their sleek scales. The coating hardened as it cooled, forming a thin armor that cracked away from the joints when they moved. The screaming reached a crescendo of pain, growing louder still until it found Death's ears in his chamber at the top of the skyscraper. He allowed his vision to drift back up from the metallic bodies littering the street until he again saw through his own eyes. Their preparations would soon be complete and they would begin their march to the west where they would wipe out the survivors he could feel gathering on the western bank of the Great Salt Lake.

III

MORMON TEARS

Adam scraped the last bite of the brown sugar-sweetened beans from his paper plate, licking off the remaining sauce, and cast it into the bonfire. The warmth of the food in his belly made him feel a million times better. He couldn't remember the last time he had eaten something that had actually been cooked. It had been before the refugee camp had been obliterated by the tank. Before wading through the endless sulfur waters in the Ali Sadr caves and the trans-Atlantic flight. Before crossing nearly the entire United States in a helicopter and on the back of a winged stallion. So much had transpired since the last time he had actually sat down with a real meal. He chuckled at the thought of what he might have said had someone told him during his last dinner that the next time he would sit before a warm plate of food would be in a smoke-riddled cave at the edge of the Great Salt Lake in Utah after the world had ended. For the life of him, he couldn't remember what his last dinner had been. He rose and stretched, his back cracking as he reached toward the roof only a couple feet over his head. The movement drew the attention of everyone else sitting in there, finishing their beans with their backs to the stone walls, but they quickly averted their eyes. Despair was a palpable aura between them, the fear and the unknown leading most everyone to turn inward, becoming silent observers in their own flesh as they waited... But for what? For someone to assume command and lead them?

Adam looked to Peckham, the ranking officer between the three of them who had been soldiers overseas before the war had escalated beyond the point of no return, but Peck just sat there with half a plate of beans cooling in his lap, staring vacuously into space. Norman's empty plate had fallen from his lap when he tipped to the side against the rocks, overcome by exhaustion. Adam knew that he should join the medic in rest, for Lord only knew when the last time he had allowed his body to recuperate had been, but he felt that there was something he needed to do first. It was an irrepressible need, a tingling sensation in his gut, but he hadn't the slightest clue what he needed to do any more than he knew where to begin.

There were about ten of them sitting in the smooth mouth of the cave now. None had ventured away from the fire and deeper into the earthen orifice leading off into the darkness, but judging by the sounds of dripping in the distance, it led at least a hundred feet back into the stone mountain. After his experience in Iran, the last thing he wanted was to be below ground for any length of time. Eventually he suspected he would have to, but he wanted to postpone that decision as long as possible.

He was just about to sit back down to tuck his chin to his chest and close his eyes when Phoenix materialized through the smoke from the fire against the gray world without.

Someone coughed in the corner, a dry barking sound that almost sounded like croup. Until that moment Adam hadn't even considered the daunting prospect of potentially having to treat all of these people medically. They had no supplies and the nearest antibiotics were surely locked in the back of a pharmacy fifty miles away in town on the other side of the lake. It was as though overnight they'd been hurled a hundred years back through time.

"You should see it out there, Adam," Phoenix said. "The lake. The beach. Everything. It's the most beautiful thing I've ever seen."

Adam smiled at the boy's unbridled wonder. Phoenix had said that he was eighteen years-old, but he still had the wide-eyed awe of a child.

"You up for taking a walk with me?" Adam asked.

Phoenix turned and looked at Missy.

"I'll bring a plate out to you," she said, stifling a giggle.

"Okay then," he said, walking back out through the smoke.

Adam caught up with him on the soft sand, throwing his arm around Phoenix's shoulder to guide him to the north and away from the others so they could have a measure of privacy.

"I believe I owe you my thanks, Phoenix."

"For what?" Phoenix watched the sand sluice between his toes. They were as red as lobsters from the cold, but he wouldn't have traded the sensation for anything in the world. Just feeling anything at all was a special experience.

"For saving us."

"You saved me, remember?"

"We helped get you out of a house. You brought us a thousand miles to safety."

"I guess we're even then," Phoenix said with a shrug.

"Not even close," Adam said, clapping him on the shoulder. He shoved his hands deep into the pockets of his weathered fatigues and looked at Phoenix. The boy's skin was pasty white, his long hair such a light shade of blonde it was almost ivory. With the pink highlights in his irises, he looked like an albino, but there was something else in those wide eyes. A light. Not just a twinkle, but a resonant glow that drew Adam magnetically to him. He had scarcely known this boy for more than a day, but already he knew that he would lay down his life without a second thought for this gawky boy.

The thought absolutely terrified him.

"How did you know to bring us here?" Adam asked, chasing the last irrational thought from his mind.

"Because this is Mormon Tears," Phoenix said, giving Adam a strange look as though it was the most obvious question he had ever heard.

Adam laughed. "I suppose it is. I guess what I was fishing for was how did you know it was here? How were you able to find it?"

"Oh," Phoenix said, blushing. "I saw it in my dreams. Well, I guess I didn't actually see it, but I knew it was here. It was more like a feeling, like how you know someone's there in the dark with you even if you can't see them. I guess once we were flying, I just kind of let the horses lead the way. I figured we'd arrive here eventually."

"So what now?"

"What do you mean?"

"Where do we go from here?"

"Nowhere. This is our home now."

Adam stopped and stared at him. Phoenix took another couple of steps before he realized the older man wasn't beside him and turned around.

"We can't stay here," Adam said. "I bought into the mysticism, the whole idea of meeting everyone here in the middle of nowhere because, truthfully, I didn't have any better ideas, but staying here is a fool's proposition. We aren't equipped to survive the winter outdoors."

"There will still be others arriving—"

"And we can leave them a map, but think about this logically. We should find a town and move inside. Houses. Apartments. Anything. Get out of the elements. We need to take advantage of the power while it lasts, and even without electricity we would have a much easier time heating smaller enclosures versus the great outdoors. Then we could figure out how to run the generators. Heck, for all we know there could be entire small communities out there in the desert powered by the wind or the sun—"

"If we leave here we will die."

Adam opened his mouth to argue, but held his tongue.

"What aren't you telling me?" he finally asked.

Phoenix looked away.

"They will be coming," he whispered.

"Who?"

"The Swarm. God's army."

"How do you know?"

"Can't you feel it?" Phoenix snapped, whirling to face him. "Can't you feel their power growing? It won't be long until they're strong enough to move against us."

"The creatures from your house?"

"Thousands of them," he whispered. A haze clouded over his eyes like milky cataracts.

Adam staggered backwards, unable to so much as blink.

"Listen carefully, Adam, chosen son of man. You must lead them. Their lives are in your hands. I have given you one last chance for redemption. You must ready yourselves for the storm, and you are already running out of time. Death's armada will descend beneath the Blizzard of Souls, and either you will triumph or all is lost."

"Phoenix?" Adam whispered. He walked up to the boy, whose entire body was stiff, as though conducting a current, the tendons in his neck standing out like cords. Adam tilted up Phoenix's chin with trembling hands, his heart pounding so hard he could barely breathe.

The swirling mist disappeared in Phoenix's eyes, leaving only that uncomfortable red stare.

"All right!" Phoenix said, brushing Adam aside. "Baked beans!"

"Phoenix!" Adam called after him, but the boy was already running down the beach to where Missy was walking toward them with a steaming plate in her hands.

"What the hell was that?" Adam said aloud, his eyes falling to the ground. The sand where Phoenix had been standing was now fused to glass.

IV

THE GATEWAY

Richard Robinson walked at the front of the pack, his tie around his head to keep the sweat and the remainder of the hair gel from running into his eyes. Fists in his armpits, he crossed his arms over his chest to contain as much of his body heat as he could. The lapels of his suit jacket were turned up to shield his neck from the rising wind that raced across the deserted highway, tearing his pluming breath sideways. The scruff on his cheeks was beginning to gray to either side of his chin in contrast to the otherwise rich black of the hair he normally kept slicked back. Lightning bolt vessels struck through the whites toward his startlingly blue eyes, the trademark that had launched his career in politics. His Italian loafers were scuffed to hell and there was precious little left of the soles, but if the sign in front of him was right, there wasn't too much farther to go.

"Mormon Tears," he said, reading the words spray-painted onto the twin rock formations that faced each other like praying children on their knees. The gravel shoulder was marred by the tire tracks turning from the road and passing through the stone arch. Twin lines stretched off across the white desert to the horizon.

He turned back to the others, the worst of the stragglers more than a half mile back down the road. She did nothing but whine about her sore feet anyway. If she didn't want to walk, there were always other options. Back in his great-grandfather's day, if a cow couldn't keep up with the herd on a cattle drive, they didn't slow their pace to wait for it. They put it down, plain and simple. That was the way of the world. Lead, keep up, or be left behind. What had they become as a people if they were willing to compromise the advancement of the group to coddle the weakest link? It was the welfare debates all over again…

"Hurry up!" Richard called back. There were seven of them in total, and so far as he knew the only ones to survive the massacre at the airport in Las Vegas. His plane had been en route to LAX when the first major wave of turbulent air hammered them from the nuclear detonation in the Middle East, forcing them to descend through an ungodly cloud of locusts to land at McCarran International Airport. When news of the first atomic cataclysm had reached Washington D.C., every legislator had already been booked on a flight back home. There was no way that any of them were going to wait around to see if the terrorists were going to strike the Capitol. Granted, the senators and cabinet members somehow ended up with chartered flights or air removal by chopper, but there was no such special treatment for congressmen. No, they had to take the first available commercial jet. It was just another unpleasant reminder of how many more rungs of the ladder he had yet to climb. Come November two years from now he would have been a senator. From there it would have only been a matter of biding his time until he could make the transition into the White House, but now…

He couldn't occupy his mind with what might have been. Those thoughts only opened the doors to the memories of the airport. He'd been furious when the captain announced that they were going to have to prepare for an emergency landing in Nevada. Didn't they know he was going to Los Angeles? He was an elected official for God's sake! And that condescending flight attendant… She didn't care who or what he was, he just needed to buckle his seatbelt with the rest of the cattle and land hundreds of miles from home. The sight of that black reptilian thing squeezing through the shattered window to rip out her throat was one of the few positives from the entire experience. After that, everything became a blur. Shooting down the inflatable slide onto a tarmac littered with bloated back corpses, amidst the clutter of clothes blowing from overturned piles of baggage. Cutting loose the luggage carts from the train led by a small white vehicle. Clinging to the back of it while one of the other passengers drove, trying to outrun the mob of creatures, listening to the screams of the slaughtered fading behind them. Driving down the long series of runways toward the desert while the first of the flames that would consume the airport rose behind them.

They'd come across the whiny woman first, sitting in the middle of the desert a half mile past the gate in the barbed wire-capped chain link fence surrounding the runways, screaming and sobbing as she pried cactus needles from her bloody feet. Apparently she'd shed her sandals on an incoming flight from Cancun and run as far and as fast as she could until she was overcome by the pain, trying not to think about her traveling companions who'd been butchered before her very eyes. Outside of Garrett, the personal trainer with whom he'd escaped Flight 721 from Dulles, she was the first living soul he'd encountered in hours, otherwise they probably would have just continued driving. But she was young and blonde with freshly tanned legs. A shivering damsel in distress, dressed for summer in the winter. And if they eventually needed to repopulate the world, she at least looked like she might be able to provide a little fun in the process.

Garrett was stocky and heavily muscled, reminding Richard more of an elementary school physical education teacher than any pretty-boy personal trainer he'd ever seen. He'd been the starting left tackle for some small college or other. Richard imagined he hadn't paid that much attention to the events that transpired between Saturdays, especially the classes, but in any sort of physical confrontation, Richard knew better than to underestimate the man's worth.

They had eventually come across an old van at a gas station with the keys still hanging from the ignition, the owner's swollen body face down on the concrete beside the open driver's side door. Fortunately, the corpse had just finished filling the tank, and so long as they stayed away from The Strip, there was space to maneuver through the stalled traffic. Once outside of town and into the desert, they'd been able to move much faster and had eventually encountered more survivors. To Richard, the others were nameless, faceless hitchhikers, whose presence was simply to be tolerated. There was the young mother, somewhere in her mid-twenties, but as plain and nondescript as wheat toast. At least that shaggy-haired little boy of hers didn't cry nearly as much as that wench with her bloody feet who even now was slowing them all down. The child was somewhere between six and ten years old, Richard surmised, but the last time he had spent any significant time with kids, he had been one himself. There was another man in a leather jacket that looked pretty warm and comfortable, and the woman with whom he'd been traveling, but they had only run into them a couple hundred miles ago. They'd run the tank dry in the van, allowing it to coast to a halt in the middle of the desert highway. They had sat there for several hours, not daring to open the doors until the sun rose over the desert. Even though the heat during the day was nearly unbearable, the chill that descended upon them during the night threatened their very survival. Leather jacket and the dark-haired woman had passed on their motorcycle sometime just before dawn. Garrett had been able to flag them down and Richard had convinced them to siphon the remainder of the gas in the bike into the van for the greater good in hopes that they would all be able to make it to the next gas station. Obviously, they hadn't, but they'd only been on foot for a couple of hours now. Two long, excruciating hours of listening to that woman shrieking about her damned feet…

"This the place?" Garrett asked, sidling up to Richard. With the faded olive jacket and days' worth of stubble, he looked like the stereotypical panhandler Richard was accustomed to seeing through the windows of his limousine at stoplights.

"Looks like it," Richard said, gesturing to the enormous letters painted on to the rocks without even attempting to mask his sarcasm.

"Are you guys sure this is where we're supposed to go?" Leather Jacket asked.

"Yes," the young mother said, looking to her child.

"This is the place I dreamed about," he whispered.

"The place you dreamed about?" Richard sneered. "Then this just absolutely has to be the place, doesn't it?"

"Leave him alone," the woman with Leather Jacket said.

The boy's mother pulled him behind her, but couldn't bring herself to look Richard in the eyes. There was something physically intimidating about him, and if there was one trait she had been conditioned to recognize after choosing the wrong man over and over, it was the subtle glimmer in his eyes that signified that he was accustomed to getting his way, whether by wit or by force.

"Wait for me!" the blonde hollered from fifty yards down the highway. "Oh please, God! Wait for me!"

Garrett turned and lumbered back down the asphalt toward her, allowing her to throw her arm over his thick neck so he could bear the majority of her weight.

"Give me a break," Richard groaned, striking off through the gateway and into the desert.

He heard the hesitant footsteps on the gravel behind him cross from the shoulder onto the sand. Without turning around, he allowed a smile to creep across his lips.

"Cattle," he whispered, picking up his pace and knowing full well that they would do the same.

V

MORMON TEARS

An endless sheet of ice stretched before her, hidden beneath several feet of snow. The wind rose with a howl, blowing the enormous flakes falling from the sky sideways, raising clouds of powder from the ground. At the furthest reaches of Jill's vision, she could see the hint of the flames burning on the distant island, a faint aura of light winking menacingly at her through the blizzard. She could smell the smoke even from so far away, knowing that it wasn't just the scent of burning wood, but of cooking flesh and boiling blood cracking through charcoaled bone. It was the surreal stench of hope's last rites.

Jill turned around and faced the sheer wall of stone behind her, now stained black by the smoke rising up from the caves. A dike of snow stood between her and their cavernous lair, long sharpened spears poking from the packed mound like a porcupine's quills. It extended as far as she could see in either direction, following the course of the bank before extending out onto the lake to encompass stretches of open black water warmed by the pyres burning so far under the beach that only the tips of the flames chased the gray smoke into the air.

Thin white clouds of breath floated from behind the snow embankment where she knew the others were hiding, waiting for their opportunity, but praying it would never come. Their fear was palpable, even though she couldn't see them.

She spun at the sound of a high-pitched hiss like steam from an industrial vat. A tide of blackness appeared across the lake, rolling toward where she stood on the frozen shore. Screams pierced the night all around her and she added her voice to the hysterical cries—

"Jesus! Is she okay?" a voice she didn't recognize said. Jill's eyelids snapped open to reveal a guy about her age, looking down at her through wide blue eyes. The bridge of his nose bent slightly to the left, knobbed as though it had been broken fairly recently. She knew she'd never seen him before, but everything about him was familiar, right down to his short dark hair.

It wasn't until that moment that she realized she was screaming.

"Are you all right?" he asked, and looked to her right. "What's her name?"

"Jill," April said, taking Jill by the shoulder and leaning right into her face. Jill recoiled at the scent of April's morning breath.

"Talk to me, Jill," the guy said. "Are you okay?"

She couldn't tear her stare from his face. It wasn't as though it merely looked familiar. It was as though she already knew him intimately. Details slowly came into focus around his face. An enormous fire burned behind him, the smoke channeling out through the open cave mouth. April was huddled against her, the blanket they shared stretched to its limits to cover Darren on the other side of April. Both looked terrified as they watched her, unable to blink.

"Was it another dream?" April asked.

Oh God, please don't let it be another dream.

I can't handle this. Make it stop!

I hope she's all right.

What the hell's wrong with that girl?

The voices swirled around in her head, fighting for dominance, chasing out her every conscious thought. None of their lips moved, yet she could still hear them, their voices assaulting her from all sides. She wanted to clap her hands over her ears to make the ruckus stop, but she couldn't, she couldn't, she could—

She's beautiful…

The torrent of words stopped and her mind cleared, leaving her focused on the boy's blue eyes.

"Thank you," she whispered.

He smiled. "Must have been a nasty nightmare. You were screaming to wake the dead." He cringed at his choice of words. "So you think you're going to be okay now?"

"Yeah," she said, blushing. "I feel like a complete idiot."

"No worries," he said through a smirk that tipped up to the right. "Given the circumstances, I'd imagine you're entitled."

"Jill has dreams," April said.

"What a coincidence. So do I."

Jill smiled and he realized how close his face was to hers and withdrew, plopping onto his rear end in front of her. The firelight flooded his face, revealing a purplish-blue mash of bruises around his eyes.

"Oh, my gosh," Jill gasped.

"I get that reaction a lot."

"I mean, your eyes… What happened?"

"They look worse than they feel."

"Jill can see the future in her dreams," April interrupted. "She's the only reason that we're still alive."

"Interesting," he said, again with that almost cocky grin. "What am I going to do next?"

"I don't know," Jill said sheepishly.

"Good. Neither do I. That's half the fun of life." He extended his right hand across her covered lap. "I'm Mare."

"Like a female horse?" Jill asked. She winced at how stupid that must have sounded.

He chuckled. "Yeah…like a female horse."

"Sorry, I'm—"

"No wait! Let me guess… Jill, right?"

"You already knew that, silly. I was going to say that I'm usually not so dense."

"I knew that."

"What are you, psychic?"

"I've been known to see glimpses of the future."

"Oh, yeah? And what do you see?"

He finally released her hand. He'd been so wrapped up in her eyes and what she was saying that he hadn't noticed when the shake had stopped and he was just sitting there holding her hand.

"I see an amazing girl—"

"Come on, Jill," April said, tossing off the blanket and climbing to her feet. "Let's get something to eat."

"But I…" Jill started, but April already had her by the hand and was hauling her up.

"Excuse us, Mary—"

"It's Mare."

"—but we'd better get some of those beans before they're all gone."

"Absolutely," he said, rising and taking a step back. He gestured with his right arm to usher them past. "It's been a pleasure meeting you."

"Don't mind April," Jill whispered as she passed. "She's a bear in the mornings."

The guy with April passed between them, giving Mare a look that could have dropped a stag from twenty yards.

"Mare," he said, offering his hand to the other guy.

"Darren," the other guy said, shaking his hand a bit too hard.

The other guy who'd been leaning up against Darren on the ground didn't stand. He just rolled over onto his side in the newly vacated space, wrapped the blanket around his shoulders, and closed his eyes again. He looked awful. His face was pale and pocked with crusted blood like freckles.

Mare looked back at Jill, standing in the short line by where an older man in a fur-lined hunting jacket ladled out beans from a soot-stained aluminum bucket. There was definitely something special about her. Nothing he could clearly identify, but he was drawn to her like a moth to a flame.

His sister turned from the front of the line and headed outside with a steaming plate of beans. He'd already seen her wolf down a mounded plate earlier before disappearing outside with that weird albino kid. Following her through the smoke, he stood in the mouth of the cave and watched her walking down the beach toward that same boy. He was about to go after her when movement from the right drew his attention.

There was a channel in the steep stone face of the mountain of rock, carved smooth by eons of water flow as the Great Salt Lake retreated from the ocean. The walls to either side had to be a hundred feet tall, creating a bottleneck of smooth white sand, the only entrance to their haven. Several figures appeared, treading cautiously out onto the beach. The man in the lead wore a suit jacket with a red and blue tie around his head, while a larger man flanked him to the right in an army surplus jacket. A man in a leather jacket and a dark-haired woman trailed half a dozen paces behind.

A man and a woman emerged from the back door of the camper parked to his left, nervously eyeing the newcomers, the man doing a poor job of hiding the shotgun behind his back.

Mare headed toward the strangers, preparing to offer his hand and an introduction, but he was interrupted by pained wails from behind them. He sprinted past the new arrivals to where one woman helped another hobble across the sand, a young boy at their heels. Ducking under the injured woman's other arm, he helped guide them out into the open and urged them along the face of the mountain to the edge of the cloud of smoke funneling out of the cave.

"Let's get you off those feet," Mare said, helping the other woman lower her to the ground. Everything from her soles clear over the tops of her feet was covered with a coating of blood-induced mud, while there were still patches from which thin cactus needles stood, broken nearly to her skin from where someone had unsuccessfully tried to pry them out.

"Is she going to be all right?" the little boy asked, unable to look away from the bottoms of her feet where fresh blood eroded the mud.

"Of course she'll be okay," he said, only to be contradicted by the woman's scream. "We just need her to stay off of those feet for a while so they can start to heal."

"And maybe sew her lips shut," the man with the tie around his head mumbled as he followed his nose toward the beans, the man in the military-issue olive jacket a half pace behind his right hip.

Mare looked at the woman, but apparently she hadn't heard the man's remark over her sobbing. "What's your name?" he asked, trying to distract her from the pain.

"Lindsay," she said through bared teeth. "Lindsay Lechner."

"I can handle this from here," Adam said from behind him, patting Mare on the shoulder.

"Ah…our resident doctor. You're in good hands now, Miss Lechner." Mare turned to the boy. "You hungry?"

The boy nodded emphatically.

"How 'bout we get you and your mom something to eat?"

"That would be wonderful," the boy's mother said.

Mare walked around Adam, who was already pouring water from a canteen onto Lindsay's feet to assess the extent of her wounds.

"I'm Mare," he said, stooping and offering his hand to the child. "What's your name?"

"Jake."

"Nice to meet you, Jake," he said, shaking the boy's hand with mock formality.

"I'm Susan," the boy's mother said, offering her hand while trying to discretely pull her child behind her back with the other.

"And there's your sister," Jake said, pointing down the shoreline.

Mare turned at the sound of footsteps in the sand behind him to see Missy and Phoenix.

"How did you—?" Mare started, whirling back to face Jake, but he was already scampering off with his mother toward the fire.

VI

MORMON TEARS

Ray knew he wasn't sleeping, but he certainly wasn't awake either. He existed between where he could only focus alternately on the roaring flames in front of him and the insides of his eyelids in a realm where he only experienced pain. His body was numbed to it, whether from the intense cold to which he'd been exposed the night before or because his flesh was simply shutting down, he couldn't be sure. The unadulterated agony that speared him was so intensely emotional that he would have traded it for the most excruciating physical torture in a heartbeat. His entire world had been stripped away from him in a single day. First his mother had been killed in the atomic detonation of New York City, and then he had been forced to watch the love of his life be torn apart by reptilian shadows.

"Tina," he whispered, blood seeping from his weather-cracked lips, battling against the vision of her decapitated head bouncing off the wall beside him to alight in a puddle of her blood.

A bitter coldness radiated from the rock floor. Even with the hooded pullover and the blanket, he was helpless against it. Darren and the girls were gone—when had they left?—leaving him alone on the hard ground in a cave hundreds of miles from his home in Eugene and the only life he had ever known. He couldn't close his eyes for fear of seeing Tina being dragged back into the stall of that restaurant's bathroom, hear her terrified screams as she was butchered in front of him, nor could he stand to leave them open to see the looks on the dirty faces of the other survivors while they pretended not to see him, like he was some sort of leper. Studying him from the corners of their eyes, but looking away as soon as he caught their stares. He needed to get out of there, out of his own head. It felt as though the walls were closing in and all of the air was being sucked out. He couldn't breathe…couldn't…breathe…

Before he made a conscious decision to stand, he was on his feet, swaying against his equilibrium. He could feel the weight of all their eyes upon him, boring through his flesh and burrowing into his marrow. Staggering forward, a woman gasped at the sight of the blood gushing out of his nostrils, but he shouldered through her, nearly clobbering her young son. All he could focus on was the gray sky outside of that suffocating cavern, but as soon as he passed through the smoke, which smelled only faintly of brown sugar and smoked bacon, he nearly stumbled into a group of people. Eyes flashed in his direction. Mouths opened to expel a cacophonous roar of voices. He had to get away from them. From everyone. He almost threw himself to the ground in his hurry to retreat, storming through the smoke and back into the cave where he was only met by more staring eyes and incomprehensible words. Ray opened his mouth to scream—

A cold hand touched his and the world came back into focus. He lowered his stare to the tiny fingers holding his, following the slender arm to the shoulder and then into the face of the young boy. Ray's eyes locked onto the child's, a shade of blue richer than the deepest arctic ocean.

"You won't find what you're looking for out there," the boy said in a voice so small Ray could hardly hear it. "You have to look deep inside." The sound of that last word lingered long after the child closed his mouth and broke eye contact. Ray followed the boy's gaze until he saw where it was focused. There was a black maw in the wall, an earthen doorway leading deeper into the mountain and a darkness as thick as tar.

"She's waiting for you in there," the boy whispered, but by the time Ray whirled to face him again, the child stood at the front of the line while the old man with the furry ring around his hood heaped a generous portion of steaming beans onto his plate.

Ray wiped the blood from his lips and chin with the back of his hand and walked to the mouth of the stone monolith, dusty, cold breath drifting into his face. Staring into the pitch black, his legs moved of their own accord, guiding him away from the fire, only now a distant flickering memory on the granite walls to either side of the corridor.

Raising his arms in front of him, he pressed deeper and deeper into the ebony heart of the rock colossus. The sound of voices faded to nothingness, replaced by the occasional drip of condensation from the darkness above and the gentle echo of his scuffing feet. It grew warmer with each step, the air thickening with humidity.

"Ray," a voice whispered from all around him at once.

"Tina?" He turned in a circle, though he couldn't pry anything from the darkness. He stopped and held his breath so as not to obscure even the slightest sound.

Plip.

A warm breeze caressed his cheek and he smelled her sweet breath.

Ploop.

His heart thumped far too loudly in his ears, his staled breath fighting to escape.

"Ray," the voice whispered again, drawing out the word.

"Tina!" he shouted, sprinting ahead, not caring if he slammed into a stone wall or tripped and broke every bone in his body. He had to scream to be heard over the thunder of his footfalls ricocheting back at him in the close confines. "Tina!"

His left shoulder scraped the wall, tearing through his sweatshirt to abrade the skin beneath, channeling him to the right. Banging into the wall over and over, smearing his lifeblood onto the rock, the tunnel eventually straightened out and he was able to run unimpeded through the blackness again.

"Tina! Where are you?" he bellowed, only this time his words sounded hollow, the echo distant and repeating into oblivion.

Slowing, he doubled over and clasped his hands on his thighs, sucking for air.

"Please," he whimpered, falling to his knees. "Please don't leave me here...alone."

"You'll never be alone," the voice whispered. He felt a warm sensation pass over his lips.

"I can't go on like this. Not without you..."

"You must be strong now, Ray. They will need your strength."

"Tina, please… I just want to be with you…"

"Soon, my love, but you have much to do first."

"Tell me… Please. I'll do anything to be with you again."

His right hand grew warm and he felt the graceful application of unseen pressure guiding it to the ground in front of him.

"Use this when the time is right," the voice whispered.

"Tina, please… How am I supposed to know when that is?"

"You're the shortest, Ray. You'll know." The whisper trailed into a wan breeze that circled him like a momentary whirlwind before dissipating.

"Tina?"

He waited, knowing deep down that there would be no answer.

"Don't leave me!" he shouted, his voice stretching into the fathomless darkness before echoing to mock him from afar.

He recoiled as something sharp poked his finger, his flesh providing precious little resistance, summoning a swell of blood. Droplets dripping from the wound, he reached back to the floor and carefully traced the outline of the object on the ground.

"Please don't leave me," he moaned. "Not again…"

Closing his fist around the hilt, he pushed himself back to his feet, and, sobbing, headed back in the direction from which he had come, the blood running from the gash on his index finger down the hilt of the knife and along the razor edge of the blade before slapping to the cavern floor with a faint *tap… tap… tap…*

VII

MORMON TEARS

Evelyn sat on the round rock, dangling her bare feet into the frigid lake. They were already a shade of red she hadn't seen before, though her toes were beginning to whiten as the pins and needles faded to numbness. She didn't know why she couldn't just pull them out of the water to warm them up. Maybe it was just nice to feel anything other than pain and sadness. The worst part was that the sensation cut through the fog in her brain and laid bare a part of her that she hadn't realized existed. Hidden in her psyche, somewhere in that normally impregnable trove of repressed thoughts and desires, was a very real part of her that resented her father for what he had done to her. The rational Evelyn knew that his accident had been just that, and not a deliberate ploy to ruin her life. She had loved him as much as any child could love a father, but when she had been forced to abandon her life and education to return to the pheasant ranch she'd worked so hard to escape, that seed of resentment had taken root like a tumor. It was one thing coming to grips with that loathsome realization, but another entirely having to mentally relive dragging his corpse out of the house and to the fire pit, where she'd already incinerated the carcasses of their stock. Screwing the spigot off the gas can to spatter his bloated black body with the remaining drops. Bringing the sky blue flame to his pajamas, watching only long enough to ensure that the fire began to consume him. The smoke from his impromptu pyre rising over the burning barn in the rear view mirror as she sped down the dirt drive and away from the smoldering remains of the dream her parents had shared.

"I'm so sorry, Daddy," she mewled, dragging the tears from the corners of her of her eyes before they could even form.

She looked out across the lake, the harsh black waves shimmering even in the absence of the sun, to the small island of stone, little more than a line against the eastern horizon. The others were a couple hundred yards to the north on the sandy part of the beach, and while she longed for even the sympathy and companionship of strangers, she craved isolation more. What kind of person was she that she would think such terrible thoughts about her own father? Had that twisted part of her soul actually been happy when he died?

The tears began to flow again, only this time faster than she could chase them away. Lowering her head, she let it bob uselessly on her limp neck with the shuddering of her shoulders. Droplets quivered on her chin before swelling enough to slip away to splash into the saline shallows.

"Mormon Tears," she whispered, shaking her head. It was a sea of lost lives and sorrow, filled by the salty tears—

Evelyn bolted upright, her brow furrowing.

It was more than a reservoir of humanity's amassed suffering, more than the beacon that had drawn all of them to its sandy white bosom.

It was their salvation.

"My God," Evelyn gasped, jumping to her feet. Between the ferocious pain and the numbness, they were barely able to support her, allowing her just enough time to grab back onto her rocky perch before depositing her in the brine. Scrabbling over the rocks, she hit the sand on all fours, crawling until she could take the maddeningly slow progress no more and fought to her feet, stumbling as fast as she could toward the bonfire and the cave where she'd left her backpack.

"Tell me they're still alive. Dear Lord, please let them still be alive."

She blew past a small group of people congregating around a camper in the bed of a pickup and another cluster where a man in army fatigues tended to a blonde woman's foot before ducking into the smoky entrance to the cavern.

"Hey lady," the old man by the fire called after her as she headed straight for where she'd set her bag against the wall. "Got any more of them beans?"

Throwing the strap over her shoulder, she raced past him and outside without sparing an answer, focused on the area down the beach where the smooth sand met with the rocky coast. After fifty yards she finally had to slow to catch her breath, seizing the opportunity to rummage through the precious few belongings she could claim as her own. When she finally found what she was looking for, she yanked it out of the backpack and let it fall to the ground. Peeling away the layers of cellophane, she unfolded the first long green-brown leaf and examined the small ball of roots. They were barely moist, but had yet to lose their elasticity. The leaf itself was beginning to wither, but it was one of the most resilient species on the planet and she held out hope, tucking the package into the breast pocket of her flannel shirt.

Clambering over the rocks, she knelt in the water and began dragging away the smaller pebbles lining the bed, the water sloshing against her waist raising all of the hackles on her skin. The soft silt beneath clouded the water to the point that she couldn't see her hands at all, but she knew she didn't have to dig very deep. Grabbing the bundle from her pocket, she lowered the first leaf of kelp into the water, wiggling it until she had the roots exactly where she wanted them, and then packed the dirt around the stem. She'd only brought a dozen plants with her as a reminder of what might have been, a security blanket amidst the chaos of Armageddon, but she planted each of them meticulously, piling the dirt over the roots and packing it just tight enough to hold them in place while still allowing oxygen to filter through. Finally, she dragged the pebbles back around the plants, using the larger stones to protect them, and pulled her hands out of the water. They were so cold that her digits were all but useless claws that she tucked into her armpits to leech the warmth from her torso, but they had served their purpose. Whatever pain may follow would be worth it.

She rose on shivering legs and sat on the large rock, tucking her knees to her chest to conserve what little body heat remained. Teeth chattering, she endured the interminable wait as the cloud of stirred sand finally settled once again and the water cleared enough to see the fruits of her labor. Exactly eleven long leaves stood from between the rocks, wavering back and forth as the gentle waves came and went.

In her past life, this would have been the culmination of her Master's Thesis, an actual physical test of her hypothesis. Her heart beat faster as the excitement claimed her. She was about to find out if her professional aspirations had been in vain or if it would have been possible to sustain oceanic crops of kelp capable of feeding entire nations and helping to heal the seas of the scars of man's incessant trespassing. More than that, she knew that these weren't simple crops that she had transplanted from several hundred miles away. They were more than single long leaves she hoped would continue to grow into mature plants; more than potential salads. This kelp was no longer the biological trash to be combed from the beaches to ready them for the constant deluge of tourists, but a commodity worth its weight in gold...

Hope.

VIII

THE RUINS OF
DENVER,
COLORADO

Death stood at the edge of the room where once a window had stretched from floor to ceiling, staring out upon what looked like the entire world from his vantage on the top floor of the skeletal black tower. Thunderheads roiled overhead, the flashes of lightning becoming increasingly infrequent, obscuring the rising sun, if it still even graced the heavens. The world outside was dead, save the mutating feral vegetation. No higher life forms moved out there on the plains, stretching away from the foothills and the Rocky Mountains behind, where once millions had thrived.

The entire Swarm rested beneath his feet, filling the floors below, clinging to the darkness. Some had shimmied into the air ducts where no sunlight would interrupt their slumber, while others were packed into interior offices and bathrooms, sealed into the ceilings where there was no chance of being accosted by even the attenuated rays of the sun. As they matured, so did their prowess. While their eyesight had grown exponentially more powerful, acclimating to seeing in perfect darkness, bright light now burned their pupils. They were the perfect hunters, and soon he would turn them loose on the dying limb of the evolutionary tree. Scourge the earth and then begin anew. Just as they had so many times before in their different incarnations.

Death had no way of knowing what the Lord had been thinking when he designed this current dominant species, for His will was unquestioned. He had created humanity in His image, but in doing so had released creatures who thought themselves gods onto a planet unable to support their destructive whims. God could be loving and He could be vengeful, and in crafting miniaturized versions of Himself, He had instilled these traits into each and every one of them. These men could hold a baby bird in one cupped palm, gazing down upon it with genuine compassion, and then pound it with the other fist. It was the dichotomous nature of the Maker Himself. He had given them the gift of divinity unfulfilled and they had used that power to destroy themselves in the name of the God who had bestowed it upon them. Their vengeful side had warred against their goodness and had annihilated it, which only seemed appropriate given in whose likeness they had been cast.

A snowflake, grayed by the ash in the sky, floated through the opening where once the window had been to gracefully land in his open palm, a pristine crystalline design atop the intricate mesh of black scales, before melting into a small droplet like a single tear to roll down his wrist and into his sleeve of tanned human flesh. More snowflakes materialized in the sky, intensifying with each plume of frozen breath escaping from his reptilian lips. More snow would come and they would travel beneath the cover of the storm. The time was finally at hand.

The winter was upon them.

CHAPTER 2

I

Richard sat apart from the others with his back to the face of the outcropping, his legs stretched out onto the sand in front of him, a plate stained with the residue of his beans resting on his lap. From this vantage, he could see all but a couple of people still inside the cave. He studied the demographics of the group as a whole to try to discover the hierarchy. As of now, they were still congregating in small groups like clans. The first step would be to unite them.

He thought back to what the boy with whom he had been traveling had said. They had still been in the van at that point, filling up at a gas station in the middle of nowhere. He had finished pumping before those braving the darkness inside the store had returned with their armfuls of food, sitting in the driver's seat, legs dangling, letting a cigarette burn between his fingers. The boy had called out from where he slept in the rear of the van.

"The war is coming," he cried. "They'll come out of the snow and kill us all!"

At the time, Richard hadn't thought a thing of it. Granted, the words, the sheer terror in the child's voice had raised all the gooseflesh on his body, but it was only a child having a nightmare. After everything he'd already survived, Richard would have been more surprised if the boy hadn't been accosted by his dreams. But now the boy had led them to the "Mormon Tears" of his dreams, to where all of the others were gathering, which lent him a new measure of credibility. So if what this kid was saying was true, then there was still fighting to come. And what was the best way to keep out of combat? To be the leader, of course. President Wallace hadn't been standing on the bow of the USS Talon when they were preparing to launch the nukes from the submarines in the Persian Gulf. Truman hadn't been strapped aboard the Enola Gay when she dropped her atomic payload on Hiroshima. FDR hadn't given the battle cry and led his troops into the trenches behind his wheelchair. No, they had all been thousands of miles from the front lines with a small contingent of highly trained soldiers at their beck and call. The safest person in any war was the man giving the orders to march the tin soldiers to their deaths. It was only fitting that he should lead. He was a United States Congressman after all. He would have been in the Oval Office someday anyway. Maybe he would never cross the Presidential Seal now. No matter. Power came from within, breeding respect in the masses. It was an elusive thing besides. There was nothing tangible about power. All he had to do was reach out and grab a handful of empty air and call it such. Cattle existed to be led. That was part of their nature. They stood around uselessly until someone came into their midst to drive them ahead.

His lot would be to lead them. Whether or not there would ever be a war was inconsequential. If an army rose against them, he would send his soldiers to their deaths with a clear conscience. If not...power did have its benefits after all. Maybe he could begin the world anew as a Pharaoh or a Caesar and let the others toil to build monuments to him. He needed to be practical, though. When food grew scarce, who would eat? When the supply of potable water was nearly exhausted, who would decide their rations? And if the time ever came to die, who would be the last in line?

It was all in the timing from here. He had to gather them around him soon, but there was no way to force them. They needed someone to rise to the forefront from the start, so he needed to observe them to see if anyone had already done so. That wouldn't deter him by any stretch of the imagination. It would only require a little more planning. People were easily enough discredited in the eyes of the masses and anyone was susceptible to the wiles of temptation. He was a politician, for God's sake. Making other people look bad came as naturally to him as passing a bowel movement. So far, however, there didn't appear to be an alpha in the whole bunch.

He needed more than just a background in civil service if he were to expect these men and women to raise arms and fight to their deaths for him. There had to be an emotional component, a battle cry to rally them to his side. These cattle needed to believe that he was more than human. After all, nearly all ancient cultures believed their rulers to be descended from divinity. If they were to blindly accept the imposition of his will, then they needed to believe that he was nothing shy of the second coming of Christ.

To his left, a boy who looked like he hadn't seen a day of sunshine in his life awkwardly flirted with a young girl who should have been well out of his league, but there was obviously chemistry between them. Neither could have been out of their teens, but he could safely eliminate them as a significant threat as none of the others flocked to them.

To his right there were several groups of people, while others hovered between as though trying to be alone amidst the congregations or gathering their courage to join them. The blonde he had come in with now had her feet bandaged and appeared to be reveling in the attention as the others catered to her, bringing her food and water along with additional layers of clothing. There were two men in full army garb, though neither exuded the aura of authority their uniforms should by all rights have commanded, though both appeared more than adept at treating the woman. Perhaps medics? The only one who looked to be potential competition was the man with the trailer, which seemed to be as good a command post as any. He sat on the step leading up into the camper with a shotgun on his lap. The others surrounded him, facing him as though he were the focal point. Regardless of whether he turned out to be the direct opposition or not, Richard knew the man would make a prime ally. The longer he waited now, the more power the man with the shotgun would assume either by choice or by gift. Richard needed to find that one special thing to unite them and bring them unquestionably into his service to support him as their leader. And he needed to find it fast...

The young boy who had led them there appeared from the cave, holding a plate in one hand and his mother's hand in the other.

Richard smiled.

This was going to be too easy. Casting his plate aside, he looked for the best and most centralized location. There was an old white Ford truck parked in the middle of the beach. He strode purposefully toward it, oblivious to the sideways glances of those who noticed him. Why hadn't he thought of it sooner? What was the best way to galvanize people?

Fear.

Fear of the unknown was an undeniably strong force, but more frightening still was the fear of what was already known. Every one of them had surely seen what those mutated reptilian men could do, and that was more than terrifying enough to get their attention.

Richard stepped up onto the front driver's side tire and clambered onto the hood, which bowed beneath his weight with a metallic thumping. Removing the tie from around his head, he hung it from his neck without bothering to tighten it. Licking his palms to smooth back his hair, he cleared his throat.

"Everyone listen!" he shouted. The din of conversation ceased almost immediately, the remaining voices dying down until Richard could see all of their eyes upon him. "We're running out of time. The creatures are still coming for us."

He fell silent, gauging their reactions. Several sobs broke the silence occupied only by the grumble of breaking waves. The hook was set.

"The time has come to ready ourselves for battle or we will bleed this very shore red." He looked to the little boy and lowered his voice to make sure he held their complete attention. "The war is coming. They'll come out of the snow and kill us all."

II

MORMON TEARS

Adam was transfixed by the man atop the truck. He felt as though he had seen him somewhere before, but for the life of him he couldn't remember where. With the tailored coat and silk tie, he looked like he must have been a lawyer or some upper-echelon businessman before everything changed. Maybe it was the fact that even under the circumstances the man looked polished, but Adam instinctively disliked him. Regardless of his first impression, however, Adam could feel the truth of the man's words resonating within him. All of them had known it on some instinctual level, but none of them had vocalized it. The man was right. The end of the world had only been the beginning for them. There were still battles to be fought and much blood to be spilled. He could feel it.

There was a tug at his sleeve.

"We must fortify our position and arm ourselves against what is to come," the man said from atop the Ford, his voice rising with the level of his conviction. "The time is nigh to rise from our own ashes and begin anew."

Adam turned to find himself face to face with a guy who couldn't have been more than twenty.

"Jesus," Adam gasped at the sight of the blood smeared all over the kid's face. His eyes were recessed into darkness; haunted in a very real sense.

"We need to get you cleaned up so I can look at your face," Adam said, already reaching for his canteen.

"No. Really, I'm fine," he said. "I just…

There's something you need to see…"

Adam creased his brow and inspected the younger man. The blood was definitely already dried and there were no visible lacerations, except for the small cuts on his lips where strands of skin had peeled away from exposure to the elements.

"What do I need to see?" Adam asked. Behind him, a smattering of scattered applause and a few calls of support accompanied the man's impassioned speech.

"I need to show you."

"Do you think that guy up there is for real?" Norman asked. When he turned at Adam's lack of reply, he saw the bloody young man. "Holy crap! What happened to you?"

"He says he has something to show me," Adam said.

"Please…you can come too. Everyone needs to see this."

"Well…" Norman said. "My schedule appears to be clear."

"Okay," Adam said, splashing the last of his water onto a shred of cloth. He offered it to the bloody man and mimed wiping his face with it.

"Thanks," he said, taking the rag and rubbing it over his mouth.

"What's your name?" Adam asked.

"Ray Gorman."

"Shall we then, Ray?" Norman said.

Scrubbing the crust of blood from his stubble, Ray turned and led them back toward the cave. When he reached the bonfire, he sifted through the ends of the thick branches hanging out of the fire and pulled one out, holding it up like a torch.

"You're going to need one of these," Ray said, already walking toward the cleft leading into the mountain.

"You've got to be kidding," Adam said, watching the shifting light from the flickering flame reach out into the darkened corridor.

"Claustrophobic?" Norman asked, removing the branch with the longest handle from the blaze. He offered it to Adam before grabbing one for himself.

"Just spent way too much time underground lately," Adam said, fighting to repress the memories of Ali Sadr and the friends he had lost in the labyrinth of caverns.

Falling in behind Norman, they passed through the opening and into a thin corridor. Every imperfection in the rock wall cast a flagging shadow animated by the flames. Ray was a dozen paces ahead, the aura of light from his torch turning him into a being of shadow. He bent to the right, momentarily disappearing from sight. Rather than the darkness bringing with it the coldness of the grave, it seemed to be warming slightly as they penetrated the mountain, rounding the corner to find that Ray had gained ground on them. His torch appeared to have dimmed, the fire dwindling, but it wasn't until they closed the distance between them that Adam and Norman could tell why.

Ray was standing in an enormous cavern, so large that the light didn't even reach the ceiling or the far walls. Norman stepped out of the earthen tunnel and into the larger chamber. He whistled at the size of it, the note echoing back at him from far off in the darkness.

It looked dramatically different even with the weak firelight. While Ray thought he had been halfway into the room before, he now realized he had only stood at the precipice of it on a rock ledge that looked down upon the surprisingly large room. He must have been nearly to the edge when he'd crouched to find the knife, now stuffed into the front pouch of his hooded sweatshirt. Another couple of steps and he would have fallen twenty feet from the edge of the cliff to the stone floor twenty feet below. He could only imagine lying there with broken bones poking out through the skin, waiting for anyone to come after him, knowing that even his most pained screams would never reach their ears. But Tina wouldn't have allowed that to happen…would she? Her appearance was now beginning to feel more and more like a hallucination from a fever dream. Had she ever really been there or had she been a manifestation of his mind's descent into madness?

"What's that?" Adam asked, pointing down into shadows so thick it looked like a lake of tar beneath them.

"Where are you looking?" Norman asked. He couldn't see a blasted thing down there.

"Straight out there," Adam said, pointing over the cliff and off to the right. At the edge of the furthest reaches of the torch light, he could see a flat portion of wall that almost looked like it had several sawed-off telephone poles poking out of it.

Their branches were beginning to burn down, throwing embers behind them as they moved slowly toward what almost looked like steps descending into the darkness. The slate had been roughly chiseled away to lead from the outcropping around the front of the cliff, winding down to the cavern floor. Adam raised his torch as he stepped down from the final stone stair, guiding them ahead. The cave floor was smooth, interspersed with clusters of stalagmites that were nearly as tall as they were, occasional droplets falling from the stalactite-riddled ceiling to land on the tips. Something off to the left reflected the glow of the flames from the floor, rippling like a small body of water. Ahead and to the right, what they'd seen from above slowly came into view. It was a manmade structure composed of straight lines and boxes, climbing several stories against the back wall of the cave. While at first it looked like adobe, the closer they came, the more it began to resemble packed mud and thatch, crumbled away in large sections to reveal an inner framework of sticks. There were no windows or apparent entrances on the lower floor, but several poles were roped together to make primitive ladders that leaned against the structure.

"How old do you think it is?" Ray asked, pulling on one of the cracked edges only to have it fall away around his feet.

"Hundreds of years, I'm sure," Norman said. "I think it was the Goshute or the Shoshone who lived in this area."

"Why do you think they built this here?" Adam asked. "I mean I've seen cave dwellings and plenty of these pueblos built out in the open, but I've never even heard of such an elaborate indoor creation."

"I know why," Ray said.

Adam and Norman turned at the sound of his voice. Ray had his back to them and was facing the stone wall where it met with the pueblo. He held his torch up to the flat rock surface, highlighting enormous primitive chalk drawings covered with a thick layer of dust. Had the torch not been so close to the designs, they might not have been able to see them at all.

"Jesus," Adam whispered, staring at the flickering image of a man with a snake's head and yellow- and black-marbled eyes. There was a red dewlap beneath the thing's chin, but it was what was beside that creature that made Adam's heart race and his breath stale in his chest.

A chalk rendition of his face stared back at him through the ages.

III

MORMON TEARS

Gray Ciccerelli sat on the fender of his pickup, watching the man standing atop the hood of the truck trying to rally the enrapt men and women to his cause. There was no longer any point in trying to hide his shotgun. Everyone else seemed to draw comfort from it and he had to admit that there was a certain measure of power that emanated from it. His power. He and his wife Carrie had been in their sleeping bags inside of their insulated tent when the mosquitoes had passed through the high country, and while they had heard the insects beating against the walls of the six-man, only a small number had managed to penetrate their inner sanctum, but they had been unable to pierce the thick waterproof hide of their sleeping bags. The couple with whom they had been camping, Carrie's cousin Jessie and her louse of a boyfriend Sam, hadn't been as fortunate. They'd run screaming from their trailer, the same one Gray and Carrie now called their own, into the swarm of mosquitoes, trying to escape those that had infiltrated the camper through the exterior ducts. Their screams had been unbearable, trilling on for what felt like forever before finally being drowned out by the humming of wings. Gray and Carrie had waited a good ten minutes before daring to climb out to investigate, all the while Gray fighting against his sobbing wife who wanted to run out to save Jessie, but by then it was far too late. They'd found their bloated black bodies lying face down in the dirt at the edge of the ring of stones surrounding the extinguished fire pit. Gray had poked them repeatedly with the end of a stick, but all that oozed out was a sappy white fluid. It positively reeked of disease. He'd seen all kinds of dead animals, and even a man's body once, but none of them had looked even remotely similar to those corpses with bluish veins rising beneath their sweaty ebony skin. Carrie had begged him to load the carcasses into the camper and take them back down into Billings, but he knew that whatever was replicating inside of them to cause such dramatic swelling was something with which they didn't want to take their chances. He'd tossed a couple shovelfuls of dirt atop them to keep them from being scavenged before they could return with the authorities, but that hadn't been good enough for Carrie, who refrained from speaking to him for several hours afterward. By now, she just wasn't doing much talking to anyone at all. She just kind of sat there staring off into space, but she was slowly beginning to come around, her eyes flashing with an occasional sentience, especially as she watched the guy on the hood of the big old Ford.

Gray had to admit that the guy was a masterful orator, but he'd known far too many people of this man's ilk in his life. They were brilliant when it came to finding the common ground to sway people to their perspective, but they always had an agenda. For the life of him, however, he just couldn't pin down this guy's ulterior motives, but give it time. Give it time. Gray had been a claims adjustor for the largest private insurance company in Montana before what turned out to be their final camping trip, so he was accustomed to dealing with lawyers on a daily basis. This guy was as smooth as they came, a real snake oil salesman. Even in those unwashed clothes with dirt and grime all over his face, this man came off as polished. He had politician written all over him. And while Gray had strong opinions about such lower forms of life, he knew they were a necessary evil.

"We have been gathered here at Mormon Tears knowing that soon we must make our final stand," the man bellowed, his voice rising with his reddening face. "Band together with me and we will triumph and usher in a new age of humanity!"

A cheer arose from the forty-some spectators and Gray couldn't help but grin. This guy knew how to work a crowd.

Richard climbed down off the hood of the truck and was immediately surrounded by people patting him on the back and hurling questions at him only to be met with that practiced smile. How did he know that the creatures would be coming for them? What could they do to help prepare? He didn't have any of the answers. Not yet anyway, but so long as though he appeared as though he did, he would be able to maintain the illusion of omniscience.

Gray slung the shotgun over his shoulder to hang by the strap. Maybe it was time that he introduced himself. Hopping from the tailgate, he eased through the mob until he reached the man and offered his right hand.

"Gray Ciccerelli," he said, his hand clasped in the well-rehearsed shake he'd expected.

"Richard Robinson." He could tell from Gray's eyes that he would be a hard sell, but there was strength in his skepticism. Richard knew he needed this man on his side.

"Familiar name. Do I know you from somewhere?"

"I'm a congressman. California. West Hollywood and Beverly Hills actually."

"That must be it," Gray said, releasing his grasp. "So what's the plan, chief? Now that you're in charge I'd imagine it's time to buckle down and get to work."

Richard could tell that Gray was still sizing him up, carefully baiting him to gauge his response. Sometimes to take a yard you had to give an inch.

"We need to find shelter for all of these people with winter coming. Maybe head into Salt Lake City and see if we can start the process of rebuilding." He paused. "Does that sound like the kind of project you'd be interested in heading?"

"I'll give it some thought," Gray said. He wasn't having much success getting a clear read on this guy, but he could definitely tell when he was being worked.

"See that you do. Well...it was nice to meet you, Gray," Richard said, clapping him on the shoulder and then turning to face the others who wanted to shake his hand and congratulate him on his quick ascension to the head of the pack.

"Oh, hey! Richard!" Gray called after him.

Richard stopped and looked back over his shoulder.

"I meant to ask," Gray said, thumbing the strap on his right shoulder, "how do you know these creatures are going to come after us?"

Richard paused and bit his lip. This was a man who wouldn't be easily placated by a smile.

"Because I've seen it in my dreams," he said, allowing himself to be guided away by the masses toward the comfort of the bonfire.

Gray watched him walk away. That last statement had caught him off guard. He wasn't a particularly spiritual man, but the last couple of days had begun to cause him to reevaluate his stance on such matters. He hadn't been to church since the last time his parents had made him as a child. He didn't believe in aliens, and the mere idea of ghosts was laughable. But the truth was that he had driven all the way to Utah based on a gut feeling, and while he had learned through the years to trust his instincts, he hadn't thought to question why he had driven away from the life he knew to end up at the Great Salt Lake. It had begun simply as progressing from one town to the next in search of help for Carrie's cousin, and then a quest to find any other survivors, but there had really been no conscious decision as to how far they would go or when they would stop. It had just felt like the natural progression. Now that he truly looked at it for what it was, could he honestly rule out the prospect that they'd been led there by something, some divine force greater than themselves? And if he gave that thought credence, was it indeed possible that this man Richard could see the future in his dreams?

He shook his head. He didn't like where his thoughts were leading him. There had to be a rational order to life. He just had yet to find it. That was all.

Something still nagged at him, however, as he walked back to his camper... If he were actually willing to consider the notion that they'd all been gathered here by some spiritual force to prepare for some great battle to come, then what would be the consequences if they lost?

IV

MORMON TEARS

Richard scared Phoenix. Not because of anything he'd said, but because he reminded Phoenix so much of the man who had kept him imprisoned in the basements of all of those different houses for his entire life. There was an aura of death surrounding him, a black haze that clung to him like crude shale. He couldn't even bring himself to look at the man anymore, for every time he did, all he could hear were the screams of the dying.

No one else seemed to notice. Not even Missy, who'd joined her brother farther down the beach so that she could hear the man more clearly. He didn't know why he felt the way he did, nor did he know how to vocalize his concerns. All he knew was that this man would bring death upon them all if given the chance.

Phoenix shivered and wrapped his arms around his chest, forcing himself to look away from the spectacle and to the lake. A small flock of birds stalked the shallows in front of him on long, spindly legs, racing up and down the shore with the tide. He couldn't tell what they were spearing on their knitting needle-beaks, but there were apparently more than enough of them to go around, the crimson birds gurgling contentedly as they choked back the morsels, down gullets that expanded like a bullfrog preparing to croak.

Rising, he waded out into their midst, startling them to flight. They swirled around him, protesting with a haunting call of mourning before alighting again, though maintaining their distance from him. The water was so cold it positively hurt, but it was a pleasant distraction from the thoughts of the man with the dark cloud of death around him.

There was a scream from above him, sending the birds scattering in all directions. He craned his neck back to stare up into the overcast sky while retreating from the water. A layer of ash still hovered above, though by now he'd adapted to the point that it no longer burned in his lungs. The lightning had petered off to the occasional violet strike that shivered from one thunderhead to the next. A flash of white winked at him before blending back into the clouds, another shrill scream piercing the day.

He looked over to the others. They were now gathered at the entrance to the cave around the roaring bonfire.

By the time he raised his gaze to the heavens again, he could clearly see the white shape, which now resembled a great cross. Another scream erupted from the thing, which began to descend as it circled around him. Lower and lower it dropped until he could clearly discern the long white feathers curled from the tips of the wings and a tail filled with streaming feathers like a peacock's. There was a sparkle of gold from its head as it released another cry. Talons unfurled from its downy belly and its wings pointed straight up into the sky. It plummeted toward the lake as though preparing to snatch a fish from the waves, but opened those enormous wings at the very last moment and swooped upward before folding them to its sides and dropping onto its feet in the sand directly in front of Phoenix.

It was the most beautiful bird he could imagine, its silky feathers so white they generated an aura around it. The feathers were so thick it looked almost like a mammal in fresh winter growth, its beak appearing as a wide golden V in a scruff of snowy down. Its eyes were rimmed with black crescents, but it was the orbs themselves that drew his focus. They were nearly as white as the shimmering feathers, but cloudy as though made of crystal balls containing a thick mist.

It stood there, more than two feet tall with those long feathers trailing along the ground behind it. Cocking its head first one way and then the other, it opened that golden beak and let out a *skree*.

"Hi there," Phoenix said, taking a tentative step forward. "What brings you to see me?"

The great white bird cocked its head again as though weighing his question. Slowly, the feathers on its crown rose like so many knives. It hopped forward in long strides until it was barely outside of his reach and looked directly up at him.

"Are you hungry?" Phoenix asked, looking back down at where he'd set his plate. There were only a couple stray beans on the tacky plate, but he would gladly share them. He was just about to head back for it when the bird let out a savage cry and opened its wings like a threatened goose.

Phoenix turned his head and brought his arms up in front of his face. Pinching his eyes shut, he prepared to throw himself to the ground.

Sharp pain lanced through his left forearm, forcing his eyes wide and a scream to his lips.

The large bird sat on his forearm. Talons curled nearly all the way around his arm just below the elbow, poking through the skin, which issued dribbling freshets of blood. It was so heavy he could barely keep his arm raised, but even the slightest movement made those wickedly sharp claws feel like they were sinking deeper into his flesh to carve through the bone. He looked up, his eyes matching the bird's, and was drawn inside. The white mist swirled as though he'd stepped into a fog, gently peeling back until it revealed itself to be a blizzard of snow assaulting him from everywhere at once. Far below, the pine trees were beginning to don their winter coat of snow, the fields now splotchy with accumulation. The lush foothills faded away, replaced by well-spaced houses that grew closer and closer together as the eastern plains of the Rocky Mountains spread out to the horizon. The snow had quenched the last of the rampant fires, leaving only the smoldering, charred skeletons of the suburbs. Wafting smoke was the only thing moving about in the piles of rubble, the snowflakes turning to rain with the dwindling heat to muddy the earth with a paste of black soot.

With a scream resonating in his ears, he banked to the north, following the ragged edge of the crater surrounding downtown. Ponds formed where businesses had once stood, black as tar pits and steaming from the trapped heat of the earth underneath. The ground was scorched, though patches still glimmered from the melted glass fused to the piles of destruction. Following the line where complete vaporization faded to mere haphazard demolition, his vision soared continually eastward until what remained of the city was behind him and fields of thorny briars covered the ground. A small fire captured his gaze and he began to descend toward it. As it came into focus, he began to decipher the details. The flames crackled from a skull turned upside down and staked atop a length of wood, funneled into a thin stream of fire by the hole in the base through which the spinal cord had once passed. Beside it, the ground was trampled into a choppy mud crusted into what looked like frozen waves by the sheer amount of footprints marring it. In the vision, he swooped down until he was skimming over the ground, staring straight ahead to where a slanting tower of darkness rose from the rubble against the backdrop of the snowcapped mountains. Tangible waves of pain and suffering emanated from it, hitting him in the face with concussive force, drawing tears from the corners of his eyes.

More of the skull lanterns whizzed by to either side, illuminating the path every hundred yards or so like runway lights. The massive black tower grew taller and taller against the skyline, the night all-but-impregnable to the light of the moon, which was unable to permeate the churning masses of clouds and smoke. Reaching the eastern edge of the crater, this time they proceeded directly ahead, weaving through the maze of solid walls that had withstood the atomic blast, under collapsed overpasses and through channels formed by fallen buildings crumbled against each other. A sound like a leaking gas pipe reached his ears, growing louder and louder by the second until it overwhelmed him.

The closer they came to the tower, the darker the ground became beneath them until a ring of bonfires appeared around the base of the monolith, churning ash up into the atmosphere. It wasn't until the flames began to cast their flickering light onto the ground that he realized it hadn't been charcoaled earth they had been cruising over, but black bodies packed shoulder to shoulder. Thousands of them, all gathered around the building, cold amber eyes staring anxiously up at the structure.

Phoenix saw the sky as the bird soared higher and then landed on a mangled girder jutting from the wreckage of the adjacent building. From this vantage, he could see the minions stretching off to his right, swarming beneath him, and the face of the tower to his left. The deafening hissing ceased at once, leaving in its stead a silence that descended upon them like cellophane.

Clop.

Clop.

A figure appeared at the edge of the third story floor, his body the color of blood beneath a brown cloak. He sat high upon a steed draped with that same brown material, skeletal legs emerging from the tatters. The beast bucked beneath him, blasting twin plumes of fire from its nostrils. The rider held up his right fist, and a fervent hissing erupted from the Swarm, so loud Phoenix's vision shook with the girder beneath the bird's feet. Every one of the creatures beneath him came to frenzied life, moshing chaotically in a flurry of slashing claws, snapping jaws, and trilling dewlaps.

He averted his eyes in horror, his gaze rising toward the heavens until it reached the top floor of the skyscraper, where a pair of glowing golden eyes stared directly at him from under a black cowl that trapped the rest of the face in shadow.

Phoenix screamed and again he was standing on the beach with the enormous bird on his arm, talons carving through his flesh in search of solid footing. Their eyes parted and the mutated falcon leapt into the air, flapping with those long wings until it reached an outcropping on the stone face of the mountain, where it perched to stare out across the lake, nearly vanishing against the pale gray rock.

"They're coming," Phoenix whispered, allowing his bloody arm to fall to his side, ribbons of life spiraling around his wrist and over the back of his hand to drip from his fingertips.

Sprinting back toward the others down the shoreline, the wounds in his arm sealed themselves up like mouths closing over a secret.

"They're coming!" he screamed, watching as their startled faces turned in his direction. "We're out of time! They're coming!"

V

MORMON TEARS

Adam stared into his own face, looking back at him from the wall through hundreds of years of dust. It wasn't a precise replica as though painted by a Renaissance master, but there was no denying the resemblance. The chalk had faded over time, and he feared brushing away the dust on it might take the faint powdery residue with it, but he could still see it clearly enough. The eyes were a match. The hair, the skin. Everything, right down to the camouflaged fatigues. In each hand, the drawing held a long spear taller than his likeness, crossing in front of his knees, sharpened ends pointing at angles toward the cavern roof. A woman had been drawn beside him, in her hands a basket full of what looked like lettuce. Her face was familiar, but not enough so that he immediately recognized her.

Raising his torch, he inspected the rest of the mural. It was massive, covering the wall to the furthest reaches of the firelight. Higher up on the wall, Phoenix hovered in midair, arms stretched out to either side and engulfed by a ball of light. It was strangely beautiful, yet at the same time disconcerting, as the boy looked like he'd been crucified.

"Jesus," Norman whispered from beside Adam, who turned in time to see all of the color drain from the medic's face. "That's me."

Adam followed his stare to the wall. There was an uncanny image of Norman looking back at him from where he'd been drawn onto the stone, only his eyes had been filled with black charcoal. He held what looked like an axe by the handle, reminding Adam of a lumberjack.

"How could someone have drawn me so…perfectly…so long ago?" Norman whispered.

"I don't know," Adam said, following the flow of the design. There were other faces he had seen outside on the beach. Many had the same black eyes as Norman, while others were normal shades of blue, green, and brown. And surrounding them all like a backdrop were yellow- and black-marbled eyes recessed into blackness.

"What's it supposed to mean? Why are my eyes like that?" Norman asked.

"I wish I knew," Adam said, unnerved by how much the eyes in the background reminded him of how it had looked in the house where they had found Phoenix.

"I've got to be honest, man. This is scaring the crap out of me."

"You and me both," Adam said, watching as Ray paused at the wall farther down to the right, bringing his burning branch closer to the wall so he could see more clearly.

There was an image of the young man there as well, left arm across his chest with a knife held high as though preparing to slash it sideways in front of him. Unlike all of the others, his eyelids were closed.

Self-consciously, Ray reached into the front pouch of the hooded sweatshirt and patted the knife.

Use this when the time is right, Tina's spectral voice whispered in his mind.

"How did you know this was here?" Adam asked.

Ray nearly jumped at the sound of Adam's voice. He'd been so mesmerized by the picture that he'd lost track of everything around him.

"I…I didn't," Ray said, walking back toward the pueblo where Norman was already climbing up one of the ladders, bouncing on the first couple of rungs to make sure it would hold his weight before continuing upward, holding the torch away from his body in his left hand while using his right to steady himself.

"Do you see any way in?" Adam called to him as Norman eased forward onto the roof, wary of the cracking sound of the mud-fused thatch beneath him.

"It looks like there's a hatch up here." Norman knelt, grabbed the wooden square by the edge, and raised it. A gust of dust belched out into his face, forcing him to cough and swat away the dry cloud. He lowered the burning end of the stick into the darkness, partially illuminating a small square room. There were no doors or windows of any kind, only a hand-woven rug on the floor, thick with centuries of dust, and what looked like hundreds of corn stalks corded together and tied off with rope made from reeds.

"You want to give me a hand?" he yelled back over his shoulder, his voice echoing throughout the cavern.

Sitting, he dangled his legs down through the ceiling of the room beneath and waved the torch through a tangle of cobwebs before dropping down to the earthen floor. He swung the torch side to side to clear away the dusty filaments connecting the walls, giving him the impression that spiders were crawling all over his skin. At just over six feet tall, he wasn't an incredibly large man, but he still had to stoop under the low ceiling. Pulling his shirt up over his mouth and nose to keep from inhaling the dust, he kicked through half an inch of grime on the floor until he reached the first bound stack. They weren't cornstalks as he had originally thought, but thin lengths of wooden dowels. He gave the reeds binding them a tug and they snapped with hardly any pressure, an avalanche of wooden posts clattering around his feet.

"What was that?" Adam asked, leaning over the hole in the roof.

"There are a ton of these things down here." Norman grabbed a couple of the poles and held them up through the hatch.

Adam set down his torch so that the burning end hung out over the side of the building and took the wooden rods from Norman. Grasping one in each hand, he leaned them out to either side so that he could get a better look at the ends, which tapered into sharp points.

His heart stalled in his chest.

Looking down at the mural where Ray still perused it by torchlight, he saw himself painted on the wall exactly as he stood at that very moment.

VI

MORMON TEARS

Jill was starting to feel more like herself. The beans she'd consumed for breakfast, which had actually been around lunch time, had helped, but it was really the fact that she'd been able to just sit on the beach with April and Darren, watching the waves roll in from the eastern horizon, that helped establish at least a few precious moments of normalcy. Her thoughts continued to drift back to Tina, especially with Ray's conspicuous absence. Nothing about her death seemed real, as though at any moment, Tina would just come bouncing down the beach, so full of life as she'd always been. At least Jill hoped it was the feeling of surreality, rather than having become so anesthetized to all of the death that even the loss of a close friend didn't affect her. She had loved Tina, almost like a sister, so it truly bothered her that even thinking about her horrible death couldn't summon a single tear.

They had wandered well away from the camp so that they could barely see the others to the south. Without all of the unfamiliar faces, it felt almost like a vacation. Just the three of them sitting on the sand, watching the strange red birds and the inland ocean. April and Darren hadn't allowed their hands to part for more than a few minutes at a time and their once uncomfortable flirting was gone. In a matter of days they'd gone from furtive glances to being almost an extension of each other. Jill was genuinely happy for both of them, but she couldn't help feeling as though the more they grew together, the further apart they drew from her. Darren turned to kiss April and Jill had to look away. A lone figure walked in their direction, so far off that she couldn't see who it was, but she had a pretty good idea.

"I'm going to head back," she said, listening to the wet caress of lips and tongues. "I'll meet you guys back by the fire, okay?"

Those last words turned to mist as they blew from her mouth. Goosebumps prickled up the backs of her arms. The air was crisp and cold as it entered her chest, and while it rarely snowed in Oregon, some part of her nature knew that without a doubt the flakes would soon fall. Wrapping her arms across her chest to preserve her warmth, she struck off down the beach.

"Are you all right, Jill?" April asked, leaning her head onto Darren's shoulder.

"Yeah…I'm fine. Just starting to get cold is all."

"Do you want us to walk back with you?" Darren asked.

Jill shook her head, but didn't look back. "No thanks. You guys just try to enjoy a little time alone."

"You'd better believe we will," Darren said.

April slid her hand down his thigh and gave him a good pinch.

"Ow! What was that for?"

"You'd better believe we will," April said, doing a terrible job of imitating his voice.

"I was just joking, for crying out—"

April cut him off by pressing her mouth to his.

Jill smiled as she walked away, partially because she knew that April and Darren were good for each other, but mainly because the person heading along the shore toward her was finally close enough to recognize.

Mare's face lit up when he saw her smile.

"There you are," he said as soon as he was within earshot.

"You were looking for me?"

"With all of the fun going on back there, I figured it would be a shame if you missed out."

"What fun?"

Mare pulled up in front of her and offered his elbow. Jill took it, despite how the cold air froze her chest in her arm's absence. They continued strolling back toward the cave slowly, alternately looking ahead and then at each other until they were caught staring and averted their eyes bashfully.

"That kid my sister's been hanging around with started freaking out, screaming about how 'the Swarm' is coming."

"It does feel like it might snow."

"Not storm," Mare chuckled. "Swarm."

"Oh…" Jill said, blushing. "There is a big difference between the two, isn't there? What *are* we supposed to do if those mosquitoes come back?"

"Everyone else thinks he's out of his gourd. He keeps saying that the Swarm is preparing to march against us."

"March?"

"Yeah… You see what I'm saying."

"We're all under a lot of stress."

"I guess. Richard says we'll be gone long before anything can march anywhere. He's planning on leaving in the morning."

"Where's he going to go?"

"Not 'he,' Jill. We. He thinks we should all go into the city to find someplace where we can try to live. Someplace where we can actually hope to defend ourselves if something does want to attack us."

"That makes sense, but I'm really not looking forward to heading back out on the road."

"Neither am I, but the prospect of having a roof over my head sounds wonderful." He stopped and held out his free hand. A single snowflake floated down and landed on his palm. "It didn't really snow in Tennessee."

"It hardly ever snows in Oregon either."

"What I don't get," Mare said, shaking the droplet of water from his hand and walking again, "is why everyone is so convinced that we're going to be attacked at all. I mean, I've seen these creatures—my dad even turned into one—but why would anyone think these things are capable of organizing into some kind of army? And marching on us? Please."

"I'm more worried about what will happen if the mosquitoes come back."

"Once winter hits and everything starts to freeze, they'll be dead anyway."

"But what about spring? Don't you think it's possible that they could have bred and laid eggs? Or maybe they're already in a warmer climate where they can wait out the cold. Will they come back then?"

"I don't know," Mare said, shrugging. "We'll just have to be prepared by then, I guess."

They slowed even more as they came upon the camp. Several people had managed to climb up onto the mountain and were hurling down small trees they'd been able to uproot from the crevasses, and any other stray pieces of wood they could find. Others were gathering and stacking them in the middle of the beach with the half-charred logs from the bonfire formerly in the cave, and anything else that looked potentially flammable. It was strange to see the opening to the cave without smoke pouring out of it, exposing those tortured souls who were where they had been since their arrival, huddled against the walls with their knees to their chests. Some shuddered as they sobbed, their anguished cries drowned out from this distance by the crashing waves, while others tried to sleep or stared blankly out into space.

"What's going on?" Mare asked a man in a leather jacket as he passed with an armful of collected limbs that looked too green to burn.

"We're having a meeting," he said, barely slowing. "Everyone needs to be there."

"About what?" Mare asked, but the man was already past him and focused on his task.

Someone had dragged a chair from inside the camper, as evidenced by the thin trails through the sand, and set it up so it faced the growing stack of wood. A man neither had seen before emptied a can of gasoline onto the pile and dropped to one knee just barely within arm's reach. He took a lighter from his pocket and stretched as far as he could toward the fuming fluid. One snap of the flint and a blue flame raced across the mound.

The sky was starting to darken, deep black smoke billowing from the wood, the pile more smoke than fire. The wind arose with a howl, chasing frigid air across the lake, assaulting them with sheets of small snowflakes.

"Feels like the temperature just dropped ten degrees," Jill said, stealing her hand back from Mare's elbow to again wrap both arms around her chest.

The clusters of people up and down the beach worked their way toward the bonfire. There had to be more than a hundred of them now. Jill hadn't seen any of the newcomers arrive, but as they gathered around the sole source of heat, she could see an old school bus that had been painted baby blue with the words Calvary Adventist Youth Group stenciled onto the side, a collection of bikes, both motorized and not, and several new tents.

"Hey, little brother," Missy said from Mare's right, ruffling his hair.

"Hiya, Miss. So what's the word here?"

"They're calling it a town meeting."

"What happened to that creepy albino kid?"

Missy socked him in the shoulder. "Phoenix went up on the mountain to help gather wood. Besides, he's just about the nicest person here."

"I'm hurt."

"You know I love you, Mare, but sometimes you can be a real—"

"Everyone gather 'round!" Richard shouted, climbing atop the lone chair so that everyone could see him.

"What's all this?" April whispered into Jill's ear, startling her.

"I'm not really sure…"

"The time has come to organize," Richard bellowed, spreading his arms out to his sides. "As you can all clearly see, winter's already here. We can't afford to waste any more time here in the middle of nowhere. What are we supposed to do when it gets really cold? What happens when we run out of our pathetic supply of food and water?"

Jill watched Richard, his presence positively commanding. He was across the fire from her, the rising flames giving him the impression of burning, his features aglow with an orange-yellow glare. His face flirted in and out of the smoke as the wind whipped it in changing directions.

"We need to find shelter before the elements kill us all, before…" Richard paused for dramatic effect, his eyes covering the crowd to draw each and every one of them to him. "They come for us."

A cloud of smoke obscured him from Jill's sight. The crowd grumbled like thunder as somewhere behind the roiling storm clouds the sun set unnoticed. A gust of freezing wind raced inland, chasing the smoke and flames sideways toward the cave.

Jill screamed.

Richard's face had become transparent, his skull clearly visible. His eyes were empty black sockets, teeth without lips chattering around his impassioned speech. Those bared teeth closed and even without eyes she could tell he was looking directly at her.

Her head started to spin and her knees gave out, dropping her to the ground on her back. She looked up into the rapidly darkening sky as people began to lean over her from all sides. April's face was the closest; Mare's and Darren's staring down at her as well. There were a couple others she didn't recognize, but the majority no longer wore their faces at all, only exposed skulls leering at her.

Screaming, she kicked at the sand to propel herself away from them, but all she could see were those animated skeletons advancing toward her.

Pinching her eyes shut, she wailed at the top of her lungs until she heard a loud slap and her head was knocked sideways. When she opened her eyes again, she was looking directly into Richard's regular fleshy face.

VII

Mormon Tears

Adam walked out of the cave and onto the beach with Norman at his side and Ray behind. He was surprised to find that the fire had been moved out into the open and closer to the water with everyone gathered around it. There were easily twice as many people now as there had been when they went into the mountain and the snow-spotted sky was darkening before their very eyes. How long had they been down there?

"Well…" Richard said, climbing back up onto the chair. He smiled for the crowd and laughed. "Now that we're all feeling better, shall we proceed?"

Phoenix appeared at Adam's side from the crowd to tug at his arm.

"What's going on here?" Adam asked.

"You have to stop them," Phoenix said, his eyes frantic. His hands shook as he pulled Adam forward into the masses. "They'll all die if they go. All of them."

"Who's going anywhere?"

"That man. He's trying to convince them to leave with him."

"We can't force anyone to stay here, Phoenix."

"You're supposed to lead us. You have to make them stay!"

"I'll do what I can, but I'm still not entirely convinced that it's a bad idea."

Phoenix took Adam by the shoulders and turned him so that their eyes locked. It was disconcerting staring through those long dirty bangs and into the boy's pinkish irises, but Adam was too surprised to resist.

"You saw the painting in the cave,

didn't you? The house of mud and straw? How can you still not understand?"

"How did you—?"

"You are the one who will lead us. You can't let them follow him!"

Adam broke eye contact and looked to the right of the fire where Richard stood higher than the rest, preaching down at them.

"We need every available vehicle ready to head out by sunrise," Richard shouted. "We can't afford to burn a single minute of daylight, especially if this storm starts to worsen. I'll need everyone with any sort of carpentry experience ready to begin construction on our fortifications and anyone with electrical expertise setting up generators and making sure that the heating works. The women and children will need to gather food and supplies."

"Adam, please," Phoenix said.

Adam looked at the boy again, tears streaming down his cheeks from his strange eyes, and sighed.

"Excuse me!" he shouted, raising his hand.

Richard flashed with anger, but hurriedly softened his expression.

"This is an open forum," he said, forcing a smile. "Please introduce yourself first."

The crowd parted to allow Adam to approach the fire.

"I'm Adam Newman," he said, raising his voice to be heard.

"We will need people like you, people of strength, if we are to rebuild," Richard said.

"People like me?"

"Soldiers," Richard said levelly.

Adam looked down at his fatigues. "I'm a doctor. I was just serving my time to pay back my education."

"Excellent. We will need physicians in our New World Order." *New World Order?* Adam didn't like the choice of words. It sounded positively fascist. "What issue would you like to address, Dr. Newman?"

"I don't think leaving is the right thing to do. We were all drawn here for a reason—"

"And now that we're here, we need to organize so that we can survive. What would you propose? Hmm? Pitch tents on the beach and freeze to death? Or maybe you'd prefer we wait around until we starve?"

"There's a big cave under the mountain with a pueblo—"

"You're a physician, Dr. Newman. To what kind of diseases would you have us all exposed? How will you even treat something as ordinarily benign as frostbite? Amputating with your teeth? Even the common cold could prove lethal out here. In town we will have access to heat and medications—"

"We can bring those things out here."

"And live in your cave? In the city we can live in actual indoor dwellings designed to accommodate human beings rather than bats. With doors that lock. We'll be able to actually defend ourselves against the coming attack."

"We can do that here. All we need—"

"With what? Sticks and stones? The one shotgun we have between us? Surely you learned a little more about defense strategies than that during your tenure in the service. I can't imagine the Army didn't teach you that we need to build a perimeter and fortify it, make our fortress impregnable. How would you defend this cave of yours?"

"These mountains form a natural bottleneck. The only access to this shoreline for miles is the way we all came in."

"Tell him they're all going to die if they leave!" Phoenix shouted from the crowd.

"I see," Richard said, allowing himself a predatory smile. "You're with Chicken Little back there. Well, if the sky's falling, I'd much rather have a roof over my head."

Laughter rippled through the crowd.

"That kid led us here. I don't know where we would be right now without him. If he says not to go, then by God I'm not going anywhere. And I hope you won't either."

"Look at these faces around you, doctor. Look into their eyes. These brave men and women have survived hell to gather here from all across the country. Would you really ask them to stay here, out in the elements, away from food and water and the benefits of modern medicine—all of the things we need to live—when they're readily available just on the other side of this very lake?"

"If we leave, we will die."

"How do you know that for sure? What is your justification?"

Adam turned and looked at Phoenix, the boy's stark white facing staring back at him, lighted by the flickering flames. The crowd fell silent.

"I've seen it in my dreams," Phoenix said.

"Your dreams?" Richard bellowed. "Well I have dreams, too. And in my dreams I've seen an armada of evil coming for us under the cover of a blizzard. Maybe even this exact storm rolling in right now."

The snowflakes reinforced their numbers as if to illustrate his point.

"Then why would you want to leave here and risk getting caught in the worst of it?" Adam asked.

"I can offer these people food. Shelter. Protection. What can you offer? Oh yeah, that's right, a cave. And how many months' worth of food do you have stockpiled in this cave? How much potable water? All I've heard to support your argument is that the sky is falling."

"Don't divide us. There's safety in numbers."

"You are the one who would divide us. Come with us. Be saved."

"You can always stay."

"Let's put it to a vote, shall we?" Richard raised his voice even higher. "Do you all want to eat?"

There was a booming chorus of approval.

"Do you want to live like human beings? Inside and out of the cold?"

The cheers grew even louder.

"Or would you rather stay here in Dr. Newman's cave with no food or water?"

The clamor of dissention was deafening.

"So I ask you, you who have already survived this nightmare… Would you rather come with me and have a chance to truly live or stay here and slowly die?"

The response was a roar of excited voices and applause. Fists pumped in the air. Richard leaned his head back to the sky and reveled in every moment of it.

Adam tried to shout, but even he couldn't hear his own voice. He turned and looked at Phoenix, catching just the shimmer of firelight on the tears trailing down his cheeks before the boy hung his head.

They were all going to die.

VIII

THE RUINS OF
DENVER,
COLORADO

War crested the western edge of the crater astride the behemoth Thunder. Trotting his powerful steed in a half-circle, he inspected his army. There were fluorescent yellow eyes as far as he could see, trailing nearly to the tower where Death stood atop the roof, watching them march from that vantage until they vanished into the mountains.

The night had finally descended, blacker than sin, nearly invisible snowflakes filling the air around them, freezing like television static with each strobe of lightning. Atmospheric electricity flashed back into the sky, reflecting from slick black reptilian skin and the hardened coating of molten metal fused to their scales. The ground trembled beneath their advance, their clawed feet hardened into steel-reinforced killing implements. Torches blazed from where the flanks carried them at the periphery, nearly out of sight through the suffocating storm.

He tugged his cowl down to keep the snow out of his fiery eyes and gave the long spines of Thunder's mane a sharp jerk. The beast's skeletal head snapped from side to side and it blasted fire from its nostrils as it turned back to the west. The snowstorm obscured the jagged crests of the Rocky Mountains, the foothills already white with snow.

Movement to his left drew War's eye, and while at first he could see nothing of import through the snow, his keen stare finally settled upon the source of the motion. A large white falcon sat atop the windowsill in the middle of a brick wall, the only standing remnant of the building now lying in rubble around it. He cocked his head at it and watched as it did the same. Without betraying his intent, War brought his hand beneath his cloak of dried flesh and took hold of the hilt of a thin bone crafted into a serrated blade. In one swift motion, he snapped back his wrist and launched the dagger at the bird, striking it right in the center of the chest before it could even leap from the ledge. The momentum carried it backward out of sight, the air filled with its dying scream and bloody white feathers.

Several more of those ivory birds rose from where they hid and flew into the storm, only now giving away the fact that they had even been there at all. Before he could reach under his cloak again, the storm swallowed them whole.

Guiding Thunder toward where he had felled the falcon, he leapt down to the ground and snatched the fuzzy white corpse from atop the blackened carcass of a sport utility vehicle. He held it upside down by the long claws, blood rushing from the wound to stain the feathers crimson like roses against lace.

In his mind he saw the surface of a choppy lake speeding past mere inches beneath him. A wall of smooth stone arose from the distant horizon, coming right at him. People took shape on the shore of the lake, gathered around a bonfire taller than any of them. One man stood above the others, the focus of their attention.

War smiled a lipless grin beneath his armored mask. Cut off the head and the body will die. Lancing his fingertips through the bird's breast, he tore it apart, throwing splashes of blood all around him before launching the tattered chunks of flesh back over his shoulder. With a frenetic hissing, the Swarm battled each other over the remains, filling the air with a momentary cloud of feathers and each others' sloppy blood. The sound of crunching in his ears, War hauled himself back up onto Thunder and clopped around the building. The same reptilian creature was behind him as it had been since they had first begun their march. It stood apart from the others, as it had a ferocious scar across its forehead, splitting its brow, and diagonally down its cheek with a frill beneath its chin the color of spilled blood. It stayed just behind the right flank of his steed, eyes affixed to the horizon while the others fought like the animals they were for their place in the pack.

Lowering a hand covered in the falcon's blood and a clump of feathers, he allowed that creature to approach and slather the mess from his palm with its purple tongue. Contented, it backed away again and issued a violent hiss, its crimson dewlap expanding to shiver like a flag in a stiff gale.

Turning his focus back to the mountain range, the only obstacle in his way, he raised his right fist and let out a war cry that sounded like boulders slamming together. A riotous hissing answered his call, shaking the accumulating snow from the rubble. The horse charged forward, the ground catching fire behind its stomping hooves. The Swarm ran through the flames behind, their rising voices the sound of the night being torn in two.

CHAPTER 3

I

MORMON TEARS

There were now only eleven of them standing on the beach, watching as the caravan fell into line and passed through the gap in the mountains and back into the white desert. Even through the dense cloud cover, they could tell that the sun had yet to rise. Every fiber in Adam's being screamed for him to go with them, but whether on a conscious level or not, he believed in Phoenix. He knew the logistical nightmare they faced. Richard was right. The others had been generous enough to leave them a small stock of canned goods, several gallon jugs of water, and a couple cases of Pepsi, but that was it. The rational part of his mind knew that they were in big trouble, but for Adam, logic had been eliminated from the equation long ago in those Iranian caves. All that remained were the spider web-thin strands of faith and they were already strained to the point of snapping.

Richard's parting words had been a standing invitation. That was the bottom line, if they failed there on the shores of the Great Salt Lake, then they could always track down their counterparts in the city. It was a wonderful safety net to have. Of course, if Phoenix was right and all of the others were going to die, then there would be nothing waiting for them in Salt Lake City when they arrived. And if that was how things played out, then they were now watching the others drive away for the very last time with death as their final destination.

Adam had tried everything he could imagine to convince them to stay, but in the end, he had failed. Perhaps it was because he lacked the strength of his convictions. He believed in Phoenix's visions and the undeniably convenient coincidences they had faced on their long journey, but what it all came down to was that he hadn't been able to make that final leap of faith, and if he were unable to, then how could he expect the others to? The more pressing question, however, the one that festered in his gut like a tapeworm, was would he be able to live with himself if they were all slaughtered, knowing that it had been within his power to stop them?

"You did everything you could," Phoenix said, resting a hand on Adam's shoulder.

"Did I?" Adam shrugged out of the boy's grasp and walked toward the tracks leading away across the salt flats. White rooster tails rose from their wake in the distance as they prepared to vanish from sight.

They had taken all of the vehicles, save one beat-up old Ford pickup and a trio of motorcycles. There were other means of transportation—they had flown in on the backs of winged equines resembling seahorses for God's sake!—but he couldn't shake the growing sense of isolation. Worse, it was a self-imposed exile in the middle of nowhere with little food and even fewer prospects for overcoming their situation. Christ…they'd already burned nearly every available scrap of wood for miles! What the hell had he gotten them into?

As soon as the vehicles vanished over the horizon, Adam turned and walked back to where the others had gathered.

"None of you have to stay here, you know," he said. "I wouldn't blame any of you for leaving right now to try to catch up with them."

There was a long moment of silence, the snow gusting around them. It had already begun to accumulate atop the sand in nearly indistinguishable swatches, small drifts forming against the base of the mountain.

"They're all going to die," Jill whispered, shivering.

Again silence.

"What do we do now?" Norman asked, looking at Adam.

"I suppose we should probably introduce ourselves first. That seems like the best place to start." No one stepped forward, so Adam assumed the lead. "My name's Adam Newman. I'm a general practitioner. Until recently I was serving the final year of my Army obligation at a refugee camp in western Iran."

He raised his eyebrows to Norman.

"Kyle Norman. I'm a medic in the fifty-first airborne. I was in the Persian Gulf when all hell broke loose." He attempted a wan smile and brushed the snow from his fatigues. "I guess now I'm just a guy in dirty clothes living in a cave." He turned to the girl with the short black hair beside him.

"Missy Stringer," she said in her sweet southern drawl. "My brother Mare and I are from Dover, Tennessee."

"Like my big sister already said, I'm Mare." He looked to his left at Jill, who had noticeably paled and appeared to be beginning to withdraw into herself.

"Jill Rayburn," she said, furrowing her brow as though concentrating. "A couple of days ago I was a freshman at the University of Oregon in Eugene. But I...I started having visions and now..." She sniffled. "Now I can't make them stop."

"It's okay," April whispered, wrapping her arm around Jill, who leaned into her shoulder. "I'm April Henson. I'm also from Eugene, and I'm only here today because of Jill's visions. If not for her, I don't know what might have happened." She squeezed Darren's hand and held on tight.

"Darren O'Neal. I came from Oregon with them. I'm a sophomore pre-med...I mean, I was a sophomore at the university." He shook his head. "I guess I'm going to have to get accustomed to using the past tense, huh?"

"I'm Ray Gorman. I suppose if nothing else I should be thankful to still be with my friends here, but along the way I lost...I lost the most beautiful girl in the world." Tears streamed from his eyes, but he swiped them away as he tucked his bangs behind his ear. "I know this is where I'm supposed to be because...because I can feel her here with me."

"I'm Lindsay Lechner," the blonde with the model looks said, standing visibly more comfortably. "I was on a plane for Vegas when everything happened. Going to try my luck as a showgirl, you know?" She smiled, her eyes clouded by unfulfilled dreams. "Eight years of ballet and tap, another four of classical. Honestly, I don't know why I decided to stay here with you guys, but the only reason I can come up with off the top of my head is because that guy Richard is such a jerk."

They all shared a moment of laughter, but it quickly faded.

"I'm Evelyn Hartman from the middle of nowhere, California. I was a graduate student in oceanography at the Scripps' Institute before my dad had his accident and I had to come back home to help out on the ranch. With his dying words, he sent me on a quest for 'Mormon Tears,' which I'd imagine is the same reason we're all here."

"My name's Phoenix," the pink-eyed boy said, "but that's about all I know. Until Adam and Norman saved me from the Swarm, the Man had kept me locked in a dark basement my entire life. I don't really know much other than that." He shrugged.

"What's the Swarm?" Mare asked.

"They're the ones who are coming for us. They are the corrupt, the sinners, the ones whose souls couldn't ascend to heaven, trapped inside the proverbial body of temptation. They are the snakes that walk on two legs, God's chosen army of destruction, the dark nature of each and every one of us. When they arrive, they will bring only pain and suffering, promising an end to man's days on earth."

"Why would you think that God would want us all to die?" Missy asked.

"I don't think He does," Phoenix said, pausing. "I think that's why we're here. Maybe we represent some part of humanity that He isn't ready to completely part with yet."

"Then why would He send an army against us?" Norman asked. "To me, that kind of makes it sound like He *is* willing to part with us. Don't you think?"

"I just don't know," Phoenix said, averting his eyes. "All I know is what I see when I close my eyes, and even then it doesn't make very much sense. It's like I see pictures of things that haven't happened yet through other people's eyes without the benefit of their interpretation.

It's only when these things come to pass that I understand their significance. I think that God's just giving us clues to see if we're worthy of survival. If we believe in Him as much as He believes in us. Kind of a last chance. But I know that if we fail when we take our stand, He will have no second thoughts about wiping us out."

II

EASTBOUND
INTERSTATE 80

Richard sat in the cab of Gray's truck, pressed all the way up against the window, watching his breath form and then dissolve on the glass as the truck passed through alternating stretches of salt flats and pine forest. The snowflakes had nearly doubled in size since they'd reached the highway and were now so thick it was like driving through a moth infestation. It covered the road, but the shoulders were still clearly discernible as they rose and fell with Gray keeping them equidistant to either side. The stalled and abandoned cars were slowly disappearing under the accumulation, crashed into the hillsides or simply dead in the middle of the interstate, but they were still able to navigate with relative ease. As there were more bodies packed in there than the seatbelts could accommodate, he didn't complain as their progress started to slow with the worsening roads.

Garrett was pressed against him from the left, their legs warring for space beneath the dashboard as he tried to keep from bumping the gearshift, his broad shoulders aching as he compressed them to afford as much room for the others as he could. Carrie sat to his left against her husband, her knees tucked to her chest, heels on the seat, to give Gray access to the stick.

Highway signs passed to the right, their faces crusted with ice, only a couple of words visible here and there. They knew they were heading in the right direction and would eventually end up in Salt Lake City regardless. It was just a matter of time.

Richard looked at the rear view mirror. The youth group bus was about fifty yards back, packed three to a seat with the aisle stuffed with bodies. It had been able to hold nearly all of the refugees by itself, leaving only a handful of stragglers to bring up the rear in their old trucks, hauling the motorcycles they'd bled dry to fuel the other vehicles. They traveled in a straight line, with those behind following in the tracks of the preceding. Without headlights and taillights, he imagined it must be difficult to keep the car ahead in sight through the storm, but that wasn't his problem at the moment. He was too busy alternately scouring the sides of the road and the horizon for the first sign of a suitable location to stop.

They needed a building large enough to house all ninety-six of them, yet small enough that it could be heated fairly easily. What did that inherently imply? An apartment building maybe? Nothing too tall as they would need to be able to defend the building from the roof. Three stories was about as high as they could comfortably get and still allow for an untrained marksman to hit the street with a shotgun or rifle. It couldn't be out in the open either. Trying to secure three-hundred and sixty degrees would be nearly impossible. They had to find a structure that allowed an unobstructed view of the surrounding area, yet at the same time limited the number of directions from which they could be attacked. That ruled out everything suburban or in the densely-populated downtown districts. Too many tall buildings would hide an advancing army until they were already upon them. What did that leave? Their fortress needed to be close to a large grocery store or warehouse with a suitable stock of dry and canned foods. There had to be a hardware store, preferably one of those gigantic mega-stores like Home Depot close by as well. That covered all of their immediate needs but water. They could melt snow and boil it, but that would be awfully time-consuming and labor-intensive. It could be done, no doubt, but not as easily as if they found some place already equipped to store large amounts of water, preferably with some sort of purification system intact. Did such a thing even exist?

"Figured out where we're headed yet, boss?" Gray asked. With the spotted houses appearing to either side of the road and the increasing number of truck stops, he knew they had to be close now, and Richard hadn't said a word since they left.

Richard couldn't afford to come across as anything other than decisive. He couldn't allow room for anyone to question whether or not he was in charge. Ever. Indecision was a sign of weakness, which engendered dissention. They couldn't permit factions to arise from their ranks or progress would be seriously impeded. He needed to answer, and it had better be good.

A sign whizzed past on the shoulder, the tail of an airplane poking out from beneath the crust of ice.

"Follow the signs to the airport," Richard said.

Gray stole his eyes from the road to scrutinize Richard.

"We can't stay at the airport," he said. "What would you propose? All of us living in a terminal and sleeping on the floor?"

"It would be impossible to secure the perimeter of an airport," Garrett said. "I don't even know how many miles of fence—"

"And that's why we aren't going to the airport," Richard said smugly.

"But you just said—"

"I said to follow the signs to the airport. I didn't ever say we were going to live in it."

Silence fell upon the cab.

"What can you always find surrounding the airport?" Richard asked. "Without exception."

"Hangers," Garrett said.

"That would be no different than living in a cave. Try harder." Richard needed them to follow his logic so they could recognize the genius of it, but he was growing impatient. Was he the only one among them with any kind of intellect?

"Hotels," Gray finally said.

Richard smiled and touched the tip of his nose. It was perfect in its simplicity. There would be a single enormous kitchen large enough to stock plenty of food and cook for hundreds of people at any given time. Every major grocery store would have a warehouse not far from the airport, and even if there wasn't a gigantic hardware store within walking distance, they would be able to find everything they needed in any of the adjacent hotels or machining shops nearby. And since the airport needed to be outside of the city proper, with so many hotels requiring so much water, there would have to be some sort of storage tower to accommodate their needs.

It wouldn't even surprise him to find a nice Hilton or something already enclosed by gates or walls they could fortify without too much effort.

"I like it," Gray said, veering off the highway and pumping the brakes to slow. The rear end fishtailed, but he was able to correct it easily and bend around the ramp over the highway and toward the airport. The signs were now clearly visible as they no longer faced into the wind.

Gray still had one major concern, though. Even if they were successful in building this fortress that Richard envisioned and were able to withstand whatever assault was coming, what then?

He watched Richard from the corner of his eye. The man sat there so aloof. He was scheming something, but for the life of him, Gray couldn't imagine what. All he knew was that he didn't trust Richard any farther than he could throw him and actually feared what he might do if given too much power. There was something in his mannerisms, but more specifically in his eyes, that made Gray increasingly uncomfortable.

III

Mormon Tears

Evelyn had walked away from the others to check on her plants, promising to catch up with them in the cave to help with whatever they needed. She didn't want to speak prematurely and raise their fragile hopes, but if she were able to get just the kelp she had brought with her to take root, then she would potentially be able to feed all of them. Kelp was as extraordinarily fast-growing species that could overtake entire coastlines if not kept in check. In many tourist traps, it was considered a pest. It was strange to think that their dreams of survival now depended on the proliferation of a weed.

She climbed over the now familiar rocks, perching atop the one closest to the edge of the water. There would be no more wading into the lake, as the temperature already had to have dropped a good thirty degrees since the previous morning. Her breath was ripped from her lips as steam to join with the snowflakes that clogged the air. The stones were slick with a layer of ice, making her balance tenuous, but she was able to get close enough that she could see down into the water. The lake was obviously cooling rapidly as it no longer generated the fog it had during the night, becoming so cold that the waves almost looked sharp. All of the plants were still there where she had left them, still buried by the roots, but they had taken on a deeper brown color and were starting to wilt.

"They can't tolerate the cold," she whispered, shaking her head. But what could she possibly do about it? She could try to uproot them and grow them out of the elements in some sort of container, but they didn't have anything larger than a single gallon, which by itself could only house a couple of plants. She could always head into town to find some aquariums, but without the full-spectrum lighting, they wouldn't have a chance, and leaving them out to be exposed to what little light reached the ground brought her right back to the exact same problem. It was a fool's proposition unless she could figure out some way to raise the temperature of the lake, and shy of opening a fissure in the earth, she couldn't think of a blasted way to do it.

She refused to give up her life's dream just yet. There had to be a way to make it work…she was just running out of time to do so.

Rising, both arms out to her sides for balance, she carefully traversed the pile of rocks until she reached the sand and jumped off. The snow was now just deep enough to cover the toes of her shoes, but based on the black clouds to the west, she could tell that they were going to see much more before the storm was through.

Evelyn had only stayed there at the lake because of her project, and now that the kelp was dying, she wondered if she should have left with the others before she began to do the same. There was something undeniably spiritual about this place, though. The expulsion of gasses from her father's dead body had sent her halfway across the country to find Mormon Tears, and thus far it had proven to be her salvation. They had found it with nothing more than those cryptic words to go on. What were the odds of that? She was fairly confident that she was where she was supposed to be, but what now? It felt as though they were simply passing time…but until what?

She walked by the remains of the bonfire to the right, in the middle of the beach. The logs were nearly consumed stacks of charcoal, only now cool enough to allow the snow to accumulate on them. The other tracks in the snow were already beginning to fill, soon to be obliterated entirely. Even the stone island far off where the lake met the sky was a white beacon barely visible through the sheeting snow.

Turning into the cave, she walked into the recess in the wall and followed its course through the pitch black, running her fingers along the walls to either side to keep from walking into anything. Wan light slowly infiltrated the smothering darkness, accompanied by the muted voices of those ahead. Finally, she stepped out into the larger cavern and stood atop the overlook.

The others were down beneath, the room dimly lit by the flickering remains of a fire constructed with all of the remaining wood. She tried not to think about their options for heat when the flames had turned what little was left to ash. Several of the others were up on the various levels of the pueblo, hauling out large sticks and other objects from whoever passed them up from beneath and tossing them down to the ground where others gathered them into piles. One of the girls was monitoring a pot of what smelled like Spaghetti-O's on the fire while another circulated the room with a jug of water.

The cave wasn't much, but it was warmer than she thought it would be, and easily twice the size. When they had said there was a pueblo inside, she hadn't known exactly what to expect, but this surpassed her wildest expectations. It looked almost like a haphazardly-constructed motel straight out of the American Southwest. She'd seen similar buildings in paintings and coffee table books, but never in person. Decomposition had set in through the years and it looked as though a stiff breeze could topple it, but they just might be able to live in it after all.

Evelyn looked around until she found the rocky staircase leading down to the cavern floor and began to descend. The mural on the wall caught her attention and she had to slow to marvel at it. The people weren't square-sided or abstract like any of the other primitive wall etchings she had seen, but true-to-life, almost photographic drawings. The level of craftsmanship was staggering.

Walking between two clusters of stalagmites, their points reaching above her head, she approached the fire to warm her hands before trying to see where they needed her to help.

"We were starting to wonder if you might have left," April said, stirring the wonderful-smelling concoction with an oversized plastic spoon.

"I was just checking on some things."

"Like what?"

"Nothing really. I just planted a couple of—"

"Oh, yeah. You're the plant lady," April said and smiled.

"What…? I don't understand."

"Haven't you seen yourself in the mural?"

Evelyn could only shake her head.

"Come on then," April said, leaning the spoon against the side of the pot. She brushed her hands off on her thighs and took Evelyn by the hand.

Evelyn stared at the chalk design as they approached, amazed by the size of it. It was still mainly bathed in shadows set to flickering by the crackling flames, but details revealed themselves with each encroaching step. From above, it looked as though the background was smeared black with chalk, but as she drew closer, yellow eyes separated from the darkness, mottled with black. She'd never seen anything like them, but they still sent a shiver up her spine.

"See…" April said, stopping right in front of the wall. "You're the plant lady."

"Oh my God," Evelyn gasped. It was like staring into a mirror. She held a basket brimming with kelp in both hands. The leaves were far too wide though, more closely resembling a species of lettuce. She grazed her fingers through the dust, but the chalk turned to powder and came away on her skin.

"Hey! Check this out!" Mare called. They turned in time to see his head pop out through the hole in the roof of the corner unit on the ground floor of the pueblo. He held what appeared to be a large black rock over his head.

"What is it?" Adam asked, setting down an armful of those long sharpened spears. He took the stone from Mare and helped him out of the room beneath. Adam pulled away his left hand and studied his palm. It was positively coated with a black chalky residue.

"Well…what do you think?" Mare asked, waiting for a response, but Adam only shrugged. "Don't you know what that is?"

"Apparently not. Enlighten me."

"It's coal. You know…extremely flammable? Produces heat? Burns hot for a long time?"

"How much is down there?" Adam asked, rolling the chunk over and over in his hands.

"The whole room is nearly filled with it."

"Seriously?"

Mare smirked. "There ought to be more than enough to last us through the entire winter."

Adam bit his lip, his brow lowering contemplatively.

"I would have thought this would have made you a lot happier," Mare said.

"I just don't understand."

"You burn it and—"

"No, not that," Adam said, passing the coal back to Mare. He turned and looked out upon the entire cave. "Don't you think this is all too convenient?"

"What do you mean?"

"The building. The mural. The coal. Everything. How could anyone hundreds of years ago have known that we would be here now, and why would they go to so much trouble to make sure that all of this was so perfectly prepared?"

"Don't look a gift horse in the mouth, man."

"That's just it. What exactly are we preparing for here?"

IV

SALT LAKE CITY

It was perfect. Were he to have closed his eyes and tried to picture the building that best suited each and every one of their needs, this would have been it. Richard couldn't help but reflect upon his own brilliance. If he had believed in fate, he knew it would have been smiling down on him at that very moment.

"Magnificent," he said, standing at the rear of the front parking lot with his back to the street and staring up at his fortress.

The Renaissance Inn had been designed to look like a medieval castle, from the large gray bricks all the way up three stories to where four red parapets crowned each corner. The only thing that could have possibly made it even more amazing would have been a thick wooden drawbridge, but just a double set of glass doors in the front and one to either side would be easy enough to defend. If indeed they would have to. That still remained to be seen.

He turned to where the light blue bus was idling near the front door and watched the boy and his mother climb down the steps and into the deep snow. Exhaust swirled all around them from the old vehicle as they walked toward the front doors where the others were already beginning to pack into the lobby. He needed to keep the boy close to him. He was like a naïve little Rasputin; the key to the power Richard needed to rule. So long as he could keep that child right by his side and usurp his dreams, he would be able to lead them as the prophet they were slowly beginning to believe him to be. So long as the others thought he was more than human, more powerful than all of the rest with his direct connection to divinity in his dreams, then they would blindly follow him to the gates of hell itself.

There was a loud clang behind him and he spun to face the road again. The last of the convoy of trucks had finally pulled through the gate where Garrett had been waiting to close it behind them. The extent of the property was enclosed by a black, wrought-iron fence that had to be close to eight feet tall, each of the vertical posts capped with a sharp spade. It would be simple enough to coil some barbed wire on the top and maybe even run some battery-powered electrical fencing through the lower portion. And with the gaps between the bars, they would have a nearly unobstructed shot straight through at whatever may attempt to storm the gates before they even attempted to scale it.

Across the street was an enormous parking lot that led back to a warehouse that could have housed a football field, the loading bays lined with a fleet of semi-trailers adorned with the Safeway logo. There were dozens of other properties just like it leading away toward the airport, and while he couldn't clearly see any details through the blizzard, odds were that at least one of them had to serve as a distributor for some chain of stores that carried hardware. And maybe one of them might even be a hub for a sporting goods store where they would be able to load up on guns and ammunition. That was the most important thing after all, wasn't it? None of them would feel safe until they were armed, and who would hold the key to the armory?

Richard beamed. Power was a wonderful thing, indeed.

He strode out of the storm and through the front doors with an unwavering feeling of confidence. Maybe his claim to divinity was more than just rhetoric. Everything had fallen precisely into place, not as he had foreseen, but as he had imagined. Maybe in this brave new world of dreams that predicted reality and unsubstantiated faith, he was more than just their leader. Soon enough...soon enough they would worship him as a god.

Richard didn't even feel the trailing edge of the freezing wind or the snow that had accumulated on his shoulders and head. He was impervious even to the chill as it melted through his loafers. When he walked through the entryway, they were all waiting for him in a silence marred only by sniffling and coughing. All eyes were upon him as he passed through the foyer and past the racks of pamphlets advertising local attractions.

His people filled the chairs and couches in the large lobby, crowding the space between. To the right was a darkened restaurant beside the front desk, aptly enough named Ye Olde English Tavern. They looked as he thought a similarly grungy and unbathed group of refugees might have passing through Ellis Island in the days of his forefathers. The cold and exhausted huddled masses not risking their lives for a mere shot at freedom, but pathetic human refuse yearning to be led to their destinies.

He grabbed the back of the closest chair, the man already sitting in it immediately hopping out, and dragged it to the center of the room beside a chalkboard advertising prime rib for two for twenty dollars. Climbing up atop it, he surveyed their faces before addressing them. Their features softened noticeably when he smiled.

"How does it feel to be inside again?" he asked.

There was a grumble of contentment.

Dim light slanted through the dramatically-arched windows at the front of the hotel, creating corridors of mote-riddled grayness to give just the impression of illumination, showcasing his misty breath when he spoke.

"First off, I want to congratulate all of you for your unfaltering strength and desire to better our circumstances. Surviving in itself is no small feat, but taking that first step forward into the unknown is downright terrifying. You all should be incredibly proud of yourselves. You are the bravest lot of men and women I have ever had the privilege of being associated with." He paused to allow their applause. "But now comes the hardest part of all. Are you guys ready to get to work?"

There was much nodding, a good portion of it obviously grudgingly, but he could see in their eyes their acquiescence, that they knew there was no alternative.

"With the storm outside adding to the lack of sunlight, we'll be lucky if we have four or five more hours of daylight out there, so we need to get started. Time is working against us. We need to have our generators running and in place to allow us the luxury of artificial light to extend our useful hours of productivity." He paused. They looked like so many beaten dogs. Perhaps the time was right to throw them a bone. He continued with a warm smile. "But first, why don't you all head into this restaurant and see if you can rustle up some breakfast?"

That set them at ease, encouraging smiles and conversation as they moved en masse into the tavern.

"Garrett," Richard said, taking the larger man by the arm before he could walk past. "I need you to do me a favor."

"Whatever you need, boss."

"As my right hand," Richard started, gauging the man's reaction carefully, "I'm going to need you to do something of the utmost importance. Confidentially. Do you think you can do that?"

"Absolutely," Garrett said, his eyes alight with his newly-designated importance.

"Here's what I need you to do," Richard said, pulling Garrett closer so he could whisper directly into his ear.

Garrett listened intently, focusing on each and every word so as not to lose any of them beneath the din. He nodded several times, peering at the crowd from the corner of his eye until he saw what he was looking for. When Richard finished, he looked the muscular man in the eyes and slapped him on the shoulder, dismissing him with a nod.

As Garrett crossed the lobby, he could feel his chest swelling with pride. He'd been a lot of things in his life and had even enjoyed a fleeting moment of celebrity playing ball in college, but until now, he'd never been anything close to truly important. Integral. Richard was counting on him and there was no way he was going to let him down.

"Excuse me," he said to the man in the Army fatigues who remained seated, apparently waiting for someone else to fix his food for him or for the crowd to thin. There was an air of depression about the man, not merely emotional sadness, but a physical malady that appeared to be draining him slowly. "My name is Garrett." He offered his hand.

"Peckham," the man said, reciprocating the gesture, his grip embarrassingly weak. His eyes reflected a level of exhaustion that unnerved Garrett as they were sunken into pits of darkness. The man was overly subdued, almost like he was drugged, and even though

Garrett was no doctor, he could easily recognize the symptoms of shock.

"Mr. Robinson would appreciate it greatly if you could spare a few minutes to meet with him on the third floor."

"I need to eat."

"We'll make sure you eat your fill afterwards."

Peckham scrutinized Garrett. He didn't like the cryptic nature of the entire conversation. If there was one thing he had learned through his years in Uncle Sam's service, it was how to sniff out subversion. The whole nature of the proposed meeting was covert.

He watched the other men and women through the restaurant's door as they gathered around bowls of croutons and pretzels. The last thing he wanted right now was to find himself in the middle of anyone else's business, but he had to admit that for the first time in days something had piqued his curiosity enough to momentarily clear the fugue that had settled upon him.

"Third floor?" Peckham asked.

Garrett nodded.

"What the hell," Peckham said, clapping his palms on his knees and rising to his feet.

"I'll meet you up there," Garrett said as he turned away, trusting Peckham to find the stairs and ascend without a chaperone. Walking into the restaurant, he scoured the crowd until he saw his targets. He pushed through the mob of people happily crunching away on anything they could get into their mouths until he reached the mother and her young son. He rested his hand on her shoulder. "Mr. Robinson would like to see you."

Susan whirled to face him, at first appearing frightened, but she relaxed fairly quickly. She had known at some point this might become a possibility, and she would do absolutely anything to protect Jake.

"Can you stay here with my son?" she asked.

Garrett looked confused. "Mr. Robinson would like to see both of you, if you don't mind."

"Why?" Susan asked.

"He will explain when we arrive."

Susan eyed him cautiously. What wasn't he telling her?

"Come on, Jake," she said, taking the boy by the hand.

He turned around at her urging, his face covered with crumbs, and shut his eyes as fast as he could, stifling a scream.

The man in front of him was drenched with blood from wide gashes all over his face and chest, his clothes torn to wet black ribbons, and his mother...she had a bloody crater on the back of her head from which blood poured unimpeded down her back.

When he opened his eyes again, everything had reverted to normal. Both the man and his mother had already started to head for the door, oblivious to his reaction.

"Please, mommy," he whimpered. "I don't want to go. Please don't make me go."

But she either didn't hear or ignored his pleas, pulling him along behind as they crossed the lobby toward the staircase door.

V

MORMON TEARS

Jill set the last of her gathered poles onto the giant pyramid in the middle of the cavern floor. There were still a ton more down in that room, but the others were now completely preoccupied with shoving blocks of coal into the fire, so she could finally sit down and relax for a few minutes. She'd eaten a plate of those canned noodles, but they sat like a stone in her gut. Maybe after she gave her system a chance to digest them before putting her body back to work she might start feeling—

Darkness descended upon her like a shroud. It was smothering. She tried to scream, but no sound came out. Pulse thumping in her temples, her eyes gradually adjusted to the blackness. She could see her hands in her lap. No…the fingers were longer and dirty, the bare legs too heavily muscled. It wasn't a thick coating of dirt on the slender fingers, but chalk, covering the hands all the way up to the forearms. The backs of the arms were forked with veins despite how thin they were.

She caught a glimpse of something drawn on the ground in front of her crossed legs and chunks of chalk scattered about. There wasn't time to clearly see the design before she raised her head and looked straight up through a square hole. Shadowed faces leered over her for a moment before they withdrew and slid something that made a grinding sound across the opening, slowly, inching incrementally over her until it sealed off the wan light, stranding her in the absolute blackness where she couldn't see a thing.

"Jill," a voice whispered, followed by a string of words in a tongue she couldn't understand. They sounded like no language she'd ever heard before, and yet at the same time somehow familiar.

She hadn't realized she'd closed her eyes until they opened and she was sitting on the ground with her back against a stalagmite, staring up at the highest level of the pueblo. The others were still gathered around the fire, which was now easily twice as tall as when she'd seen it last, divvying up the remainder of the Spaghetti-O's. She felt disoriented as though she'd fallen asleep, but she couldn't possibly have allowed her lids to close for more than a couple of minutes.

There was something about the third story of the structure that wouldn't allow her to steal her gaze away for even a second. It was no more than a single cube stacked atop the others, a lone room at the pinnacle of the non-symmetrical building. Rising to her feet, she shuffled over to the pile of spears and took one in her right hand, her legs guiding her to the ladder leaning against the pueblo. She climbed upward, reaching the first roof and finding another ladder to her right, which she used to reach the roof of the second level, where she stood and stared at the windowless walls. There were no entrances of any kind, the two walls terminating against the cave to either side where they met with the rock, the seams crumbled away over time.

"How are you supposed to—?" Jill started, but realized what she needed to do. Setting down the pike, she grabbed the top rung of the ladder she'd just used and pulled it all the way up. After a moment of fighting with its weight, she leaned it against the wall.

Taking the pole in her hand again, she climbed upward until she reached the roof and stepped off. There was no large square stone as she had expected, but rather a flat surface marred by only a single mound of the adobe-like substance. She raised the spear and pointed the sharpened end at the edge of the mound. With a grunt, she rammed to tip into the roof, which cracked away to reveal the edge of the square rock. Again and again she jammed the spear until she'd freed all four sides, scraping away the remainder of the mud and straw until she could force the tip under one side of the rock. Using the staff as a lever, she pulled down on it until the rock slid back just enough to release a stale breath of dust from the hole. Casting the stick aside, she sat down and braced her feet against the edge of the stone and pushed as hard as she could. It slid away with a loud scraping sound until it was nearly halfway across the opening. Scooting closer, she struggled to straighten her legs, nearly screaming with the strain, until the rock slid past the far edge of the hatch.

Rolling onto all fours, she scurried toward it, holding her breath to try to keep from breathing the dust. She began to cough so hard that she had to pull her shirt up over her mouth and nose, but lowered her head through the hole regardless. The darkness beneath was so thick it looked like the room was filled with oil.

"I need light," she gasped, ducking back out and looking over her shoulder. There was a burning branch wedged into a fissure in the cavern wall a level down. Hurrying down the ladder, she exhumed it and nearly extinguished the flame in her hurry to again ascend the ladder, scrabbling to the edge of the square entryway and lowering the fire through.

The torchlight was nearly consumed by the thick cloud of dust and strands of cobwebs that filled the room, but she was able to make out a vaguely human shape on the floor directly beneath her. Jill looked back to the others, but they were still down below reveling in the massive amounts of heat produced by the coal.

Lying on her stomach, she tossed the burning branch down into the room, off to the right so as not to land on the outline of the person. As soon as it hit the ground, the light drew contrast along the contours of the shape. Skeletal legs crossed Indian-style terminated in bony feet, the lap the unmistakable heart shape of a bare pelvis. The skull slumped forward onto an exposed ribcage while two limp arms hung to the sides, hands resting on their backs so that the fingers curled up toward her. The ground was black with liquefied skin and tissue.

"Jesus," she whispered, pursing her lips against the ungodly stench that rose from the corpse.

Closing her eyes, she took a deep breath and maneuvered herself until her legs dangled down through the ceiling. She dropped down into the room with a furious cracking sound of the deteriorating floor beneath. Fortunately, it was built upon rows of logs the size of telephone poles or she could have fallen right through to her death. She needed to be more careful.

Lifting the torch, she stamped out a small section of the floor that had begun to burn and inspected the skeleton. The hollow eye sockets were filled with spider webs and the decayed carcasses of their former inhabitants. Whether induced by the firelight or not, the entire body took on a manila cast. All of the teeth were intact, though the mandible had fallen away and rested in its lap. Some of the ribs had broken over time as the cartilage decomposed and the body slumped forward. The walls were bare with the exception of the wall to her right, which served as the front of the structure. It had been carved away from within in jagged sections that could only have been clawed by fingers.

Kneeling, she looked first into the expressionless face, and then to the ground in front of it. Chunks of colored chalk littered the floor in the deep accumulation of dust. She blew gently across the ground, scattering the dust, which rose into the air with a fresh swell of putrescence that made her retch. Lowering the torch until it illuminated the drawing, she marveled at the intricacy. It had obviously been drawn by the same person who had done the cave wall. There was the image of a hand extending a finger to touch another hand, though the second was skinless, merely a collection of bones.

Jill raised her eyes to look into the long dead face, momentarily sensing a sentience like unseen eyes looking back at her.

"Is this for me?" she whispered, lowering her gaze to its hand. Slowly, she reached toward it until her fingertip touched the pointed tip of the corpse's finger.

A blinding white light grew from the eyes of the skull and Jill had just time to open her mouth in surprise before being drawn into it. The light peeled back to reveal a blizzard so oppressive she could barely see the dark shapes trudging through the deep snow ahead of her. Like a poorly spliced film, the next image was of a group of people in the cavern holding their torches aloft. They were clad in animal skins: the hairy hides of both brown and black bears, the shorter fur of elk and deer, and even one with the shaggy mane of a bison hanging down his back. Then the furs were gone and dark-skinned men and women in tanned brown leather slaved to build the pueblo, while a lone woman with long black hair drew on the wall beside the burgeoning structure. Another disorienting cut in the continuity and the pueblo was complete. As was the mural on the wall. Several older men with wrinkles like melting wax gestures toward the drawing. And while Jill couldn't understand their words, the fear in their voices was unmistakable. The woman stood in front of them, tears streaming down her face, her abdomen swollen by pregnancy. A wrinkled man, hobbled by time, extended a knobby finger toward her and touched her belly. All of the onlookers were somber, burdened by the weight of the monumental decision they shared. And again she was inside the room, watching the stone slide over the hole again to seal her inside the darkness of the tomb. There was a flash of brightness and she saw a torrent of snowflakes. Men and women walking through the knee-deep snow until they could walk no more, collapsing into the accumulation, unable to rise. She heard screaming and her fingers exploded with pain, nails ripping from the cuticles, blood rushing from the rent skin as she tried to claw her way through to help them, watching them die in her mind before slumping to the floor of the room to the tune of sobbing.

Jill gasped and fell onto her rear end, panting as she apparently hadn't been breathing.

Her eyes shot to the skeleton. The skull leaned forward and broke free from the cervical spine, hitting the ground with the crack of sutures breaking. It rolled away from the legs and came to rest in the middle of the drawing.

Jill lifted it carefully and was about to try balancing it on top of the vertebrae again when she noticed that something about the drawing was different. Someone had smeared a finger through the chalk to write the words Blizzard of Souls. Perching the head atop the shoulders, she looked at her hands. The tip of her right index finger was covered with colored powder.

There was a scream above her.

Jill looked up and saw a great white falcon perched on the edge of the opening with blinding white eyes that looked remarkably familiar.

VI

Salt Lake City

Gray had been helping comb the kitchen for food and had just set out a wholesale-sized bag of peanuts when Garrett had walked into the restaurant. He didn't know the man well enough to read his expression, but he could tell by the way the man shoved through the crowd as though with a purpose, eyes darting from one side of the room to the other, that he was looking for something far more imperative than a handful of pretzels. At first he thought that maybe he was the object of the search. He knew it wouldn't be long before their self-anointed ruler called on him, but when Garrett stopped beside the mother and child with whom they'd traveled, talking to them only briefly before escorting both back into the lobby, he could tell that something strange, something that none of the rest of them were meant to see, was transpiring. It wasn't the culmination of a string of logical thoughts that led to that conclusion, but a gut instinct as powerful as any he'd ever experienced. It felt like someone had reached inside of him, curled their fingers through coils of his bowels and started to twist.

"Load up your pockets for me, Care," he whispered into his wife's ear. "I'll be back in a few."

"Don't do anything stupid," she said, taking him by the arm with a genuine look of concern in her eyes. Could she feel that something was amiss as well?

He turned to face her and allowed a cocky smile. "Me?"

"I know that look, Gray. What are you sniffing out?"

"Just following a hunch."

"Keep your head down and your nose clean, you hear?"

"Don't I always?" he said through the wavering smirk.

She rolled her eyes. It was the first time that he had truly seen the real Carrie through the fugue that had settled over her. Maybe she was going to come out of it after all.

He turned without another word and passed through the dining area and into the lobby just in time to see the door to the stairwell close to the right. Turning the knob without a sound, he opened it and ascended into the shadows. Footsteps echoed hollowly above him like thunder. Using them to disguise his own, he pulled himself upward by the railing, carefully planting his feet to keep from betraying his advance. Rounding the first landing, he continued on until he reached the next. A door closed above him, the only remaining sound his harsh breathing. When he finally made it to the top floor, he pressed his ear to the cold metal door, but he couldn't hear a thing. Holding his breath, he twisted the knob and opened the door just far enough to see into the hallway.

Soft voices trailed from his right where he could see a dim glow from what appeared to be a pair of flashlights pointed around the corner where the hall terminated and bent to the left. Slipping through the gap, he closed the door softly behind and eased down the corridor until he was nearly to the end, pressing his back against the door of one of the rooms.

"…why I need you all right here beside me," Richard said. "I won't pretend that in this situation we're all equal. We need to clearly identify our strengths in order to best utilize them for not just our survival, but our future prosperity."

Gray slid along the wall until he was at the very edge and dropped to one knee. Keeping his back firmly against the wall, he peered around the corner. Richard and Garrett both held long broad flashlights that they must have found in emergency roadside kits, while the military guy listened beside the mother and child.

"But why do you need us?" the woman asked.

Richard smiled. "Your son has a special gift, Susan. We need to both use it to our advantage for the good of all, and protect him from those who would exploit him."

"He's just a little boy."

"With precognitive abilities that could mean the difference between life and death for all of us."

"I can't allow you to use him. He's a kid, for God's sake."

"All I'm suggesting is that you and Jake stay by my side. In the grand scheme of things, he is far more important than I. Take the room next to mine. Think of your son. I can't imagine that there's a safer place to be right now, can you?"

"No," Susan whispered, looking at the other men.

"Good," Richard said, clapping his hands. "And Sergeant Peckham…as Chief of Security, your first task will be to acquire a room for these two."

Peckham stepped forward and rattled the handle on the door. Without the key card for the electronic lock, there was no way it was going to open, and even then, without electricity, it would be futile. He looked at Richard, who simply nodded. Raising his right boot, Peckham kicked the door as hard as he could. The lock gave way with a loud crack, taking a chunk of the trim with it, the doorknob slamming into the drywall behind.

"Don't worry," Richard said. "I'll have someone get right on that lock." He gestured for them to enter. Their eyes never left his as they crossed the threshold. "Why don't you two try to get some rest? You're both excused from this afternoon's work."

"We can help just like everyone else."

"Societal standing does come with certain perks, dear," Richard said, pulling their door closed. "Take whichever rooms you guys want. Just make sure you leave me the corner suite next to theirs."

"Sure thing," Peckham said, walking down the hall to the next available room on the right and kicking through the door. He ducked inside to explore his new home.

Garrett waited until Peckham was out of sight and escorted Richard to his suite, kicking the door in himself. The two stepped inside and closed the door.

Gray darted across the hallway and pressed himself into the corner.

"The mother isn't going to let us get too close to him," a voice whispered from inside the room.

"Well, she isn't going to have to now, is she?"

"She hasn't let him out of her sight for a minute this entire time."

"It doesn't matter. We need him. Not her. He's the key to our survival."

"His visions, anyway."

The voice was silenced by a slap.

"My visions."

There was a moment of silence. Gray held his breath to listen.

"Why don't you go get something to eat with the others?"

"Richard…"

"It's okay, Garrett. I'm the one who should be sorry. You're my number one. I need you more than all of the others combined."

"My fault, Richard. I shouldn't have said anything."

"Tell you what… After you get some food, I want you to make this kid your only priority. Bring him as much food as he can eat and anything he wants to drink. Make sure he doesn't have any reason to leave the room."

"What about the mother?"

"Treat her like a queen. Just make sure that they both stay in that room."

"And what if they won't?"

"Make sure that they do. Understand?"

"I think so…"

"Good." There was a long pause. "We only need the boy."

Gray struggled to breathe. Were they saying what he thought they were? The door beside him opened without warning. Pressing himself into the corner, he prayed that the shadows would conceal him.

Garrett and Richard walked down the hallway away from him without looking back. Opening the door to the stairwell, they stepped inside silently. As soon as Gray heard the booming of their tread echoing from the other side of the closed door, he allowed his stale breath to rush out.

He should never have followed them upstairs. He could have been downstairs with his wife and a bowl of peanuts. Instead, he was hiding in the darkness on the third floor trying to talk himself out of doing what he knew he had to do. They had given themselves over to a power-hungry madman, and they were going to die if he didn't do something about it. The feeling was so intense it caused him to shiver.

He needed to get Carrie out of there. They could head back to the Great Salt Lake with the others or maybe just keep on driving. Maybe find a hut on a beach somewhere tropical and—

A small face appeared to his right, peeking out at him from the second door down. Gray couldn't see the eyes in the darkness, but he could feel their stare.

He couldn't leave them here. Might as well bury them himself.

"It's okay," the boy whispered. "We'll be fine."

They wouldn't be though, and Gray knew it.

VII

Mormon Tears

Phoenix sat around the fire with the others. They had already unloaded the contents of the rooms, leaving only the front chamber filled with coal, which had already proven to last far longer than any amount of wood and burned hotter to boot. Their brief break had been well earned, but now they had to begin preparations for what was to come. They were quickly running out of time.

He looked at Adam through the smoldering flames. As did all of the rest.

"The first thing we need to do is secure our perimeter," Adam said. "The way I see it, there are two direct points of access. The first is through the passage in the mountain; the other is from across the lake. I think we ought to make the passage our priority. Does everyone else agree?"

"How do you propose doing it? I mean, how are we supposed to block off an entire corridor large enough to drive through?" Darren asked.

"And even then, how hard was it for us to climb up onto the mountain to get that wood?" Mare added. "All they'd need to do is scurry up it from the other side and drop right down on our heads."

Adam looked at Phoenix, who answered his unspoken question with a shrug.

"Anyone have a better idea?" Adam asked. "We can't just allow them a free run at us."

"No," Norman said. "That's exactly what we need to do."

"You're out of your mind," Missy said, shaking her head. "What chance do we have against these things? We'll be slaughtered."

"We all agree that by blocking off the road they would only have to go over the mountain to circumvent our blockade, right?"

"Yeah, but we can't just not try to block off the entrance," Mare said. "They'd just come pouring right through."

"I'm not suggesting we don't build a barricade," Norman said, allowing a sly half-smile to creep up his cheek.

Adam finally understood. "We want them to know they can't break through our barrier and come over the mountain instead. They'll think they have the upper hand."

"Bingo," Norman said.

"Why would we want them to come over the mountain?" Mare asked. "All that would do is buy us a few more minutes to dread dying."

"I don't know about you, but I don't intend to die out here," Adam said. "We want them to come over the mountain if they attack from across the salt flats. They'll have to get down off the cliff above us, right?"

"You're proposing an ambush," Evelyn said.

"They'll know we'll be waiting for them," Darren said. "If we're really lucky we might be able to kill a handful at most."

"Heck, no," Norman said. "We can't try to engage them. There's no way we could beat them in a fight. We need to outthink them. They'll come flying off the edge of the cliff knowing that with their superior numbers they'll be able to overwhelm us, but the surprise will be on them."

Norman rose from beside the fire and walked to the enormous pile of long sticks, raising one and planting it on the ground so that the tip pointed straight up into the air.

"So they'll think we're waiting down below to fight," Evelyn said, "but instead—"

"They'll be shish-ka-bobbed," Mare said with a grin.

"Exactly," Norman said.

"So where will we be?" Lindsay asked.

"Some of us will have to stay on the beach," Jill said, recalling her vision. In her mind she could see the snow bank with the spears standing from it, but more disconcerting was the smell of cooking flesh wafting across the frozen lake from the stone island against the horizon. "They'll need to be able to see us. They aren't stupid. They'll attack from across the lake as well."

"In what?" Ray asked. "Boats? Or are they going to swim?"

"No," Jill said. "They'll cross the lake on the ice."

"Ice? A natural body of water this large isn't about to freeze solid anytime soon."

"It will," Jill whispered, trapping his stare.

"Lay off, Ray," April said.

Ray debated arguing, but decided to save his breath. While it sounded completely asinine, if Jill had seen this in one of her visions, then he wasn't about to browbeat her with it.

"In my vision, I saw myself standing out on the beach with a wall of snow at my back, staring out across the lake through the blizzard at that island. I could see a fire—or at least the smoke from a massive fire—across a sheet of ice buried beneath several feet of snow. I don't know for sure what they were doing out there, but I could…smell people burning on the fire."

They all sat in silence for a moment. Some looked into the fire between them while others looked at anything else.

"They will come under the Blizzard of Souls," Phoenix said.

Jill looked at him, blinking. "That's what I was shown in the vision I had in the room up there where that woman was entombed. Alive. Is it possible that what's outside right now is that storm?"

"I don't know," Phoenix said. "We know they're coming for us soon, so it definitely could be. It would be so much easier to tell if I could understand why it was called the Blizzard of Souls."

"Whether it is or not is irrelevant," Adam said. "We need to get everything ready now. If they catch us unprepared, we're as good as dead anyway."

"Thank you, Mr. Sunshine," Evelyn said, standing and rubbing at a knot in her lower back. All of this sitting on rocks was beginning to take its toll. "On that cheery note, I suppose we should get to work."

"We haven't even figured out where to begin yet," Adam said.

"Well, it's not going to be in here, is it?" she said, casting Adam a wink before heading up the stone staircase.

Adam just stared at her as she walked away.

"You can close your mouth now," Norman whispered into his ear, giving him a pat on the back.

"Did she just put me in my place?"

"Indeed she did, my friend. Quite nicely, too," Norman said, offering Adam a hand.

The others were already ascending the stone stairs, following Evelyn, who disappeared into the darkened tunnel leading toward the outside world. Adam brought up the rear, still mesmerized by the woman's wink. It was strange to feel anything other than fear and a certain measure of desperation. What exactly was he feeling now anyway? Certainly she was an attractive woman, but was it possible to generate any sort of emotions under such duress? He didn't have the time to occupy his mind with such thoughts. The others were counting on him not just to lead them, but to keep them all from getting killed. Maybe sleep deprivation was finally beginning to get the better of him. God, when was the last time he had actually closed his eyes long enough to—?

He bumped into Norman from behind, barely able to see the other man's silhouette in front of him. They were nearly to the cave by the beach as evidenced by the freezing wind that lanced right through him, tousling his hair with snowflakes.

"How long were we down there?" Evelyn asked from somewhere ahead.

"What is it?" Adam asked, standing on his toes to try to see over Norman's shoulder.

The procession slowly moved forward, each step bringing a dramatic drop in temperature. Adam could see only their cumulative breath around him like a fog. The dampness in his lips felt like it froze a heartbeat before they split, summoning just a swell of warmth that immediately chilled. By the time he passed out of the tunnel, the others were already huddled together in the mouth of the cave. The storm had intensified to the point that it looked like a sheet of snow in front of him, whipping from side to side at the behest of the screaming wind.

"Jesus," Mare said, wrapping his arms across his chest and stepping out of their protective enclave. The wind nearly drove him to his knees, causing him to stumble into snow that was nearly to the middle of his shins.

"I've never seen anything like this," Adam said. "Even growing up in Colorado, I never even heard of snow that got this deep so quickly."

The beach was barely visible as white contrasting the black water on the shoreline, which vanished from sight no more than a few feet out.

"The Blizzard of Souls," Phoenix whispered.

"How can you be sure?" Adam asked, but the answer was obvious. Flirting in and out through the driving snow were ghostly eyes. Hundreds of them. Whiter even than the accumulation. The wind shifted with a shriek and he could see them… tall white birds standing in the snow with crowns of feathers like headdresses. As one they raised their golden beaks to the heavens and released a furious cry.

When the wind shifted again, they were gone.

VIII

THE RUINS OF
DENVER,
COLORADO

Death stood again at the edge of the roof, looking out across the vast wasteland. The briars had grown to the size of shrubs, nearly obscuring the torch-lined path. Soon enough the fires would run out of fuel, but it didn't matter now. His army was more than large enough to make short work of the survivors. No amount of readiness would prepare them for the sheer enormity of his Swarm. They were outnumbered more than a hundred to one. Even as more stragglers joined his encampment, he simply directed them toward the mountains to join with their brethren. Let them butcher the last of humanity and then turn upon each other. Once the stain of man had been bled into the earth, the way would be paved for evolution to begin anew, though even he knew it was only a matter of time before another species assumed dominance and began the process of self-annihilation. Even were he capable of feeling pity, he wouldn't have spared an ounce for these glorified apes who shunned the most precious gift that God could bestow. They had no concept of the sanctity of life.

He would revel in their merciless slaughter.

Closing his eyes, Death urged his mind to take flight. When he opened them again, he was standing at the edge of a great valley of snow. The sun was beginning its descent above the horizon, a mere circle of weak light through the thick storm. Down the steep, pine-infested slope, mountains gave way to foothills, which in turn succumbed to a flat sheet of white that extended from the edge of the Sangre de Cristo Mountains in western Colorado to the border of Utah where another distant mountain range stood like tombstones. By the end of the coming night, his forces would be in those mountains. The following night they would lay siege to their prey. When the sun rose again on the following morning, two days from now, the world would be bereft of the destructive urges of man, free to begin the process of healing. There were a handful that the Almighty had singled out to take a stand against him, though. A dozen-plus-one who it would pain Him to eliminate, but Death would do so without reservation. He was God's chosen son, and as such he would carry out his Father's wishes.

Through War's eyes he turned from the western horizon and back to the east. Thunder dropped to its front knees, blasting twin plumes of fire from its skeletal nostrils, sensing Death within its master. He favored it with a glance, the deep snow melting away from its elongated snout.

He stomped down the slope from just above timberline to where the dense pine and juniper forests encroached upon the rocky hillside. The ambitious snowflakes had nearly filled the tracks of his minions, who were hidden from sight. It was as though he stood all alone in the middle of the forest, miles from the nearest living entity. Until he looked up…

They filled the trees, packed close to the trunks and shielded from the sunlight by the thick branches beneath a burial of snow. With claws latched into the pulp, seething with amber blood, they clung however they could. Upside down, right side up. Hanging from branches and crumpled into the nooks. Black scales and hardened metal, the occasional yellow crescent of an eye opening to salute his presence before hurriedly closing. Dewlaps drawn tightly against their necks, they blended into the shadows so well that if he hadn't instinctively known they were there, he might never have seen them.

Death looked down the slope, sensing that nearly every tree within his field of vision was filled with his armada. Closing his eyes again, he left War to watch over the sun slinking behind the clouds to the west and again found himself atop the black skyscraper with the snow swirling around him. The wind battering him from all sides at once, he turned and stormed back into the tower to observe his own preparations for the future…just in case the softness he sensed in the Lord, this momentary sentimentality He felt for His wayward children proved to be His Achilles heel.

Death knew he had been summoned for this one purpose, and be it his Master's ultimate will or not, he would answer the calling and wipe every trace of Homo sapiens from the face of the planet. And perhaps this time, he would be able to claim what was left.

CHAPTER 4

I

SALT LAKE CITY

Gray stood on the loading dock at the Home Depot warehouse, trying to see the hotel through the blizzard. The tracks they'd laid on their way in were already filled with snow, leaving only the faint impression that they'd ever been there at all. He wished he could talk to Carrie, just to make sure that everything was all right. It made him paranoid even thinking about what he was preparing to attempt with all of the talk of dreams and visions. Was it possible that his thoughts weren't even safe? He knew that Richard wasn't the kind of man you wanted to cross, but he didn't know to what lengths the man would be willing to go to stop him.

God, if he'd done anything to endanger Carrie…

There was no doubt in his mind that he needed to get the woman and her child out of there, but still he was terrified of the consequences. Carrie was his love and his life, the woman he'd sworn to lay his own life down to protect. He'd made no such vow to that lady and her kid. He could just grab his wife and get the hell out of there. No looking back. Just load her up in the camper and drive off into the storm. No one would come looking for them. They could settle anywhere in the world. Maybe way down south on a beach in Aruba where it was warm and there was no snow or threat of attack—

It's okay, the boy's small voice repeated in his mind.

But it wasn't. If he left them there, Lord only knew what Richard might do to keep them all to himself and his secret safe. The man was a power monger. If he was using this kid's visions to make the others tow his line, then losing the child would threaten the entire foundation of his burgeoning rule. And if he and Carrie screwed up, he knew an example would be made of them. It would be the opportunity Richard was waiting for to flex his empirical muscles. The people followed him because of the dreams he claimed to have, but fear was a far better tool. Give him both and Richard's reign would be unquestioned, his power unopposed. And that had been the whole cause of their problems. The source of the evil that had given rise to weapons of mass destruction had placed them in the hands of men like Richard who just couldn't wait to use them.

"Truck's loaded to the gills," a man said from behind Gray, nearly causing him to jump.

Gray turned and nodded, his heart beating so fast that he was unable to speak. His first thought had been of his shotgun, but it had already been requisitioned by the recently designated Chief of Security.

"You okay?" the man asked. He was burly, but affable, a bald man whose smile was at odds with the prison-green tattoo of a coiled snake on his neck. "We got the whole trailer packed with enough wood to build another hotel around ours and enough PVC to plumb it."

"What about the barbed wire?"

"Left on the first truck. They should already be stringing it by now."

"And the generators?"

"Man, you worry too much. Just 'cause they put you in charge don't mean the rest of us are stupid."

"I'm sorry, I—"

The bald man laughed. "Heck, bro. I was just messin' with you. I'll grab you a beer when we get back. You got to learn to relax a little. After all, it ain't the end of the world."

Gray forced a smile.

"That's better, m'man. Now let's get back inside before we start pissin' icicles."

Nodding, Gray walked around to the front of the cab and climbed up. There was a rumble as the other man dragged down the trailer gate. He appeared through the passenger door and hopped up beside him.

"Heck of a storm," the man said, watching the windshield wipers drag arcs through the snow as they rolled out. There had been many trucks on the lot, but the majority hadn't worked. For whatever reason, only the older trucks that hardly looked roadworthy would even start. One of the other men had said something about an electromagnetic pulse knocking out any equipment that ran on computer chips, which did make a fair amount of sense. The camper in which they'd crossed the country was a relic itself, and, come to think of it, every other vehicle they'd come in with had been ancient. It made him wonder if trying to set up the generators would be a complete waste of time. They'd probably be better off sitting in a cave around a fire.

Gray laughed at the thought.

"What's so funny?" the man in the passenger seat asked as they slowed to approach the gate that would grant them access to the hotel parking lot.

"Everything."

"That's the spirit," the man said with a chuckle. "Name's Oscar. Oscar Dominguez."

"Gray Ciccerelli." He offered his hand across the console and Oscar shook it firmly.

Gray recognized his shotgun pointed at them through the iron gate. The man in the Army gear held it leveled at them through the front windshield. It seemed astoundingly excessive. If they'd wanted to get through the gate badly enough, Gray could have just pinned the gas and plowed right through. The man on the other side of the gate knew that too. It was merely a demonstration of power and authority meant to both intimidate and inspire a sense of subservience and security.

Peckham lowered the shotgun from Gray's face and unlocked the gate, drawing it back through the snow and ushering them past.

Everyone turned from their posts to watch the semi pull into the parking lot. A dozen men lined the fence, standing atop chairs from the lobby, coiling barbed wire over the horizontal rail of the fence so tightly that it looked impossible to climb over without flaying oneself. He didn't know how long they'd been out there in the gloves and parkas they'd obviously only recently procured, but they were nearly finished stringing the entire front of the property and had already moved around to the far side of the building.

Gray was startled by tapping on the driver's side window and turned to see Peckham preparing to rap again with the barrel of the shotgun. The soldier mimed for him to roll down the window.

"You've got to be freezing out there," Gray said, doing as he was instructed.

"Any more trucks in your caravan?" Peckham asked.

"Nope. We're the last."

"What's your cargo?"

"We've got about a million two-by-fours and a ton of PVC piping."

"Back it up by the front doors as soon as the other truck pulls out."

"Just leave it here for now then?"

"Pull up about twenty feet against the curb."

"Done deal," Gray said, allowing the truck to ease forward when Peckham turned his back. He parked against the edge of the sidewalk and killed the engine, shoving the keys into his pocket. Snow blanketed the windshield as soon as the wipers stopped.

Tossing open the door, he hopped down into the snow and walked around the front of the truck toward the hotel entrance. Garrett burst through the front doors and cut across the middle of the parking lot toward Peckham, who had just finished closing and locking the gate. Taking the other man by the arm, Garrett drew him close and whispered something into Peckham's ear, eliciting a nod. Both men hurried back into the hotel, nearly bowling Gray over in the process.

"What's going on?" Gray asked, but neither man so much as slowed. He followed them through the foyer and into the lobby. They crossed through straight toward the door to the stairs and climbed into the shadows as the door fell closed behind them.

"They were in some kind of hurry," Carrie said, appearing at his side and taking him by the hand.

"Something's going down," Gray said, still staring at the closed door, biting his lower lip. "Do you still have the keys to the truck?"

"They're with our stuff in the room. You should see it. I found us a place on the second floor with a hot tub and everything. Do you want me to—?"

"No," Gray said, pulling the keys to the semi from his pocket. "Take these. There's a semi-trailer at the north side of the parking lot out front—"

"What's happening, Gray?"

"Just listen to me!" he snapped, turning to face her and taking her by the shoulders. "Grab only what you can carry and go get that truck started."

"You're scaring me."

"Just have the truck running and be ready to go," he said, releasing her and turning to dash across the lobby.

"Where are you going?" she called after him, summoning the attention of those laboring around her, moving all sorts of crates and boxes into the lobby. They all averted their eyes from hers when they noticed the tears streaming down her face.

"I'll be right behind you," he said, throwing open the door to the stairwell.

Carrie turned and ran for the foyer, pausing only long enough to grab a coat and some gloves from the communal piles by the front desk where they were being collected as they were unloaded from the trucks.

Bursting through the front doors and into the snow, she veered to the right and sprinted toward the old yellow cab parked at the far end of the lot. Clambering up and out of the accumulation, she jammed the key into the ignition and started the engine with a roar.

"What are you doing up there?" she whispered, turning on the wipers and craning her neck so she could look at the upper floors of the building.

She could see only the hint of light through the third floor windows, vacuous eyes leering back down at her. Lowering her stare, she noted that there was just a hair over half a tank of gas in the truck. The gearshift looked like nothing she'd ever seen before, so she climbed across it and sat in the passenger seat to ensure that she wouldn't have to drive, no matter how much of a hurry they were in.

Gray had been acting strangely since the moment they arrived. She'd tried to coax whatever was troubling him out into the open, but, as always, he was just too stubborn to allow her to help. He'd said something about Richard and a kid who could see the future, but had clammed up after being unable to clearly vocalize the connection. All she knew was that Gray had told her they wouldn't be staying long, maybe a couple of days at the most, but had then gone with the other men to help secure supplies from the surrounding warehouses. It didn't make a whit of sense, but she'd learned through the years to let Gray have his—

Boom!

She jerked her head skyward toward the source of the sound. A drift of snow fell from where it had been perched on the roof of the castle, landing in a pile on the sidewalk in front of her. Those who had been working on the fence slowly abandoned their tasks and wandered closer to the hotel, staring toward roof like tourists.

Boom!

Someone screamed as glass exploded from one of the third story windows, sending shards flying in every direction and a splash of blood onto the hood of the semi.

II

MORMON TEARS

◉

"What do you think is going to happen?" Missy asked. She was carrying as many of the poles as she possibly could.

"I wish I knew for sure," Phoenix said. They'd been hauling armfuls of those spears out of the cavern and to the edge of the beach for what felt like hours. His arms ached, as he was unaccustomed to physical labor after spending his life locked in a basement. Missy was smaller than he, but was only now beginning to fatigue. "All I know is that they're going to be coming for us soon."

"You haven't had any more visions?"

They walked out of the tunnel and nearly to the mouth of the cave where the accumulation of snow slanted up toward the buried shore, where it had to be several feet deep by now.

"No," he whispered, dropping his haul onto the growing pile with a clatter. He could see the others out there through the blizzard. Most of them remained closer to the steep rocky face of the mountain, staking the poles into the ground every couple of feet with the points to the clouds. They weren't as close together as they had originally planned, leaving enough room to walk fairly comfortably between them. Hopefully it wouldn't matter. They needed it not to matter.

Adam was farther down the bank, nearly to the lake, walking behind the white pickup. They'd strapped a half-dozen poles together and tethered them to the rear of the vehicle. As the driver fought through the snow, Adam kept the makeshift plow angled so that it carved a trench into the ground, piling sand and snow to either side. Several of the others followed behind, shoving the pile closest to the water across the cut and packing it against the other, which was now so tall that the undercarriage of the pickup wouldn't be able to clear it on the next pass. They would have to continue moving closer and closer to the lake to gather enough sand and snow to make the barricade as tall as they wanted. It wasn't turning out nearly as well as they'd hoped, but it was still far better than their efforts at blocking off the road leading into their haven.

Without any sort of construction materials, they'd been limited to using whatever sand they could fire from the rear wheels of the truck, which dug so far down into the beach that it left a slanted hole like a swimming pool. The wall of sand was maybe ten feet tall at the most, but could hardly classify as a speed bump for their purposes. All someone would have to do from the other side was simply scramble up it and then slide down into their midst. They needed to make a run into town to gather more formidable supplies if they wanted to even attempt to fully block off the passage, but the old Ford was already running on fumes. While none of them wanted to vocalize their barely restrained panic, it was evidenced in each of their eyes. The harder they worked and the more exhausted they became, the more it started to look as though they would be easily overcome and butchered.

"Well?" Missy said. "What do you say?"

"Hmm?" he said, obviously having tuned out part of their conversation. He scoured the storm for white bodies and even whiter eyes, but saw nothing. There was something comforting about knowing the birds were out there, but not being able to see them engendered the terrifying feeling of abandonment.

"I said, are you ready to get the next load?" She smiled at him, amused by the embarrassed expression that crossed his face, reddening even the tip of his nose. There was definitely something endearing about his innocence and lack of self-awareness. All of the other boys she'd known were always putting on an act. Trying to be anyone other than they were. Phoenix, though, he was so lacking in pretension that everything about him was genuine. He wore his emotions on his sleeve and had none of the filters that prevented him from saying whatever came to mind. That made him even cuter.

"Sure. I was just seeing how they were doing out there."

"Not as well as you'd hoped, I take it."

"They're working so hard…" he said, brushing his bangs out of his eyes.

"Here," Missy said, pulling a hair tie from her pocket. She gathered his hair behind his head, trying not to tug on any of the tangles. Looping the band around the handful, she tucked the stray strands behind his ears. "That's better."

"How do you maintain such a wonderful attitude, especially with everything as it is now?" he asked, staring deeply into her eyes.

"What's the alternative?"

"I don't know," he whispered, taking her by the hand. Warmth flooded up his arm from her touch.

"We can either try to live our lives—such that they are—or just accept the inevitable."

"You mean death."

"We're all going to die someday, right? You have to make the most of every moment."

"You're even more amazing than in my dreams."

He felt her breath on his lips a heartbeat before she kissed him. Her life force poured into him, filling him with a tingling sensation that was positively electric. The fine hairs on his back straightened electrically when her arms wrapped around him. He reciprocated, pulling her tightly to him, their hips merging. It was the most wonderful experience of his entire life, so unlike when the Swarm descended upon him to steal his energy, sapping his very life from him. Missy instead transferred her energy into him, their combined life force a blinding supernova. When she finally withdrew her lips, her eyes lingering on his, he couldn't help but feel as though she took a part of him away with her.

"Thank you," he whispered.

"You don't have to thank me," she said, smiling slyly. "It was beginning to look as though if I didn't do it, it might not ever happen."

"That was the most incredible moment of my life."

"Tops my list, too."

"Can we do it again?" he asked, unable to contain his smile.

"I'd imagine there's probably more of that in your future."

Someone cleared his throat behind Phoenix, startling both of them so badly that they released each other and dropped their arms to their sides.

"Um… Sorry to interrupt," Mare said, grinning so widely that it appeared close to tearing his cheeks. "I'd tell you to get a room, but I'm way too cold to even try to be clever."

"What do you need, Mare?" she asked.

"More of the poles. That is…if you can spare a few minutes of your precious time."

She looked at the stack, preparing to tell him to grab any of the number they had just thrown onto the pile, but they were already gone. How long had she and Phoenix been kissing? It had felt like only a moment…

Outside, the snow had to be several inches deeper and the barricade between them and the lake was nearly tall enough to obscure those walking on the other side of it. The truck had obviously burned through the remainder of the gas, as exhaust no longer poured from the tailpipe. Poles stood from the ground everywhere in front of her, a maze she would have to navigate to reach the open stretch of snow.

She looked at Phoenix, who seemed every bit as confused.

"I thought…" she started, but he silenced her with another kiss.

"So did I," he said, withdrawing and walking toward the mouth of the cave. He scooped up a large snowball with both hands, closing it under his bright red fingers.

"So, um, the poles?" Mare said.

Phoenix opened his hands to reveal not merely a snowball as Missy had expected. A single green blade grew from the packed snow. As he held it, the plant thickened and grew to form a stem before blooming into what looked like a dandelion painted the colors of the sunrise. The flower yawned wide and then died back, turning into a collection of wispy seeds.

"Make a wish," he said, offering her the plant.

Missy closed her eyes and placed her hands over his. Drawing a deep breath, she blew on the feathery seeds. Some clung to his coat, while the others flew over his shoulder to be stolen by the wind and blown out into the storm.

"I think I'm going to puke," Mare said, rolling his eyes.

"What did you wish for?" Phoenix asked.

"If I tell you, it won't come true."

He smiled and held her hands.

"I think it just might."

Behind him, several thin green blades rose like grass from the snow, the union of their palms wet with his blood.

III

Salt Lake City

Gray heard shouting before he even reached the top floor. Easing up the final staircase, he pressed his back to the wall and opened the door just wide enough to see with one eye into the hallway. Kerosene lanterns were positioned on the floor beside every doorway, the small flames lining the walls with dancing shadows. The corridor was empty as far as he could see, the heated voices coming from around the corner. With the flickering fire and the yelling, the whole scene reminded him of how he imagined hell.

"You aren't getting past me!" a female voice screamed.

"I heard him through the wall," Richard said, his voice low and menacing. "He's having one of his dreams. I know it."

"He's only a little kid! Why can't you just leave him alone?"

"His dreams are the key to our survival."

"You told everyone that you were the one who had visions. They all think you're a prophet."

"What can I say?" He lowered his voice even more. "I lied."

A thick silence filled the hallway like a sentient entity.

"That's why you need us," Susan said. "You need to know Jake's dreams so you can claim them as your own, don't you?"

"Clever girl. I thought it would take you much longer. I'm impressed."

"You're not using my son."

Gray opened the door quietly, holding his breath so he could hear even the slightest sound, and sneaked out into the hallway.

Turning the handle, he closed the door and allowed the latch to settle back into the wall. He darted across the hall and pressed his back to the wall, inching his way toward the origin of the voices.

"How about we make a deal then?" Richard said from just around the corner. "You just report everything he dreams about to me, and in return I'll make sure that neither of you want for anything. Food. Water. Clothes. You name it and it's yours."

"All I want is for you to leave my son alone. Don't you think that this has been hard enough on him already?"

"It could always be so much harder."

"Are you threatening me?"

"Just stating the obvious," Richard said. "I'm offering you so much more. The world outside may be a much different place now, but that doesn't mean that you should have to live like paupers."

"Leave us alone."

"Susan… You're being unreasonable."

Gray reached the end of the wall, sliding along in almost imperceptible movements as the lanterns cast his shadow on the wall around the blind corner.

"I don't care what you think. He's my son!"

"Don't rush to any rash decisions you might regret."

"Another threat?" she screamed. "We'll see how almighty powerful you are when the others learn just how much of a prophet you really are."

"I can't allow you to do that, Susan."

"You can't stop me! I'm taking my son and we're—!"

"Susan…"

"Get out of my way or so help me I'll scream as loud as I can and you'll have to try to explain this to everyone!"

Gray leaned just far enough around the corner to see that Richard was standing between Susan and the door to her room. Garrett was in the middle of the hall with his back to Gray while Peckham stood several paces directly behind Susan with his back to the wall opposite her room. His fingers played nervously on the pump and the stock of the shotgun.

Jesus, Gray thought, watching both Peckham and Garrett shifting nervously from one foot to the other, tossing each other the occasional wary glance. Back down, lady. Just back down.

He looked across the hall to the open doorway leading into Richard's suite, now lit by a string of lanterns running the length of the countertop past the door. At the far end of the room he could see a sliding glass door. He hadn't noticed from the front of the hotel, but apparently the rooms on the back side had balconies.

"You don't want to do that," Richard said, taking her by the hand.

"Let go of me!" she shrieked, yanking her arm away. "Don't you ever touch—!"

There was a loud slap and Susan's head snapped to the right. Richard had moved with such astounding speed that by the time Gray saw his arm move, there was already a welt forming on the woman's cheek.

She looked back at Richard in disbelief, tears pouring down her face.

"You were starting to become hysterical," Richard said, justifying his actions. "Why don't you take a few minutes to calm down and reconsider—?"

Susan screamed and launched herself at him, slamming him against the door. Fingers curled to claws, she slashed at his face, banging his head repeatedly against the wood, throwing curls of skin from beneath her nails.

Garrett grabbed her by the arms and pulled her away from Richard, holding her to his stout chest with her arms pinned behind her. She continued to scream and kick at Richard.

"Crazy bitch!" Richard spat, smearing the blood from the diagonal lacerations on his cheeks to inspect it on his hands. He held up his bloody palms. "Look what you've done to me! Look what you've done!"

Gray was frozen where he stood. He could feel deep down how this was going to play out, but he couldn't seem to force his body to react. The whole scene played out in front of him like a movie.

"Peckham," Richard said without taking his eyes from Susan.

The soldier just stared blankly at him.

"Peckham!"

The chief of security raised the shotgun and seated the butt against his shoulder, pointing it at Susan, the tip of the barrel only inches from her left temple.

"You're going to stop screaming right now," Richard said, regaining control over his rage, though with his wild eyes and the blood running from those cuts he looked insane. "You don't want to orphan our little Jake, do you? Don't want him to hear the walls being painted with mommy's brains."

Dear God, the boy was still in the room!

Silence filled the hall, smothering. Gray couldn't even breathe.

"Please," Susan whispered. "I'll do anything you want."

Richard smiled, the rivulets of crimson racing around the corners of his mouth to drip from his chin. "Good girl."

Garrett looked to Richard, who nodded back at him. Slowly, he released Susan's arms and took a step back. She stood there, chin to her chest, shoulders heaving with the onset of hyperventilation.

"Please…just let me go back in to be with him."

"Of course," Richard said, stepping to the side, his smile never faltering.

Susan walked sluggishly as though in a trance, refusing to look at any of them. When she reached for the doorknob, Gray sensed her moment of hesitation, but he couldn't respond quickly enough. She grabbed Richard by the arm and pulled him in front of her, closing her hands around his neck from behind and curling her fingers over his trachea so hard that the nails drew crescents of blood. Richard opened his mouth like a fish, choking as he gasped for air.

Peckham took one strong stride forward and pressed the barrel to the center of her forehead.

"Back off!" she screamed. "Don't come any—!"

Boom!

Gray jumped, unable to close his eyes fast enough to keep from seeing everything above the bridge of Susan's nose liquefied and pounded into the wall with a fiery spray of steel. Smoke lingered around what remained of her head, mixing with the chalk released from the holes in the drywall behind.

"Christ!" Richard bellowed, clapping his hands to his ears. His entire face and shirt were awash with blood and gray matter. "You could have blown my head off!"

Susan's fingers fell away from his red neck as her body slid down the wall into a sloppy heap on the floor, leaving a smeared trail of blood.

Gray's whole body trembled. He couldn't believe they'd just killed her. He turned and looked at the doorway leading to the stairwell, his gaze lingering long and hard on the doorknob, but he just couldn't do it. The urge to save his own skin was overwhelming and he knew what fate would befall him if they found out that he'd witnessed Susan's execution, but he couldn't leave that little kid at their mercy.

"She was going to tear out your windpipe!" Peckham shouted. "What was I supposed to do, let her?"

Gray looked back around the corner. All three had gathered around the woman's corpse and were leaning over her as though waiting for something to happen.

It was now or never.

Gray dashed across the hallway and through the door to Richard's room, straight through the patio door and onto the balcony. A painted cinderblock wall separated the balcony from the one beside, the rest enclosed by a white railing. There was no time to think. He hopped right up on the rail and stepped around the wall onto the adjacent railing, dropping down onto the cement without looking first. The wind screamed its displeasure, battering him with snowflakes, but he already had the sliding glass door open and lunged into the room.

Pinpricks of light shined through the pellet holes in the front wall beside the door, allowing the scent of gunpowder to creep through. He scoured the room for any sign of the boy. The covers had been tossed from the bed, revealing nothing but a plain white sheet atop the barren mattress. There was no one in the chair beside it, the wind billowing the curtains inward to prove that Jake wasn't hiding back there either. Gray raced through the room, past a round table with another pair of chairs and a miniature refrigerator. Clothes and empty plates littered the dresser beside the useless television. Veering to his right when he reached the front door, he carefully slid open the closet door. Nothing. Heading into the bathroom, he threw open the shower stall door. Empty. Where the hell was he?

"Get her out of the hallway!" Richard shouted from the other side of the wall, his voice obscenely loud to compensate for the ringing in his ears.

"What are we supposed to tell everyone else?"

"Tell them she tried to kill me!"

Gray ducked back into the main room, his head on a swivel. He could still hear the men bickering on the other side of the door behind him, but he couldn't make out their words. He couldn't afford to waste another second. If they found him in there...

The bed.

He ran toward it and dropped to his stomach, lifting the blankets to find himself staring directly into the boy's frightened eyes.

"Come on!" he whispered, dragging Jake out by his wrist. The child's face shimmered with tears, but he managed to hold his hand over his mouth to keep from sobbing aloud.

Gray pulled him to his feet and led him out onto the balcony, lifting him by the waist until Jake was able to balance his feet on the icy railing. With a groan, Gray heaved Jake around the wall and onto the adjacent balcony, listening for the thump of the boy dropping to the concrete pad. He followed without hesitation to find Jake waiting for him. Scooping the child into his arms, he ran for the door, but stopped when he heard voices.

Gray peered down the hallway. Had any of them turned around, they would have been looking directly at him, exposed in the middle of the open doorway. They rounded the corner at the far end of the hallway at the front of the building with Garrett and Peckham both dragging Susan by a leg. Richard trailed behind, careful not to step in the fluids that sloshed out of the crater where her cranium had once been.

As soon as they disappeared around the bend, Gray sprinted toward the door to the stairwell, throwing it wide and thundering down. He passed several faceless people, shadows against the darkness ascending to investigate the sound of gunfire from above. They just watched him fly past, holding Jake as tightly as he could to his chest so he could bound down the steps two at a time. They blew through the door and dashed across the lobby toward the front entrance. Wide-eyed faces passed to either side, unable to hide their dawning fear.

"Go!" he shouted as soon as he shouldered through the glass door, but Carrie was waiting in the passenger seat. Exhaust plumed from the tailpipe and the headlights highlighted twin circles of light on the wall. A crowd had gathered around the truck, all eyes raised to the top floor where a silhouette appeared in the shattered pane. Leaping over a steaming wash of red melting into the snow, he rounded the front of the semi just as Carrie leaned across the driver's seat and opened his door.

"Gray!" she screamed. "What's happening?"

Out of breath, he could only shove Jake at her and climb up into the bucket seat. Before he even closed the door, he popped the clutch and the semi was rolling in reverse. They needed more speed! Pounding his foot on the gas pedal, the trailer rocketed backwards. He looked back over his shoulder to navigate, trying to steer that enormous trailer through the center of the gate.

Boom!

The windshield shattered, glass shrapnel slicing his right cheek and ear, tearing through his hair and cracking the glass behind him.

The truck slammed into the gate, tearing the lock with a metallic scream and wrenching the gate from its hinges to slam to the street beneath their tires. He cranked the wheel and the trailer jacked to the right, the cab swinging around until it faced down the road to the south. Stomping the clutch and slamming the gear into first, the tires spun before finally catching and sending them rocketing forward, snowflakes blowing straight through over the hood and smacking him in the face.

Jake was crying beside him from beneath the dashboard where Carrie had shoved him.

Merging into the right lane, he exited onto the ramp that would lead them onto the interstate.

"Are you okay?" he asked, too nervous to steal his eyes from the road for even a second for fear of launching them off of the highway.

Jake sobbed even louder in response.

"Carrie?"

As soon as the truck straightened out on the interstate, he looked to his right. Carrie was leaning against the side window, blood pouring from beneath her hairline.

"Talk to me, Carrie!"

He slowed the truck to reach for her, the change in speed causing her to slump forward, leaving a wet mess of blood on the window.

"No!" he screamed, grabbing her by the shoulder and pulling her toward him.

The entire right half of her face was torn to ribbons. Fractured bone stood out of the pulpy swelling of red flesh, soggy crimson bangs flopping down in front of her face.

"God…no! Please…not my wife…"

IV

MORMON TEARS

They were dying and there wasn't a thing she could do about it.

Evelyn steadied herself on her rocky perch and jabbed the ice with the stick, breaking it into pieces small enough to slide atop the thicker ice surrounding the section she was trying to keep clear above the kelp. There was only a thin line of saltwater against the shore, the rest now hiding beneath a crust of ice close to half an inch thick and buried under the rapidly accumulating snow. It covered the lake as far as she could see into the storm.

"Don't die on me," she said, staring at the brown leaves wilting down to the roots like rotting lettuce.

So much for her thoughts of sustaining them all on kelp. They were already nearly through the remainder of the stock of food and were down to a single gallon of water.

Like the kelp and the dream that those plants embodied, they were going to die.

She thought of the mural in the cave, but chased away the budding sense of hope before it could be crushed.

"Wishful thinking," she said, rising carefully and hopping back down to the beach, now invisible under several feet of snow. Granted, her specialty was oceanography, but she'd passed enough biology and ecology classes to know the kind of storm they were up against. The accepted theory of the extinction of the dinosaurs held that after the impact with the great asteroid, the resultant cloud of dust it had thrown into the atmosphere had shielded the planet from the sun's rays, ushering in the ice age. She imagined that this was no different. The nuclear and atomic detonations had done just that, sending tons of debris into the air on massive mushroom clouds to be trapped in the sky. Worse still were the clouds of radiation and God only knew what else that roiled above them. It would eventually clear, she knew, but how long would it take? Weeks? Months? Or, heaven forbid, years?

She wished she could go back in time and beat some sense into the politicians and religious zealots who had damned them to this fate. Surely there wasn't a bible or Koran that stated that their god would only be appeased when the entirety of creation was decimated. What kind of god would hate his own children so much as to demand they destroy themselves? Hers was a God that smiled down upon them in the majestic colors of the sunset and showed His face in the miraculous first breaths following childbirth. Maybe it was a fool's dream, like following a rainbow to the end in hopes of finding a pot of gold. Perhaps it was simply time to allow that idealistic image to fade. If this is what God wanted: pain, suffering…death…then she wanted absolutely nothing to do with Him.

Tugging the ancient blanket tightly around her shoulders, she tucked her chin to her chest and walked into the stiff wind, which pelted her with snowflakes the size of dimes and ripped her frozen breath back over her shoulder. She stopped when she saw movement in front of her.

One of those enormous white birds of prey stood in front of her, head cocked to the side, eyes locked on hers.

"What do you want from me?"

The feathers on its crown rose to erection and its throat swelled like a goiter. It gagged several times, its head rising and falling repeatedly before it spewed a mess of what looked and smelled an awful lot like fish guts onto the snow. Its wings spread wide and with a single leap it was airborne, swallowed by the blizzard.

"Ugh," she gasped, looking at the foul-smelling sludge melting into the snow.

A glint of something shiny caught her eye. With the toe of her shoe she shoved aside a pink coil of half-digested intestines to find a gold coin…just like those that might fill a pot at the end of the rainbow.

All she could manage to do was stare at it. What a humbling experience. It was as though God had heard her thoughts and doubts and had seen fit to send a message just for her. A message of hope.

Maybe whoever had drawn the mural in the cavern had more faith in her than she did. There had to be a way to save the kelp, she just hadn't thought of it yet.

"You're just in time," Lindsay said, appearing in front of her. "Oh. Gosh. Are you all right?"

Evelyn looked up at her, noting Lindsay's pursed lips and the way she was just staring down at the pile of bird vomit.

"That isn't mine," Evelyn said with a chuckle, having to take a second look at the ground. The coin was no longer there.

"Good, because I didn't even want to speculate as to what all of that crap is." Lindsay kicked snow over the festering puke. "Now hurry up so you can see the test."

"What test?"

"Would you just come on already?"

Lindsay bounded ahead, leading Evelyn back toward the camp, weaving through the slalom of sharpened poles lining the beach. They were everywhere, from the face of the mountain halfway to the shoreline. The others were gathered ahead, spear-tips standing above their heads. They looked as one to the top of the mountain.

"Is everyone here?" Adam shouted down to them. He was barely a spectre all the way up there through the storm.

"Yeah," Lindsay shouted. "Finally…"

"Just do it!" Mare shouted.

"On three," Adam said. "One… Two…"

A body appeared from the snow, plummeting down toward them. Evelyn screamed as it landed on one of the spikes, which gored it straight through. She ran toward it, falling to her knees and grabbing—

A handful of straw?

The others let out a riotous cheer.

"Did it work?" Adam called down.

"Perfectly!" Lindsay shouted. She rested a hand on Evelyn's back. "You didn't think that was Adam…did you?"

Evelyn held up a shirtsleeve stuffed with musty old grasses they must have pulled out of one of the disintegrating walls of the pueblo. A belt had been tightened around the bottom of the shirt to affix it to a similarly-stuffed pair of pants.

The spear had passed so cleanly through the scarecrow that the shirt hardly even appeared ripped.

"You did, didn't you?" Lindsay said, unable to hide the lilt of amusement in her voice. "He is pretty cute, isn't he?"

Evelyn looked up at her, angered by the comment, but for the life of her she couldn't understand why. Was it actually possible that she was developing feelings for a man she didn't even know?

Lindsay picked up on the cue and tried to have a little fun with her.

"You know, I was thinking of maybe seeing if he was available." Evelyn shot her the look she had expected. "I mean, if you aren't interested, of course."

"I'm not," Evelyn said far too quickly.

"Oh. I see. Then you wouldn't mind if I—"

"Not at all," Evelyn interrupted.

Lindsay smirked. "I guess if you're sure…"

"Hey!" Norman shouted from above where he and Adam were preparing to descend the far slope of the mountain again, fortunately minus the unwieldy weight of the stuffed clothes. He was jumping up and down and waving his arms. "Over here!"

"What is it?" April called.

Adam ran back to the edge of the cliff where they could see him. "There's a car coming!"

"A car?" Lindsay said, forgetting all about tormenting Evelyn for the moment.

Ray ran ahead of them all, scrabbling up the mound of sand blocking the road and down the opposite side. The others followed, though at a greater distance. It had been a while since anyone else had arrived at the camp, so none had realized just how rapidly they had become wary of outsiders. All of the preparations for the coming battle had altered their mindset from one of gathering as a people to an increasing level of suspicion.

Evelyn ascended behind Phoenix and Missy, who now held hands everywhere they went, with Lindsay to her left. April and Darren followed behind with Jill and Mare bringing up the rear. When she reached the crest, she could see a cloud of snow rising behind the advance of a large vehicle. Standing atop the knoll, she raised a hand to shield her eyes from the assault of flakes, watching as the yellow cab of a semi-truck came into focus. It was nearly brown with accumulated ice and dirt from the road, the front windshield completely absent. The driver slammed the brakes when he saw them, the trailer jackknifing sideways, kicking up a spray of sand until it stuttered to a halt.

Norman jumped down from the rock formation first, followed by Adam, who headed straight for the driver's side door, which opened outward, nearly knocking him back. The sludge-coated headlights stared blankly at the others as they slid down the hill of sand.

The driver leaned to his right and lifted something large and heavy from the passenger seat. He climbed down with whatever he had grabbed across his chest. When he stepped out from behind the door, it became obvious what he was holding. Lifeless legs dangled over his right arm, while a head lolled over his left, arms hanging down so that the backs of the hands grazed the powder.

He looked back over his shoulder as a kid dropped down into the snow behind him.

"I need to bury my wife," the man said, his emotions finally tearing through and dropping him to his knees. He nuzzled his face into the corpse's chest and began to sob.

V

SALT LAKE CITY

Richard stood at the front of the lobby, preparing to address his followers. How had he allowed everything to get out of his control? The boy's mother had been a necessary casualty, one he had planned on from the start. It had happened far sooner than he had predicted, but it was a contingency for which they had been thoroughly prepared. The others had been instructed to keep to the lower two levels from the start, and even though they weren't physically on the same floor, he had known they would hear the shots. Of course, none of them would know in which order the killings had transpired, so they would easily be able to enact his plan. He and Garrett would say that Susan had cracked under the strain, the same overwhelming pressure that each and every one of them felt, and had attacked Peckham. As newly anointed Chief of Security, they could claim that he had tried to calm her down, but he had underestimated her deteriorating state of mind and approached her too casually, allowing her to wrest the shotgun from him. They could then say that she had blown his head off. After all, the evidence of that would be everywhere. Leave it to Peckham to screw that one up, though. He had recognized their plan and tried to stop Garrett, the tussle causing him to step in front of the window as the gun went off, creating a dozen potential witnesses down in the parking lot.

That was the first big problem they were going to have to deal with.

The second stemmed from their plan for Susan's death. The idea was that after she shot and killed Peckham, Garrett would overpower her and accidentally shoot her in the process of trying to subdue her. That would leave Richard as the humanitarian hero who would swoop in and take her orphaned son under his wing to raise as his own. In his suite, away from prying eyes. Now that the boy was gone too, that created the biggest problem of them all. Not only would he be unable to play the role of the good guy, but without the child—and more importantly, his precognitive abilities—his power to rule the cattle was now tenuous at best. They would expect more visions and he would have to indulge them with fiction. And when his predictions didn't come to pass…

He hadn't had the time to sufficiently prepare the official account that everyone was waiting to hear, but he knew that the others would accept no delay. Everything that had transpired had done so for all to see. If given enough time, even these people would be able to align the events and piece the story together. He needed to produce a plausible account to keep them from even beginning to wonder. Give them facts to gnaw on so there would be no room for speculation, but at the same time, he needed to use the day's events to galvanize them, not just together, but together under him. They needed to know that he could protect them. After all, their Chief of Security had been shot to death in their midst. That in itself didn't inspire much confidence. He needed to be proactive, show them that he would not stand for violence against any of his followers. They needed something tangible at which to direct their mounting anger, the source of the fear he could already tell they felt building inside. He needed to give them an enemy to hate. A face to embody the source of their rage. It wasn't until he opened his mouth to speak and all eyes were upon him that he knew precisely what to say.

"Please, ladies and gentlemen, we have much to discuss." He held out his hands and waited for the rumble of conversation to cease. Instead of allowing the smile he felt to cross his face, he feigned concern mixed with anger, mirroring the looks on all of their faces to draw them to him. "It's important that we open a frank and honest dialog in hopes of not only understanding, but preventing a recurrence of what happened here today, inside this very shrine housing our hopes and dreams for the future. The future of mankind.

"It all happened so quickly that even now I am still trying to comprehend this tragedy and the even more staggering implications. I will try to explain what I witnessed as I remember it, so please reserve your questions and comments until the end."

He studied them from where he stood, this time opting to stand on the floor just outside the entrance to the restaurant while they sat in the chairs and on the floor surrounding them. It was important in this instance that they see him as one of the people, on their level rather than above.

"I'll be the first to admit that I was naïve. I am human after all, looking for the best in people rather than the worst. When we abandoned Mormon Tears in search of a better life, those we left behind became jealous. They wanted the power that you entrusted in me. I was blind to their envy. In fact, the last thing I said to them was that they were welcome to join us when we arrived here if they wanted to better their overall circumstances. I invited them into our sanctuary." He paused, reading their confused expressions with practiced ease. "But they wanted more than to be accepted among us, into the safety and prosperity that our new home promised. They wanted more and I...I didn't recognize it in time. My visions told me to be wary, but I didn't heed their warnings. I believed that we could rally together as a species and approach the future with a shared sense of hope. I erroneously believed that we who were spared from the mass casualties that befell nearly our entire race were all inherently good, that together we could make our stand against the forces of evil lusting for our extinction.

"I was wrong...and I failed you."

He lowered his head and pretended to wipe his nose, instead pinching a pair of hairs and yanking them from his nostril. Listening to the soft genesis of voices, he allowed them not only a moment to wonder what he had done so wrong, but to sympathize with him as he absorbed the entirety of the blame. When he raised his face again, there were tears in his eyes.

"The others, those who exiled themselves to the caves, sent a spy among us and we drew him to our bosom with open arms. Surely you all recognized him, for he wore the face of one of us, but beneath he was a conniving demon sent to infiltrate our ranks and throw us into chaos. His goal was to assassinate me, to destroy our very way of life. Sergeant Peckham, our fallen Chief of Security, was the first to discover his nefarious plan. That poor, courageous man. He confronted my would-be killer on the third floor and a scuffle ensued, right outside my quarters even as I was in the process of planning for the battle to come. The ruckus drew the attention of a young mother named Susan, who tried to help Sergeant Peckham, only to be gunned down when the shotgun discharged during the fracas.

"I came out of my room at the sound of gunfire, barely entering the hallway in time to see the good sergeant relinquish his firearm to use both hands to try to save the woman. I ran to his side, as did my most trusted confidant Garrett, the sight of both of us startling the killer, who ran into Susan's room. When he emerged a moment later, he was holding her young son in front of him. Using that innocent child as a human shield."

A spontaneous groan arose from the masses, their features betraying the repulsion they felt on the most basic, fundamental level.

"None of us dared to move, for what kind of men would we be to jeopardize the life of a young boy? We would have been lowering ourselves to his level, metamorphosing ourselves into monsters like him. So we allowed him his retreat, all the while with Garrett shielding me from the assassin's bullet with his own body. It was Peckham who seized the opportunity to try to save the boy when it presented itself. He managed to chase the man down the hallway, where he paid for his nobility, his ultimate sacrifice, with his own life. From there we had no choice but to allow this demon to escape. He had already demonstrated not just a willingness to take life, but an unquenchable bloodlust that demanded it. Coward that he is, he ran away down the stairs and compromised our defenses by crippling the iron gate securing our compound."

"Hey!" someone shouted. "I saw that guy!"

"Me, too!"

A rumble passed through his people as they compared their stories of witnessing portions of his account. Some saw the man dragging a little boy through the lobby, while others saw him tossing that same child into a truck that was already idling in wait outside. The fevered tales escalated as Richard had known they would in a classic exercise of one-upmanship, until there were some who claimed to have seen him shoot Peckham through the window from outside and still others who heard that man plotting something devious when he thought he was out of earshot.

"Please forgive me," Richard sobbed, falling to his knees and burying his face in his hands. His shoulders and back shuddered as he wept.

The gathering became quiet. None dared to speak, barely able even to watch him until one woman rose from where she knelt on the floor and walked over to him, gently placing her hand on his back.

"It's not your fault," she whispered, tears in her eyes as well. "He fooled all of us."

"Don't blame yourself," a man said, following her lead. "If you had tried to do anything more, that kid would be dead now too."

"You can't beat yourself up," someone else said. "You did everything you could."

More soothing words poured down on him until after a moment there were hands all over him, trying to comfort him. They didn't blame him, they said. He was braver than any of them. They needed him. They loved him.

They worshipped him.

Richard rose to his feet, standing in the middle of the flock that had swarmed over him.

"I made a promise," he said, wiping away his tears. "I made a promise to that woman."

They were all silent, hanging on his every word.

"I promised that if anything ever happened to her I would look after her son, that I would treat him like my own and see that no harm ever came to him. And I failed her, as well."

"We'll get him back," a man with a gruff voice said from the back of the room, followed by a chorus of assent.

"This is my responsibility," Richard said. "I made a vow that I intend to keep, and I refuse to risk any of your lives in the process."

"We will get that boy back," the man at the back said again. "Whatever it takes."

Richard smiled.

He would have the child back, and nothing would stand in his way.

VI

Mormon Tears

Jill sat atop the enormous pile of sand, tears streaming down her face. Watching that man commit the love of his life to the earth was more than she could bear. Gray stood down there on the beach at the foot of the hole they'd helped dig while he said his goodbyes with her body curled in his lap. The others maintained a respectful distance from him, allowing him all the time he needed before burying her beneath the mound piled above her head.

"This is my fault," he whispered, his breath wrenched away and downwind. The snow was already piling on his head and shoulders, but he was oblivious.

The child walked up beside him and took his hand, joining him in mourning.

"She's with God now," the boy said, knowing the words would be of no comfort, for they were of no help to him either. "And my mom."

Gray looked down at Jake, giving that small hand a gentle squeeze before lifting the boy to his chest. Together they stared at his wife's body until he could take it no more and turned his back on the grave. The others moved in behind him, shoving the sand into the hole by whatever means they could. He walked off toward the cave and sat down in the snow, pulling Jake's blanket around both of them. The child leaned into his shoulder and together they looked out across the lake at nothing in particular.

Jill had to close her eyes. It was both the most tragic and most beautiful thing she had ever seen in her life. It positively hurt to observe, even from the distance, but she knew that she would only serve to increase the man's suffering were she to be down there too. There had been so much death on such a grand scale that it seemed surreal, but the death of one woman, a wife whose husband had loved her more than anything else in the world, brought the reality of it crashing down upon her. So many lives had been snuffed out with casual disregard... Mothers. Fathers. Children. Not just casualties of war, but of a cosmic indifference that broke her heart. Their lives had mattered to those who had loved them, but taken as a whole of the world's population, their deaths hadn't.

She opened her eyes at the clapping sound of Mare brushing the sand from his blazing-red bare hands. He sat down beside her without a word, joining her from her vantage, where she could see the others dispersing from the mound of sand, which would eventually be hidden beneath feet of snow, the woman's life marked by only a bump on the beach over which they had planted a thin cross made from a broken pike, lashed together by a shred of fabric.

Several small flowers bloomed from the snow beneath the cross, droplets of blood against the ethereal whiteness from afar.

"Please hold me," she whispered, leaning into him, allowing him to slip under the Indian blanket with her. He offered no sarcasm or insecure wit, only a warm body to absorb hers and chase away the cold, if only momentarily.

Her breath on his neck, Mare held her tight, wishing more than anything that the sun would part the clouds and shine down upon them. He wished he could say something to make her feel better, to offer some semblance of hope, but his life had been an exercise in hiding from the physical and emotional pain inflicted by a father who couldn't find a way to love him, burying his feelings beneath an impenetrable shell. He didn't know the words to console her, having conditioned himself to mask his feeling with humor. Maybe his silence would be enough for now.

"He loved her so much," Jill said. "She was everything to him."

Mare raised her forehead with his chin, summoning her eyes to his.

"Love like that can survive even death," he whispered. "They'll be together again."

He hadn't planned it, but before he could stop himself he leaned in and kissed her, tasting her salty tears on her lips. Her hands moved against him as her lips parted for their mouths to join. He'd felt passion and lust before, but never such an all-consuming emotional bond. He didn't just want to get her out of her clothes, but rather to become one with her, to make everything all right with her world.

Her tongue touched his, softly, inviting his to pursue. He raised his hand to stroke her cheek, caressing it down the side of her neck. Her tendons grew tight, straining against his fingertips as her muscles flexed, her body becoming rigid. He barely had time to withdraw his tongue from her mouth before her teeth snapped closed.

Mare opened his eyes and stared directly into hers. The lids fluttered over not her beautiful blue eyes, but the vessel-streaked whites.

"Jill," he said, shaking her gently.

His voice faded as she was absorbed in the blinding white light, peeling back to reveal the blizzard over the frozen lake. Again, she was standing on the shoreline with the barricade at her back, accosted by the scent of burning flesh, but this time something was different. Two figures, black shadows against the sheeting snow, staggered toward her. One supported the other as best he could, while the one who could barely walk had both hands pressed to his face, blood streaming through the gaps between his fingers.

"Hurry!" she screamed at them as a wall of darkness rose behind them. Golden eyes shined like captive suns and she screamed—

Her voice still trilled as her eyes snapped down. She was lying on the sand with her head propped on Mare's lap, staring up into his frightened face.

"Tell me you're okay," he whispered.

"Yeah," she said, raising her hand to wipe the tears from his cheeks. "I'm fine."

"You scared me pretty good." He forced a weak smile.

Her frame of vision expanded and she saw that most of the others were now standing over her.

"Was it another vision?" April asked.

Jill could only nod.

"What did you see?" Darren asked.

"The same thing as before. Only…" She scanned their faces until her eyes settled upon Ray's. Blood poured from his black eyes. She blinked and the image was gone.

"Only what?" Ray asked, uncomfortable under the weight of her stare.

Jill was too scared to speak.

"It's me they want," Jake said, stepping out from behind Gray. They had come running when Mare had shouted for help, hovering at the rear of the crowd. "They'll kill you all to get me back."

"No one's getting killed," Gray said. "And no one's ever going to take you away."

A sad smile spread across Jake's lips. "They won't stop until they have me all for themselves. The bad man needs me to control the others. They would be lost souls without him."

"Who's the bad man?" Adam asked.

"The man who killed my mom and will lead all of the others to their deaths."

"Richard?"

Jake nodded.

"He's willing to sacrifice them all to get me back."

VII

SALT LAKE CITY

Richard stared at his reflection in the mirror, the flickering flames from the lantern accentuating the gashes on his cheeks. Tracing them with his fingertips, his anger swelled to a crescendo of rage. They would scar, there was no doubt about it. The edges had curled away from the scabbing stripes, creating thick shadows that made him look like a monster.

He roared and punched the mirror, large triangular shards cascading to the dresser top.

"You okay?" Garrett asked, bursting through the doorway from the hall.

Richard turned to face him, blood draining from his knuckles. The impact had left a starburst of crimson on the wall. He shook his stinging hand, spattering Garrett with droplets of blood, but the larger man didn't even flinch.

"Are they ready?" Richard asked.

"Your hand… Are you all right?"

"I said are they ready?" Richard shouted, spittle spraying from his lips.

"Yeah," Garrett said, wounded. "They're down in the lobby waiting for you."

Richard smiled and walked up to Garrett, placing both hands on the other man's shoulders and giving them a solid squeeze. Garrett could feel the warmth of Richard's blood soaking through his jacket and onto his skin.

"I'm counting on you, Garrett," Richard said, his breath beginning to sound raspy, labored. "You're my number one, you know."

Garrett only nodded, unable to look away from Richard's face.

"By the time I return, I expect this place to be a fortress able to withstand a nuclear assault."

"You know it will be."

"Of course," Richard said, his features softening. "I wouldn't doubt you for a second."

He removed his hands from Garrett's shoulders and clapped him on the back.

"You sure you don't want to bandage that hand before you go?"

"I said I'm fine!" Richard shouted, but then lowered his voice. "We need to get that kid back before we come under attack. There's no time to waste, especially to bandage my stupid hand."

Garrett nodded and slipped back out into the hallway, leaving Richard alone to watch as the blood rolled from the ridges of his knuckles. Dabbing the tip of his left index finger into the mess of fluids, he drew a streak under each eye.

"War paint," he said aloud, chuckling to himself as he headed down the hall and descended the stairs to the main level.

Eight men waited for him in the lobby, bundled in multiple layers of clothing with scarves drawn across their faces so that only their eyes were visible. Each had either a rifle or shotgun slung over their shoulder and across their chests, the front pockets of their jackets bulging with square boxes of ammunition.

"We aren't coming back without the child," Richard said.

The men nodded solemnly, understanding the gravity of Richard's words.

"We travel through the evening and night so that they won't see us coming." Richard donned the gear they had reserved for him as they waited patiently. By the time he was finished adding layer after layer of pants and snow pants, several jackets and a hooded sub-arctic coat, he felt like he was in a rotisserie. "If any of you have qualms about doing whatever it takes to free the boy, then you need to state so now. No hard feelings and no judgments. Just turn around and walk away." He studied their firm expressions. "Good."

He tugged a ski mask over his face and pulled on the faux fur-lined hood, making his final stop the row of tables buried under a display of firearms. Lifting a shotgun that appeared to be the right length, he sighted down the barrel. Content, he slung it over his shoulder and stuffed his outer pockets with boxes of shells. As he was turning away, something caught his eye. With a smile, he took the sheathed hunting knife from the table and gripped it by the hilt. With a snick he withdrew the blade and held it up to the light. The back edge was deeply serrated, the front designed to be sharp enough to cut a deer's hide from the meat. Definitely sharp enough to slit a man's throat with ease. Tucking it beneath the jacket and into the pouch of the pullover beneath so he could feel it against his belly, he led the men through the foyer where many of the others had gathered to see them off.

"We shall return!" Richard called back over his shoulder as he shoved through the front doors. Their cheers resonated in his ears long after he climbed into the passenger seat of the pickup truck. Two men clambered in through the driver's side door, the truck shaking as the remainder bounded up into the bed behind.

The driver cranked the key and pinned the gas, urging the truck to life with a roar. Jamming the stick into reverse, the tires screamed on the ice before gaining traction and firing backwards. It slid sideways as the driver cranked the wheel and punched it into gear, sending the vehicle rocketing forward through the gap where the gate had been. Instead of turning to the left toward the highway, they veered to the right for several blocks before taking a left and driving back through the warehouse district until they saw what they were looking for.

Enclosed by a chain link fence capped with barbed wire was an enormous lot with several acres containing motor homes and trailers as far as the eye could see, but that wasn't why they had come. The driver designated a section of fencing at random and launched the truck from the road, plowing right through. The wire gouged through the paint, but parted easily enough. High-end recreational vehicles passed to either side as they drove deeper into the lot, motor homes larger even than Richard's first apartment. They became smaller in size the farther they worked away from the main road, until they came across the display they had been told would be there in front of the warehouse where they were stored.

There was a line of snowmobiles in front of the metal platforms that held the premiere models aloft so they would be seen first. The truck coasted to a halt right in front of them, the freezing men in back hopping out of the bed and into the accumulation before the pickup even stopped. Richard opened his door and joined them as they marveled at the sleek machinery.

"I still say we could move faster in the truck," the driver said, rounding the hood to stand beside the others.

"There would be too many variables outside of our control," Richard said, noting that the keys hung from the ignition of each of the speeders as he had hoped. "We could always slide off the road and get stuck in a snow bank. And since by now they have to know that we're coming for the boy, they could already have set up roadblocks or any number of traps. In one vehicle, we'd be an easy target. On several with the capabilities of fast maneuvering and off-road evasion, they'll have a much harder time trying to account for all of us at once."

"But it will take twice as long, if not longer."

"Were you not listening?"

The man fell quiet, knowing that any further protests would be summarily dismissed.

"I want these things gassed and ready to go in under half an hour. Find spare gas cans and load four onto each. Strap them to the backs and take care of whatever other business you may have," Richard said, walking away from them.

"Where are you going?" one of them called after him.

"If there's a repair shop, there will be vending machines. If you guys are even half as hungry as I am, then we'll need all of the food we can carry."

He crossed the lot toward a shiny glass building with enormous RVs all around it. Raising his right boot, he simply kicked through the glass and sauntered inside. At the back of the showroom, he could see a pair of bathrooms with an unmarked door between, surely the break room where he would find whatever food they stocked, but it was what he saw behind the sales counter to his left that piqued his curiosity.

There was a display of road hazard gear. Flashlights and blinking emergency beacons. Flat tire foam and triangular wheel blocks. The item at the far end of the top shelf drew his eye.

A flare gun.

Stepping behind the counter, he pulled it down and set it beside the register just long enough to unzip his winter parka. He shoved it into the pocket of his interior jacket with the knife and took the remaining reload canisters as well. One could never predict when a towering blaze just might come in handy.

MICHAEL McBRIDE

VIII

SANGRE DE CRISTO
MOUNTAINS,
WESTERN
COLORADO

They were on the move before the sun even set. With the storm clouds and the blizzard adding to the already thick haze overhead, the sun vanished long before it officially set. Given the unexpected extra hours, they might even be able to reach the suburbs of Salt Lake City before the sun again graced the day. If all went according to the revised plan, not only would they be able to lay siege to those occupying the hotel the following night, they would be able to advance upon the others on the banks of the Great Salt Lake, those the master saw as the true threat.

Thunder raced up the slope, flames licking at its bony heels. When it crested the hill, it brought its legs to its chest and soared with its momentum, fire streaking across the sky like exhaust from a jet, before landing in stride, the earth quivering beneath its stomping hooves. War rode low on its back, tugging on its mane of long sharpened spines to spur it even faster. The skeletal beast was inexhaustible, like the Swarm sprinting behind it, hurdling boulders and slaloming between trees with sinuous agility. They used their claws to gain leverage, propelling them forward to alight on legs that ran with such long, fluid strides that they appeared not to touch the ground at all.

Frozen streams passed beneath, cleared in effortless leaps; gullies and rivers proving to be of no consequence. Only the sheer faces of stone slowed them, forcing War to stick to the paths cut by what had once been deer and mountain goats, but were now something else entirely, something that knew better than to be out in the open when War's armada passed through. The Swarm, however, could scale even the steepest formations, latching their sharp claws into the smallest imperfections in the stone to ascend vertically like geckos, arriving on War's heels so as not to delay their progress longer than absolutely necessary. They bled from the wounds inflicted by their brethren, who scrabbled over each other in the chaos, jockeying for position and their master's favor, but they were oblivious to the pain and the pasty white sludge that slopped to the snow from the gashes.

They hissed from behind him with their mounting bloodlust, spurring War to drive them that much harder. Thrilling in the hunt, he barely noticed the scenery flying past to either side as the ground leveled off and the trees grew farther apart. The snow and ice covering the hidden lakes melted under the intense heat of his stallion's thundering hooves, sending dozens of those reptilian creatures splashing into the bitterly cold water to sink like so many stones to their deaths, the shock of the subzero temperatures overwhelming their central nervous systems, which only resumed command of their physical forms after inhaling that fatal lungful of water. It didn't matter, though. His army numbered in the tens of thousands, more than enough to make swift work of the remainder of man. Soon enough they would learn from watching their kind fall through the ice and avoid traveling directly behind him. If indeed they were actually capable of such higher thought, as many still raced along behind him in the flames, their flesh cooking until they just collapsed forward into the snow to be overcome, every iota of meat picked from the bones left to sink into the soil. They were the perfect mindless killing machines, save that one with the scar across its eye and the dewlap to match the crimson of War's armor. It maintained some semblance of sentience, even after its rebirth into the minions of the damned, its eyes burning with a fire that transcended even death.

Crossing the border into Utah as the mountains obscured the setting sun, the world falling under the blanket of darkness, their eyes cast an eerie light across the fields of snow, the smoke from Thunder's fiery advance hovering over it like a Scottish moor. There was but a single mountain range left to ford, rising like a wolf's teeth against the horizon of night, and they would easily clear it before that celestial orb was a glimmer on the horizon behind.

Little did mankind know that the coming sunrise would be its last, that when it rose again in little more than a day and a half, the few rays that permeated the dreary sky would shine only upon the chalk of their shattered bones, ground beneath War's heel.

CHAPTER 5

I

MORMON TEARS

They were all going to have to labor through the night if they had any hope of being ready in time. It had been Adam's idea to work in shifts. Each and every one of them would expend maximum energy for two straight hours, pushing their bodies to their limits before earning the luxury of passing out from exhaustion, only to throw themselves back into the work again. There would be plenty of time to rest when all was said and done. Either they'd miraculously survive the assault and thrill in the prospect of once again sleeping with both eyes closed, reveling in the promise of being able to sleep through the night without being slaughtered, or they would fall, and eternal rest would be theirs. At the moment, both options held a certain appeal.

It had taken nearly an hour by itself, but they had managed to back the semi-trailer sideways into the passage through the mountains after unloading its cargo, abutting the mound of sand so that it could be shoveled against the trailer to reinforce it. Using it as the foundation, the construction had begun on the vertical wall above it, using two-by-fours like pickets to build rows of fencing, one atop the other until it stood nearly as tall as the mountains to either side. It shuddered with each stiff gust of wind, but it would only have to hold for so long. Besides, it was only a deterrent. Considering they'd siphoned the last of the gas from the semi to douse it when the time came, they didn't need it to stand so much as they needed it to burn.

Evelyn's project, on the other hand, required more careful planning and implementation. Time was of the essence. The kelp was starting to look as though it was past resurrection, but she simply couldn't allow it to die without a fight. She'd been working straight through the night, and now, only hours from sunrise, she was finally ready to put her design to the test. They had dug a large hole in the sand twenty feet from the frozen shoreline. It was only four feet in diameter and maybe five feet deep, but the true challenge had been in hauling the rocks from where they had been embedded in the ice over to the pit and stacking them on top of each other, packing them into the dirt walls to give it the small measure of structural integrity they needed. For all intents and purposes, it looked like an old well that couldn't possibly hold water, but they didn't need it to. All it had to do was keep the sand from collapsing down upon the coal.

They'd carved several long trenches leading away from the pit to the edge of the lake, and then broken through the ice to clear a ten foot square patch. Using the PVC piping from the semi, they'd fashioned four long, straight tubes using four eight foot sections of piping and coupling them together. At one end of each was a ninety degree bend and a four-foot straight length coming out the other side. All four had been lowered into the trenches in parallel so that the tubing hung over the edge of the rocks above the center of the hole, while the other end stretched all the way out into the water where they were able to balance the ends between rocks so that the four-foot sections pointed straight up from the water into the sky like so many smokestacks. Now that the pipes were buried and packed into the earth and they had finished creating a lid, leaving a single four-inch square hole in the center, it was finally time to either save the plants or give up the ghost.

"Is that enough?" Mare asked. Both he and Darren were covered with black dust from lugging load after load of coal out of the cavern.

"At least for now…I think," Evelyn said. She couldn't think of a time in her life when she'd been this nervous. "Maybe just a few—"

"We're ready!" Mare shouted back to the cave, cutting Evelyn off mid-sentence. She'd already sent them back two more times than necessary and his shift had been over for ten minutes already. He'd be damned if he didn't at least get to see if his labor bore fruit.

Jill was waiting in the cave with a burning wooden post, out of the wind and snow, waiting for her summons. She knew that once she ran out into the elements that the flame would extinguish, but they were planning on the embers rekindling the flames just enough to ignite the coal. At the sound of his voice, she shielded the fire with her body and dashed out into the night, using their tracks as a guide. She didn't even slow when she reached the hole in the ground, the elevated lip around it ringed with rocks like a campfire, launching the makeshift torch down to the bottom.

Its end was little more than smoldering black charcoal, but the occasional golden ember winked with life. Thin tufts of smoke twirled up out of the pit to be tossed aside by the wind. None of them dared to so much as breathe for fear of creating that one fateful current of air that would kill the hopes of rekindling the fire. They could always start again with a new torch or somehow carry out an already burning coal, but they'd invested so much time into getting to this point that none of them could stand the prospect of waiting a second longer.

With a crackle, one of the dim embers sparked, a small flame wavering in its stead, growing incrementally larger until another sprung up beside it, the two of them joining to begin consuming the wood anew. Characteristic deep black smoke billowed from the coal beneath, making them cough even as the wind wished it away.

"Just a little more," Evelyn said, raising the lid in preparation of dropping it over the pit.

"Won't that hole just allow the smoke to vent first?" Jill asked.

"It ought to allow just enough air in to stoke the fire and create a buildup of smoke to be forced out through the tubes."

"I still don't think the smoke will be hot enough," Darren said.

"It only has to be warm enough to keep the ice from forming and raise the ambient water temperature into the low fifties."

"Like I said—"

"Shh!" Evelyn shushed him. Maybe he was right, but they were so close now. So close. And until she saw it fail with her own eyes, she wasn't about to entertain the notion.

Flames licked the rocky surface of the coal, taking root with a radiating warmth that they all felt sigh from the mouth of the well.

"Okay," Evelyn said, her heart beating so fast that she could hardly breathe. "Here we go."

She lowered the wooden flap forward until the others could reach it from the other side to help her seat it in place atop the lip. A rush of smoke billowed from beneath the closing lid before being shunted. A thin column of smoke plumed from the hole in the cover, diffusing onto the wind. They all turned and stared toward the lake, slowly walking down the beach to the shoreline. Evelyn bit her lip in anticipation as the others nervously looked out across the water to where the four two-inch wide columns stood erect from the deceptively placid surface.

"Maybe the wind's blowing the smoke away," Jill whispered.

"We'd still be able to see it," Mare said.

"It's just taking a while to get through the tubing," Evelyn said.

"If it is at all," Darren said, turning back to the cave where the others had gathered to watch with great interest before starting their shifts.

"It'll come," Evelyn said.

"What if it doesn't?"

"It will."

"All I'm saying is we should have some idea of what to try next if…"

His words trailed off as the first finger of smoke bloomed from the pipe on the far right, followed in short measure by the two to the left, and finally by the lone remaining.

"It's working," Evelyn whispered, her long-trapped breath escaping her in a sigh of relief. It still remained to be seen if the smoke would be hot enough to heat the water by osmosis, but they could always throw on more coal. The point was that her theory was sound. It had passed the first test, and if it worked, they could manufacture these pits up and down the coast to culture acres of kelp.

"You did it," Adam said, smiling. He placed his hand on her shoulder. "What a brilliant idea. If it works like it's supposed to, then we'll all—"

Evelyn squealed with excitement and clapped her hands. Whirling to face Adam, she grabbed him by either side of the face with her dirty, frozen hands and kissed him right on the lips. She spun again to watch the smoke rise triumphantly, only realizing what she'd just done at that precise moment. Her face ran the gamut of reds and she clapped a hand over her mouth. Did she really just kiss him?

She turned again, slowly, her mind racing to come up with any plausible excuse. It had been the excitement. She would have kissed whoever was standing there. She was coming down with a fever, maybe even delirious.

But when she finally faced him, he walked directly up to her and wrapped his arms around her, drawing her to him. She barely had time to lower her hand before his lips met hers.

"It's a serious burden always being right," Lindsay said, but Evelyn ignored her, rejoicing at the spark that was now a flame burning inside of her.

II

SALT LAKE CITY

He should have gone with Richard. He had sworn to protect him after all, maybe not aloud and to his face, but it was a vow he had made to himself and he took such matters very seriously. Richard had entrusted Garrett with so much more though, and he knew it. He was now responsible for close to ninety lives, and on top of that, he had been delegated the paramount task of making sure that the hotel would be ready not only for Richard's return, but for the coming battle. Having seen what these creatures could do, he needed to ensure that their fortress was impenetrable, that it could withstand even the most violent attack. Their best shot would be if they were able to hold the enemy back beyond the perimeter where they would be able to snipe them from the roof with rifles, but if their outer fortifications were breached, they wouldn't stand a chance.

"You down there!" Garrett shouted from the roof. Three men looked up from where they leaned against the front of the building, preparing to take a nicotine break. "Those windows aren't going to board themselves up!"

"…take a stupid break…" one of them grumbled in a tone meant to elude his ears.

"You can take a break when you're dead! Now get back to work!"

"We're exhausted!" the man shouted back up at him. "We've been working non-stop since—"

Garrett pointed his rifle at the man, inching the sight to the side just enough to miss his head, but close enough to make sure he heard the bullet passing right beside it.

Bang!

"Jesus Christ!" the man shouted, dabbing at his bloody ear. The bullet had grazed it just enough to tear away the outer conch. "You... you shot me!"

"Get back to boarding up those windows or I guarantee those monsters will do so much worse!"

The other men flung their cigarettes into the snow and went right back to task without looking up. Still cupping his tattered ear, the third man leaned against the sheet of plywood to hold it in place so the others could board up the glass.

Gotta break some eggs if you want to make an omelet, his father had always said. Of course, he had worked in collections, and by eggs he had meant legs, but Garrett still subscribed to the principle. In his football days, he had intentionally gone for the defensive linemen's knees, and in the scrum for a fumble had done many things that should have drawn a flag. Gouging his thumb into an opponent's eye. Giving a groin a solid squeeze and a twist. Bending fingers backwards, clawing skin. A man had to be willing to do whatever it took in any given situation to come out on top. It had brought him collegiate acclaim as an All-American, at least until he'd blown out his knee at the scouting combine, but more importantly, it had prepared him for life. Without football, he'd been as ordinary as the next guy, only a heck of a lot stronger and more intimidating, which had served him well in stints as a bodyguard and a bouncer.

His father had been right...for the most part. When it came right down to it, success wasn't about breaking eggs, but simply the willingness to do so without a second thought. He'd found that by making an example of someone, others would learn what kind of consequences they faced. That's where he and Richard were so similar. Killing the woman had been regrettable, as had shooting Peckham, but it wasn't about either of them as individuals. It was all about the others who needed to know that someone had taken charge to guarantee their safety. Lying about the events had made him uncomfortable, though. He had no problem with taking responsibility for his actions for the sake of the greater good, but he understood

Richard's motives. No one wanted to see the chef cracking the eggs or milking the cow or butchering the pig, they just wanted to sit down with a steaming omelet and not have to think about anything other than the marvelous taste.

So be it. They would all survive and prosper thanks to a pair of broken eggs.

Garrett stepped over the smoldering gold casing melting through the snow and walked across the roof to look down upon the rear courtyard. The workers down there must have stopped when they heard the gunfire, but quickly resumed when he appeared, pretending as though they hadn't seen him.

They'd completed the circuit of barbed wire atop the fence and were coiling more into the gaps with the remainder. As they were on the front side, they were boarding up the windows on the lower level and would soon appear on the balconies of the second story to do the same. A tractor trailer cruised slowly through the back lot, allowing the group of people trailing it to unload every scrap of wood they could fit on board from the open rear, tossing them into haphazard piles against the base of the fence. Another pickup followed behind, the two men standing in the bed dropping full plastic containers of gasoline into the snow.

When the man with the telescopic sight atop the parapet to Garrett's left saw the first sign of advancing forces, they would douse the wood with gas and set the piles to burning. Let those monsters peel their skin from their bones climbing the fence and wriggling through the razor wire, only to drop into a wall of flames that would consume their remains. If by some miracle they were lucky enough to make it that far, they'd be easy pickings through the sight of a rifle. Richard was going to be so proud of—

Light flooded out onto the balconies attached to the rooms below, his instincts bringing the butt of the rifle to his shoulder.

A cheer arose from all around him at once. Everyone stopped what they were doing to look up at the artificial illumination. Garrett had no choice but to allow them to enjoy this small victory. It was an accomplishment to be shared by all. A sign of hope and the undying human spirit. It espoused the belief that they would not only make it through the coming trials, but would soon be able to begin reclaiming their former lives. It was the first baby step that would eventually lead to home-cooked meals and hot showers, central heat and air conditioning, and maybe even one day radio and television. They would be able to electrify their fences and install sophisticated defense systems. The opportunities were limitless.

Garrett turned back to the roof and headed for the doorway leading down into the building, the formerly dark stairwell now well lit. For a moment he even thought he felt air flowing out of the ductwork. He rounded the corner and opened the door onto the third floor.

"You shot me," a level voice said from behind him as he entered the hallway.

Garrett whirled to face the man.

"Consider it a warning," he said.

The man peeled his hand away from his crusty ear. It looked like something had taken a bite out of it and ripped the flesh along the side of his head away with it, closely-cropped hair and all.

"This doesn't feel like a warning. Does it look like a warning?" The man's eyes were wild and unblinking, the tendons taut in his neck, stretching the tattoo of a snake.

"We either get the work done or we die. Do you understand that?"

Lips curling angrily, the man extended his index finger and jabbed Garrett in the chest.

"Or maybe it's just you who's gonna—"

Garrett grabbed the finger and bent it sharply in the opposite direction. With a loud crack, the jaggedly fractured phalanx ripped through the skin.

The man howled, dropping to his knees and cradling his hand against his chest.

Garrett took him by either side of the face, squeezing so hard on his cheekbones that the man's eyes started to bulge, and then squeezing even harder. Releasing the man's now bloody face, he closed his fists around either ear and jerked the man's head forward at the same time as he raised his knee.

With one final crack of snapping bone, the man toppled to his back on the floor.

"Eggs," Garrett said, taking the man by the collar of his jacket and dragging him down the hallway into his room.

III

THE EASTERN
BANKS OF THE
GREAT SALT LAKE

Richard throttled the speeder and gave it some gas, sending it rocketing forward as soon as the ground leveled off. He should have known better than to expect the state-of-the-art snowmobiles to work. The other men had hauled them down from the racks, but hadn't even been able to get the engines to turn over. Useless computer chips. Fortunately, they'd been able to find some older models in reasonable shape at the back of the lot, clunky old junkers that barely resembled their streamlined successors. They reminded him more of tanks than anything else with the way the rider was forced to sit erect to accommodate the battery-powered engine and none of the fancy bells and whistles, but they would get them from here to there, and that was all that really mattered.

The remainder of the fluorescent orange discounted price tag he had scraped off marred his vision through the windshield, but to nowhere near the extent of the blizzard that choked his headlight nearly back to the lens. All he could do was balance his speed against the visibility and dodge whatever he could before slamming into it. Lowering his head even further to try to prevent the wind from cracking open the chafed skin around his eyes, he tried not to think about the pain in his toes or the prospect of them turning black before they reached their final destination.

A glance at the side mirror confirmed that the others were lagging. As they were traveling in a single-file line, he could only see the headlight immediately behind him, but barely, as it faded in and out through the snow. He tapped his toe on the brake repeatedly to make the red taillight flash, trying to get their attention to urge them on, but it had quite the opposite effect. The light behind him vanished into the storm. He stopped and waited for the others to catch up, but when it became apparent that they weren't going to, he turned the snowmobile around and followed his tracks back to them. When the headlight finally reappeared, he could see their silhouettes standing in front of it.

"What the hell are you doing?" Richard shouted, hopping off his sled and stomping straight over to them.

"You wanted to stop," one of the men said, his frozen breath gusting through the hole in his ski mask.

"I wanted you to speed up. You were falling behind."

"We've been driving for hours without a single break. Probably time we took one, don't you think?" another said, sloshing a fifth of vodka before taking a swig and passing it to Richard, who knocked it back and coughed out the fumes. He was prepared to verbally lash them for wasting precious time, but he needed something special from these men, something that they wouldn't do simply because he told them to.

He was going to need them to kill for him.

"You're right," he finally said. "I have been pushing you kind of hard."

"Kind of?" one of them men said, causing them all to laugh.

Richard bit his tongue hard enough to fill his mouth with warmth.

"I just keep thinking about Jake," he said, readjusting the shotgun strap across his chest. "Lord only knows what they're doing to that poor child this very moment or if...he's even still alive."

That sobered them up, their laughter a distant memory.

"If they've so much as bruised him, they're dead," the man behind the others said from where he stood outside the range of the headlights. Richard recognized the voice as that of the man who had rallied them to his crusade at the hotel. "I promise you that."

"You're a good man..."

"Bruce," the man said.

"You're a good man, Bruce."

"Good has nothing to do with it. The kid reminds me of my boy.

Looks like him anyway. When my old lady left me, she took him with her. The guy she split with beat her, beat them both. Only he beat my boy just a little too hard."

They all fell silent.

"I'm sorry," Richard said, trying to read the man's eyes, but they were hidden in shadow.

"You and me both. I didn't get a chance to pay a visit to the bastard before…this." He held his hands out to either side to gesture at everything in general before clenching them into fists and dropping them again to his sides. "I think this is fate's way of giving me a second shot at retribution."

Richard nodded and turned to look back in the direction in which they had been headed. A dozen paces away, there was a line bisecting his tracks. He walked toward it, watching the line widen to a full-fledged crack, but it wasn't until he was directly above it that he understood. He tapped his toe on the line, listening to the splash of water and the crack of breaking ice. Their path hadn't flattened onto a meadow or salt flat buried by snow. He'd driven right across the beach and onto the frozen lake.

"Well… What do you know?" he said, looking again toward the horizon. His plan had been to follow the shoreline around the periphery of the lake, using it as a guide until they were able to sneak up on the others in their precious cave, but it now appeared as though they had stumbled upon a shortcut that could potentially save them hours in transit.

He walked gingerly forward, listening for the sound of ice disintegrating beneath his weight, knowing that if he fell through into the freezing water that the resultant death would be agonizingly slow, but there wasn't a sound or the slightest bit of give underfoot. After another couple of steps, he started to stomp. Two more steps and he stomped again.

"What are you doing?" one of the men asked. There were now three of them out on the ice and it was as solid as ever. He'd driven the snowmobile out onto it already and it had supported the weight just fine, but his speed could have contributed to luck in that regard.

"This is the lake," Richard said. He stomped again to illustrate his point. "See? Frozen solid."

Both men jumped back as though they'd been standing in a nest of serpents, one of them sprinting back to join the others.

"Jesus," the remaining man whispered. "How did it freeze so fast?"

"I've learned never to question opportunity when it presents itself. You just have to seize it."

"You're crazy if you think I'm going to drive out onto this," the man said, still retreating.

"Then I suppose you'll have to take the long way."

"That's cold."

"No. Cold is spending needless hours on the back of a snowmobile in a blizzard while the rest of us have already reached our destination and are sitting around a warm fire hashing out the details of our plan."

"I hear drowning's the most peaceful way to die," the man said, stomping gingerly on the ice before finding the confidence to jump up and down. "And I do like the idea of that fire."

Richard smiled as he approached the man, clapping him on the shoulder.

"Sounds to me like you've made the smart choice," Richard said, heading back to where they were all parked.

The others had been watching, but were apparently reserving judgment for the time being.

"That's the lake, you say?" Bruce asked.

Richard nodded.

"Frozen, huh?" Bruce shrugged. "What are we waiting for then?"

"Lead on, my friend," Richard said, climbing onto his speeder. *Good*, he thought, *if the ice breaks, he'll be the first to fall through*. Maybe that would afford him the split-second he would require to avoid the same fate. He was about to make the engine roar when movement caught his attention.

Sitting still, he didn't turn to face the source of the motion, but rather inspected it from the corner of his eye, slowly un-slinging the rifle from his shoulder. It was hardly a shade of white apart from the snow. Wedging the stock against his shoulder, he pointed the barrel out across the lake, leveling the sight. He held his breath and swung the rifle to the right, pulling the trigger as soon as the crosshairs centered on the ivory body. Wide wings spread far too late, the bullet pounding through the chest of the great bird, the body hurtling backwards amidst a spray of its blood.

He heard the other men shouting, drawing their weapons and swinging them in every direction, expecting to find themselves under attack, but Richard calmly climbed off the snowmobile and walked into the deep snow away from their path. Scurrying over the large rock on which the bird had been perched, he knelt over the remains, downy feathers blowing across the snow like tumbleweeds. Taking it by the ankles, he hung it upside down, rivers of blood running down the silky feathers and over the golden beak to drip to the ground.

"What is it?" Bruce asked, leaning over the boulder with his sights trained on Richard.

"Just a bird." He tossed it off into the shrubs and was preparing to head back when he saw the pattern of blood on the accumulation. The droplets had fallen in such a way as to form two words in crimson, the warm fluids eating through the snow.

Richard scoffed and kicked the words into an indistinguishable mound of snow.

"We're wasting our time," he said, this time skirting the rock to head back to the snowmobile.

Bruce lowered his weapon, studying the bloody heap of snow and looking at Richard before slipping the sling over his shoulder and following him back to the others. In the heartbeat before Richard had kicked the powder, he thought he had seen the blood form words on the snow through the scope.

Turn back.

IV

MORMON TEARS

Adam stood on the beach in knee-deep snow, staring toward the eastern horizon, where somewhere behind the low-lying banks of clouds the sun was rising into the sky. Even though he could only vaguely sense its presence as a faint gray aura, he drew a measure of comfort from it. They had survived another night. There had been so much in his former life that he had taken for granted, even something as commonplace as the sunrise. He'd never truly appreciated the magnitude of such a profound celestial event from which nearly all life was derived, nor had he ever wondered if he might be witnessing it for the last time. As he did now. Wrapping his arms around his chest to stifle the goosebumps that the thoughts had generated, he turned back to the stone cliff he now called home, wincing at the knot in his lower back from sleeping on the rock floor, if indeed closing his eyes sporadically through the night could be called such.

The dike they had crafted ran the length of the shoreline in front of him, not quite as tall as he was, but high enough to hide the others from sight. The sharpened tips of the poles poked several inches out of the embankment in twin rows, hopefully soon to be covered entirely by the falling snow. They had rammed them straight through the wall of sand so that the trailing ends projected behind, where long boards were waiting. When the attack finally came, all they would have to do is align the lumber with the ends of the poles and lower a shoulder to it, goring whatever tried to scramble over from the other side. It was a flimsy plan at best, but it was only meant to slow them down while they fell back to the cave. There was no way they would be able to face down the Swarm and survive. Their entire scheme was predicated on using the element of surprise to postpone what was beginning to feel like the inevitable.

He climbed over the mounded sand and slid down the back side, careful not to dislodge any of the spears. Ahead and to the left, the sand slanted up to the top of the semi trailer, its roof barely visible. There were five rows of fencing above it, so poorly nailed together that it looked as though it might topple of its own accord, were it not for the haphazard Xs of wood holding one row atop another and the slanted wood appendages propping it up. The blowing flakes actually helped to strengthen it, drifting into a crust of ice and packed snow on the opposite side. His only trepidation was that when the time came, it wouldn't burn as well or as quickly as they needed it to.

To his left, a spire of flames rose out of the hole in the scorched lid over the pit. It had taken several more trips to secure all of the coal they required, but Evelyn's contraption was now working far better than any of them had thought it would. The water wasn't warm enough to bathe in by any stretch of the imagination, but the pipes heated the water enough to keep the ice from forming, and even appeared to be melting it back a little to free even more surface area. Lindsay and April slaved a good dozen feet out from it on the thicker ice, mounding and packing the snow to form an extension of the wall along the shore to shield the kelp garden. Not only would it slow down the forces crossing the lake, but it would protect the open water from the wind to slow the cooling process.

The kelp had almost immediately regained its original form, the leaves brightening from brown to an olive green and new plants were budding out of the silt from the expanding webwork of roots beneath. Evelyn had already convinced Darren and Mare to build a matching system all the way down the beach past the cave since they had done so well on the first, giving them time to bring the saltwater up to temperature before transplanting some of the kelp. Right now she was back in the cavern, curled up by the fire under a blanket, catching up on some of the sleep she had forsaken during the night.

Adam made his way to the cave, weaving through the maze of tall spikes. They were nearly as ready as they would ever be. Their defenses were primitive at best, and more than likely pathetic, but according to Phoenix, they were now just about out of time.

He passed through the cave and continued into the passage leading into the mountain, thankful to be out of the blizzard and the wicked wind. It warmed significantly with each step, starting to dry his wet jacket, the ice now falling from the fabric. His eyes burned with sleep deprivation and his head throbbed, but he couldn't afford to allow his body to undermine his will. Soon enough he would be able to sleep, but for now they were all counting on him for the strength and courage he could feel draining from his tired body. He'd never been meant to lead. He was a doctor by trade, blessed with the ability to heal and the compassion to do so. The Army had paid for his education, but in no way had they made a soldier out of him. His worst nightmare was not that he would be killed when the Swarm descended upon them, but that he would allow the others to suffer that fate. The mere thought was more than his conscience could bear.

Navigating the tunnel by heart now, he rounded the final bend to see the light from the cavern. Norman and Gray were on the elevated cliff in front of him, putting the final touches on a makeshift vehicle they had aptly dubbed "The Last Resort." It was an awkward looking creation: the leading surface a flat slab of two-by-fours nailed together to form what looked like a barn door with long nails poking out of it, while behind it they had affixed the rear tires of Evelyn's truck, which was now sitting uselessly outside on the beach collecting snow. Some sort of pushcart system had been mounted to the wheels from behind. If their outer defenses failed to withstand the assault, they would all make a made dash for the cavern. After the last of them passed through, they would run the cart down the tunnel until it met with resistance in the form of the reptilian bodies impaled on the nails while the others stacked the boulders they had collected behind the wheels until they had built an impromptu stone wall.

There was no plan in place for what they would do afterwards. They would have blocked off the lone point of access and there would be no way out, leaving them trapped inside what would become their tomb. There was a vent in the roof that served as a sort of chimney for the smoke from the fire, but it was far too thin to allow them to wriggle out to the surface above. With the way that everything around them seemed to have a purpose in the grand design, he hated to speculate as to the function of the pueblo, but it only stood to reason that such a structure's sole purpose would be to house them for an extended period of time. The very idea was positively demoralizing.

"Anyone behind you?" Norman asked.

"I don't think so," Adam said.

"I'll run down and check," Gray said, disappearing into the tunnel.

Norman smiled at Adam. His eyes were bloodshot and bruised bags hung beneath. "How are you holding up?"

"Fine," Adam said, looking down to the cavern floor where the others were asleep around the fire.

"You aren't fooling anyone, you know."

"I'm no worse off than anyone else."

"You look like death warmed over. You should try to get some shuteye before…" Norman stopped short of vocalizing it.

"Before tonight," Adam said somberly.

"Yeah."

"I don't think I could sleep even if I wanted to."

"I'm sure you'd be surprised. The human body is a miraculous creation, but I don't have to tell you that, do I, Doctor?"

Adam smiled, highlighting the weary lines of exhaustion on his face.

"You're a good man, Norman. I don't remember if I ever formally thanked you for saving my life—"

"No need, my friend. Just make sure you return the favor if needed," Norman said with a wink.

"I told them all to stay clear," Gray hollered over the sound of running footsteps. "Let's take this baby out for a test drive."

Norman's eyes lit up like a child with a new toy as both walked around behind the construct, shouldering up against each other and grabbing onto the horizontal piece of timber above the wheels.

"On three," Gray said. "One… Two…"

Both grunted as they shoved, the cart rolling forward slowly at first, the bottom edge of the wooden blockade scraping the stone floor, but rapidly gained speed. It raced straight into the tunnel all the way to the bend before becoming lodged at an angle. There was maybe a six-inch gap above it, but the sides were wedged snugly against the walls to that point that it was a struggle for them to pry it free to drag it back out of the tunnel.

Adam listened to them congratulating each other for a moment before descending the rocky stairs to the bottom. He watched Evelyn as he neared the fire, wanting nothing more than to gently raise the blanket and curl up beside her. Her hair had fallen down over her face, blowing on each soft exhalation. Kneeling beside her, he stroked her long bangs back over her ear. She was so beautiful. So amazing. He leaned over to place a tentative kiss on her forehead, his lips barely grazing her smooth skin—

A scream erupted from behind him and she jerked her head up, banging his. They turned to see Jake sitting upright with his blanket bunched around his waist, eyes rolled back into his skull.

V

SALT LAKE CITY

Garrett sat on the balcony from his room, enjoying a moment of peace as he stared out across what under other circumstances would have been an amazing city. The taller buildings of downtown looked stunning against the backdrop of the distant snowy peaks. He could see the domed facilities they'd only recently built for the Winter Olympics, a sad reminder of a better life. There were houses and churches as far as the eye could see with yards buried beneath feet of snow and skeletal deciduous trees standing sentry over those monuments to the American Dream. They were domiciles where families had gathered to share their love and lives with one another, where they had hoped for the future and told stories of the past. Where they had knelt at the altar of the God that would forsake them in their hour of utmost need, leaving their bloated corpses to rot through the floorboards and eventually dissociate back into the earth. He could only hope that their souls had departed gracefully from their flesh, abandoning the surely overwhelming pain of their black bodies swelling like boiled sausages. Had they been spared from the agony and called to their Father's side? Were they the chosen and those who remained behind the damned?

He looked to the gray sky, but there were no answers to be found. No glint of heaven's pearly gates or the hand of God reaching down to reassure him that everything was going to be all right.

Such introspection was foreign to Garrett. He had lived his entire life by his own will, not by that of some greater power. Why then was he now mourning a town he had never known and its people whose lives had never intersected his? It had to be the lack of sleep. He was going on close to seventy-two hours without by now. Maybe more. He might have lost track of a day somewhere in there. Or maybe this was the manifestation of an altogether new emotion for him, one that he had done everything in his power to avoid throughout his life. Could this possibly be what it was like to feel afraid?

Again he found himself staring off at the mountains. They were out there somewhere, weren't they? Were they watching him now just as he watched them? Or were they closer, hiding in the surrounding buildings, keeping to the shadows just outside of sight through the windows? There was nothing to be gained from obsessing about it. They would come, most likely under the cover of night, but they wouldn't find their prey cowering and unable to put up a fight. Stand or fall, they would battle with everything they had. They would not go quietly into that good night, but would rage against their fate, going down screaming and clawing if that was their lot.

His primary concern now was whether or not Richard would make it back in time. He could only imagine what would happen if they caught him out in the open. He was a strong man, but no amount of strength or firepower could withstand superior numbers for very long. Worse still...what would become of the rest of them if anything happened to Richard? He was their leader in every sense of the word, the centipede's head to their minions of legs, without which they would be left in chaos.

He had recognized the look in Richard's eyes. Like his father, there had been no denying him. Garrett had learned never to stand in the way of a man so possessed. Men of singular focus could be incredibly dangerous, even to their friends. He trusted Richard. He believed in him. But that didn't mean that the next arranged accident wouldn't be his.

Walking back into his room, he yanked on the curtains, tearing them off the rings and kicking them to the side. Grabbing the first of the plywood sheets from where they leaned against the wall, he lined it up in front of the patio and nailed it to the wall. He did the same with the other two panels, effectively sealing off the glass. Flipping the bed onto its side, he slid it up against the boards for good measure.

They were now as prepared as possible. Men were rotating through the watch atop the parapet every hour to keep them sharp, while eight others were posted with rifles or shotguns at each of the four corners of the roof with another between to cover all angles. Sixteen more patrolled the perimeter inside the courtyard. Lord only knew if any of them could shoot straight, but he suspected that any opportunity to pull the trigger from the ground level would be at close range. Their instructions were simple, like using a camera: point, click, and shoot. That would have to be good enough. Women and children provided constant refills of coffee and cider to keep all of the mugs hot while others created what was to be a celebratory banquet late in the afternoon. They would have to be ready by nightfall. Setting them on watch with full bellies worried him. It would slow their reflexes and make them lethargic, neither of which were ideal traits for a sentry, but he couldn't deny them their elaborate feast, especially if it proved to be their last.

He sighed at the completion of his task and headed for the bathroom. They hadn't figured out how to run the plumbing, so no one dared to flush yet, but that wasn't why he had entered the small room. The man who had accosted him in the hallway sat on the toilet. His wrists were taped behind his back and his legs were similarly bound from his knees all the way down to his ankles. Chin slumped to his chest, he simply sat there with blood crusted over his eyes and nose. Thick scabs covered his face, which was startlingly white in contrast to the browning blood congealed on the tape across his mouth. He'd been alive when Garrett had brought him in and restrained him. Peeling the tape off, the body fell forward off of the commode, still bent at the waist, as though in the throes of rigor mortis. It would be easy enough to discard with the rest of the corpses following the battle. For now, however, the time had come to join in the revelry. He would refrain from eating, trusting the pangs of hunger to keep him alert, but the troops needed to be rallied. They needed one of those famous Vince Lombardi pep-talks to work them into a frenzy before the big game, and it would be his job to deliver it. His calling. All of those years in all of those locker rooms, injecting steroids to bring out his animal aggression and intravenous fluids to stave off the cramps, painkillers to deaden some pain while banging his head and fists on lockers to heighten others. It all boiled down to this. He would deliver a speech that would endure through the annals of time, that would be passed down through future generations of survivors. His name would live on long after his body nourished the soil.

Allowing his chest to swell with pride, he walked out into the hallway and closed the door behind him.

Had he lingered outside the doorway instead of heading straight for the stairwell he might have heard a gasp for air or maybe the scuffing sound of clothes scraping linoleum. Perhaps he would have noticed a groan or a meek sobbing.

Maybe he should have checked for a pulse.

VI

The Great Salt Lake

Snow flew from the runners as they sped across the interminable whiteness, crusted with ridges as though the lake had frozen with the waves precisely as they had been when the storm descended. Smooth rock formations passed to either side, former islands now landlocked by the rapidly accumulating snow. They traveled in a wide V formation like migrating geese, spreading their weight as far apart as possible. So far, not a single section had threatened to collapse and whatever qualms they had once shared were now completely gone. Richard felt a certain sense of invincibility, a growing power that radiated from every pore.

He had underestimated the size of the lake. It was more of an inland sea, isolated from the oceans as they retreated from the shifting continents. It had taken nearly half a day to drive around by highway and easily as long on the snowmobiles, though they cut straight across. They would have wasted nearly an entire day had they tried to follow the shoreline. He didn't know how much farther it would be to the western coast, but the ride had afforded him plenty of time alone with his thoughts to formulate a plan. They could easily just walk into their encampment and slaughter the others, take the boy, and be following their tracks back across the lake fifteen minutes later, but Richard knew that this was the perfect opportunity to write his own legend. He pondered what a Caesar would do. Lao Tzu had called war an art, and as such, Richard had a masterpiece to create. He needed to be seen by his followers as larger than life, feared and respected, his intellect and will unquestioned.

And he knew exactly what to do.

Scanning the horizon, he watched for the distinctive profile of the rock formation that he had seen from the opposite side when it had been an island. From the western shore looking to the east, it had reminded him of a great sea monster, its humped back cresting the surface before lowering toward the water and rising again like a sinewy tail. How much different could it possibly look from the other side? They couldn't afford to overshoot their mark or they would soar right out into the open and give up the element of surprise. Approaching the rock from behind would allow them the time they needed to ready themselves for the confrontation, and he knew with the utmost confidence that there would indeed be one. Only it would be on his terms in a situation where he could control all of the variables.

The snowflakes had grown so large and the wind so violent that the visibility was essentially nil, the horizon appearing only momentarily while the wind drew a deep breath to blow again in another direction. Without the sun, there was no way of accurately estimating the time, but Richard suspected they were coming upon midday. By nightfall they would have the boy and would return to a hero's welcome the following morning. If Garret had done his job as he had promised he would, the hotel would be a venerable fortress with heat and electricity and armed guards on duty around the clock. They would be ready to withstand an army, and with Jake by his side he would be able to predict when the showdown would come. Everything was falling into place precisely as he had envisioned it. His followers would coronate him their king and worship him as a prophet, blindly follow him as their leader and fear him as their ruler. He would have everything he had ever dreamed of.

He would be a god. Through the curtain of snow he thought he saw another of those white falcons, but when he turned it was gone. He debated heading back to see if it had left tracks in the snow, standing there in the middle of icy nowhere, but he was too eager to reach the island. There was a part of him that wanted more than anything to kill another one of those birds. The words formed by the last one's drizzling blood must have been an illusion, a random pattern of dots rationalized by his brain into a coherent form, but it had appeared clear as day, as though written by an invisible hand. But he had kicked snow over it as a knee-jerk reaction so that none of the others would see. If he could just kill another one, he could prove that theory, if only to himself. The thought of being sent a message—especially one so contradictory to his well-calculated plans—in the blood of a dead animal was absurd. Turn back? There was no way he would even consider that option. After working his entire life toward a goal that was now just outside of his reach, he would sooner die than allow it to slip through his fingers.

With a howl, the wind shifted again, battering him from the left so hard that he could feel the snowmobile slide sideways. Tightening his grip, he drove into it to straighten his path, looking ahead through the windshield—

There it was. He was sure of it.

It looked like the sea monster was swimming in the opposite direction, but its silhouette against the gray sky was exactly how he remembered it. Speeding up, he passed by Bruce to his left to attract his attention, signaling for him to slow. The others veered in from the flanks, just close enough to be able to communicate without amassing their considerable weight on one section of ice.

"That's where we're going," Richard said, pointing at the rocky island, which was immediately consumed by the storm.

"What's the plan then?" Bruce asked.

"We come upon it slowly to quiet our engines and moor the snowmobiles on the eastern edge."

"You heard the man," Bruce called to the others, again heading forward into the snow, though at a dramatically reduced speed.

The noise was still too loud for Richard, but there was nothing they could do about it shy of abandoning their sole mode of transportation, which was completely unacceptable. When the time came to leave, they would need to do so in a hurry. He giggled at the thought. That little albino freak who had opposed him and divided them would never even see it coming. Unless he were truly psychic as the others claimed... Then he would surely be nowhere within a thousand miles.

The shadow of the island took form through the snow, rising steadily until it towered over them. The ages had buffed the stone round and smooth, like staring at a cluster of mushroom caps. It was far larger than it had looked from the western coast, close to a hundred feet in height with various levels and roughly half a mile long, surpassing even his wildest expectations. From afar it had resembled a single mound of rock, but in actuality it was a large spiral-shaped cluster of stones of various sizes.

He killed the engine and coasted to a halt with the front runner abutting the rock. Climbing off, he hopped up on the lowest level, a long slanting section that led away from the lake and up to the right behind the larger section that eclipsed it. The others ascended the stone, allowing Richard to lead them along a winding course until they reached the pinnacle, lowering themselves to their bellies to crawl far enough forward to be able to see the opposite shore.

It was barely visible through the storm, but there was no mistaking it. A sheer face of stone lined the entire beach, fading intermittently at the behest of the savage assault of snowflakes. He couldn't see any of them out there, though from this distance he was sure he wouldn't have been able to regardless of the smothering storm.

"That's it all right," one of the men said. "So what's the plan from here?"

Richard looked past him to where a large clump of dead shrubbery grew from the cracks between rocks, filled with sticks and straw from whatever birds nested there in the spring and summer.

"We announce our presence," Richard said.

"I thought we wanted the element of surprise."

"We have it."

"Then I don't understand. If they don't know we're here, why would we want to give up that advantage? We could just cross the ice and take the kid back from right under their noses."

"Then we'd be just like them. Sneaking into their midst to steal a child. That was what was wrong with the world. Armies fighting undeclared wars. Terrorists hijacking planes full of civilians to crash into buildings and fashioning dirty bombs to leave in markets or send into an elementary school in their own kid's backpack. We started it all. While the British formed battle lines, we picked them off from the trees. We invented guerilla warfare and cried about it when others used our own cowardly tactics against us. Vietnam. Iraq. They were direct consequences of our own actions. If we've been given the chance to begin anew, then we need to do so like men. We need to declare our intentions so that we leave no doubt as to what is to follow."

"But then they'll know we're coming. You said you wanted to use the cover of night and the storm to hide our advance so we could catch them by surprise."

"And we have. Right now, they have no idea what we intend to do. They can't see us from all the way over there and couldn't possibly have heard our snowmobiles. We have surprise on our side, but it's only a tool. Fear, on the other hand, fear is a weapon. Fear breeds chaos and dissention. That, my friends, is what we need to capitalize upon."

Richard rolled onto his side and craned his neck to see around the man to where Bruce lay on his stomach, using the rifle's sight to view the far shore more clearly.

"Bruce," Richard said, drawing the man's eye from the scope. "Feel up to a hike?"

"I thought you'd never ask." He stood and slung the rifle back over his shoulder.

"Tell them they can either send the boy back with you or be prepared to negotiate their surrender."

"And if they don't want to play your game?"

"They will."

"But if they don't?"

"We'll come running at the first sound of gunfire."

Bruce nodded. That was all he really needed to know.

He followed the cut back down to the snowmobiles and began his trek around the island.

"What's there to negotiate?" one of the men asked Richard. "I thought we were here to get the kid back…whatever the cost."

Richard smiled. "We're negotiating how many of them will die."

The wind screamed and pelted them with snow, silencing any further questions. Bruce appeared on the frozen lake off to the left, walking due west. Richard watched him growing smaller and smaller until he was nearly out of sight.

"Go get me one of the gas cans," he said to no one in particular.

The men only stared at him quizzically.

"Now!" he shouted and three of them leapt to their feet.

Richard knew the timing would need to be precise, so he borrowed a rifle from one of the others to use the scope and marked Bruce's progress. When Bruce finally disappeared completely, he couldn't have been more than a hundred yards from the bank.

"Here," a voice said from behind Richard, panting from the exertion. He shook the can for effect.

"Thank you," Richard said, setting down the rifle and taking the plastic container from him. Walking over to the clump of dead shrubbery, he opened the spigot and doused the sticks, the snow melting away at first contact.

"What are you doing?" one of the others asked, but Richard had no time for asinine questions.

He unzipped his coat and reached into the pocket of the jacket beneath, producing the flare gun and cracking it in half to open the chamber. Pulling one of the silver canisters from the pouch, he pressed it into the gun and with a flick of his wrist, sealed the chamber. Pointing it into the glistening collection of branches, he pulled the trigger and launched a ball of fire into the shrubs.

Deep black smoke gushed from the small flames, growing larger as they burned through the gasoline and into the wood, the blaze soon rising above his head.

"We're going to need more gas," Richard said, walking past the dumbfounded men to assume his post on the ledge, staring across the lake through the crosshairs.

Waiting.

VII

MORMON TEARS

Jake continued screaming until he was finally able to rationalize his surroundings. He had woken everyone around the fire, and it felt as though they were all standing over him, so close that he was suffocating. His eyes shot from face to face, not recognizing any of them at first, half-expecting to see his mother's loving smile, to see her reach down for him and cradle him to her bosom. But that was impossible, he knew. She was dead, and that thought allowed reality to bludgeon him back to his senses.

"They're here," he whispered, tears pouring down his cheeks. "They've come for me."

Gray dropped to his knees in front of him and wiped the dampness from his cheeks. He hesitated, as though debating whether or not to hold him to try to comfort him. Jake settled the inner dilemma for him, leaping to his feet and throwing his arms around the surprised man's neck.

"You're safe," Gray said. "No one's going to take you anywhere. I promise."

He looked back over his shoulder to Adam, who was still rubbing his chin from where Evelyn's forehead had slammed into it when the screaming had roused her. With a nod of understanding, Adam headed back across the cavern toward the stone stairs and ascended with Norman right at his heels and the others following behind.

"Wait!" Phoenix called, bounding up the stairs to catch up with Adam before he could head into the tunnel.

Adam turned and waited, his pulse thundering in his temples.

"Are you ready?" Phoenix asked. "This is where it all starts."

"You've seen this in a vision?"

"Parts."

Adam waited for him to elaborate, but when Phoenix offered nothing more, he had to ask. "Anything you'd like to share?"

Phoenix looked nervously at Norman, and then back to Adam. "No."

"Thanks, kid," Adam said, turning to head into the dark tunnel. "You've been a big help."

"There are things I can't tell you or they won't come to pass. Your decisions—all of our decisions—can't be influenced if we are to stand a chance. Our greatness will be defined by moments, foresight can only lead to hesitation and we may miss those moments."

Adam continued walking, trying to comprehend Phoenix's words. They made sense, obviously, but he didn't like the idea of walking blindly to his fate if there was information that could prove invaluable. He didn't know what precisely was awaiting him out there in the storm, only that something definitely was.

Bracing for the cold, he passed through the cave and trudged into the snow. He had barely reached the middle of the beach when there was a flash of light on the horizon. As he watched, it grew in size, billowing a pillar of black smoke before the wind chased it away.

"Oh, God," he whispered, a lump rising in his throat. His first thought was of the sheer terror in Jill's eyes as she had described her vision.

A figure appeared from the snow, the shadow of a man walking toward them through the blizzard. What looked like a long pole pointed diagonally from the right shoulder of the silhouette, but Adam quickly recognized it as the barrel of a rifle.

The spectre stopped at the edge of the lake, inspecting the dike they had built to fend off attack. He climbed over it and slid down the back side, stopping a dozen paces from Adam, behind whom all of the others gathered.

Adam looked to his right to find Norman standing at his side, biting his lip nervously.

"We've come for the child!" the man shouted, his voice echoing from the face of the cliff.

"You can't have him!" Gray yelled from behind Adam, who tried to calm him by holding up his hand.

"Who are you?" Adam asked, trying to keep his tone as level and non-threatening as possible. His eyes flicked from the man to the fire on the island and then back again. He shuddered at the thought of Jill's words.

Cooking flesh.

"My name is Bruce." The man took several strong strides forward until Adam could have reached out and touched him. "I'm here to give you just one chance to hand over the boy."

Adam could barely keep his feet planted in the snow against the urge to retreat from the man's advance.

"You aren't coming anywhere near—!"

"Gray!" Adam shouted, silencing him before he could finish his epithet. He kept his eyes focused on the other man's, the fur framing the hood around Bruce's head making him look like a wild beast. "The child's safe with us. You can rest assured that no harm will befall him."

Bruce laughed, a deep guttural sound prematurely silenced by his bared teeth.

"I don't believe you understand me correctly," Bruce said, his eyes wide and unblinking. "This isn't a visit from child welfare. We're taking the boy with us. Period."

"And if we refuse?"

"Personally, I'm hoping you do." He grabbed the rifle strap across his chest. "I'd like nothing more than to find out how fast I can reload this thing."

"Is that a threat?" Norman said.

"I thought it was clearly stated."

"If you had wanted to use that rifle, you could have easily already done so," Adam said. "What is it you really want?"

"I've been instructed to offer you one chance to send the boy with me. If you decide not to, you'll be given the opportunity to negotiate the terms of your surrender, and I promise you that one of them will be that you turn the boy over to us. Either way, we're taking that kid where you won't ever be able to hurt him."

"Hurt him?" Adam said. "What would lead you to believe that?"

"Shut up!" Bruce bellowed, startling Adam so much that he flinched. Richard had been right about fear. They were terrified of him, even standing alone against all of them. "Am I to assume that you're declining to send him with me willingly?"

Adam looked back over his shoulder to the others before replying.

"Yeah," he said, matching stares with Bruce. "He isn't going anywhere."

"Good," Bruce said with a smirk. "I was hoping we could do this the hard way."

Adam looked past Bruce at the fire on the island, sparkling against the storm.

"So what happens now?"

"You come with me," Bruce said, slipping out of the sling and holding the rifle across his chest. "By choice or by force. Your call. I'm sure you know which one I'm rooting for."

"No need for the gun," Adam said. "Where are we going?"

"To the island. Richard's waiting."

"We can take him," Norman whispered into Adam's ear.

"Try it," Bruce said, chambering the first bullet and clicking off the safety.

"Lower the weapon and I'll come with you now."

"You're in no position to make demands."

"Then he isn't going alone," Gray said, stepping forward while pushing against Jake's chest to make sure the boy wouldn't follow.

Bruce's eyes lit with recognition. Just the man he was looking for.

"I wouldn't have it any other way."

"Me, too," Lindsay said. She'd traveled with Richard and had seen the way he looked at her. The implications of what she was thinking scared her to death, but in a pinch, she might be able to use that to her advantage.

"I should go," Norman said.

"Why don't we all go?" Bruce said. "Make a day of it. Pack a picnic lunch." His face burned red with anger. "I'm taking you and you." He pointed at Adam and Lindsay, and then to Gray. "And you'd better believe you're coming too."

"No!" Jake screamed, fighting out from behind Evelyn, who had stepped in front of him in Gray's absence. "You can't go!"

Gray turned at the sound of his voice and was nearly bowled over by Jake, who wrapped his arms around his legs.

"Please don't go," Jake sobbed. "Promise. Promise you won't go."

"It's all right," Gray said, peeling the boy off. "I promised you that you'd be safe."

"But you won't come back…"

"I'll be back before you know it." Gray's eyes filled with tears.

"No, please! They're going to kill you! Please, Gray… Please…"

Evelyn and Jill each took the boy by a shoulder, drawing him close enough to hold him back.

"Let's get this over with," Gray said, walking toward Bruce, whose expression was no longer one of rage, but bewilderment.

Bruce looked at Jake, wailing as the two women knelt in the snow and held him. There was something wrong with the way this was playing out. He'd heard of Stockholm Syndrome and victims sympathizing with their captors to the pointing of aiding them, but this was just a little boy. Kids could see through all of the idealistic garbage and weren't swayed by politics. They were by nature self-serving and ruled by their emotions. After watching his mother die before being kidnapped, he should have been screaming for Bruce to save him. He'd expected to find the boy locked up or under some sort of guard, not out in the open where he could easily run away. The bottom line was that he had come to liberate the child, but Jake wanted to stay by choice. The entire situation reeked. He had no allegiance to Richard, and certainly not to any of these others. He had come to save the boy, and that was exactly what he was going to do.

He took a step toward the sobbing boy, but the women turned him away and a couple of teenaged boys stepped between them. These were unarmed kids, putting themselves in harm's way for a boy they couldn't possibly even know. Until he knew what was really going on here, he would have to be extremely cautious.

"Start walking," he said, gesturing toward the mound of sand and snow with the barrel of the rifle.

Adam moved first, fighting with his legs to keep them from trembling. He cast a glance back to see Evelyn watching him, mortified. Phoenix was behind her, paler than he had ever been before.

"Turn around," Bruce said, following behind the three of them as they crossed over the hill they had built and stepped out onto the ice, heading toward the island with its crown of flames that would soon enough know the taste of human flesh.

VIII

THE RUINS OF
DENVER,
COLORADO

Death descended the piles of rubble and debris into the subterranean levels, skirting the bones of the saved that had been gnawed clean by the damned. The air was rife with putrescence and rot, but he was immune to it by now. He could see through the eyes of War that the final battle would soon be at hand, but there was a growing sense of unease chewing at his insides like worms in a corpse. The Lord was showing favor for his mortal children that He hadn't in the past. It was almost as though He Himself had set against the legion He had spawned to wipe the slate clean. It was the dichotomous nature of the Maker, Death knew, but his biological drive had become an imperative. He had been placed upon the earth with a single goal, a mission that was outside of his power to resist. The human portion of him was dead, its remains boiling in a burbling cauldron of hate that rose from his stomach and burned in his throat.

He found himself in a position he could never have foreseen. He was pit against the God who had birthed him, in a battle where the Almighty had a stake in both sides. Had he been aligned against them not as their executioner, but merely to test them to discover their worthiness? The idea was unthinkable, and yet that was precisely what he was doing. Were they toy soldiers set in opposition for some kind of cosmic amusement? Even so, he knew nothing but destruction. He reveled in the exquisite pain of the dying and the sloppy flesh of the dead. It may have been the Lord's will that had cast him into this pathetic sack of skin, but it was *his* will that would bring about the end of mankind. God had loosed him upon them and turned away, only this time, He had peeked. And now, whatever side his Master secretly hoped would triumph, he would fulfill his destiny and decimate what little remained of humanity.

Whether God wanted it or not.

Reaching the lowest level, so far beneath the ground that he could hear the heart of the Earth beating, he weaved through a maze of toppled cabinets and crushed tables, through a minefield of feces left by the Swarm that had infested the darkness before being sent to battle, and to a short hallway that would lead him to his quarry. He had seen through the eyes of Pestilence and Famine, but this…this he wanted to see with his own eyes.

The sounds of heavy, raspy breathing reached him before he even saw the entrance to the room. His brother and sister of the apocalypse had been sequestered down there for days, working by the dwindling torchlight to create the most ferocious creatures to ever set foot on the planet. In his fervor to please the Lord and ensure that even should man survive the Swarm, they would fall to the second wave of His wrath, had he actually defied Him? It was a simultaneously frightening and liberating idea. God had seen fit to give them the power to birth the Swarm, but at that very moment they were taking the next step. Had this been His will, would they not have created these beings from the start? And if their experiments were contrary to His grand design, and He hadn't punished them or struck them down, was it possible that their power was independent of His? Had He turned them loose on the planet without a leash? Could they exert their influence regardless of His wishes?

Were they free?

The buzzing of mosquitoes welcomed Death into the chamber, taking flight from the walls and bodies to fill the air around him. Pestilence opened her mouth and drew them all back into her diminutive form, her parchment skin cracking against the strain of the bodies writhing inside of her. She stood over a long table with what had once been a man staked to it, the body brown and slick with the spew of locusts. Famine hovered behind her, his blind white eyes scouring the entire room at once, his insect minions scurrying under his pale skin like raindrops down glass.

They exchanged glances in silence, their thoughts on the same frequency. This was the one. The culmination of all of the vile experiments to which they had subjected their prey. All of the tearing skin and tortured cries came down to this specimen, its eyes wide open despite the physical agony it surely endured, pinned down like a butterfly by jagged stakes formed by sections of copper piping ripped out of the walls.

It roared and strained against its moorings, leathery skin like a bat's wings tightening over bulging muscles. Long, coarse black hair grew in tufts from its shoulders, a long mane of it running down the thing's back from its forehead all the way to its rear. Opening a mouth that split its face nearly from ear to ear, it displayed hideously sharp teeth in rows that pointed back into its mouth like a great white's. Its eyes were useless black coals, barely able to see their vague outlines against the firelight, though it could easily triangulate their locations in its mind, sensing them by sonar. Though unlike its winged brethren, it issued not an inaudible shriek, but a guttural roar that shivered dust from the ceiling above, their every contour coming into perfect focus.

Death nodded his approval, walking along the side of the table until he reached the monster's fingertips, curled around the end of the stake, trying to jerk it free. He pulled one of the fingers away and straightened it so that the hooked talon at the end pointed straight up. Opening his palm, Death pressed down on the nail, barely feeling the pain until after the tip of the nail poked out through the back of his hand, passing through his tough scales without the slightest resistance. Excellent. They would be able to see through even the densest smoke and make short work of their prey. They were a life form like nothing that this planet had ever seen: able to hunt under the worst conditions and on the darkest of nights. Though they had yet to truly test the creature's strength, the musculature was superhuman. All that remained to be seen was how fast it could run and if it could indeed reproduce.

Death looked at Pestilence, who answered his unvoiced question with a deliberate nod.

Perfect. These beasts would dominate whatever survived the coming battle between the humans and the Swarm, and usurp the top position on the food chain. And best of all, they would pay their allegiance to Death, who was beginning to think that he just might want to stick around for a while.

Damn God and damn the consequences.

CHAPTER 6

I

MORMON TEARS

Adam trudged straight ahead, the storm swirling snowflakes all around him, shifting from side to side in an effort to knock him from his feet. Lindsay walked to his left; Gray to his right. Bruce followed behind with the rifle pointed directly at his lower back where a single bullet could sever his spinal cord and paralyze him. The thought of bolting wasn't even an option, though. The others were counting on him to do whatever he could to not only guarantee the boy's safety, but all of theirs as well. He didn't know Richard well at all, but he'd seen in the man's eyes a determination that promised he would do absolutely anything to get what he wanted.

It felt as though they'd been walking forever, surrounded by nothing but snow, when the island of rock came into focus, wavering in and out of the sheeting flakes, black plumes flagging from atop it like an industrial smokestack. The stone face towered over them, even larger than it had appeared from the distance. He looked all the way up to the top and caught the familiar glint he knew all too well. The scope of a rifle.

"To the right," Bruce called to be heard over the whistle of the wind along the rock wall, waiting patiently for them to veer along the smooth stone before resuming his guard behind. He couldn't chase the image of that little kid's eyes from his mind. The boy had been scared of him. Not the others who gathered around him. Not those who had abducted him from the hotel and killed two people in their rush to escape. It had been he who frightened the boy. And that sat like a hatching egg sac of spiders in his belly.

They skirted the island with the wind at their backs, rounding the side to find the wind waiting to batter them directly in the face. Leaning into it, they stumbled through the drifting accumulation until they reached the spot where a group of snowmobiles was parked in a small cove created by large round stones.

Adam looked back at Bruce, who pointed to a path of sorts that led diagonally up the island on the right, winding around smooth formations and through channels of stone. With Lindsay on his heels and Gray trailing with the barrel pointed between his shoulder blades, he scrabbled up the icy slope, following the path through the piled snow until he reached the top.

Richard stood in front of him, sighting down his forehead through the high-powered scope.

"I take it you didn't want to do this the easy way," he said, grinning, with his cheek against the stock. "Just as well."

He lowered the rife and invited them toward the fire with a gesture of his arm.

They followed, sliding down a rocky slope to alight beside a large cluster of shrubs that had been set ablaze. There were five other men standing on the far side, training their weapons on them through the fire.

Seven men, Adam thought. All armed. They outnumbered these men nearly two to one, but each of those weapons held at least three shells and wouldn't miss inside of fifteen feet. Conflict would only result in their swift extinction.

"Please," Richard said, sitting on a rock at what appeared to be the head of the fiery negotiation table. "Have a seat."

Adam decided it would be best to humor him. Richard was firmly in control of the situation and the last thing they wanted to do was incur his ire. He dropped to his haunches and then plopped to his rear end on the rock. Lindsay and Gray followed his lead, Gray's eyes never leaving Richard for a second.

The wind screamed past overhead, stealing the black smoke from the fire and absconding with it on gusts of white flakes, urging the flames higher and higher. At least they were out of the snow and in the radiating warmth of the bonfire, though it was nowhere near enough to steal away the chill.

"Let's dispense with the song and dance," Richard said, resting the rifle across his lap and leaning forward, his stare seeking out Adam. "You have something I want and I'm not leaving without it."

"You're not getting anywhere near that boy!" Gray shouted, preparing to lunge forward, but Adam held out his hand to try to keep the other man from getting himself killed. "I saw what you did to his mother."

"I tried to protect her from you…but sadly, I failed."

One of the men from the other side of the fire rose and rounded the snapping flames to stand beside Gray.

"From me?" Gray gasped. "I wasn't the one who shot her point blank in the face."

Richard nodded to the man, who casually stepped behind Gray and lowered the barrel of the shotgun to the back of his head.

Before Adam could even cry out, there was a thunderous boom. The fire hissed under the assault of Gray's blood and brain matter. Gray's body slumped forward, fluids pouring from the fractured remains of his face. The man placed a boot on Gray's back just above his rear end and shoved his corpse forward into the fire.

Lindsay screamed.

It had all happened so fast…so fast… Adam hadn't even seen it coming. He looked away from Gray's body as his clothing started to burn and at Richard, unable to hide the fear and sheer hatred.

"There's no room in these negotiations for a kidnapper and a murderer," Richard said.

Adam heard the man shuck the shell from the shotgun and felt its awful one-eyed stare on the side of his head.

"He didn't kidnap the boy," Adam said through bared teeth. "He told us all about what you did to Jake's mother. What you did to Peckham."

"He lied," Richard said, the flames reflecting in his eyes. "I can't believe you would take the word of a scoundrel like him."

"I didn't. I took Jake's word."

Bruce flinched behind him as if he'd been slapped. This was spiraling out of control. First, they'd shot the man in cold blood and now, listening to Adam talk, he couldn't help believing him. With two guns pointed at him and the smell of his friend's roasting meat on the wind, instead of giving Richard what he wanted, he was defiant. Nothing made sense. There were too many stories. Too many lies. And now the stench of cordite and death.

Richard laughed. "That boy would say anything to keep the man who had killed his mother from doing the same thing to him. Christ. He's just a kid."

"That's right," Adam said. "He's just a kid. A kid who isn't going anywhere with you."

"Wrong decision," Richard said, pointing the rifle at Lindsay. She screamed and covered her face with her hands.

"Drop the rifle!" Bruce shouted, pointing his at Richard. From the corner of his eye, he saw the man who had just executed Gray turn his shotgun on him. "And tell this jerk over here to throw his weapon down or I'll put a hole through your head big enough to crawl through."

"You're making a big, big mistake, Bruce," Richard said, resting his rifle on his lap and dismissing the other man with a nod. The man set the shotgun on the ground and walked to the other side of the fire behind the men lining Bruce up with their weapons low enough that he couldn't see them though the fire.

"No mistake. No one's moving an inch until I know exactly what's going on here. Someone's going to start telling the truth right now or I'm going to—"

"What?" Richard said. His calmness was unnerving. "Shoot us all? That wouldn't do you much good now, would it?"

Bruce looked at the scabbed slashes crossing Richard's cheeks. They were the kind of ruts that could easily have been inflicted by a woman's fingernails.

"How did you hurt your face?" he asked, carefully scrutinizing Richard's reaction.

"I cut myself shaving," he said with a laugh. "What do you think? I gashed my face open leaning through the broken window in the room where that murderer shot Peckham. There were still jagged shards in the frame, but I wasn't concerned for my own safety. I had just watched that man," he nodded to the fire, "shoot him in the chest. Someone needed to call down to the others for help."

"You're lying."

"That's a serious allegation, Bruce. You'd better be able to back it up."

"I saw all of the proof I needed in that little kid's eyes. They weren't holding him captive. He was there because he was terrif—"

Boom!

A bullet sang past Adam's ear, a funnel of flame trailing it out of the fire. *Thuck!*

Adam turned to see Bruce lifted from his feet with a crimson amoeba around a hole in his chest. Sloppy down stuffing blossomed from the hole in the jacket. The rifle fell from Bruce's hands as he slammed to the ground, his head hammering the rock so hard that a spout of blood fired past his lips. His eyelids blinked spastically, his fingers dabbing at the blood pouring from the wound guarded by shards of his fragmented ribs.

"J-Jesus," he spat, crimson pouring from his mouth.

Richard walked right up beside Bruce, pressed the barrel to his forehead, and tugged the trigger.

Boom!

The bullet caved in Bruce's frontal bone as it passed through with such velocity that it hit the rock behind and ricocheted out the side of Bruce's head, taking gobs of his brain along with it. There was a spark as it careened off another stone surface before flying out over the lake.

Richard growled as he balled his fists into Bruce's jacket and yanked him away from the rock. Blood trailed from a spattered star shape down the rock, the flow sluggish from the mess of tissue running away from it like a gutter full of slush. Heaving the body from the ground, Richard cast it into the fire on top of Gray's.

"Anyone else want to challenge me?" Richard shouted. His eyes were wild, the seams along his cheeks opening to issue fresh blood from the exertion.

"We aren't all your enemies," Lindsay said, reaching with a trembling hand to touch Richard's. "Some of us find power so attractive—"

Richard stole his hand away and slapped her across the face so hard that she toppled into Adam, already beginning a sob as her cheek swelled to an angry red.

"I'm not stupid," he growled, walking back to sit on his rock throne by the fire. "You have two hours to bring the boy to me."

"Or what?" Adam asked, cradling Lindsay's head to his shoulder and helping her to her feet.

"Or we're going to kill you all!" Richard shouted, his voice echoing off into the storm.

II

SALT LAKE CITY

War stood atop the roof of the Mormon Temple, staring out across Temple Square toward the distant horizon. He could see the structure where his prey hid, and he was sure that if they looked really hard, they just might see a lone masked man wearing a cloak of flesh, waiting for the sun to fall just a little farther toward the western edge of the world. Thick black storm clouds waited to descend, preparing to smother it. Then it would be just dark enough to set loose the Swarm to fulfill its wicked destiny. They were mayflies thrust upon the earth not in a frenzy of breeding activity, but in a massive fit of bloodlust and carnage.

He turned away from the skyline and walked back toward the entrance to the stairwell. There was something about this building that he absolutely loved. The architecture was almost gothic in contrast to the rites of worship performed within. Three parapets stood to either side, the middle one taller like a finger extended to the heavens, each corner capped with a thin cone. It was ornate in its simplicity, a bland gray structure of mortar and stone that dominated the landscape with power and grace. The windows on the third story beneath him were round, while those on the preceding two floors were gabled. In an obscene way, it reminded him of the Tower of London, where once upon a time they had housed the most vile prisoners and staked the heads of the enemies on pikes as a warning. It was somehow fitting that this should be the staging grounds from which they would launch the final strike. A shrine of the Lord's love and his wrath, an apropos reflection of the inherent dichotomy of the Father that had brought them all to this point, the culmination of His grand experiment called mankind.

An experiment that had failed miserably.

Descending the grandiose staircase of the Mormon castle, he stepped out onto the third floor. The rooms lining the hallway were brimming with his legions, clinging to the high ceilings and walls, packed shoulder to shoulder where they stood in their own filth and excrement. Eyes closed, they waited eagerly in the solitude of the darkness in their feeble minds, salivating at the thought of what the coming night would bring.

War passed doorway after doorway, the wan light shimmering from the black scales within like the rooms were filled with oil, until he reached another stairwell. Bodies were latched to the walls by sharp nails and clung to the rails to dangle above space, leaving him just enough of a path to continue downward until he reached the main level. He entered the elaborate temple proper, a massive, vaulted room of congregation with throngs of pews that could have seated his army, were they not hanging from the ceilings and walls, biding their time until the darkness outside summoned them back to consciousness.

A lone creature dangled from the wall behind the altar, arms and legs wrapped around a great golden cross, its head nuzzled into the crook where the crossbar met the post. There wasn't another one on that entire wall, as though avoiding even touching it, instead covering the ceiling and walls like living black paint. Only this single minion adorned the wall, clinging to the cross as though for dear life.

When he approached, he could clearly see the crimson dewlap sucked back under its chin as he had expected. It was the same one that was always at his heels, the one that showed a startling amount of higher functioning compared to the others. It was an enigma; the person whose form it had shed to join their ranks obviously pious, yet at the same time damned.

He ascended the stairs to the stage and walked behind the altar, reaching up to grab that creature and yanking it down. Instead of releasing the cross, it held tight, causing War to tear the entire works out of the wall and send them crashing to the ground. The creature's eyelids parted slightly, crescents of golden light causing the cross to glow.

"Child… mine," it said in a voice that was almost human, the final syllable degenerating into a hiss.

War's eyes narrowed behind the ragged slashes in his mask. Had he lips, he would have smiled. Obsession. It was the fine line a man walked between God's favor and the pleasures of the flesh. This man had tried to cling to both, refusing to relinquish either in his final heartbeat, his obsession strong enough to carry over even through his damnation.

Shadows descended across the windows, slowly at first, but faster with each passing minute. Yellow eyes opened all around him, chasing back the darkness with their vile yellow stare. They shined down on him from the ceiling and the walls, focusing on him to the point that he glowed like a birthing star. He raised both arms over his head, and his cloak of diseased skin fell to the ground, revealing his intricately sculpted, blood-red armor. Hissing rained down upon him over the clamor of nails carving into wood, of fists and feet pounding on every available surface. The entire temple shook to the point that the altar toppled sideways and clattered to the stage. With a *bang* like gunfire, the front door exploded inward to reveal Thunder on its hind legs, now kicking at the empty air.

Its skeletal hooves slammed to the floor, bringing down sections of the outer roof to pound the ceiling. The steed walked down the main aisle toward War, leaving flaming hoof prints in its wake. Fire lapped at the pews until it took root in the fine polish, racing away from the central walkways, the blue flame rising higher and higher until smoke built up against the ceiling, forcing the bodies hanging up there to rain to the floor as one. The earth trembled and the pews fell backward, the Swarm standing in the midst of the flames, oblivious to the pain.

When Thunder reached the stage, it turned to face the burning masses, eyes ablaze. War lowered his arms to his sides and waited for the incessant hissing to cease.

When finally the only sound was the crackle of God's House burning, he leapt onto Thunder's back and took hold of the spiked mane. It rose to its full height, slashing burning front limbs at the air and then slammed its hooves to the ground. The towers atop the roof crumbled, falling down upon the upper levels, which gave way without a fight. Tons of stone and cement crashed down upon the inner sanctum as bodies leapt through windows and poured out of doors, swarming Temple Square like so many rats abandoning a sinking ship. They crowded around that crimson figure on his skeletal steed, pressed closely together while the temple groaned with the last of the collapsing stones, filling the sky with dust.

War raised his right fist and was rewarded with hissing screams. When his fist fell, the hissing grew impossibly louder as his minions swarmed, crashing through the square like an unstoppable tsunami.

III

MORMON TEARS

Lindsay clung to Adam's hand as they stumbled back across the lake toward Mormon Tears. She had been sobbing hysterically for most of the journey and had only now brought herself under control, sniffing back the tears and snot. The rocky crag came into view through the blizzard as they tried to follow the path they had forged through the accumulation on their way over, though it was nearly obscured by the wind blowing the snow back up into the air from the ground.

Adam still didn't know what he was going to tell them. Either they sent the boy back across to the island or they would all be slaughtered. It was as simple as that. They had prepared for an all-out assault by an unarmed force of thousands, but weren't anywhere close to being ready for a small battalion of armed men. What were they supposed to do? Raise their spears and try to lure them close enough to fight? By the time those men were within range of their sharpened poles, they'd be plucking birdshot out of vital organs. He knew that they would expect him to have a plan, but the best he could come up with was to give Richard what he wanted. After all, Richard wouldn't have gone to so much trouble if he intended to harm the child. He needed Jake for his dreams, but the rest of them were expendable. He had no doubt that Richard would lead the others against them and it would be a massacre.

When he and Lindsay were within sight of the beach, the others walked down from the cave, where they'd been waiting out of the elements. There would be no mistaking that something had gone wrong as they would only see the two of them heading inland. He only hoped they wouldn't begin to panic until Adam was able to speak to them, but his legs were so tired that he simply couldn't make them trudge through the deep snow any faster. By the time they reached the barricade at the shore, Adam could hear Jake crying.

"We could smell…" Norman started, helping Lindsay over the mound of sand. He lowered his voice and leaned into Adam's ear after he skidded down the mound. "We could smell someone burning." He paused and looked back at Jake. "Gray?"

Adam nodded. He couldn't bear to hear the words aloud.

"We heard two shots," Evelyn said, running to him and throwing her arms around his neck. "I was so worried that—"

"Shh," he whispered, giving her a gentle kiss to silence her. When he withdrew she could see the fear in his eyes.

"What is it?" she asked, but Adam was already pulling out of her grasp and preparing to address them all.

"Everyone gather in the cave," he yelled to be heard, already pushing through them toward the steep stone face and the dark mouth beneath. The others had built a fire out of the wind from a pyramid of coal, the smoke staining the wall black. He stood with his back to the corridor leading into the mountain so that he could see all of them and the island at the same time.

"Where's Gray?" Mare asked, restarting the child's whimpering in earnest as it had nearly tapered.

"He didn't make it," Adam said, looking at Jake.

"I told him not to go," Jake whimpered. "I knew…I knew what was going to happen…"

"How?" Missy asked.

"They shot him in the back of the head. He didn't feel anything."

"How many are there?" Norman asked, his jaw muscles visibly clenching.

"Six," Adam said. "All armed."

"Jesus," Norman gasped, turning to stare out across the lake.

"Can I ask a stupid question?" Mare said. "And I don't want you to take this the wrong way, but why didn't they kill you guys too?"

"They sent them back to deliver a message to all of us," Phoenix said.

Jake stepped forward, steeling his chin even as the tears streamed down his cheeks.

"I'll go."

Adam had never seen such a beautiful display of courage, even from men three times the boy's age. Moments ago, he had given in to the thought that handing over Jake was a foregone conclusion, but now, looking into that brave child's eyes, he knew that he couldn't allow it.

"No," he said firmly, the sound of his own voice startling him. "We'll find another solution."

"What did they say?" Darren asked.

"They said we have two hours to send Jake across or they're coming to get him."

No one needed to ask what that meant. They all knew.

"What are we going to do then?" Norman asked.

There was a long moment of silence.

"I wish I knew," Adam finally said. He could feel the weight of their stares boring holes into him.

"Let me go," Jake said, wiping away his tears with a hand from under the blanket. "They won't hurt me if I give them what they want."

"Gray didn't die so that we would deliver him to them," Lindsay whispered. "They killed him because he…because he would sooner die than let them have Jake."

"We can't beat them," Norman said. "We don't stand a chance against any amount of firepower."

Phoenix took Norman by the arm and whispered something into his ear.

"We can barricade ourselves in the cavern," April said. "That's what we were planning to do anyway, right?"

"I don't know if anything we could use to keep them out would withstand gunfire for long," Adam said, watching curiously as Phoenix led Norman out into the storm.

"We can run," Darren said.

"They have snowmobiles," Lindsay said. "We wouldn't get far."

"And the Swarm is still coming," Jill said. "Don't forget that."

"What do your visions tell you?" Ray asked from where he'd been leaning quietly against the wall. "You were the one who warned us about cooking flesh and I don't know if you've noticed, but I'd imagine that's exactly what that mouthwatering aroma is."

"Back off, Ray," Mare said, stepping in front of Jill. "I don't see you coming up with any ideas."

"I'm not the one who's psychic."

"Boys!" Evelyn snapped. "We're wasting too much time arguing. Unless you have something productive to say, just keep your mouths shut."

Both boys shrunk away. Mare took Jill by the hand, while Ray leaned back against the wall, wincing as something sharp prodded his stomach. He dropped his hand and felt the hard shaft of the knife's hilt.

"I'm the shortest," he whispered, wrinkling his brow. Finally, Tina's cryptic words made sense. He took a stumbling step forward and announced his revelation. "I'm the shortest."

They all looked at him as though he'd lost his mind. He walked over to Jake and stood beside him.

"Don't you see?" Ray said, whirling so they could all clearly see him and pulled Jake in front of him, looking across the top of the boy's head. "I'm the shortest."

IV

MORMON TEARS

All Norman could think of was his image on the cavern wall while Phoenix spoke, only hearing half of the words the younger boy was saying. Phoenix had climbed up into the back of the dead Ford pickup, digging through several feet of snow until he found a locked toolbox running the width of the bed beneath the rear window of the cab. He unfastened it and rummaged through wrenches, hammers, and a million other tools until he'd found the object of his search, which he now held up so Norman could clearly see. It was an old rusted hatchet. It had been at the bottom of the bin with spilled nails long since rusted to the metal floor, the wooden handle so ancient it looked frayed like an old rope. The sharp end was crusted from the last time it had been used however long ago, the thinner trailing edge so thick with curling layers of rust it looked like a good whack would cause it to disintegrate.

"What am I supposed to do with that?" Norman asked.

"You haven't heard a thing I've said, have you?" Phoenix said. He tossed the ax down into the snow and hopped over the side of the bed, landing in a drift nearly to his waist.

"It's just that…thing. I mean, there's a picture in the cavern of me holding that thing drawn hundred of years ago and you just whip it out of there like it's nothing. Like you knew it was in there all the time and were just waiting for the right moment to give it to me."

"That's right," Phoenix said. "Is that so hard to understand?"

Norman let out a nervous chuckle. "When I got out of the army I was going to get formal paramedic training and drive an ambulance. Maybe meet a nice girl and have a couple kids. And a dog, a golden retriever. Make enough in the market so I could retire early and work on my golf game." He shook his head. "How many countless hours did I waste pondering all of that?"

"It's a wonderful dream," Phoenix said through a weak smile.

"You don't get it, do you? It's all so matter-of-fact for you that you can't see what you're asking me to do. You're just following some cosmic directions and checking us all off on some sort of list. Were the last twenty-four years just a waste of time? I could have skipped out on high school and just partied all the time. Instead of joining the Army I would have been living it up in Vegas or something. No drill sergeants. No fighting. No wars. I could have just played golf all day without a care in the world, and now you're telling me that my entire life boils down to my ability to swing a hatchet."

"There's so much more to it than that," Phoenix said, taking Norman's hand in an entirely unselfconscious gesture. "You have been chosen to save all of us. Not just the twelve of us here, but our entire race. I can't imagine golf can compare to that. Besides, what's the difference between swinging a club or an ax?"

"Was that…was that a joke?" Norman asked, unable to hide his smirk. "I don't believe I've ever heard you make a joke before."

Phoenix blushed and handed Norman the hatchet. Norman could only stare at it, feeling its awesome weight in his grasp.

"So, I'm supposed to…?"

Phoenix nodded.

"For how long? How far?"

"You'll know when you're through," Phoenix said. The levity in his voice disappeared.

Norman took a practice swing, slicing through the air. His shoulders already protested, weary from shoveling so much sand to form the barricade by the shore.

"You're the boss," he said, leaning it against his shoulder like a lumberjack. He started walking toward the sand wall.

"You're a good man," Phoenix called after him.

"Remind me again when I get back and I'm looking for someone to take my frustrations out on."

Phoenix smiled, but there was a sadness in his eyes that terrified Norman. He nodded and turned back to the task at hand, scaling the mound and sliding down the opposite side, careful not to dislodge any of the spear tips. As the storm closed in around him, the intensifying flakes making it so he could hardly keep his eyes open, he stepped out onto the ice and stole a glance back over his shoulder at the face of stone and the dark mouth of the cave. Could this be the last time he would ever see it? He shivered at the thought, his legs momentarily betraying him before finding the courage to trudge forward into the unmarred white snow.

"No turning back now," he whispered. He whistled a nameless tune as he walked.

As soon as he reached the point where he couldn't see land behind him, he dropped to his knees. With the beach to his left and the island to his right, he raised the hatchet and slammed it down into the ice, parting the accumulation cleanly and sending ice chips in all directions. He scooted backwards and swung the axe again. Repeating the process over and over again, he finally had to shed his jacket and tie it around his waist. He was so hot and the layers of clothing against his skin were dripping with sweat.

He laughed as the frigid wind knifed through him. It was a delightful sensation, but that would pass soon enough. Besides, the jacket wouldn't do him a whit of good if he fell through the ice.

Swiping the sweat from his brow, he scanned the line he'd left through the snow nearly as far as he could see. The wind had already blown snow back over it in spots, but that was what they wanted anyway, wasn't it?

He switched the ax into his left hand and began the process anew, chopping and chopping and chopping...

V

SALT LAKE CITY

The cheers were deafening. Garrett fed upon them as he stood atop one of the tables in the restaurant, beaming like a child on Christmas morning. He could see why Richard loved this so much. The roar of approval. The clamor of applause. All for him. He felt like he'd somehow plugged himself into a wall socket, his entire body alive with electrical current, tingling from his groin all the way out through his fingers and toes where it crackled and snapped like fireworks.

The words had come with unprecedented ease as he had congratulated the masses on their diligence and hard work, their devotion to one another and the survival of their species, and their courage in the face of tribulation. Most importantly though, he used his speech to rally them for the coming siege, to bring grown men's blood to boiling, and women and children to want to take up arms in defense of the new dream they had all built together and shared, not just as a hodgepodge gathering of refugees, but as a family. Come nightfall all of them, from the burliest of men to the daintiest of women, would be prepared around the clock to fend off an assault that could very well mean their deaths. And he had done it all on his own. He had achieved the grandest of all destinies. He had created a legacy of his own design, and now, like Martin Luther King, Jr., John F. Kennedy, and his personal idol, the great Vince Lombardi, he needed to finish with a tag line that would survive the ages.

He could smell the lasagna from the

kitchen and knew he would lose them soon. Now was the time.

"Today, my fellow survivors…today we take our first steps into a brave new future. United as a people. United by God and by faith and by a bond that can never be broken. We will take our stand against an evil hell-bent on our eradication, against an army of abominations the likes of which has never graced this good earth before. And whether they descend upon us today or a week from today, we will face them together. And we will win. We have courage on our side. We have the strength of a people who know nothing of defeat. And most importantly, we have the right. With God on our side we will survive…and we will prosper. For today is the day our destinies intertwine as one. Today we will take our first strides toward a better future, toward a world where our subsequent generations will never know war. We will fight this one last battle. The war to end all wars. And we will begin anew in peace. Today is the day, ladies and gentlemen. We are the future. We *will* triumph!"

The applause grew so loud that Garrett couldn't have heard himself scream. They rose from their seats, one by one at first, and then in waves until they were all standing and cheering for him. There were whistles and hoots and even a chant of "We will triumph!"

He watched them all, looking from face to face. All of them looking back at him with expressions he was unaccustomed to seeing. Respect. Adoration. Awe. All were for him and him alone. It didn't matter now whether Richard ever came back. These were *his* people now. *He* had led them though the rigors of construction. *He* had united them. *He* had given them new life and new hope in the face of a formidable armada. And *he* would lead them to victory.

Garrett absorbed their affection like a sponge until he knew the time was right to let this feast of celebration commence. When the door from the kitchen swung open and the first of the apron-clad woman appeared carrying a steaming stainless steel tray, he climbed down and allowed the attention and the cheers to turn to her.

"Eat up!" he shouted over the din. "I want everyone ready to take post in ninety minutes! Sunset's in exactly…" He checked his watch. "Two hours and twenty-seven minutes."

He surveyed them for the moment, sharing in their moment of happiness. For a while there, he had thought such emotions out of their reach forever.

Turning, he headed out into the lobby and grabbed the mound of clothes he had shed onto one of the chairs, layering himself as he opened the door to the stairwell and ascended. It was a strange sensation climbing up the stairs under the artificial light, but one he would definitely be able to get used to in a hurry. They had electricity and warm food. Soon enough there would be hot showers and DVDs playing on the televisions. They were so close to resuming their normal lives and civilization that he could hardly contain his excitement. All they had to do now was survive the impending onslaught, if indeed it was really coming. After all, they were relying on the dreams of a child in that regard. And they were more than prepared to withstand an army in a Branch Davidian kind of way. He was certain that their compound was impregnable. No one was getting over that fence without being shredded by the barbed wire, and even then they would drop down into a trough of fire. And all the while they would be under fire from snipers on the roof. All of the windows and doors were boarded up, leaving the only entrance as the solitary door on the roof.

As soon as that man in the tower raised the alarm, their defenses would be ready and the slaughter would commence. Not their slaughter, but the merciless killing of anything brave or stupid enough to approach their perimeter. It was positively airtight. Their ordeal would soon be over, paving the way for life to begin again.

Reaching the top level, he zipped up his jacket, donned the hood, and shouldered through the door onto the roof. His men were still at their posts as he had hoped, though by now they looked antsy with the aroma of lasagna wafting up from below. The snowfall seemed to have increased even in the hour he had been inside, the flakes now so large and swirling so quickly around the rooftop that the others appeared to strobe. There one moment, gone the next only to reappear from the whiteness closer than before.

"Your replacements will come relieve you as soon as they're done eating," he called, but none of them heard him over the rising wind. "Hey!"

The closest man to his right turned to face him, acknowledging him with a nod. He walked over to Garrett and slung his rifle over his shoulder.

"Did you say something?" he asked, nearly yelling to be heard even from a couple feet away.

"I said as soon as your replacements are done eating, it's your turn."

"Awesome!" What Garrett had mistaken for a man from afar was a boy who couldn't have been more than sixteen years old. "I'm starving. And I tell you, that smell's just about to drive me out of my mind."

Garrett smiled and clapped him on the shoulder.

"Almost there," he said. "Then just eat until you pop, okay?"

Beaming, the boy raced off to pass along the news to the others.

Garrett turned and headed back for the stairs leading into the parapet, and what the men had affectionately nicknamed "The Crow's Nest." He would take over the watch personally to allow his people to finish off their meal. Lead by example, he'd always said. It just wouldn't be right for him to be sending his men up onto the roof while he was sitting down there stuffing his face. Besides, the earlier he took his shift, the more likely he was to get a little shuteye during the night. Both outcomes served him especially well. And if those creatures came during the night like the boy had predicted, his shift would be over barely half an hour after sundown. He ascended the thin staircase, stepping across the threshold and into the small round room. There were four arched windows, presumably granting access to the matching directions of the compass. In the center of the room was a placard showing a map of Salt Lake City and the surrounding area, each of the major points of interest marked by a bright red arrow. The majority of the map was crusted under a layer of ice and snow like the rest of the room. The overhanging slanted roof kept out the brunt of the storm, though the ferocious wind chased the flakes through one window and out the opposite side. A quarter-operated scenic viewer was positioned in each of the windows, but the man on watch was using a pair of binoculars and pacing from one window to the next with his rifle slung over his back.

"Why don't you go ahead and get a start on dinner?" Garrett said, his voice startling the man who fumbled to draw his rifle, but only ended up dropping it on the ground. "I'll take over a few minutes early."

"You sure?"

Garrett looked at the gun on the icy floor. "Yeah," he said. "I'll be fine."

"You're the boss," the man said, shoving the binoculars into Garrett's chest.

I am, aren't I? Garrett thought with a smile. In Richard's absence, they had accepted him as such without question. He loved Richard like a brother, but his tears would dry quickly enough if Richard never returned.

"There's still some coffee in the thermos," the man called back over his shoulder, the thud of his boots pounding down the stairs fading to nothingness.

Garrett walked toward the window facing the city proper, grabbing the rifle along the way. Slinging it over his shoulder, he stood before the gabled opening, the snow blowing sideways in front of him, and looked out upon the city. He'd never truly appreciated how intricate a mere collection of houses and streets could be. There were the ivory bubbles of the Olympic domes and buildings as far as he could see. At the center of it all was the great Mormon Church, an imposing monolith of gray stone with towers like a European castle. He brought the binoculars to his eyes and studied the amazing structure. The upper windows were circular while the lower windows were arched, snowflakes blowing against the face and through—

Hadn't there been glass in the windows before? He hadn't been paying very close attention, but he was sure....

Setting the binoculars on the sill in front of him, he hauled the rifle over his back and rested the butt against his shoulder. The church grew much closer through the scope, giving him a magnified view of one of the windows. Snowflakes that appeared to be the size of elephants obscured his view, but he could vaguely make out what looked to be jagged triangles of glass poking from the seals, smeared opaque with something white.

His heart leapt in his chest, beating so hard his vision throbbed.

He swung the rifle toward the ground at the base of the church, but his view was blocked by numerous buildings.

There was the scuffing sound of footsteps entering the room behind him, but he couldn't afford to steal his eye from the sight.

"Weren't the windows still intact in the church?" he called back over his shoulder. His circle of vision crossed over rooftops, flashing across the façade of a bank before reaching a distant park, the trees blanketed with snow like marshmallows.

The footsteps approached, but no one answered.

Garrett had already moved the sight on to the houses beyond before realizing what he had seen. At first, he thought there had been a statue in the middle of the square, a monument cast of iron or stone of a man on a horse, but it had moved right as his vision crossed over it. Or at least it looked like it had. When he redirected the scope onto area where it had been, there was now a trail of fire burning in the snow, and behind…behind it a wall of darkness swept across the park. Set into the blackness were golden twinkles, like so many fireflies. No not fireflies…

Eyes.

Thousands of yellow eyes. Looking directly at him as they raced across the park. Bodies took form, all black limbs and legs.

"Oh, God," he whispered, lowering the rifle to see the army through his own eyes. It encompassed what looked to be dozens of acres swarming with ebony bodies like so many ants.

And it was only a block and a half away.

He opened his mouth to raise the alarm, but someone wrapped an arm around his head, turning it sharply to the side. Something sharp pressed into the soft tissue on the exposed side of his trachea.

"My name is Oscar Dominguez," a voice rasped into his ear. With a grunt, the man drove the shard of glass from Richard's shattered mirror into Garrett's neck, releasing a gush of warmth from his carotid. "You should have killed me when you had the chance."

Garrett shrugged free of the smaller man's hold, dropping the rifle to grab for the triangular shard jutting from his neck. His heels snagged and he fell to his back, staring wildly up at his assailant while he pawed at the glass, unable to decide whether to try to remove it or hold the flesh together around it.

The man with the snake tattoo on his neck that he had erroneously assumed to be dead dropped to his knees on Garrett's chest, knocking the wind out of him.

"In prison, you learn to play dead," Oscar said, maneuvering his legs to pin Garrett's arms. "The big ones…they like it when you put up a fight. Not me. I like things short and sweet."

He grabbed the glass with both hands, the edges slicing his palms, gave it a firm twist and ripped it to the side. A spring of arterial blood splashed his face and there was a whistle from the opened windpipe before the dying gurgle of air was drawn through the rush of fluids.

Oscar spat in Garret's face and staggered toward the stairs, dizzy from the concussion and blood loss, breathing through his mouth, as there was no hope of moving air through the pulpy remains of his nose, fighting through the stabbing pain of what felt like a dozen broken ribs, but content that justice had been served.

He couldn't wait to tell the others about the monster he had saved them from.

VI

THE GREAT SALT LAKE

◉

"How much longer do they have?" the man to Richard's left asked.

"It doesn't matter," Richard said. "They'll bring the boy."

"What makes you so sure? I mean, if they went to all the trouble of spying on us and kidnapping the kid, why would they give him up without a fight? I mean unless…"

"Unless what?"

"Nothing," the man said, pressing his eye back to the scope of the rifle to make sure he saw them coming before they emerged from the snow. He'd seen what had happened to Bruce for questioning Richard about what had transpired at the hotel and didn't relish the idea of joining the other men's scorched bones in the blaze. Right now he just wanted to get this whole ordeal over with and get back inside where they surely had the electricity running by now. With or without the kid, if need be. He couldn't help but wonder whether or not Richard had falsified some of his story, but right now he just didn't care. He just wanted to go home.

"Are you sure?" Richard asked. He could sense the man's hesitation, but it was of no consequence now. He just needed that simpleton to keep an eye on the horizon. After that, he was expendable. Perhaps an accident would even befall him on the journey back to the east. Firearms did have a tendency of discharging accidentally from time to time.

Richard turned and hopped back down from the rocky ledge to stand by the fire. There was only one other man there now as the rest were gassing the snowmobiles in preparation for a fast getaway. The man had his chin to his chest and his hood pulled down to hide his face from the cold, but Richard knew that he was watching what had once been living breathing human beings turning to charcoal. Bruce had planted a seed of doubt in the minds of these men, he was sure, but it mattered for naught. They feared him now, and there was no better inspiration for allegiance than that.

"Some weather we're having," Richard said. When the other man raised his frightened eyes, Richard cackled, scaring the man even more. So what if they all knew now. He was their overlord, their god, and none of them would even dare to raise their voices to him.

He sat down on his rock and warmed his gloved hands over the flames, rubbing them together until he could smell the Gore-Tex burning. The coals crackled and spit out a black skull, launched out of the fire by the explosion of the heated core of a vertebral disk. It rolled toward his feet until it nuzzled his toes, coming to rest on the occipital bone. Black eyes full of burnt tissue stared accusingly at him.

Richard pulled off his gloves and set them in his lap, his eyes never leaving those hollow sockets. His fingers unconsciously sought his face, prying at the thick scabs on his cheeks until his fingernails drew fresh blood. He was oblivious to it as it drew lines down his cheeks.

"Stop looking at me," he whispered, nudging the skull with his toe, the entire front row of teeth snapping off. "Stop looking at me!"

Richard leapt to his feet and stomped the skull, the bone giving way easily for his heel to squish out what little of the liquefied brain remained. He stomped again and again, finally kicking it back into the fire with a cloud of black dust.

Panting, he plopped back onto his rear end on the rock, still peering into the fire at the remainder of the corpses. It took a moment for him to remember that he wasn't alone. When he looked across the fire, the man was staring directly at him through wide, unblinking eyes. Richard smiled and the man looked away so quickly he toppled off his seat. Laughter exploded from Richard and the man scurried off, mumbling something incoherent about checking on the others.

Richard felt the trickle of fluids on his face and smeared it away, his entire face below his eyes now covered with blood. The dampness allowed the frigid air to nip into his skin, so he found his gloves on the ground and shoved his hands back in, again holding them over the fire. Flames slowly took root in the singed fabric, but the warmth felt magnificent. He left them there until he could take it no more and pulled out twin hands of fire, watching them burn. Waving them in front of his face only fanned the blaze, forcing him to find the nearest patch of snow into which to shove them. When he finally pulled them back out, his black fingernails poked out of the burnt ends. His first thought was of watching his diabetic grandfather peel off the dead nails from his necrotic toes and wondered how it might feel.

"Hey!" a voice shouted from above. "They're coming!"

Richard launched himself forward and scrambled up the rock to where the man was still flat on his belly sighting the rifle.

"Out of the way!" he snapped, shoving the man so hard that the rifle clattered from his grip. Richard pulled it to his shoulder and pressed his cheek against the cold steel, seating his eye against the scope. Two figures faded in and out of the storm, trudging directly toward the island. As they approached, he recognized the one on the left as the albino boy who had opposed him on the far shore what felt like a lifetime ago now. One simple squeeze of the trigger and he could pay back that freak, but it would spook the man to his right, who carried a bundle of blankets across his chest. But he knew good and well that those weren't just blankets. Beneath was the key to his rule, the tool that would metamorphose him in the eyes of his people from their ruler into something far greater. Inside that bundle was the catalyst that would transform him into a god.

"That's far enough!" he shouted. The figures stopped where they stood. Waiting.

Richard heard the other men scamper up the rocks behind him so they could see, winded from running all the way up the stone slope from the snowmobiles. He sighted the man holding the bundle. It was the same man who had met with him earlier, the one who appeared to be in charge. What was his name again? Adam?

"The albino kid stays right there!" he shouted. "If he moves a muscle, we fill him full of holes! Understood?"

Both of the figures nodded.

"I want to see the boy!" he screamed. Licking his chapped lips, he watched Adam fold back the blanket to reveal a white face with a stocking cap pulled nearly down over its eyes. A plume of exhaust escaped the boy's lips and Adam covered him quickly back up.

"You promise to leave us in peace?" Adam's spectral voice called.

Richard passed the rifle back to the man who'd been on watch. "Don't let either of them out of your sight." And then to the others, "I want another one of you to cover them from where they can't see you. Blow them to hell if they try anything funny. Two more... Get on your snowmobiles and go get that kid!"

"I said, do you—?" Adam called.

"Of course!" Richard shouted, turning to shove the men to motion. "I'm sending two of my men down. You give them the boy and you'll never see us again, but if you even think of trying to trick us, you're dead! You hear me? Dead!"

"We hear you," Adam called back.

A scream filled the air behind Richard and another immediately joined the chorus. The wail of the engines softened to a buzzing sound and he waited breathlessly for the snowmobiles to appear from around the side of the island to his left. With a squeal they flashed into view, headlights scanning across the snow. The two figures faced the approaching snowmobiles, which stopped about twenty yards away so as not to be in the line of fire.

Adam walked toward them, struggling with the weight in his arms.

"Keep your crosshairs on his forehead," Richard said.

It felt like it was taking forever for Adam to reach the snowmobiles. Richard's rage bubbled in his gut and he wanted to scream for his men to just shoot him already.

Adam stopped about five steps from the nearest snowmobile and shouted up to Richard. "I need your word that you aren't going to hurt him!"

"The child will live, but you will not unless you pass him over right now!" Richard bellowed, his voice echoing off through the storm.

Adam hesitated, staring back up at Richard before closing the gap and setting the boy on the snowmobile behind the man with his shotgun pointed right in Adam's face.

Snow fired from the tread and the engine wailed as the snowmobiles turned around and sped back toward the island.

"You still have him in your sights?" Richard asked.

"Yes, sir" the man replied.

"Shoot him."

VII

SALT LAKE CITY

Oscar stumbled through the doorway onto the roof, ill-prepared for the weather. Snow buffeted him in the face before he even took his first step into the accumulation, though the cold was a welcomed sensation against his broken nose and stinging eyes. The mixture of tears and Garrett's blood tightened on his face as it froze, the sudden drop in temperature doing little to dampen the adrenaline rush. Clutching his bleeding hands to his chest, he shuffled across the roof, which felt as though it teetered from side to side beneath him, toward the first person he saw. The man had his back to him, looking out over the edge of the roof toward the city, steam rising from the thermos in his grasp.

Oscar hadn't gone into prison as a criminal, but had emerged with all of the tools of the trade. He had been a nineteen year-old punk who took a ride with a buddy when he shouldn't have. When the cherries had blossomed in the rearview mirror, he'd known he was screwed, but not nearly to the degree he had been. Hector had tried to race away from the cops and failed miserably, wrapping the hood around a streetlight. He'd been able to outrun Oscar though, and so long as there had been a Mexican to collar, the cops had been happy enough. The stolen car alone wasn't nearly as damning as the heroin in the trunk. Maybe the grand theft auto charge would have gotten him six months of cable and free food, but the drugs earned him five solid years. Five years of sleeping with his eyes open and doing whatever it took to survive. He couldn't bear to rehash the thought. Maybe the other people mourned the end of the world, but not him. As far as he was concerned, the world got what was coming to it. Just like that guy who had beaten him, tied him up, and left him for dead. Some people said that two wrongs didn't make a right, but as far as Oscar was concerned, no amount of wrongs could ever make things right.

But this...this was his chance to start anew. No LAPD waiting on every corner to pitch him that third strike. No more factories and foremen who made sure he was never paid for his overtime. No more coughing up ten percent of his check just to get it cashed or getting coke for his parole officer and paying for the privilege. This was the only way he would ever be given a fresh start, and he had begun with the most valuable skill he had learned in the joint.

He had killed a man...and he'd never felt better.

"Hey, buddy," he said, approaching the man at the ledge.

The man turned to face him. "Jesus," he gasped, his thermos falling to the ground, the hot coffee eating a brown puddle into the snow. "What happened to you?"

"I was born again," Oscar said, smiling around blood-stained teeth.

"Hey, Chaz!" the man shouted, "Come give me a hand!"

"What is it?" the other man called, tromping through the snow from his post at the corner of the rooftop. "They come to spell us so we can finally get some of that wonderful smelling...?"

Oscar watched the color drain from the man's face, his eyes widening. The man jerked his shotgun to his shoulder, his hands trembling so badly that the barrel shook.

Following the man's eyes, Oscar looked over the edge of the roof.

An enormous man sat atop a tall steed, just on the other side of the fence. He raised his hands from where he clutched a mane of spikes poking from the equine's skeletal head. Curling his claws into the hood shrouding his face, he peeled it back and dropped the black cloak from his shoulders. Some sort of crimson-colored armadillo hide formed a suit of armor over him, his face shielded behind an arched shield with ragged holes slashed across eyes that burned with fire.

He jumped down to the smoldering ground and his stallion rose to its hind legs, its front legs waving hooves shod with molten metal and flames. It made a screaming sound like a choir of slaughtered goats and slammed its hooves back to the ground, shaking the building on its foundation. Fissures opened in the earth, racing through the asphalt and concrete like lightning bolts. A loud hissing sound erupted all around them as though they'd been set down in the middle of a stadium of angry spectators.

"Please, God…" the man whimpered, pulling the trigger over and over, deafening them to the sound of their impending demise.

Black bodies poured out into the streets from behind buildings and out of alleys, jumping down from rooftops and leaping over parked cars. The Swarm raced toward them, shoulder to shoulder, claws curled in anticipation of the slaughter. Their dewlaps unfurled in their excitement, capes the colors of autumn leaves trilling beneath their chins.

"They're here!" someone shouted behind them, dashing for the door and shouting down into the stairwell.

A dozen men and women sprinted toward the gas cans beside the piles of wood lining the fence to light their flaming barricades, but they never had a chance.

The Swarm hit the iron fence from all sides. Some flattened themselves and slipped between bars without breaking stride, while others climbed atop them, throwing their bodies right into the tangles of barbed wire. The sharpened points tore away chunks of scales and gouged deep lacerations into the flesh, but it didn't even faze them. Gushing white blood and flashing rows of sharp teeth, they joined in the fracas. The people below were torn apart before their very eyes, attacked by so many claws and teeth at once that gobs of flesh and spatters of blood filled the air.

The creatures flooded the courtyard, and still they crowded the streets in a seemingly endless parade of evil.

Shotguns blasted and rifles blazed from across the rooftop, but if they had felled any of the creatures there was no way to tell as more and more packed in to wedge the dead on their feet.

"Give me a gun!" Oscar screamed, whirling in a circle, but none of the others even looked his way. He leaned over the ledge and looked down. The creatures blew through the plywood over the windows and doors on the bottom floors as though they were no more substantive than spider webs.

Screams tore though the twilight from below.

War still stood on the other side of the fence, his minions flowing all around him as they poured across the fence. He took a single stride forward and raised a mighty hand, flicking his razor-honed fingertips to the sky before slashing straight through the iron bars, leaving the severed ends glowing orange. One more slice from his other hand and a large section of the fence fell inward, clattering atop the mounds of sticks his prey had never had the chance to light. He stepped through and walked toward the building, his legion parting for him like the sea before a cutter.

Standing at the base of the hotel, he looked straight up at Oscar, who screamed at the top of his lungs. The fire in War's eyes enveloped his forehead in response as he slammed his right palm against the bricks, the talons latching into it, and then his left. His whole head now ablaze, War began to scale the building.

Still screaming, Oscar whirled and ran toward the door, turning back in time to see the other guards sprinting after him.

War crested the roof and stood on the ledge, the Swarm clambering over the edges all around him like bathwater spilling over the edge of a full tub.

Oscar threw open the door to the stairs and was assaulted by agonized screams. A splash of blood patterned the wall in front of him as a reptilian head peered up from the landing below, trilling a rust-colored frill dripping with blood, yellow- and black-marbled eyes looking directly into his.

He slammed the door shut and felt a body slam into it from the other side. The other men were nearly to him before being dragged down from behind and mercilessly ripped apart. Blood spattered all over his face, but he couldn't force himself to close his eyes. Limbs were torn from joints, flayed to the bone by claws like knives, and shoved past greedy, scaled lips.

The creature on the other side of the reinforced steel door was banging so fiercely it knocked him away and to his knees in the snow.

The snarling creatures closed in, their expanded dewlaps flapping so hard they fanned the snow from the rooftop back into the air.

And then they stopped.

Oscar could feel them all around him, the roof bowing beneath their weight. They snapped at him like rabid dogs as he looked from one to the next, hatred radiating from them nearly as strongly as their hunger. Black blotches swam on those golden eyes.

The ground shook beneath him and he heard the sound of cracking joists.

"Valleys of shadows and darkness," Oscar mumbled. "Temptation of shepherds. Yea though I walk." The sea of blackness parted for War to step through, the whole building threatening to collapse under each footfall. He stopped right in front of Oscar, looking down on him through eyes that blazed hotter than the sun.

"Just get it over with!" Oscar screamed.

War's hands struck like vipers, the talons carving through the muscles in his shoulders. In one motion, he lifted Oscar and held him several feet off the ground, his legs flailing uselessly. Blood poured from the wounds, dripping from his fingertips for the Swarm to slither in and lick from the snow, darting back like mongrels afraid of the master's stick.

"What are you waiting for?" Oscar screamed, his head bucking back in pain.

"For God to look away," War said in a voice cast from the epicenter of an earthquake.

He snarled and jerked his hands apart. Oscar's wail of pain terminated in a wet splash and the clatter of snapping teeth.

VIII

MORMON TEARS

"It's not too late," Adam said, readjusting the weight against his chest. His back hurt so badly he could hardly keep his eyes open. Even forming words tested his resolve. "We can still turn back."

"I'll be fine," a voice said from under the blanket.

"You know...you know what they're going to do to you, don't you?"

Silence from beneath the covers.

Adam nodded, if only to himself, and looked up toward the top of the stone mountain ahead. He could only vaguely discern a pair of silhouettes against the gray sky.

A pair of headlights appeared around the southern edge of the island, bringing with them the high-pitched whine of engines. Snowflakes cut through the beams, creating shadows like clouds passing over the sun. They slowed and stopped at a safe distance, the snow thrown up in their wake overtaking them before being chased away by the wind. There was a single shape on each of the snowmobiles, barely visible behind the halogen glare directed right at them. The light glinted from the barrels of the weapons the men pointed at them.

"God help us," Adam whispered.

Hefting the kid up to get a better grasp, his biceps and forearms feeling like the muscles were being torn apart strand by strand, he forced his trembling legs to move. It took every last ounce of his courage to walk toward the snowmobiles. He could sense the awesome weight of the twin barrels on him and wondered if he would feel the steel shot tear him to ribbons before he died. The headlights stretched his shadow across the snow all the way back to where Phoenix waited behind.

Adam stopped when he was nearly to the vehicles and looked back up at Richard.

"I need your word that you aren't going to hurt him!" he shouted.

"The child will live," Richard's voice drifted with the wind, "but you will not unless you pass him over right now!"

Adam's heart was beating so fast that he couldn't make his legs move. He'd be killing this kid if he crossed the final five feet.

"Go on," the voice said from under the blankets.

His legs moved of their own accord, leading him to the closest snowmobile. The driver clambered off and thrust the shotgun into Adam's face, but he continued on, gently setting the boy, blankets and all, onto the long seat. He stepped away, all the while the driver keeping the end of the weapon so close to his face that he could smell the gun oil.

When he had finally retreated a dozen steps, the driver slung the gun back over his shoulder and both of the snowmobiles spun one hundred and eighty degrees, showering him with a spray of snow.

"What have I done?" he asked aloud, tears rolling from his eyes.

Adam looked up the steep stone of the island until he could see Richard, still standing there, watching him. There was a flash of light to Richard's right and Adam felt a splash of warmth hit his face. A great boom! echoed all around him.

He wiped the crimson spatters from his face, pulling his hands away to reveal not only blood, but a couple snow white feathers. On the ground before him lay the exposed breast of an enormous ivory bird, wings folded under its back, its beak askew. Blood poured from a crater in its chest beneath its left wing. As Adam watched, a spectral outline grew around the fallen bird's corpse, forming the shape of a human's body superimposed over the bird's, like a double exposure. He caught a glimpse of long dark hair and even darker eyes, clothed in the skins of some hairy animal.

"Run!" Phoenix shouted.

Adam spun to face him. The younger boy was already upon him and tugging at his arm. When he looked back to the ground, the image of the woman was gone, leaving only the shredded, feathered lump. Slowly, the pieces fit into place as Phoenix urged him backwards away from the dead falcon. The bang had been gunfire directed at him, and the bird…had the bird taken the bullet for him? And the spectre lingering around it, had that been some sort of human soul inside of it?

Phoenix turned him and they ran toward the far shore. The reports of rifle fire crashed everywhere around them like thunder. The storm enveloped them, making it so they could neither see the shore ahead nor the island behind.

Adam doubled over to catch his breath, slowing to a walk.

"What…What happened back there?" he gasped.

"The Goshute," Phoenix said. "The Indians who lived here hundreds of years ago. They gave their lives to the storm. Their souls now live in the blizzard."

Adam was speechless as a dozen more falcons emerged from the snow and landed all around them, standing atop the deep snow before completely vanishing into it.

The sound of repeated cracking joined them on the breeze, rhythmic, haunting, like a lone woodsmen chopping down a tree from a great distance.

"Come on, Adam," Phoenix said, placing a hand on his shoulder. "The time has come."

His mind swirling with thoughts of Indians and birds, metered by the monotonous chopping, Adam followed Phoenix back toward the cave. They had only made it ten yards before the sounds of screaming pierced the gray of the falling night.

They both turned and looked back toward the island, invisible through the blizzard.

CHAPTER 7

I

SALT LAKE CITY

War surveyed the lobby of the hotel, disimpassioned to the carnage. The walls and ceiling were positively covered with blood. He could still hear the screams of the dying lingering in his ears, reveling in their exquisite agony. The Swarm filled the room, fighting for the privilege of gnawing the remaining flesh from the bones scattered throughout. Sharp teeth clattered against the hard calcification while the sounds of slurping were everywhere. They lapped at the walls, slathering their tongues over floors and sucking the juices from the carpets. War let them have their feast, for they would need every ounce of their strength for the final leg of their journey and the penultimate battle.

The humans didn't stand a chance, but he knew better than to underestimate them. His minions would be prepared to lay siege to the last remaining sanctum, and mankind would be no more.

Outside, the sun set on that ungrateful species for the last time. When it rose again, it would do so on a land no longer plagued by the scourge of man. But there was something more this time. He could feel it.

Resentment.

He could feel his master's growing discontent like so many ulcers eating through him from the inside out. Death was the chosen son of the Lord, the one who had been gifted with power to do that for which God no longer had the stomach. His lot was to clean up the mess the Maker had made, to eliminate a race that would have annihilated the entire planet if given enough time. But God had double-crossed him, hadn't He? The Lord was playing both sides at once, favoring his useless creations to his own children.

Death's will was solidifying. Somewhere in that great black tower, Death was creating the next dominant race, not in God's image, but in his own. They would claim this world rather than spend another eternity waiting to be birthed into physical bodies. This time they would use the power they had been bequeathed for their own purposes.

The heavens shook with rage, but it was too late to stop them now. His army would swarm over and decimate the last of mankind with a savagery that would hail the end of the Lord's reign on earth. Theirs would be a race that worshipped them, feeding their power until they were gods themselves.

There was still the task at hand, however. The time was nigh to rally his troops, to work them into a bloodthirsty frenzy.

All of the creatures around him froze, the lobby falling silent, save the dripping of blood from the ceiling. Every black and yellow eye rose from the reeking remains to focus upon him.

The flames in War's eyes flared above his head like horns and the building shook around them. Tables rattled and chairs toppled to the floor. Glass shivered in its frame before shattering and tinkling to the floor. A rain of blood and plaster shivered from the ceiling. A riotous hiss arose from the Swarm, trilling dewlaps flapping like wings. They snapped and nipped, slicing each other with claws from reptilian feet and hands, their furor rising to a state of unrestrained excitement.

War's eyes burned white hot and they sped past him, funneling through the shattered front doors, nails clacking on the boards they had torn away, before falling silent as they dashed into the snow. As they had done before, they squeezed through the fence and scrabbled atop the masses to peel their own skin in the barbed wire. Those stuck and wriggling in the coiled metal snare only served as leverage for hundreds of others to climb over.

Thunder waited out front, fiery eyes locked on the western horizon, beyond warehouses buried with snow and the useless stretches of runways and hangars. The sky was now as black as it had ever been, only the storm clouds serving to lighten it by degrees of shadow. War leapt astride the stallion, tossing aside the drape of flesh over the animal's skeleton and wedging his toes between the exposed ribs.

He bellowed a sound like the start of an avalanche, summoning a stabbing display of lightning from the sky. Thunder bucked and sprayed fire from its nostrils. Slamming its front hooves to the ground, the beast launched forward, clearing the gate in a single leap and hitting the ground at a gallop.

The ground trembled.

The heavens shook.

The end of man was at hand.

II

MORMON TEARS

Under the shroud of blankets, Ray focused on his breathing. He was going to die. There was no doubt in his mind. Holding the bone dagger against his chest, adjusting and readjusting his grip, he focused on his breathing, trying to occupy his mind with anything other than his current situation, but it was impossible. The snowmobile vibrated under him, the runners rising and falling like a ship on rough seas as they blew through the drifts formed by the frozen waves. The engine buzzed and thrummed as the driver had to constantly reach back to grab him to make sure that he was still there.

"Are you still with me, Tina?" he whispered, but only the chill answered, stabbing him through the blankets with needles of ice. She said he'd know when the time was right, when he was supposed to use the dagger in his sweaty grasp, but he'd never even been in a fistfight. Did she really think there was a part of him that would be able to kill a man?

The snowmobile slowed and his heartbeat accelerated. There was not only the sound of the engine beneath him, but another off to the right. Fear seized him, tightening his chest to the point that he couldn't breathe, causing his entire body to shake.

"Please don't let me die," he whispered as the snowmobile coasted to a halt.

The driver killed the engine and the shuddering beneath him ceased, replaced by the howl of the wind and the patter of snowflakes.

"Come on," the driver said, nudging Ray as he climbed of the seat. "You're safe now. No one's going to hurt you here."

But for how long? As soon as his face was revealed...

He stood before they could assist him, knowing that the illusion would only last so long. Were they to feel his body beneath, he was as good as dead. He stomped his feet to sink deeper into the snow.

"Hey, Richard!" the man called.

"We've got what we came for," another voice, presumably that of the other driver, said. "Let's just head back. They'll catch up."

"Relax. It won't be long now. Just keep thinking about that nice hot mug of coffee that'll be waiting for us when we get back."

"I'm imagining an electric blanket and a bowl of soup. Chicken noodle. Man, oh man would that hit the spot right now."

"I'd settle for a—"

"Excellent job!" Richard said, sliding down the slick rocks to where they waited. He tromped through the snow until he stood in front of Ray, watching frozen breath seep out from the small gap that revealed only Ray's chin. "We've come a long way to make sure you were safe. Did they hurt you, Jake? You know we did everything we could to protect your mother, and we'll do the same for you. Once we get you back home, I'll personally make sure that nothing ever happens to you. We can be a team, Jake. I'll take care of you like my own son. What do you say?"

Ray gripped the hilt of the knife in both hands, pointing the tip toward the sound of the voice.

"How about it, Jake?" Richard reached out and lifted the lip of the blanket that hung down over the boy's face.

Ray saw Richard's face register surprise and thrust the blade forward, meeting with resistance, but only momentarily.

Richard howled in pain and shoved him in the chest, the blankets tangling around his legs and depositing him on his back in the snow. Cold air blew through the hole he had torn in the blanket, cooling the warmth that poured down the blade and onto his hands.

"Jesus Christ!" one of the men shouted. "He stabbed him!"

Richard fell to his knees in the snow, both hands pressed over the bleeding wound in the lower left quadrant of his abdomen. It felt like there was still something inside, digging deeper and deeper into the fathomless laceration. He reached his left hand through the rip in his jacket to try to hold the lips of the cut closed, staring down at the massive amount of blood dripping between the fanned fingers of his right.

With a roar, he leapt on Ray, who had the presence of mind to slash at him, but only succeeded in opening Richard's right palm. The pain served to enrage Richard even more.

"Hold him down!" Richard yelled at the shocked men, unable to raise their rifles, as they had been caught so off-guard.

Both men dropped their shotguns into the snow and grabbed Ray by either wrist, pinning him in place. Ray fought against them, but with Richard's weight atop his chest he could barely breathe, let along fend off the two larger men.

"You thought you could fool me! Me?" Richard was so angry that he shouted through bared teeth, freckling Ray with droplets of blood. He slammed his right hand down over Ray's mouth, the pressure straining the roots of his teeth, popping his lips like blood-filled juice vesicles. "I gave you a chance and this is how you repay me?"

The other men could only hold on and watch, terrified by the look in Richard's eyes.

"Give me the knife!" Richard bellowed. "I said give me the goddamned knife!"

One of the men pried it out of Ray's grasp, dislocating his index finger in the process. He quickly tossed it to Richard and wiped all of the blood on his pants.

"I'm going to give you a message," Richard growled, pressing even harder on Ray's mouth. "You go back. You walk back across the lake and you tell your friends. Tell them that they're all going to die!"

Ray closed his eyes when Richard brought the knife to his face. The sharp tip pressed into the flimsy skin above his right eyeball. He screamed at the top of his lungs, experiencing a pain like he'd never thought possible as Richard forced the knife deep into the socket. Nerves severed and connective tissue tore, but that was nothing compared to the agony of Richard jerking the knife away, taking with it his eyeball and the entirety of his upper lid.

Blood poured from the gaping hole, washing over his cheek and into the snow.

His cries intensified when Richard slammed the knife into his other side, this time spearing the orb with a sickly pop and twisting it like a corkscrew to rip everything near it out as well.

The men released his wrists and staggered away, but Ray was unable to see their fear or the look of revulsion on their faces. He didn't even hear them start the snowmobiles over his screams.

"Get up!" Richard yelled, grabbing Ray with his bloody right hand by the newly fashioned holes in his skull. The bones felt as though they were going to break and the fingertips on his nerve ending sent fiery bolts of pain throughout his body. Richard jerked upward and Ray had to force his arms and legs to push him up to his haunches.

Richard let his face go and Ray collapsed forward into the snow, the cold slush packing into the sockets, keeping him from passing out. He brought his trembling fingers to his eyes to try to pry the clots of snow out, but Richard kicked him squarely in the back.

"I said get up!" Richard yanked on Ray's hair, the first handful ripping out, but a second handful granted the leverage to pull Ray to his knees.

Arcs of snow fell on them both as the snowmobiles raced off in the other direction, the engines whining from being taxed to their limits.

Richard didn't seem to notice. His only thoughts were of Ray, who he finally urged to his feet. He gave the younger man a shove in the back to get him moving.

"You tell them!" he screamed, his voice cracking. "You tell them I'm going to kill them all!"

Ray staggered into the storm, hands pressed to his eyes in a futile attempt to slow the blood that rushed from the sockets. The pain banished all conscious thought, leaving him at the mercy of his instincts. All he could do was walk, stumbling and falling, but pushing himself back up again.

"I love you, Ray," the wind whispered, summoning tears that would never flow again.

Blood spattering the snow, he headed in the direction of the voice.

III

MORMON TEARS

Jill huddled with the others in the cave, just outside the reach of the wind and the snow, the hunks of coal in front of her turning gray and breaking apart and turning to ash. None of them spoke. They all simply stared straight ahead, into the storm, waiting to see who would return...or if anyone would return. Spears stood erect from the ground in front of her, alternately flashing with visions of monsters impaled upon them, blood spiraling down the wooden poles. Perhaps it was her growing terror, but she couldn't seem to make the visions stop. It was as though she stood at the edge of reality, watching her dawning insanity breaking through. Or maybe it was just that the closer they came to facing their ultimate nightmare, the more her mind allowed the images to slip through. Either way it was all so real that she had to scream.

Everyone turned to look at her, but none of them wanted to know. They didn't need to be able to see her visions to know what was coming, nor were they willing to risk learning the answers to ask what she saw. At his point, it was almost better not knowing the details. They knew that Richard and his men would be coming with their guns blazing and they knew that the army of the Swarm would descend upon them soon enough. They knew they were going to die, but there was some small measure of comfort in not knowing how.

Mare wrapped his arms around Jill from behind, drawing her to him. Her screams faded, but none of the others could look at her for fear of seeing how she looked back at them.

"It's all right," he whispered into her ear, but she hardly heard his words.

Ahead, she could see the snow and sand barricade beyond the broken and bloodied poles and the black creatures folded over them, impaled several bodies deep. The beach was littered with them, as those who'd managed to tear themselves free had crawled off into the snow to die. Sections of the wall were caved in, the bodies skewered on the other side permanently draped over the barricade with white ooze pouring out of their mouths. That same white film floated on the warm water where the kelp was now growing wild, with broad leaves poking out of the water amidst the wreckage of tubing. She tried not to look at the tattered clothes and butchered bodies lying where they had fallen for fear of recognizing who they were and losing what precious little control she maintained over her mind. Instead, she looked out across the lake. So much of the ice had broken away that she could see stretches of black water and chunks of ice moving in it like small bergs. The flames had died on the island as she had known they would, only she knew that many of her newfound friends had as well.

A silhouette materialized from the snow, a lone figure that appeared to be walking on the exposed portion of the lake, but the vision faded and the person crossed the ice toward them. They all held their breath. Three had left and only one was returning. Details finally came into focus as the figure reached the shoreline.

"Phoenix!" Missy shouted, dashing off into the snow. She met him after he'd slid down their side of the barrier, wrapping her arms around him and immediately kissing him.

"Oh, God," Evelyn gasped. "Adam…"

"Where's Ray?" Darren asked, even though when they'd parted, he had known he might never see his friend again.

Missy kissed Phoenix with everything she had, holding him with her fingers clenched in his jacket, refusing to let go. Her tears trailed down over their lips, his skin so cold it hurt to touch, but she couldn't tear herself away for fear she may never get the opportunity again. Finally, he withdrew and looked her in the eyes.

"You know I'll always come back to you," he whispered. "Nothing on his earth could keep me away."

She sniffled and kissed him again, releasing his jacket and taking his hand.

"What about the others?"

"Adam went back for Ray. I don't know what's going to happen from here."

She nodded, squeezing his hand and leading him back to the cave. The others waited expectantly, hoping he would volunteer whatever he knew about the other two. For the first time, he honestly didn't know whether one or both would come back and chose not to answer their unspoken question.

"Now is the time we've been preparing for," Phoenix said, hoping his voice sounded stronger than he felt. "The Swarm will be here soon. I can feel it."

"What are we going to do?" Mare asked. "Adam and Ray are gone, and no one knows where Norman is. That just leaves the nine of us against an army of monsters. And what about Richard and his men?"

"Two of them will come back," Jill said. "That much I know. I think Ray will be one of them. I remember seeing something…something abut his eyes…like they weren't even there."

"All we can do is ready ourselves," Phoenix said. "We won't get another chance."

Phoenix walked past them to the rear of the cave and grabbed two of the jugs of gasoline they'd siphoned from the semi. Passing them to Mare, he grabbed the two remaining and headed out into the storm with Mare right behind. They followed the face of the mountain to where it ended at the road. Climbing the hill of sand and snow, they both uncapped the jugs and sloshed the gas all over the fence they'd erected from the top of the semi, throwing arcs of fluid as high as they could. Setting the empty containers against the base of the barricade, they headed back into the cave. Phoenix reached right into the pile of coals with gloved hands and exhumed one that still glowed bright orange. Juggling it from hand to hand, the heat both delightful and painful at once, he rushed back up the hill and pressed the black rock against the fence. He held it there, waiting, and when he was just about to give up and grab another, a faint blue flame raced along the gas-darkened wood. The fire grew higher with each passing second, the flames turning yellow and then finally orange as they ate into the grain and expanded from the sections of fuel to the bare wood.

The others gathered around him, watching as the entire wall of wood started to burn, ten-foot high flames chasing a thick black cloud of smoke into the sky.

"What now?" April asked, pulling Darren's arm around her.

"We wait," Phoenix said, finally turning away from the fire and heading back down to the beach. He took his post behind the dike, barely able to see over it. The others lined up to either side, watching the far horizon where the bonfire still burned on the distant island, wavering in and out of the sheeting snow.

IV

The Great Salt Lake

"Oh, my God. Oh, my God. Oh, my God," Kevin said. He'd run the snowmobile's tank dry without even noticing until the engine seized and he coasted to a halt. His hands were shaking so hard that he was pouring more of the gas onto the side of the tank than in it. "Jesus…Jesus Christ! Did you see that? He just…just cut that kid's eyes out."

Jerry was using the opportunity to fill his tank as well, though with slightly more precision.

"I don't want to talk about it."

"God! There was so much blood and his eyes, man, they just popped right out of his sockets."

"Shut up."

"What the hell are we going to do?"

"I said shut up."

"What are we supposed to tell the others? I mean, they'll never believe us. It's just so… so…"

"Shut up!" Jerry shouted, his voice echoing off into the pine thickets.

Kevin flinched as though he'd been slapped. His mind was reeling. There was a part of him that was convinced that he couldn't possibly have seen what he saw. There was no way that a man could drive a knife into another man's eyes and gouge them out. It was sick. Barbaric. He'd never witnessed anything so horrific in his life. All he wanted to do was just get on that snowmobile and drive as far and as fast as he could.

"What do you think he'll do to those people?" he whispered.

"None of our concern," Jerry said.

"He's going to kill them all, isn't he?" Kevin's voice rose an octave, his breathing bordering on hyperventilation.

"Why do you think we went there in the first place?"

"I thought we were just going to take back the kid before they could hurt him."

"How did you think we were going to do that, huh? Didn't you think about that when we all got guns?"

"I didn't think we'd actually use them."

"What? And just wave them around? How naïve are you?"

"But, I thought—"

"But. But. Shut up."

The gas began to overflow from the tank. Jerry shook the container to see if there was enough gas left to try to salvage before tossing it into the shrubbery. Capping the tank, he brushed several inches of new accumulation from the seat and plopped down.

"Don't leave without me!" Kevin said, now on the verge of tears. He couldn't catch his breath, couldn't think. The world was spinning around him. A week prior he had just started his new job in social services. He'd been groomed to liberate children from bad situations. He'd hunted deer twice with his uncle, so he was no stranger to firearms, but he'd never once considered the prospect of raising one against another human being. The contents of his stomach revolted before he even knew they were coming, spattering his legs and the seat.

"Oh, for God's sake," Jerry said, revving the engine of his speeder. The last thing he wanted right now was to have to babysit a grown man. The time had come to just suck it up and save their own skins, and he was saddled with the biggest pansy on the planet. He would be better off leaving this guy before he had to tow him like an anchor. That was the way of the world anyway, wasn't it? Only the strong survived. Let this sissy get dragged down like a wounded gazelle. They would both probably be better off. He was about to just pin the gas and speed off when he heard a high-pitched roar, like the winds before a tornado.

He looked up at the trees, but the upper canopy hardly jostled. Yet still the sound grew louder, reminding him of the noise of a football stadium from afar. To his left, Kevin had stopped whining long enough to drop the gas can and scan the horizon, the same puzzled look on his face.

"Can you hear—?" Kevin started before Jerry hushed him.

Jerry killed the engine so he could better hear, amplifying the sound tenfold. He rose and stepped back down into the snow. The earth trembled slightly as though from distant aftershocks. His reflection vibrated in the side mirror of the snowmobile. Far ahead, the higher reaches of the trees shivered off their snow mass to reveal brownish-green needles that hung down like noodles.

"Get on your snowmobile," he said, backing toward his own.

Kevin stared at him, uncomprehending.

"Get on your damn snowmobile!" Jerry shouted, leaping on and cranking the engine, which screamed and fired a flume of snow from the rear.

It hadn't been the wind.

Not even close.

As the sound grew louder, it was clearly decipherable as hissing. And it was coming closer with each passing second. The ground now positively rumbled as Jerry spun the snowmobile and sped in the opposite direction.

Kevin had heard Jerry's cries, but he was paralyzed by fear, terrified by the line of trees in front of him. They shook off the snow, dropping it to the forest floor. The darkness of the underbrush wavered as though ripping itself apart before golden dots appeared, filling every available iota of space until the entire area positively glowed.

Kevin screamed, finally willing his legs to move. He leapt onto the snowmobile and cranked the ignition. The engine sputtered, drawing new life from the gasoline and releasing a roar, but he never even had time to throttle it.

Hundreds of bodies tore through the undergrowth, the headlight glinting from claws and teeth, shimmering on the outline of slick black scales. They poured over him, burying the entire snowmobile. The windshield shattered and Kevin screamed, but the sounds were drowned out by the hissing. Talons ripped through his skin to the bone, peeling away layers of flesh to be snapped up by greedy jaws and torn away. The pain was excruciating, though mercifully brief. His windpipe opened and his lungs were torn through fractured ribs, his skull shattered like impacting a solid wall at high velocity.

When the Swarm passed over, there was nothing left but an idling snowmobile with a shattered headlight and grooves carved into the metal. Stuffing protruded from the shredded vinyl seat, a trail of blood and jaggedly-broken bones coating the footprint-riddled snow for a good twenty yards behind it.

Jerry pushed the speeder as hard as he could, but each time he looked into one of the side mirrors, the eyes had grown larger. Trying to stabilize the rudder with one hand, he unslung the shotgun from his back and fired blindly over his shoulder, again and again until the chamber was empty and he threw the gun behind him into his snowy wake.

He lowered his head behind the glass and tucked his knees into the sides of the seat to streamline himself, but even that wasn't enough. Baring his teeth, he growled as the hissing overcame even the sound of the motor. The rear of the snowmobile kicked to the side as it was battered from behind, the final warning he would be given. Claws tore through his jacket, looping under his skin like fishhooks. The snowmobile raced away from beneath him, slamming into a tree trunk, but he was already flat on his back in the snow, surrounded by a wash of his own shredded flesh and spatters of blood.

V

MORMON TEARS

Adam had trudged halfway back to the beach with Phoenix before turning back. There had been a part of him that knew he had potentially sent Ray to his death and had willingly accepted it. With so many people dying all around him, he had allowed himself to become anesthetized to it. But there was a part of him—the better part—that wouldn't allow it. He'd warred with his conscience while Ray's screams echoed like gunfire in the confines of his skull. It felt as though each agonized cry stripped away part of his humanity. Phoenix had told him that it was his destiny to lead them, and he'd grown to accept it. Rushing in to try to save Ray would jeopardize his life, and should he fail, the lives of those entrusted to his care as well. He tried to convince himself that his decision to abandon Ray was in the interests of the greater good, but what it all boiled down to was the fact that he was scared. Scared of being killed. Scared of letting down those who counted on him. But most of all, he was scared of failure, which meant more than just the end of their lives. It meant the end of their race.

Was their species worth saving if one life could be deemed inconsequential versus the greater good? Regardless of the personal consequences, he couldn't allow life to lose meaning. It was far better to give his life in the attempt to save another, even if in vain, than to turn his back on a single soul that just might be within his power to save. The thought that he had even considered doing so sickened him, but perhaps there was still a chance to atone.

Though the snow was well past his knees and he had to use his hands to push off and propel himself forward, he scrabbled toward the island, ears tuned to what he hoped would be the continued sound of screaming. There was only the wail of the wind and the unheard noises beneath. The silence terrified him. If Ray's cries had fallen quiet, then that could mean only one thing.

"Ray!" he shouted against his better judgment, expecting to be barraged with a flurry of bullets. He couldn't see a thing through the storm ahead, and looking back could only weaken his resolve. The wind had already buried their tracks, so he didn't even know if he was heading in the right direction.

He wouldn't be able to live with himself if Ray was dead. How had he allowed himself to be talked into such a foolish scheme in the first place? They should have taken their stand as one, rather than sacrificing Ray. And for what? To buy them just a little more time? Was that the value of life?

The thought drove him harder, every muscle screaming in protest, his lungs unable to keep up with the oxygen demands. Mucus froze on his stubbled upper lip, his teeth aching from the cold. A small voice in the back of his mind pleaded for him to just lie down and rest for a few minutes. Just a couple lousy minutes for his body to recuperate. Maybe just close his eyes for a few precious seconds…

"No!" he bellowed, his eyes snapping open by will alone before he could pass out into the snow. There was no time for weakness. He bit into his lower lip, the genesis of pain focusing his attention, the resultant blood creeping out of the corners of his mouth.

Barely able to keep his eyes open against the furious snowflakes, he fought onward. A gentle sound materialized beneath the storm, not the tormented wails he had expected, but a soft mewling.

"Ray?" he said, veering to the right and hurrying toward the sound. A dark shape appeared against the endless white, a hunched body that took several steps forward before collapsing into the snow. Trying to rise on its legs alone, the shadow stumbled, only to fall again. "Ray!"

Adam ran toward the younger man, who toppled face first into the accumulation, only this time he didn't even try to get back up. His hood hung loosely to the side, his hair thick with ice, minus one bloody swatch of bare skin. Grabbing him under the arm, Adam eased him to his knees.

"Talk to me, Ray! Are you hu…?" His words died when he saw Ray's imprint in the snow beneath him. It was pink with blood. "Jesus."

"Please," Ray whispered. "Just kill me."

He turned as though to look at Adam, blood pouring down his cheeks from sockets black with clotting blood. A layer of frost was already forming on the congealing fluid.

"Oh, God, Ray…" Adam said, barely able to keep from turning away in horror. He slid his left arm beneath Ray's right and wrapped it around the poor kid's back until he could grab a handful of jacket under Ray's left arm. Helping him slowly to his feet, bearing an inordinate amount of weight on his shoulders and legs, Adam started back toward the shore. "I'm so sorry. This is all my fault. Please forgive me…"

Ray coughed out a mouthful of blood and tried to look at him. Warm fluid poured down into his throat from his sinuses. "You shouldn't have come back for me."

"I shouldn't have let you do this in the first place."

Ray tried to laugh, but the pain was too great. "You wouldn't have been able to stop me."

"I can't believe…I can't believe they did this to you. I'm so…sorry." The words sounded hollow even to Adam as he spoke them.

"I kind of had it coming."

"Not this. There's nothing you could have done to deserve…this."

"I stabbed Richard in the gut."

"Is he…?"

"No," Ray said, gently shaking head. "It only pissed him off."

"So he was the one who did this to you?"

Ray said nothing.

"I'll kill him," Adam said. The statement was so matter of fact that it startled him. In his military experience, he'd always known that there might come a time when he would find himself in a position where he would have to take another man's life to save his own, but as a physician, the odds were definitely in his favor of staying away from the heaviest combat. He had never actually imagined that he could ever lust for a man's blood, though. He was in the practice of saving lives. The urge was contradictory to his very nature, but this wasn't just a man. Richard was the embodiment of evil. What kind of person would gouge out a man's eyes and send him out blindly to stumble to his death in the snow?

"He sent me ahead to warn you," Ray said. "He said he was going to kill you all."

"Then we'll be ready," Adam said, his jaw jutting forth. "We'll be ready all right."

They continued to the west—or at least what felt like the west—the distance seeming interminable. With each labored step, Adam feared that rather than approaching their camp, they were wandering farther onto the lake, paralleling the shore. If that were the case, then they could end up walking forever, or at least until they passed out from exhaustion, never again to wake. He looked back over his shoulder, but here was no sign of the island. The only sound other than the wind was a metronomic *thuck…thuck…thuck*…almost like the sound of someone chopping wood at a great distance.

He was just about to alter their bearings when a light flickered into view ahead and to the left through the worsening storm. The massive flakes flew sideways in an attempt to steal it from sight, but Adam knew exactly what it was. More importantly, though, he knew what it meant.

They had set fire to the wooden barricade.

The battle was upon them.

VI

THE GREAT SALT LAKE

Three men remained with Richard, though they did their best to keep their distance. He sat on his rock by the fire, holding his knife in the flames. His glove burned and the skin on his hand was starting to blister, but he couldn't feel it at all with the horrendous agony in his abdomen and the sheer amount of adrenaline coursing through his blood. Were it not for the all-consuming rage, the pain would have driven him to unconsciousness. He held the seething wound closed with a blood-soaked glove, his innards fight to squeeze out like canned cheese. His clothes were sopping with blood clear through to the skin, drenched from his chest all the way down to his shins.

He was going to kill them for what they'd done to him. He was going to shoot each and every one of them in the knees or the stomach and watch them die the slowest, most wretched death he could imagine. Watch them bleed out into the snow, the color slowly draining from their faces, their eyes sinking into darkness. He wanted to hear their cries, but more than that, he wanted to hear them beg. Not just for their lives, but to be put out of their misery.

Pulling the knife from the fire, he peeled aside his jacket with his dripping left hand to reveal the slobbering maw in his gut. He pinched the lips closed and brought the glowing orange blade to his belly, lining up the broad side with the pursed edges, and pressed the knife against it.

Richard screamed, a blood-curdling wail that ripped his throat on the way out. Tendrils of smoke wafted from the burning flesh, bringing with them the aroma of fried burgers. Buckling back forth, he forced his trembling right hand to steady the blade until it cooked the skin to the point that it stuck and he had to pry it away. The slanted gash looked like it had puckered, the upper strata a livid red, blood weeping from the sores formed where the knife had torn away. The union of flesh was sinewy and raw, branded by the hunting blade.

His screams carried on and on until he was able to pack a handful of snow atop the wound. Casting the knife aside, he doubled over, eyes pinched against the searing pain. Blood drained in lines from his mouth, dripping into the snow. Each breath brought a new level of agony.

"Get over here!" he shouted, gritting his teeth. "Now!"

He opened his bloodshot eyes and looked around the dying fire, waiting for any of them to crest the rocky slope.

"I said get over here!" His voice grew into a bellow of rage.

After a moment that allowed his anger to fester like his abdomen, a face peeked up over the rock. It was shielded by a ski mask with a furry hood drawn over it. The man's eyes were impossibly wide, only latching onto Richard's for a split second before looking away.

Richard tried to smile at him, but only succeeded in baring his bloody teeth.

"It's time to go to war," he said.

"You know, Richard," the man said, climbing to the top of the hill, but keeping the fire between them. "Me and the guys…I mean, really the guys…they were thinking we might just head back to the city, you know?"

"The city. Really?" Richard lifted his rifle from the ground and rested it across his lap.

"Yeah." The man rocked from one foot to the other. "This whole thing… It really hasn't gone at all like we thought it would. We…I mean they were thinking we'd be better off just cutting our losses."

"You know they're laughing at us across the lake. They're sitting there in that little cave talking about what a joke we are."

"Me and the guys, we aren't so worried about that. Let them, I say." He chuckled nervously.

"I don't think that's the right decision, friend."

"Well…we were hoping you'd come with us, but, um, we're going to leave now regardless."

Richard leaned back, sliding his left hand under the barrel of the rifle and his right over the stock until his index finger was beneath the trigger guard.

"It's because I cut that kid's eyes out, isn't it?" Richard's voice was cool and calm.

The man didn't say anything for the longest time, as though surprised by Richard's candor. He finally just shrugged.

"He stabbed me," Richard said, lining up the barrel through the fire. "Surely you remember that."

"We're all in over our heads here. Man, things are just getting out of control so—"

There was a crack of rifle fire and the man flew in reverse, his heels dragging though the snow.

Richard rose and chambered another load, pressing his left hand over the bulging mass of tissue under his jacket, and limped over to where the man was sprawled on his back, both hands toying with a mess of blood above his right hip.

"J-Jesus, man. You…you shot me," the man said, trying to kick at the snow in retreat.

"Hurts, doesn't it?" Richard said, lowering the hot barrel to rest on the man's forehead, the skin sizzling like bacon. He pulled the trigger again and the upper half of the man's head exploded. "Not so much anymore though, I'm guessing."

The roar of engines filled the air as the other men sped away from the island.

"Cowards," Richard said, kicking the body for good measure. The man's hands fell away from his hip to release an arterial spurt that spattered Richard's boots. He paid it no mind as he dropped the rifle and exchanged it for the corpse's shotgun. His limp growing more pronounced with every step, Richard descended the path toward his snowmobile.

He could see the tracks the others had laid, but there wasn't even a hint of their taillights on the horizon. When he returned to the hotel, he would make them pay. Make them learn what he thought of traitors. The thought of marching them out through the gates when they spotted the creatures coming made him positively giddy. His head swam from the loss of so much blood, his thoughts buoying in a discombobulated manner that left room for his singular will alone. Swinging his leg over the seat of the snowmobile, he plopped down, the jolt firing a spatter of blood past his lips and onto the windshield. He set the shotgun on his lap, where he could easily reach it when the time came, and cranked up the engine. His head lolled forward, but he righted it and managed to get the sled moving, speeding along the face of the island until he reached the southern end. Rounding the corner, he pushed the motor to its limits. It growled in protest, but launched forward toward the western shore. He didn't care how loud he was now. They knew he was coming, but there was absolutely nothing they could do to stop him. They had no weapons, no cover. He imagined them huddled in fear in that stupid little cave and wondered how many he could fit into the expanding pattern of steel from his weapon. Their screams in his mind urged him faster, faster.

The flakes flew past to either side like stars as he rocketed through hyperspace. He rose and fell on the drifted snow, which launched him into the air to alight with an explosion of powder. Raising the gun, he tried to balance it atop the sloped windshield and against his shoulder so he could use the headlight as his sight-line.

Blood leaked into his lap, the jostling reopening the deep hole, but he could always close it again. Nothing mattered now but vengeance. He didn't even care about the boy anymore. They had all been a party to his humiliation. No one treated Richard Robinson that way. They would all know pain for what they had done, and he would go back to Salt Lake City and they would either accept his rule or face the same consequences. He was out of patience. No more psychology. No more manipulating people to achieve his goals. They would either give him what he wanted or they would die. Plain and simple. For all of the hoopla surrounding democracy and the misguided notion that the people had a say in their government, in the end it had proven to be their ultimate undoing. An iron-fisted rule would have saved the world. When those Middle Eastern sand-jockeys had started poking their sticks at the American Empire, they should have just come down upon them with their giant heel. Then none of this would have happened. He had learned that lesson, and he would not make the same mistake. Not a chance. People were either with him or they were dead. Period.

The vague outline of the cliff rose from the skyline, wavering through the snow like a ship in the fog, only the entire mountain appeared to be on fire. Flames raced toward the clouds, the scent of burning wood finally reaching him on the gale. More smoke seemed to come from the beach, lingering around him in a haze.

With a loud crack, the front rudder bent upwards, launching the snowmobile into the air at an angle. The right runner landed first, his weight toppling it to the side and sending the whole works torpedoing into the accumulation.

Richard pried his right leg out from beneath the weight of the sled and pushed off on the ice on the lake, emerging from beneath the snow sputtering mouthfuls of bloody slush. The barrel of the shotgun poked out of the white mat to his right, the mangled runner to his left. The spring shock had snapped, leaving the short ski dangling uselessly. With a cough, the engine shuddered and died.

All he could think to do was to jerk the gun out of the snow and continue walking. Left hand fighting against the opening wound, shotgun in his right, he stumbled through the snow. Large white birds flapped at the furthest reaches of his peripheral vision, feathers clapping, before disappearing back into the storm, following him just out of sight.

At first he thought it was a mirage, but there appeared to be a wide silhouette ahead. No. There were two heads. Two bodies leaning against each other as they trudged toward land.

Richard smiled and brought his sloppy left hand to the pump of the gun to brace it, wedging the butt against his shoulder. Blood poured past the tattered edges of the cauterized wound, but he didn't even notice, for his time had finally arrived.

Let the slaughter commence.

VII

THE GREAT SALT LAKE

The two snowmobiles streaked eastward across the frozen lake. Neither man looked at the other, only at the sheet of white ahead, praying to distance themselves from the island and the hell they had endured. That was how they were forced to rationalize it in their minds. Both had been willing participants in a situation that had escalated beyond the point of no return. They had been willing to attack their fellow survivors at Mormon Tears to save the boy from them, though neither had figured it would ever reach that extreme. Their adversaries had been unarmed and they had known that fact all along. All they would have needed to do was brandish their weapons and they would have had the boy back with them in no time. It had become a series of lines in the sand, faint at first and easily enough crossed without even noticing, but as those lines had become more clearly defined, the ramifications had become readily apparent.

People had died.

At the time, they had felt the power of righteousness even though they had essentially stood back and observed. It was staggering how much right and wrong actually looked alike in retrospect. Neither of the men had pulled the trigger that ended Gray's life, but neither had they tried to stop it. To say that it had been beyond their control was a copout. Either could have interceded at that crucial juncture when violence had appeared imminent. Maybe at the time they hadn't clearly recognized the signs, but looking back, they would have had to be blind to miss them. They had been strung along, taken down a path neither even wanted to follow, of their own volition, without even knowing it. When Richard had cut out that kid's eyes, it had been like waking from a dream into a nightmare. He had gone too far. They had gone too far. And now, rather than trying to right their wrong, they were running away. Like cowards.

Maybe that was too cut and dried. Richard wouldn't have hesitated to kill either of them, as he had the man who had drawn the short straw and been designated to tell Richard of their plans to head back to Salt Lake City. They hadn't seen the man die, though as soon as they heard the shots, they were on their snowmobiles and speeding across the lake. For all they knew, both men were gut-shot and bleeding to death by the fire, but they couldn't bring themselves to turn around. Too many bad things had happened on that island and there were no signs of it relenting. They just needed to get back to the hotel with the others and prepare to fend off those creatures. Even that battle had lost its imperative in the face of all of the bloodshed they had witnessed. They had all lost their way…

The ground shook beneath them, causing the snowmobiles to lose traction momentarily, sliding as they sought purchase.

They had taken the ice for granted and both knew it. And now they were going to pay.

The storm had gathered its strength to cut them off from the rest of the world, the flakes clogging the air to the point that they could barely see the halos of light around the head and taillights of the speeder right beside them, though still they tried to watch the ground. Both expected chunks of ice to rise like jagged tombstones from the white as it fractured to reveal the lake, but the accumulation never wavered. Still the ground shuddered beneath them as though a giant stomped across the lake, its monstrous body hidden by the snow, or before the advance of a great army…

Neither even had the chance to ease off the gas. Black bodies materialized from the sheeting snow already within the range of the headlights, which only glinted from the metallic armor on the smooth scales, highlighting the tips of teeth and claws before they were upon them. A cresting tide of darkness crashed over them, cleaving them from their seats and into the snow so fast that by the time either felt the impact they were buried in the snow.

The snowmobiles continued on without them like missiles until they ran out of steam and were stampeded into the snow. Windshields were shattered and seats shredded, but neither man would ever know, as they were already collections of broken bones littering the bloodstained snow and dribbling down the chins of so many savage monsters.

War paused atop Thunder long enough to study the crimson snow angels before crunching the bones beneath his steed's fiery hooves. He looked up to the horizon and kicked the beast in the exposed ribs with spurred heels, urging him to race directly ahead to where the island was a distant black mound peeking out of the blizzard.

The flames rose so high from War's eyes that they scorched the armor over his face, a trail forming from Thunder's heels like the tail of a comet. They could all feel what was coming. The final battle at long last was at hand. They would tear through the last of them, and their task would be complete. The planet would be purged of the taint of man and the process of rebuilding could begin anew. Only this time…this time the dominant species wouldn't be cast in the Lord's image, but in that of a new form entirely. Now was the time to seize their rule. They were the Lord's children and rightful heirs to His throne. They were going to take what was theirs this time.

And they would never again relinquish it.

Thunder pounded up the face of the island, the ice on the smooth stone not even slowing it, and stood atop the highest knoll. The Swarm seethed over every inch of rock, covering the atoll like flies on a corpse. With the smell of charcoaled death lingering around them and fresh meat carried along the wind from the far shore, War sat high atop his stallion, consumed by its flames of desire. Hissing erupted all around him and he could positively feel their excitement. It was all his minions could do to await his command, knowing that the first of them to reach the island would be the last to enjoy human meat, and it was such a divine taste.

A fire several stories tall burned ahead, black smoke chasing away the snow. He couldn't help smiling beneath his mask. So they thought themselves ready for what wouldn't even qualify as a fight. A wall of fire was no deterrent to his Swarm. They would simply go around it, attacking from all sides at once. They would pour over the mountain from the west and launch a full-frontal attack across the lake. The humans would barely have time to understand what was happening before they died.

Battle? It was going to be a massacre.

War raised his right fist. Thunder bucked onto its hind legs and stabbed the air with fiery front hooves. The hissing escalated to deafening levels, the earth quaking. He jerked his fist to either side and hundreds of black creatures sprinted away from the island to the north and south to sneak around the mountain and descend upon them from behind their pathetic flaming barricade. The vast majority remained, sensing that by the time the others reached their destination it would be all over. They would leap down onto the ice and barrel toward the shore.

Jerking his fist down, War bellowed a war cry that shook the heavens. The Swarm leapt down from the stone formations, hitting the ground at a sprint even on legs broken from the fall. The ground shuddered beneath their terrible rumbling advance.

The earth would soon taste the last drops of the spilled blood of its mortal plague.

VIII

MORMON TEARS

Norman's shoulders burned white hot, his breathing now so labored he could hardly move. He didn't know how long he'd been chopping, only that he had nearly exhausted his reserves of energy. Fingers frozen around the hatchet, he no longer even felt its weight as he swung it, over and over, groaning with the exertion. The conversation with Phoenix that had led him out onto the ice with the ax had left the most important thing unspoken, but he had seen it in the boy's eyes.

He wouldn't be coming back.

The tears froze on his cheeks, his lashes so thick with ice that they scraped his eyes. There was a part of him that wanted to scream and run away, but he knew he had no choice but to accept it. There was a certain measure of calmness that came from that revelation, especially knowing that his life would be given in exchange for the prospect that the others might live. He was a military man after all, and such altruistic motives lent a measure of nobility to the art of war. While he had been in Iraq, there had been what they liked to call "civil unrest" at home. People screaming and protesting in the streets about the military's involvement overseas, burning flags in effigy and filling the internet with all sorts of left-wing propaganda designed to further some fat cat's political agenda that they bought hook, line, and sinker. It didn't matter though. It never did. He never expected a hero's welcome and only hoped no one would spit in his face when he finally returned home. It was enough just knowing that he was willing to sacrifice himself for them if need be, for a concept greater than any one person and the very dream that gave them the ability to speak out in a matter that would have led to execution in more countries than not. It was about more than oil, more than anything even dirty Washington money could buy, more even than freedom.

They fought for hope.

Hope that one day there would be no need for an eight year-old Saudi child or his counterpart in Compton to carry an automatic rifle. His army, the army he joined fresh out of high school, had learned that providing hope for a thankless nation that criticized them while they drank their five dollar lattes had to be enough. It didn't matter if back home they slashed the budget for veteran's hospitals or cut their pensions, for if they could help save the world, if only for a single day, it would all be worthwhile. And even today, there was no way of knowing if his endeavors would be in vain or his life for naught, just so long as he had given his friends the hope for survival. He could hang his hat on that.

A loud sound that he at first erroneously thought to be the wind rose from across the lake to his left. He allowed a wan smile to cross his lips. He'd seen the best winds Mother Nature could offer in the middle of the desert and in the hurricane gales on the high seas. This was something else entirely.

"Showtime," he whispered, rolling onto his haunches.

A shriek answered him from his right.

When he turned, he saw nothing at first until the tall bird hopped through the deep snow to stand beside him, cocking is head at him quizzically.

"I don't suppose those wings of yours are strong enough to fly us both out of here?"

It opened its golden beak and screeched at him.

"I'll take that as a no."

The ground shook so hard beneath him that the fissure he had carved into the ice made a loud crack that sounded like the earth had split down the middle.

He finally understood.

"Better get out of here," Norman said. "I can't imagine you're the world's best swimmer."

It shrieked again and hopped up onto his thighs. His eyes locked onto the birds and that milky white faded away to show him a glimpse of several shadows emerging from a cave onto a beach littered with black corpses. The sun shone down on them through the dissipating clouds and he could see the joy on their faces, but most of all, in that spotlight cast from heaven, the look in their eyes was unmistakable. Maybe he had never seen it before and most certainly never would again, but he recognized it nonetheless.

Hope.

With a cry, the bird leapt into the air, sharp talons tearing through his pants and ripping his flesh, but it didn't matter. Those long white wings clapped in front of his face before blending back into the snow.

"Thank you," he whispered, though even he didn't hear it over the rumble coming toward him like an earthquake racing from its epicenter. The ground rose and fell, but he managed to fight through it until he stood and faced the east.

He tasted tears in the corners of his mouth and raised his chin. Black shadows raced past him at the edge of sight, all but invisible in the blizzard. The hissing rose to a level that positively hurt his inner ear, drowning out the sound of the crack he had created as it widened to the point that he could see the black water a foot ahead. Jagged fissures raced away from the main crack, expanding under the snow like lightning bolts. A section of ice broke away to the left, followed by more and more. The ground beneath his feet tipped upward, forcing him to grab hold of the highest edge as an army of monsters appeared, darkening the entire horizon.

They fell through the ice as it disintegrated beneath their awesome weight, and into the painfully cold lake. He was blessed with watching those that dropped beneath the surface become rigid with shock, sinking out of sight into the darkness. Many clung to chunks of ice as he did, their claws so sharp they gouged trenches into the surface before either sliding to their deaths or freezing from the feet up and dropping away. Their dewlaps trilled and they hissed through their dying breaths.

Many of them managed to perch atop the bobbing sections, leaping from one to the next, followed by those who had been far enough back to watch the others fall in before them. The underwater equines, the same seahorse-looking steeds that had brought them there, threw their bodies against the ice from below, toppling creatures down into the water, sticking their heads out long enough to grab hold of ankles and feet, dragging more and more to their demise. A trail of fire rushed toward him, the horse and rider consumed by flames. He saw a blur of skeletal legs moving so fast they never even touched the ground, turning the water to steam.

Legs sopping wet and numb, he struggled to his feet and faced what he knew to be his end. Taking a deep breath, he clenched his fists at his sides, and stared down the rider. In those fiery eyes, all but hidden behind a mask the color of blood, he could see the fires of hell, but he wasn't afraid.

And even in death they couldn't take that away from him.

"We will surviv—!" he shouted, only to be cut short by the hand that reached down from atop the horse. Fingers like knives lanced through the soft tissue beneath his chin, curling underneath to scrape bone. War's palm slammed into his face so hard that his nose flattened.

The almighty War held onto his chin as Thunder stampeded past, ripping Norman's head backwards with such force that his spine easily snapped. They rode on with War carrying Norman's head like a football helmet, leaving his decapitated body to sink slowly down into the Great Salt Lake.

CHAPTER 8

MORMON TEARS

Jill stood on the far side of the sand wall as she had so many times before in her dreams. It felt as though the world had frozen all around her, leaving her standing in the middle of a vortex. She couldn't breathe or think. All she could do was survey the beach around her. A glance back over her shoulder confirmed what she already knew. The others were back there, hunkered down behind the barricade, only their breath rising above before being swept sideways by the wind. To either side, smoke drifted from the smokestacks in the open sections of water where the kelp grew at such an accelerated rate that the leaves now broke the surface of the water. Twin pillars of fire rose from the vents over the pits full of coal on the beach. Turning her attention ahead again, as she knew she would, she waited for the final act of her vision to unfold.

Her body cried out for her to whirl and sprint back into the cavern, to find a nice dark corner and curl up into a ball, but she was rooted to the ground. A passenger in her vessel of flesh. She was like a marionette, forced to stand her ground until the moment she was released, but then what? Her visions had only shown her so much. Beyond that, she was as blind as the rest of them. Or was that simply the end? Had they lined up along this frozen stretch of sand merely to be annihilated?

She shook her head. That couldn't be it. They had been guided here by powers beyond their understanding and whatever it was—be it God or fate or some cosmic hand—hadn't summoned them all through such arduous trials simply to be put down like dogs in the middle of nowhere beneath a nuclear winter of their own creation.

Her heartbeat accelerated when the first two silhouettes materialized from the snow. One leaned on the other, both struggling through the deep snow, falling forward before fighting back to their feet. They staggered toward where the burning blockade cast her shadow out onto the snow. She tried to run out to help them, tried to turn and run away, but she couldn't move.

Another human shape appeared behind them and she screamed.

The first shot threw up a cloud of snow beside Adam before the report echoed from the face of the mountain. She watched in horror as Adam glanced over his shoulder, then looked back in her direction with eyes wide in terror. He grabbed hold of Ray—Dear God! His eyes! They'd carved out Ray's eyes!—and tried to pick him up, but both men just fell into the accumulation with a pattern of steel whizzing over their heads to tear up the snow nearly to her feet.

Jill jumped away, still screaming, but the shot had freed her body from its stupor. She took her first stride toward them and saw more silhouettes knifing through the snow behind the man with the gun, who stumbled after Adam and Ray, holding the shotgun to his right shoulder.

"Hurry!" Jill shouted, running toward them.

Someone ran past her to the right and she caught only a flash of blonde hair. Lindsay reached them a step ahead of Jill, who ducked under Ray's opposite arm to help ease Adam's burden.

"Oh, God, Ray. I'm so sorry. So sorry. I knew…I knew this was going to happen," she blubbered.

"Shhh," he whispered into her ear, giving her shoulder a reassuring squeeze.

Lindsay grabbed Adam by the hand and started to pull him forward. She looked past him and recognized Richard's blood-drenched face leering at her down the barrel of a gun. There was no longer anything human about him. Whatever monster looked out from behind his eyes was even more frightening than the creatures sprinting out of the storm past him.

The left corner of Richard's mouth raised in a mockery of a smile.

Lindsay didn't even have time to cry out. Pellets pounded her chest, tossing her backwards like a feather on the breeze. A spatter of blood washed over the snow before she slammed backwards into it, still clinging to Adam's hand and jerking him down on top of her. His left shoulder landed first, driving his weight firmly into the sloppy remainder of her thoracic cavity, breaking away already fractured ribs and pulping an indecipherable mess of internal organs. His face landed in the snow beside hers. He recoiled, coughing out a glob of slush, and stared into her glassy blue eyes. Her face was freckled with blood, streams pouring from the corners of her mouth.

"No," he whispered, trying to push himself back up, prying his fingers from her death grip. Enraged, he looked back at Richard as more steel flew past, the warm wind of its passage on his cheek. A splash of wetness slapped his other cheek and he knew the pellets had robbed Lindsay of the last remaining identifiable part of her.

He hadn't heard the shot. How in God's name had he not—?

The Swarm rose up behind Richard, whose maniacal eyes had him dead to rights down the sightline of the weapon. Adam spun and propelled himself toward the shore. Jill was having a hard time keeping Ray on his feet, but they had gained a good five yards on him. The others were climbing over the barrier, sliding down and running out to help them.

"Go back!" Adam shouted, waving his arms.

There was no way they would hear him over the loud hissing.

They all froze in place and looked out across the lake.

"Go back!"

But they weren't looking at him.

They were looking past him.

II

MORMON TEARS

Richard felt his heat draining down his left leg, but the rest of his body was growing colder by the second. The frozen lake teetered to either side as the lightheadedness worsened, now spreading through his chest and into his arms in numbing waves, his movements far too slow and deliberate. Only one thought permeated the fog settling over his brain as he leveled the barrel of the shotgun at the two figures in front of him.

Kill.

He squeezed the trigger and the butt kicked him in the shoulder, his shot firing wide and to the left in the snow beside the two figures.

So much for the element of surprise.

He urged his legs faster, kicking up snow all around him. It sizzled on the smoldering steel as he lined up the second shot, shucking the smoking shell into his wake. The person on the left glanced back and Richard recognized him with a grin. It was their leader. Cut off the head and the body would thrash around and bleed to death. Aligning the back of Adam's head with the small sight, he stopped to steady the gun, pulling the trigger and bracing himself for the recoil. His targets stumbled and fell, his shot skimming over Adam's head to tear up the snow all the way to the shore, where someone else stood, screaming as the steel shot raced toward her feet. She jumped away, but instead of running back up the beach, she dashed out onto the lake toward him.

That would only make it easier for him.

The rest of them climbed over the

wall from where they'd been hiding and slid down the sand into plain sight. What were they, stupid? It was like fish jumping into a fisherman's boat. Might as well pass around the gun and let them all do themselves for him. Nah, where was in fun in that? He wanted the pleasure of doing it himself, of feeling the kick against his shoulder and smelling the gunpowder as their lifeblood exploded out the far side. He wanted to see the look of recognition in their eyes when they realized their lives were over and it was he who had killed them. He wanted their last thoughts to be of regret for trying to trick him, for defying him. But most of all he wanted to see their pain, the excruciating agony of hot steel searing through them, shredding bone and organs alike, leaving only the exposed nerves to send their message of suffering to the brain.

Another person sprinted toward his targets, reaching Adam's side and trying to hasten his progress. She looked at him and his blood boiled. It was that same blubbering woman whose feet had cost them hours of travel time and whose incessant whining had driven him up the wall. He'd give her something to really gripe about this time.

He swung the shotgun slightly to the left and fired, a blossom of red bloomed in the middle of her chest before she was launched back into the snow, pulling Adam down with her. There had been only a transient expression of fear on her face, the rest happening so quickly that he couldn't revel in her pain. He fired again, but missed Adam, the pattern of steel pounding Lindsay's face into oblivion.

Roaring his displeasure to the heavens, he shucked the spent cartridge and tried to load another, but it closed on an empty chamber. He jammed his bloody left hand into his jacket and tore off the lid of the box of shells, grabbing a handful and pulling them out. Half a dozen flew from his grasp and dropped into the snow and out of sight, but he retained enough to shove them up into the shotgun. By the time he chambered the first load, his quarry was already to the shoreline. The others stood facing him, wide-eyed like so many deer on a highway.

This was going to be too simple. The least they could do was try to run and create a little sport. What the hell were they doing, anyway? Did they want to be shot?

He ran at them, resting the shotgun against his shoulder and trying to steady the barrel on Adam's back.

Why were they just staring at him? It was as if...

Richard stopped and turned around. He never even got off a shot. Three reptilian humanoids slammed into him as more raced past on either side. Claws tore through his clothing and lacerated his flesh. There was a flash of color like the setting sun from beneath their chins before he saw nothing but teeth. They hooked beneath his skin and ripped away strips, revealing the juicy muscles beneath. His nose was torn away and choked back down an eager gullet. Several of them fought over what appeared to be his hand, which explained why he couldn't seem to get a grasp on the shotgun. Teeth lanced into the meat of his shoulder, jerking from side to side until muscles were torn from tendons, baring his electric nerve endings.

He screamed as he experienced a pain beyond anything he had dreamed possible. There was crippling agony in places he didn't even know were capable of sensation. His rage kept him conscious, acutely aware of every inch of his body, every nerve bundle singing in sheer torture. He couldn't allow himself to be cheated. He had to deliver his vengeance upon those who had defied and openly mocked his power. Pain was only a state of mind, while passion was all-consuming.

Raising his gushing stump, he punched one of the creatures in the face and tried to rise, but fell right back down. He rolled to his side and managed to get to his knees, straightening his legs until he stood. One arm, the bones in the shoulder exposed, dangled limply at his side, the other wedged into his shirt to staunch the arterial rush, he swayed back and forth, the blood loss toying with his equilibrium.

"Where's my shotgun?" he railed, blood draining past his lips and running off his chin.

The Swarm encircled him. They kept their distance as though sizing him up, picking the best cuts of meat.

"Is that...?" he sputtered, his eyes rolling upward, but he forced them back down. "Is that all you've got?"

A blinding light appeared in front of him, his attackers shrinking away from it. After a moment, he rationalized it as fire, the flames revealing a horse larger than any he had ever seen, its skin and flesh stripped away. Astride it was what had once been a man, though he radiated a level of power unlike anyone Richard had ever encountered. The man wore blood-red armor and sat in the middle of the flames as though immune to them. In his left hand was a severed head.

The man reached toward him with a heavily muscled arm and extended his index finger to point right at him.

The creatures descended upon Richard from all sides, though instead of shredding him, they grabbed him and pinned him down, slathering bulbous purple tongues over his exposed flesh, hissing and flapping the scales under their chins. One grabbed him around each ankle and they sprinted back out across the lake. His head dragged though the snow, his arms trailing behind.

"No!" he screamed as the beach fell farther and farther behind.

He couldn't allow them to keep him from completing his mission. He still needed to kill them. It couldn't end like this.

"Nooooooo...!" he screamed, his words fading as unconsciousness finally claimed him.

III

Mormon Tears

Evelyn swept Jake up in her arms, bringing him to her chest. He clung so tightly that she could barely breathe, his legs squeezing her hips. His cries pierced her ears, his tears momentarily warming her neck as he buried his face against it. The last thing she saw before she turned and climbed over the barricade was black bodies rushing inland toward the shore. There was no way they would be able to hold them off. They would crash down upon them and exterminate them mercilessly. They had never stood a chance. All along, despite their best preparations, they had been doomed to extinction.

She slid down the slope, catching her heels on the board bracing the spears and sending them both tumbling into the snow. Battling to her feet, she looked up and saw movement on the cliff above the cave. Large white falcons lined the stone. There were easily a hundred of them, motionless like gargoyles standing sentry over the beach. Where had they all come from? She tried not to imagine them like vultures picking knots of cartilage from their bleached bones where they fell. But animals always knew. They could sense these things.

The others scrambled over behind her, the sound of hissing growing steadily louder.

"Spread out and brace yourselves," Adam shouted.

"Oh, God. Oh, God," Evelyn whispered, turning and looking back out across the lake. The Swarm emerged from the snow from everywhere at once. Golden eyes bored through her from the slick black creatures, trilling straps of brightly-colored scales.

She grabbed hold of the horizontal two-by-four standing from the mound of sand and looked to her right. Her eyes caught Adam's, which were startlingly wide and white in contrast to the blood covering his features. He was similarly poised to shove another long board forward.

"Wait until they're already on the wall!" he yelled to her. "They can't see it coming!"

She nodded back to him, already beginning to hyperventilate and unable to form words.

Past Adam, Mare gripped the plank in front of him, licking his lips nervously as he watched the Swarm closing the gap far too quickly. Jill was ten feet past him with Ray crumpled at her feet, pressing his palms to his useless eyes and trying simply to keep from passing out from the pain.

To her left, Darren positively shook as he waited. She could tell by the way he constantly glanced back toward the cave that it was everything he could do to keep from bolting, but he held his position. He leaned to his left and shouted something to April, but Evelyn could no longer hear anything over the hissing. She was able to read April's response on her lips, though.

I love you, too.

The sentiment hurt Evelyn, her chest heavy in the face of such beauty while the world was crashing down all around them. She didn't even know she was crying until the cold stung the wet corners of her eyes. What had these two kids done to deserve all of this? What kind of God would allow it?

Beyond April, Missy readied herself, adjusting and readjusting her grip on the wood. She looked like a little girl who should have been more worried about what she would wear to the prom than whether or not she would have the strength to push hard enough to drive the spears through the opposite side. Phoenix was at the very end. Of them all, he appeared the most calm. He merely stared out at the monsters barreling down upon them, a pillar of strength.

She turned back ahead and felt her breathing cease. They were close enough now that she could see the glinting of metal armor and scales, claws on the end of elongated fingers, muscles bulging with the exertion. She could see past rows of teeth and deep purple tongues into the gaping maws of their throats.

There had to be at least a hundred of them.

Ten yards and closing fast.

"Not yet!" Adam shouted, but his voice was overcome by the thunder of footsteps and the frantic hissing.

Five yards.

Jake trembled against Evelyn's chest, his small body tightening as he screamed.

Evelyn could see the black shapes marbling their golden eyes, the spittle flying from their savage jaws. And she could tell that they clearly saw her as well, the hunger and rage in their eyes burning like embers.

An inhalation finally reached her lungs and she released it as a scream, throwing the entirety of her weight against the two-by-four. It slid forward until it met with resistance and a wash of warmth rained down on her from the other side. Sinewy arms struck at her from the top of the dike, snapping jaws tossing more white blood onto her.

She stumbled away, unable to pry her stare from the bodies flailing against the spears that moored them. One was simply draped over the sand from a fatal puncture, but the others seemed only angered by the poles jutting out of arms and legs and abdomens, yet unable to pull themselves off.

The creatures behind the first wave slowed, caught off-guard by their trap when they had been expecting zero resistance.

This was their chance.

Evelyn whirled and raced for the cave, her eyes fixed upon the darkened corridor at the very back. Shadows passed over her from above, darkening the sky, but she never looked away from the mountain even as more fluids spattered her from both sides and the hissing metamorphosed into screams.

IV

MORMON TEARS

Darren could only watch the wretched black wave of creatures crashing toward him, parting the driving snow like a curtain. He could clearly see their eyes, the moving black blobs on irises that shined like headlights, could feel them lock upon him, their hunger and hatred shredding his resolve. When they snapped open the scaly flaps of flesh under their chins and shook them, deep red and yellows shimmering like they were breathing fire past wicked rows of teeth, his heart dropped into his stomach.

They didn't stand a chance. The tide would wash over them and wouldn't recede until there was nothing left of them but gnawed bones and bloody slush.

He glanced at April, who was already looking at him through wide eyes.

"I love you!" he shouted, though he couldn't hear his voice over the deafening roar.

She smiled hesitantly, tears lining her face and repeated the words back to him. As he read her lips, he wished to God to be able to hear her words one last time.

One last time.

When he turned again to the lake, they were nearly upon them. All he could see were black bodies dashing through the storm. He couldn't draw air as he watched them, tightening his hands over the board in front of him. He should have practiced with it more to make sure it worked. What if he shoved it forward and missed? Or what if he threw his weight against it and the poles broke off or were frozen in the sand and snow?

It was too late now. He could only trust in the same destiny that had brought them to the banks of the Great Salt Lake from Oregon, across hundred of miles of rapidly changing landscapes and through perils that by all rights should have ended their trek. This time, though, this time something felt different.

The Swarm collapsed upon them. He felt the barrier shudder, nearly knocking the two-by-four from his grasp, throwing ice and sand into his face. It burned beneath his eyelids, grinding as he tried to blink it out.

Darren shouted and shoved the board as hard as he could, the spears firing out the opposite side and skewering the first wave of creatures. The heat of their fluids splashed down on him from above, though he still couldn't see a thing through his watery eyes. He tried to pull back on the board to drive it forward again, but it was lodged in place. The bodies pinned to the other side of the mound flopped against it, punching and kicking, the whole works starting to crumble away.

Dragging his coat across his eyes, pain bloomed in the corners as the dirt scraped the ultra-sensitive tissue. He could finally see enough to get his bearings, but everything still looked like he was viewing it through a kaleidoscope. His tears refracted the light and he could barely keep his lids apart, but there was a small channel through the middle. Nails slashed at him, inches from his face, teeth snapping in front of him like bear traps.

Now! Now! Now!

He whirled to run, but stopped when he looked down the barricade to where April stood. The plank in front of her was still a good half foot from being flush against the sand, the lengths of pole still visible between. She threw her body against it repeatedly, but was unable to drive it all the way through. The sharp tips had done their job on the far side, but not nearly well enough. The creatures were already pulling themselves off of the pikes.

"Run!" he shouted to her.

She looked up and the panic in her face was unmistakable. Her wide, unblinking eyes issued rivers of tears and a scream parted her lips.

To his left, the others were already retreating toward the cave, falling back to the next level of defense.

Biting his lip and tasting blood, he sprinted toward April through the drifting snow. A long black arm reached over from the other side, its claws slicing through April's hood to get a handful of hair. She grabbed it by the wrist with both hands and tried to pry it away. Thin trails of blood poured down her forehead from the gashes on her scalp, frightening her even more. Screaming and stomping her feet, she strained against the thing's grip as it fought to pull her closer to its hissing mouth.

Darren seized the dark forearm with both hands, trying to jerk in opposite directions to break the bones, but it almost felt as though they bent slightly to accommodate the pressure. He had no weapon of any sort to try to saw or hack the arm, so he beat at it with his fists until April finally fell forward into the snow, her momentum dragging the creature over the wall behind her. It dropped the handful of her hair to brace for the impact. No sooner had it hit the ground than it was back on its feet, swaying and pouring white sludge from the gaping wound left by the stake. It had been gored straight through the abdomen, tearing clear through to exit its left flank above its hip. Its brethren on the wall worked themselves into a frenzy at the smell of blood all around them, human and reptilian alike. They ripped though their own skewered muscles, leaving behind chunks and appendages to throw themselves over the wall.

Darren grabbed April around the waist and pulled her to him, his eyes meeting hers. Crimson ribbons twirled over her brow and around her eyes. She bucked into him, arching her back and issuing a scream that spotted his face with blood. Her hips thrust against his and her neck snapped back, a geyser of scarlet firing up into the sky from her open mouth.

"No!" Darren screamed, trying to pull her away with him, but she was stuck. He looked down to see her stomach bulge outward under her jacket and sharp claws slash through the fabric, puncturing his thigh.

He screamed and pulled away, blood seeping into his pants from the stinging lacerations. Stumbling in reverse, his heels snagged on the snow and dropped him onto his back. April appeared to hover in front of him, the tips of her toes an inch above the accumulation. Her legs dangled limply, allowing the steaming blood to wash over her waistband and down their length to drizzle onto the snow. The hand poking out of her midsection jerked back and forth as the creature behind her tried to pull it back without having to relinquish any of the meat.

"P-p-please…" April sputtered, her head flopping forward.

Darren stood and walked toward her, lifting her chin so that he could see her face. Time slowed to a crawl as he wrapped his arms around her, giving the creature the leverage it needed to jerk its fist back out. He nuzzled his forehead against hers, tipping her head up just enough to see into her eyes, so full of blood that it flowed from them like tears.

"P-p-please…"she garbled. He tasted the blood on her lips. "Save your…self."

With her blood inside of him and their flesh separated only by layers of clothing, he felt as though they were one.

"I'm not leaving you," he said.

"Darren…"

"I love you, April."

The touch of a smile graced her bloody lips before her head rolled to the side and fell to his shoulder. Her blood cooling on his face, he saw reptilian shapes converging on him from all sides. He could only hold her against him, their bodies merging together. Closing his eyes, he lowered his face to her shoulder as she had to his.

Talons slashed.

Hooked teeth parted flesh.

Darren refused to relinquish his hold on April as they parted his flesh from bone.

Even in death.

V

MORMON TEARS

Claws tore through Phoenix's jacket and gashed his chest, but he threw himself backwards to the ground and out of reach. The Swarm was frenzied. Even staked to the ground, they thrashed around uncontrollably, just like he remembered from his basement prison, which now seemed like a million years ago. Struggling to stand, he looked to the top of the mountain in time to see all of the birds spread their white wings as one and swoop into the air. A wall of darkness swelled just beyond them as they flew over the field of spikes with talons opened and golden beaks screaming.

Like a tsunami, the Swarm crested the top of the stone formation and leapt into the air.

Phoenix ducked instinctively and ran toward the cave. The birds soared directly above his head to strike at the creatures racing inland from the beach, who were no longer slowed by witnessing the others being impaled along the dike. Hooked talons sought reptilian flesh while razor-honed beaks stabbed at eyes.

He caught a glimpse of Missy from the corner of his eye and veered toward her, reaching out and taking her hand. She was screaming and blood drained down her forehead from a cut along her hairline. She flinched when he touched her hand, but as soon as she recognized him, she grabbed his and squeezed as hard as she could. Together they slalomed through the maze of poles toward the cave, as ebony bodies rained from the sky.

The air shivered with hissing like static

electricity before exploding with spatters of white that rose in opposition to the snow. So many bodies slammed down onto the spears at once that the ground shook.

Phoenix swiped their sickly blood from his face while dodging arms and legs and gnashing teeth, pulling Missy behind him so that she could traverse the same ground. He bore the brunt of the assault for both of them. Nails like daggers slashed through his thighs and forearms, tearing his coat clear down to his chest and into the muscle. His cheeks opened and his lips split, but there was no way he was going to allow anything to happen to Missy. He had loved her in his dreams, but even more in real life. He would sooner die than allow her to feel even the slightest pain.

They were all around him, some staked standing up, run through from below, from their groins through the crowns of their skulls, others lying flat on the ground on their stomachs or their backs as they had seen what awaited them below and tried to flip away. One had nearly avoided the spears entirely, but had snagged its chin and was clawing at the sharp tip poking up between its eyes, what looked like pus spurting from the wound. More fell down atop the others, crunching them down to the ground to die slowly beneath them. Stakes broke along the shaft, leaving the creatures that had fallen on them to try to pull out the jagged edges.

The snow melted with the heat of so much spilled blood, the staked bodies straining against the poles like so many junkyard dogs against their chains.

A crowd of the Swarm stood high upon the mountain, having witnessed what had happened to their faster brethren. They cocked their heads as they studied the carnage, before lowering to their bellies and slithering down the steep rock, claws seeking any minor imperfections in the surface.

Phoenix ducked into the cave below them, barely able to stand. The pain was excruciating, but he would recover. All that mattered was that Missy was safe for the moment. He tugged her out from behind him and pushed her ahead toward the corridor leading into the heart of the mountain right behind Evelyn and Jake.

Releasing her hand, he turned again to face the shore.

"What are you doing?" Missy yelled.

"I'll be right behind you."

"Don't go back out there!"

He looked back at her and smiled. She gasped and clapped her hands over her mouth in shock at the sight of so much blood. It covered his face and was already soaking through his clothes.

"I won't let anything happen to you," he said, staggering back out into the blizzard.

VI

MORMON TEARS

Mare grabbed Jill by the arm and pulled her away from the mound of sand. She had thrust the spikes outward with all of her might, but it hadn't been hard enough. The creatures were stunned, but by no means paralyzed. They screeched and hissed as they pried themselves from the tips of the dowels, but were already freeing themselves far too quickly and tumbling over the crest of the barricade onto their side of the beach. Farther down he could see them hurdling uncontested over the wall, splashing down into the warm water, trampling the kelp and kicking through their system of pipes. When they reached the land they broke into a sprint directly at them. Their best defense had merely slowed them down.

They were straight up screwed. Hell, in for a penny in for a pound.

He pulled Jill right up to him and kissed her on the lips, staring right into her startled eyes. Releasing her, he shoved her in the opposite direction.

"Go!" he shouted, dropping to his knees beside Ray.

Wrapping his arms around Ray's chest, he groaned as he heaved him to his feet and tucked his hand under Ray's elevated arm, bracing the other guy's weight against his hip.

"It's just you and me now, buddy," he said, though he was certain that Ray couldn't hear him. Ray's chin bounced against his chest and what little skin was visible beneath a mask of blood was pallid. Ray's legs dragged uselessly through the accumulation, making each step a challenge.

The thought of dropping Ray and leaving him on the beach flashed across his mind, followed by images of Ray's body being scavenged by those creatures, but Mare shook it away. There was no way he was leaving him behind. Ray had sacrificed his eyes, and quite possibly more than that, for Jake, for all of them. What kind of man would he be if he weren't willing to do the same?

But he was just a kid himself.

No… He had shed the last of his adolescence with his tears over his father's reptilian corpse.

An enormous white bird screamed over his head, forcing him to duck under its fanned talons. He didn't need to look back to know what the bird was attacking. The hissing had reached a fever pitch and sand patterned the back of his jacket like buckshot from the creatures slashing at the wall to try to free themselves while others clambered over their backs and leapt down in pursuit. They were relentless.

Jill stopped and turned to face him, her eyes widening as the tide of black bodies rolled over their seemingly insignificant barricade.

"Just go!" Mare bellowed, waving his free arm at her.

She paused before shaking her head and running back toward him.

"No!" he screamed.

The sky darkened overhead.

Jill ducked under Ray's opposite arm and together they hurried toward the cave as black shapes plummeted from above. They struck the spikes all along the beach, hissing angrily as they were impaled. Claws raked their legs from floundering forms pinned like so many butterflies, but they were able to avoid the rows of teeth that snapped at their heels.

The Swarm attacked from the sky like meteorites, staking themselves atop those who had leapt ahead of them, while even more raced inland from the beach. Fragments of wood and splinters tagged Mare and Jill from either side, the piles of writhing bodes all around them more than waist deep even on top of the snow turning to bloody slush. They had to turn sideways to navigate the maze of bodies, stepping over the corpses while trying to stay out of reach of the living, whose nails rent their clothing, tearing the skin. Mare screamed in pain but pressed on, knowing the only alternative was death. Even were he willing, there was no way he was going to let anything happen to Jill. If that meant his skin would be flayed from his bones, then so be it. All they had to do was make it to the cave and down the tunnel. From there they could barricade themselves in there until…until what? Forever?

He dared to look away from the slashing arms and teeth to the cave in time to see Evelyn disappear into the darkness with Jake. Phoenix was leading his sister through the melee ahead and off to his right, allowing himself to be carved like a Thanksgiving turkey to protect Missy. In that moment, he completely changed his opinion of the albino kid.

Phoenix shoved Missy into the cave and turned back to face him. Mare couldn't believe the sheer amount of blood covering him. There were gashes all over his face and arms, across his chest and down his legs. Not the white sludge that coursed through those creatures, but his own crimson life soaking his tattered clothes. Mare didn't even want to know if he looked a fraction as bad.

They stepped around Phoenix, who just stood there looking past them, oblivious to their presence. Mare helped Jill through the stone doorway, grateful to be out of the snow and wind, and into the darkness, walking backwards to carry as much of Ray's weight as he could. The tunnel seemed interminable, but finally wan light stretched over his back and highlighted Jill's face. Even with her hood pulled down over her eyebrows and the tears frozen on her cheeks, she was just about the most beautiful woman he'd ever seen in his life.

"Help me set him down," he said as they stepped out of the corridor and into the cavern. Leaning Ray's back against the wall, they lowered him to his rear end, trying to prop his head upright.

Mare headed back toward the tunnel to the outside.

"Where are you going?" Jill asked.

"I've got to go back out there."

"You need to stay here…with me." She looked up at him with those stunning eyes shimmering.

"I'll be back before you miss me," he said, flashing his trademarked cocky grin, though he was so terrified he felt like he might hurl.

"But you're cut all over," she said, placing her hands on his cheeks and pulling them away bloody.

"When I get back you can do whatever you want to me." He froze. "I mean…you can take care of whatever… Aw, screw it." He ran back and kissed her.

"Please," she whispered, unable to meet his eyes as she pulled away. "Don't go."

God, how he wanted to stay with her, but his destiny was outside in the storm. He could feel it twisting around inside of him like a tapeworm.

"I…I gotta go," was all he could think to say. Tearing away from her and hearing her start to cry physically pained him.

"Mare!" she called after him, halting him no more than a couple of steps back into the darkness. "Just promise me you'll come back…"

"Count on it," he said, though as he ran back down the corridor, his blood draining in rivulets down his skin, he prayed he was right.

Exiting the cave, he came upon Phoenix from behind and sidled up to him.

"Thanks for taking care of my sister," he said, following Phoenix's line of vision in the direction of the shore to where a crowd had swarmed into a cluster of striking arms and snapping jaws just their side of the barrier and off to the left. Shreds of clothing and flesh flew from their midst, enticing even more to throw themselves into the fray.

"God have mercy," Phoenix whispered.

Flames rose from the shoreline, burning through the blowing snow.

The shadow of a man stood between them and the rising blaze, which grew taller and taller until, like a comet, it soared over the sand barrier.

A fiery horseman atop his monstrous burning steed.

"Jesus Christ," Mare gasped. "What the hell is that?"

"War," Phoenix said, his whole body shaking. "The time has come to make our stand."

VII

MORMON TEARS

Adam finally had to turn away from the scavengers tearing each other apart over what little remained of Darren and April. Watching them meet their fate in each other's arms was like the most beautiful sunset. He couldn't steal his eyes away even though it positively hurt to watch. There was such nobility in their sacrifice that he couldn't imagine anything more touching. Halfway between the shore and the cave, he had seen those who would make it to momentary safety vanish through the dark corridor and those who would not fall before his very eyes. There was nothing he could have done to change anything. It had all transpired too quickly.

He could still see Lindsay's blonde hair out on the lake beside a starburst of her blood. A crimson trail led away into the storm from where Richard had been dragged off into the night. The Swarm was only now dissipating down the beach, leaving in their wake piles of bones amidst the carnage of man and beast alike.

So many of his friends had already fallen…

A dawning sense of awareness blossomed within him. He could feel Evelyn's fear as she stood in the shadows with Jake against her chest, the child's cries in her ear and her eyes affixed to the mouth of the tunnel, waiting for…him. Jill knelt over Ray, alternately checking for his pulse and feeling his shallow breathing on her cheek. Missy stood in the center of the tunnel, wishing for nothing more than to run down the corridor and drag Phoenix back with her, kicking and screaming if she must. Instead, she knew what she needed to do and walked over behind the wheeled contraption. Soon enough she would have to charge into the darkness behind it.

Adam saw all of these images in a single flash before they were stolen away and replaced by a feeling of terror that raised every goosebump on his flesh. He turned and looked to the cave, seeing the same expressions on Phoenix's and Mare's faces that he felt upon his own. They sensed it too…the calm before the wrath of the storm, the gentle inhalation of a bomb before exploding.

The snow no longer gusted sideways, but rather fell straight down. The creatures crowding the beach stood still in anticipation, studying them before looking back over their shoulders at the frozen lake. The flock of falcons circled nervously overhead, blending in and out of the snow. For the first time in what felt like forever, the lapping of distant waves reached the shore. It was as though the entire universe held its breath in anticipation of what all knew was to come.

Silence washed over even those dying on the pikes, their blood merely pouring out as they watched the eastern horizon with glazed eyes.

A muted aura of light stained the snowflakes before separating by degree. Flames drew contrast against the night, celestial tendrils of fire that issued no smoke, only the savage heat from the heart of hell and the stench of brimstone. A shadow took form in the core of the blaze, moving toward them across the ice in strong, steady strides. A large, elongated equine head materialized atop a broad body with thick, bony legs. As it drew closer, its skeletal contours became clear. It appeared to be the source of the fire, rising from white hot orbs and burning hooves.

The rider astride it was enormous, easily a full head taller than anyone Adam had ever seen, an imposing, wide-shouldered mountain of a man. He wore skin-tight armor that looked like armadillo hide, fitting together in sections to accommodate fluid motion. A smooth shield covered his face, marred only by two ragged slashes for eyes. Spikes stood from his skull and shoulders like an ancient gladiator. And even as the fire consumed him, he appeared impervious to it, feeding on the flames. He was the color of blood, as though he had been bathing in a lake of it.

Adam's mind raced back into his memories of the caves in Ali Sadr.

Lakes of blood. That thought triggered the memory of something else…of lying on his back in the bed of a convoy truck in the Iranian desert and looking back through the dust raised by the tires to the mountain he had only narrowly escaped. Four figures had emerged atop a rock cliff…four silhouettes to match the four friends he had lost in the depths of that earthen tomb.

"Keller?" Adam whispered.

As if his voice alone had shattered the calm around him, the wind arose with a furious wail, battering him with snowflakes. The rider jerked on reigns of bony spikes and spurred the massive steed to rise to its heels, kicking flaming front hooves at the air before slamming them down, already charging toward the beach.

Adam whirled and sprinted toward the cave, where Mare and Phoenix were waiting in its open mouth.

"Run!" he shouted, waving his arms frantically.

Mare snapped out of his stupor and turned to race back into the tunnel, but Phoenix placed a gentle hand on his shoulder and he stopped. Phoenix whispered something Adam couldn't hear, to which Mare responded with a nod.

"What are you doing?" Adam shouted, preparing to throw both boys over his shoulder if he had to. "It's right behind—!"

Phoenix cut him off by taking him by the arm and slowing him.

"No more running," Phoenix said, his pink eyes unflinching. "Now we must face our judgment. Stand or fall, we shall do so right here and now."

The ground shuddered beneath their feet from the thunderous advance of the red rider. Angrily roiling clouds split with lightning, stabbing the ground all around them, striking the poles and shaking to rip free. The smell of cooking flesh from the dead and dying staked to the ground filled the air with deep black smoke that choked back even the storm, covering the entire area like a fog.

Adam looked deeply into Phoenix's eyes and for the first time since they'd rescued him from that basement in Pennsylvania saw the tremor of fear. The younger boy took him by the hand and gave him what should have been a reassuring squeeze, but to Adam it felt more like a parting gesture. When Phoenix finally released his hand, Adam turned away from the blood-drenched boy to face the shore.

The stallion slowed as it reached the mess of death and the spears standing from the carnage. The giant man surveyed his fallen army as the electricity continued to strobe the sky, striking the ground all around him until the black creatures began to openly burn. Behind him, the Swarm closed rank, choking off any possible access to the lake. They watched through glowing eyes, dewlaps flared and trilling, claws clattering anxiously.

Adam couldn't breathe, the oxygen deficit slowing his thoughts to the point that he could only focus on the man in crimson, who trotted his steed sideways to block off the lone remaining path away from the cave. The red rider raised his left arm and held high a large spherical object, which he threw toward Adam. It bounced along the snow until it came to rest at his feet. Adam feared taking his eyes from the man for even a moment, but risked a glance at the object.

Twin burned sockets stared up at him from the charcoaled skin, the mandible newly ripped off, hanging broken and askew by a single attachment. The teeth were the only part of it of any color, stark white against gray gums. Despite the fact that the lips and ears were burned to nubs and there was no hair remaining, Adam could tell exactly whose head it was.

"Norman," he gasped, raising his stare to meet the horseman's. Their eyes locked, the snow blowing between them, and Adam began to hyperventilate. Not from fear, but from an unadulterated rage that radiated outward from his chest and into his fingertips in searing hot waves. Lips writhing over his bared teeth, he lunged to his right and grabbed the nearest sharpened pole, bracing his foot on the cooked corpse and jerking it out with a slurp.

His shoulders heaving, Adam grasped the pike and held it across his chest.

War's eyes narrowed behind the slits in his mask, the flames rising even higher, and Adam could tell even without seeing the monster's mouth that he was smiling.

Mare walked tentatively up to Adam's side and pulled another pole from one of the dead bodies and tried to look formidable, even though he felt like he was about to wet himself.

War's head snapped back until he was looking up into the flashing clouds and he bellowed a war cry that shook the heavens and earth alike, the sound like two airplanes slamming into each other in midair, of the roar of fission at ground zero.

It was the sound of impending death.

The sky came to life with movement, the world around them turning white. Wings pounded Adam and Mare in the face as hundreds of falcons descended as one, battering them until they had to raise their arms to shield their faces, watching the golden beaks and talons through the gaps between their forearms. When the assault passed, they were still facing the horseman, feathers floating to the earth with the snow.

But War was no longer looking at them, but past them into the mouth of the cave.

When Adam turned, he was unprepared for what he saw. All of those great white birds were attacking Phoenix, pecking with golden beaks now red with blood and slashing with talons dripping with it. Spatters of crimson flew in all directions, patterning the snow in an abstract design of pain. He saw Phoenix's eyes through the flapping wings. They were cool and calm, barely even blinking as his face was sliced over and over.

The flock of falcons arose into a churning chaos of wings and bodies, sloppy beaks screaming as they swirled overhead, creating a rain of blood.

Phoenix attempted a smile, but even that was too much pain. He felt as though his entire life force had bled out of him. He dropped to his knees in the snow, a fresh layer of blood covering every available inch of skin, darkening his jacket from the multitude of wounds beneath his tattered clothing. His eyes rolled upward and he fell forward into the accumulation, unconscious long before he could attempt to raise his arms to break his fall.

"Phoenix!" Adam shouted, running to his side and thrusting his hand under the boy's zipped jacket to feel his carotid pulse. It was weak and thready, but present nonetheless.

He again stood and faced War, the sky overhead alive with enormous birds circling over the beach. They let out a shrill cry that split the night and were answered by a fevered hissing.

Adam lowered the spear and pointed it at War.

Lightning pounded the trembling ground.

And from the black soul of bedlam, the nightmare siege commenced.

VIII

MORMON TEARS

Adam charged through the smoke toward the glow of the flames, aligning the tip of the pole with the point where he imagined War. He was only going to get one good shot at this, and Lord only knew what would happen if he missed.

Screams echoed in his ears as ivory shapes knifed from the sky, swirling the snowflakes and smoke around him. He expected to feel avian talons gashing his skin, but they sped past and around him, barely clipping him with their long wing feathers. The flames grew brighter as he ran until they towered over him, the dark shapes of the mighty steed and its master forming within the ethereal core of the blaze. The horse bucked and shrieked, but it wasn't until Adam was within striking distance that he saw why.

The entire flock of falcons had descended upon War, slashing at him with claws and beaks still wet with the boy's blood. Where the talons struck, the armor split, issuing fingers of steam as though their avian weapons were coated with acid. Sections fell away, revealing black skin the consistency of charcoal. They attacked over and over, dropping onto him, slashing and nipping, before rising back into the whirlwind of feathers and bodies above him. He swung at them with fists from which sharp spines stood from the knuckles, but it seemed that for every breast he pounded and dropped to the ground, two more fell upon him. His mask was slashed diagonally in half from above his left eye across his nose. Swatches of ebony flesh were exposed on his chest and abdomen, the shield over his neck cast aside onto the piles of feathered bodies on the ground. Chunks of armor fell from his arms and legs, and where their bloody claws raked his skin, it parted like scorched sausage to weep pustulates.

Yet still he battled against them, Thunder bucking beneath him and rising to its full height to strike at the flock with fiery hooves. They clawed at the beast's burning eyes until the flames were doused, leaving only sightless black holes in its skull. It shook its head in rage, flailing so violently that War leapt from its back into the snow. Where his feet struck, fissures opened in the beach, racing away from him in all directions, sand and snow pouring down into the widening cracks. Reptilian corpses fell into the maws on cascading sand, the long wooden spikes now leaning at angles to each other.

Thunder stomped the ground and bolted blindly toward the cave, racing away from the birds that still dove at it from all angles. Mare froze as the stark white skull aligned with him, its spiked mane standing above its head. Raising the pike, he pointed it at the stampeding stallion, his feet rooted to the ground.

The spear trembled in his grasp, or maybe it was the earth rising and falling under those massive fiery hooves, but he managed to keep it directed ahead, watching as the beast shook its head violently, snorting fire in all directions. Mare bellowed in terror as Thunder bore down upon him.

Crack!

The pole shattered the steed's frontal bone just above its left eye before it collided with Mare, its massive chest throwing him into the snow.

Mare's breath escaped in a scream, his fractured ribs prodding him internally. A rear hoof stomped on his ankle, pain racing up his leg and into his hip. He managed to roll over onto his stomach, choking for air, each failed attempt at inhalation bringing with it a brand new level of agony, and watched the flaming hooves race away from him.

Thunder still shook its head to try to dislodge the pole standing from its skull like the horn of a unicorn. Adam threw himself to the side to avoid the collision, the steed blowing past him into the shadows. It impacted the rear wall of the cave with such force that the spear was driven through the back of its cranium. Bones shattered and an enraged equine scream was cut short. The skeletal stallion swayed from side to side momentarily before collapsing. Bones clattered to the ground as joints dissociated, the fire it produced sweeping across the remains to finally consume that which had held it at bay so long. The bones blackened instantaneously, returning the beast to the death that had befallen its mortal form.

Wrapping his arms around his chest, Mare finally drew breath, struggling to rise to his knees. The pain was beyond anything he had ever experienced. A glance behind him confirmed what he already knew. His right foot bent away from his lower leg at a sharp angle, the toe of his boot pointing at his face. He felt unconsciousness rising within him in bleak waves, but couldn't allow it to claim him.

Adam turned away from the dwindling flames and charred bones that lit the mouth of the cave. Phoenix lay face down in the accumulation in front of it, bleeding the snow a meek pink. Mare was still somewhat alert, though he couldn't seem to make it to his feet and was crawling far too slowly toward him, using only one arm for leverage, the other cradling his chest, his useless leg dragging behind. Ahead, War faced him down through the snow-clogged smoke, the falcons still swooping at him, but their talons no longer appeared to have the same effect. He simply swatted them away, unfazed by those that passed through his defenses, their dry claws only glancing off his armor. The Swarm gathered behind him, a wall of evil revealing itself through the storm. They stood or crouched, dewlaps folded to their necks.

Waiting.

The last of the falcons flew away from War, unable to flutter very far on its broken wings before taking a nosedive into the snow.

Adam had no idea what to do. Charging would surely mean his death and running would only stall the inevitable.

He dropped the spear and ran to Phoenix, grabbing him beneath the shoulders and pulling him up out of the snow. Wrapping his arms around the boy's chest, he dragged him toward the cave in reverse, never taking his eyes from War, whose left eye flamed from the exposed half of his burned face.

War strode forward, crunching the carcasses of fallen birds, clenching and unclenching his fists. One was still armored, the other bare and black. The Swarm advanced with him, allowing the scaly capes to unfurl beneath their jaws.

Adam growled with the strain, urging his tired legs to move faster and faster until Phoenix's trailing heels slid out of the snow and onto the smooth rock floor, where he rested the boy gently on his back. He ran back out into the storm and grabbed Mare beneath his arm, eliciting a scream of pain, and helped slide him through the snow and into the cave beside Phoenix. When he turned again, War was only a dozen paces ahead and closing fast, the Swarm right on his heels.

Adam scrabbled forward and pulled his pole out of the snow, flipping it around to direct the tip at the red rider. His eyes scoured War's body for its most vulnerable point. Armor still shielded the majority of his head. A portion of the abdomen was exposed, but best case scenario, all he could hope for there was a wound that would slowly bleed him to death or lead to a terminal septic infection.

War closed half the distance, now so close that Adam could see the muscles working beneath the charred skin where it had been freed from the crimson throat plate.

The horseman's neck was exposed, but he guarded it with his tucked chin. That left only the half of his face where Adam could see the barred teeth and the contours of bone.

And the fiery eye.

It was his only chance. If he failed, they would make short work of Mare and Phoenix, who he prayed to God were trying to crawl back into the cavern where they could barricade themselves inside. But when he looked back, they were no longer alone. Missy and Jill had come out of the tunnel and were trying to help drag Mare and Phoenix into the mountain.

"Hurry!" Adam shouted, his head snapping around to face War, who was nearly upon him.

The giant man raised a fist and Adam lunged toward him, holding the long spike high above his head and slamming it forward with all of his might. The tip struck where he prayed it would, the pointed end pounding straight through the burning socket and out the other side.

War roared in rage and pain, a sound like a sonic boom. Rocks cracked and fell away from the face of the cliff. His lone good eye focused on Adam with such intensity that his prey could feel its heat. He grabbed the pike with his right hand in front and his left behind, and rather than trying to pull it out either side, he snapped it in two and cast the splintered halves into the snow. Adam's heart sank and his breath staled in his chest.

He had failed them all.

And as War lumbered toward him, he could feel death was at hand, his soul weighted by the promise of the slaughter of his friends and the knowledge that it was all his fault.

CHAPTER 9

MORMON TEARS

Even at the far end of the tunnel, Missy could hear the eruption of hissing and the shrieking of the birds. It echoed behind her in the cavern like the moaning of the ghosts of warriors yet to fall. Piercing her ears, it lanced through to her very soul, tearing her apart inside. What were they doing? They were cringing in the shadows while the others faced an entire army of the creatures her father had become. If there was one thing she had learned from that man, it was that only bad things could happen when you tried to hide from the world. She and Mare had witnessed it on countless occasions, their teenaged lives deteriorating to parallel their father's self-destruction. Yet Mare was still out there in the blizzard, risking the only life he had against seemingly insurmountable odds, while she listened to the rising sounds of his impending demise. And then there would be no one left to stand in the way of the mutated armada. They would fire down that tunnel like bullets through a rifle. Maybe they could impale a handful of them on their spiked battering ram, but then what?

There were five of them: three women

barely out of their teens, one blind man who, for all she knew was already dead, and a child. By the time they moved all of those heavy rocks behind the blockade to keep the Swarm from shoving it back down their throats, the cavern would be crawling with them.

She looked to Jill, who had managed to at least clean up Ray's face with a rag soaked in a puddle of water. The melted water trickling down through the fissures was anything but clean, but it was the best they could do. It wasn't going to heal any of Ray's wounds, but it felt criminal to do nothing. Jill raised her eyes to meet Missy's stare, and within she could see the same doubts and hopelessness. It felt as though they were lying in their graves just waiting from someone to come along to bury them.

"They need our help," Missy said, her voice echoing into the darkness.

"The plan was for us to stay here."

"And listen to them die?"

"I didn't say I agreed, but what good can we possibly do?"

"More than we can here, that's for sure."

Missy glanced at Evelyn, who stood behind the fortified pushcart, pacing back and forth in an attempt to soothe Jake, whose tears had finally run their course. His head rested on her shoulder, his eyes closed, only his quiet whimpering betraying his consciousness. Evelyn had been watching them, following along with their conversation. Her bland affect tipped nothing of the though processes behind, her feelings a mystery until she finally spoke.

"We can't hide in here while the others die," she said, her eyes steel.

"So what can we do?" Missy asked. "We're unarmed and outnumbered, and I don't know about you, but I've never even been in a fight in my life."

"Neither have I, but what choice do we—?" Jill started, but she was blinded by a light that transported her in her mind. The light peeled back and became millions of snowflakes choking the sky. She saw Missy standing in the mouth of the cave, screaming, her entire body covered with blood. Phoenix crumpled against the rock wall, head hanging limply forward. Mare on his back, crying out in agony. A giant armored monster beyond her worst nightmares tromping through the snow, crunching the carcasses of dead birds so white they were nearly indistinguishable from the ground. And behind that blood-red monster, his cooked flesh showing through where the armor had been knocked away, was a gathering of those creatures, held at bay by their master's outstretched arms. The scent of death was all around her. Not the smell of cooking flesh as before, but of raw flesh torn asunder, of fresh blood rising to the surface, and formerly trapped gasses escaping from butchered bodies.

Lightning slashed the sky, freezing the falling flakes in midair like a camera's flash, and she screamed.

"Jill!" Missy shouted, shaking her by the shoulders, their faces only inches apart. "Are you all right? What's happening?"

The red glow of flames faded from Jill's vision to reveal the dimly-lit cavern, her cries still echoing in its depths. She dropped to her knees, slipping from Missy's grasp, exhausted. The vision had drained her of her strength, the speed and ferocity of its onset punching her like a fist. Panting, she looked up at Missy, who teetered from side to side until the floor finally held still beneath Jill, her equilibrium rushing back with a wicked migraine. She opened her mouth to warn Missy not to go outside, not to rush to the aide of the others, but she held her tongue before she could speak. If she had learned anything from these glimpses into the future, it was that these events were already destined to come to pass. Instead of trying to run from them, she needed to find the strength to learn from them. Courage in the face of adversity was one thing, but courage in the face of destiny was another entirely. She knew what lay in wait for them at the end of the tunnel. If they were going to face their fate, then she couldn't betray it to Missy and risk allowing her to succumb to it rather than raging against it. She would have to summon enough bravery for both of them.

"God! Did she have a stroke?" Missy called to Evelyn who was already rushing to her side.

"I'm fine," Jill said, her voice trembling despite her best efforts.

"What did you see?" Evelyn asked.

Jill felt a cold hand on her shoulder as she rose and looked up to see Jake's teary eyes staring back at her. He smiled and gave her shoulder a gentle, reassuring squeeze.

Drawing strength from his affirmation, she planted her feet solidly and engaged first Missy and then Evelyn.

"I saw Missy and myself outside in the storm," she said. "And I saw an army preparing to fall."

Missy stared at her as though searching her eyes for the truth she was hiding.

"Then what are we waiting for?" she finally said, turning to the tunnel from which a chilling breeze rushed. She took the first step forward into the shadows. Jill balled her hands to fists, her fingernails digging into her palms, and followed the sound of her footsteps.

"Wait!" Evelyn called after her. "What am I supposed to do?"

"Take care of Jake and Ray. They need you more than we do."

And with those parting words, Jill hastened her pace to catch up with Missy, the temperature dropping with each step until the light began to grow from the far end, highlighting Missy's silhouette. Jill nearly stopped at the sound of hissing, which muted even her thumping pulse in her temples, the pounding of her heart in her chest. She'd never been so terrified in her life.

Missy stepped out into the cave first and paused, making it so that Jill had to slide around her against the wall to enter. Snowflakes billowed through the opening, and there beyond was the man Jill had seen in her vision, with only Adam standing between them. He was a monster of a man, if there was indeed anything remotely human about him, standing nearly a full foot taller than Adam, wide shoulders capped with spikes. He reminded her of a gladiator in his almost-primitive shielding and imposing stance. She felt a scream rise in her throat, but her breath seized when she saw Phoenix lying on the ground. Mare was off to her left, crawling toward her, his face a tortured mask of pain, his shattered ankle dragging behind him at an absurd angle to the rest of his leg.

Dwindling flames lapped at a pile of soot, only the wooden staff still actively burning, though there were still distinct bones in the ashes. A savage gust of wind blasted her in the face, extinguishing the fire and scattering the ebon dust.

"Phoenix!" Missy screamed, running to his side and raising his head into her lap. Her hands shook at the sight of so much blood, the sheer number of lacerations making her cringe. Even the slightest touch opened one gash after another, his outer skin the consistency of cubed steak. She tore off her jacket and tried to mop up the slick layers of blood, even the soft fabric eliciting a hideous moan with each gentle dab. Sobbing, tears freezing on her cheeks, she raised him and wrapped her arms around his slender chest, his head falling against her shoulder. She leaned Phoenix against the wall and staggered to her feet.

Missy stood in the mouth of the cave, dripping with Phoenix's spilled life, and screamed so loud it even quieted the hissing.

In the moment of silence that followed, Jill grabbed Mare by the wrists and dragged him into the tunnel toward the cavern, not knowing how the battle would play out, but certain there could only be more pain and bloodletting.

II

MORMON TEARS

Adam reached to his right, his eyes never leaving War, his hand snatching at empty air until it wrapped around another pole. He jerked it out of the ground with a geyser of rapidly cooling reptilian blood and held it out in front of him, but he was too slow. War grabbed the upper end and snapped it in the middle, stealing both ends from Adam's grasp and hurling them behind him. There was a high-pitched shriek as one of the poles skewered an angry black creature just beneath the right clavicle. It shivered its orange dewlap, tossing blood onto those around it, breaking them out of their trance. They pounced on it, tearing it apart so quickly and methodically that there was nothing left but the bones to clatter into the snow with straps of ripped skin.

War's fist slammed into Adam's midsection and he doubled over, draped over War's forearm. The fist remained where it was, the sharpened scales on his knuckles embedded nearly a full inch into his belly. His warmth rushed out onto that large red hand, which felt as though it was hooked so deeply inside of him that War might never be able to remove it. Even the slightest pressure pulled his skin away from the layers of fat beneath, though he continued to push against War in an attempt to extricate himself, but to no avail. It wasn't until War raised his other fist and pounded it into Adam's face that he tore away with the sound of ripping skin. He landed on his back, the taste of blood filling his mouth and sinuses, and looked up at War.

The crimson goliath towered over him, studying him through that one good eye behind what remained of the mask. One of the creatures lunged at War's bloody fist, managing a quick flick of its purple tongue at the blood before he knocked it aside. The others held back, though the hissing rose to a crescendo.

"Keller," Adam whispered. "I know you're in there…somewhere. You have to fight against it."

There was no sign of recognition in the horseman's eye, only the fire that burned with the intensity of his hatred. The way he looked down upon Adam, as a man might look upon a spider, he knew he was going to die. His right hand fell to his abdomen, pressing on the wounds to hold them together as he kicked at the snow to try to propel himself away. For each increment he retreated, War matched his progress effortlessly.

War stopped and balled his fists, the fire from his eye spreading over his entire head.

Adam prayed for it to be swift.

A scream erupted from behind him and a figure flashed into view from the periphery. War's good eye narrowed in momentary confusion, and he turned his attention from Adam to the blur that leapt over the fallen man and hit him squarely in the chest. The red rider may not have known fear, but he recognized pain, rocking his head back and blasting a sound into the heavens that sounded like the combined wails of all of the tormented souls in hell.

Adam scurried out of reach, but it was only when he turned back that he realized what was happening.

"No!" he screamed, prying another pike from the nest of corpses. Stealing his bloody hand from his stomach, he grasped the spear and raced toward War.

The Swarm was now frenzied, their golden eyes glowing even brighter, the capes under their jaws snapping wide and shaking in anticipation. They darted in and out like jackals at a lion's meal, smelling the blood on the air and that which would soon be spilled.

III

MORMON TEARS

Missy looked out from the cave, her vision red from an overwhelming combination of rage and fear. Her brother lay on the ground in more pain than she had ever seen him, his ankle obviously broken. Phoenix was crumpled against the wall under a skein of his own blood, shimmering in the dying flames from the skeletal horse. His wounds may not have been too deep, but they were positively everywhere. He looked like he'd been dragged through a tangle of thorns, summoning the skein of blood that now soaked her. Everyone she loved was dying around her. The emotional pain was crippling, fueling an anger she never even suspected resided inside of her. She couldn't help her brother any more than she could help Phoenix. Adam stood alone before a monstrosity that would surely crush him, the Swarm going crazy as they waited to kill whatever remained. And for the first time in her life, she felt as though hope had abandoned her.

There was only suffering.

Adam raised a spear in a pathetically futile attempt to engage the armored man, who moved so much faster, snapping the wood and casting it off into the snow. He followed with a fist that caught Adam by surprise, bending him in half. Blood dripped from Adam's midsection, patterning the snow beneath him. He no longer even appeared capable of moving.

All was lost.

Missy screamed as War threw Adam to his back in the accumulation, allowing the emotional fire to consume her. Images of all of her friends flashed before her eyes. Phoenix and Mare broken and beaten. The starburst of blood in the snow where April and Darren had fallen. Lindsay buckling backwards as the steel shot tore her apart. Ray in the cavern with the scabs on his eyes where his orbits had been carved out. Adam lying in his own blood with the monster standing above him. When War's head caught fire, she could bear no more. She sprinted out into the storm, still screaming in anguish. Leaping over Adam, she launched herself at the horseman, trying to knock him down, but it was like hitting a brick wall.

He didn't see her until she was upon him and was unable to get his arms between them to fend her off. She smacked into his chest with a wet slap of blood-drenched clothing, reaching for the burnt tissue exposed by the broken mask with curled fingers. Clawing at his face and eye, she slashed at anything her nails could reach. War's head snapped back on his shoulders and he screamed so loudly that it sounded like the sky would crumble down. The fire burned her hands, and yet she still flailed at him until he was able to push her far enough away from his body to punch her squarely in the chest. She flew in reverse, tripping over Adam and collapsing to the ground.

Missy rolled over onto all fours, sucking at the frigid air to replenish the lungful that had been knocked out of her. Whatever rush of anger had incited her was now gone, leaving a cold, scared little girl to stare back up at War through tear-blurred eyes. She had given everything she had and yet he still stood, her actions only serving to intensify his hatred. They had lost. They had taken their stand and lost. There was nothing left to do now but die.

Exhausted, she couldn't force her body to move. War took a great stride toward where she knelt beside the bloody impression in the snow where Adam had been only a moment prior. Black spires of smoke wafted from his armor and the disintegrating seams. Adam stepped between them, raising the sharpened pole. War paused and clawed at his chest, the smoke growing thicker and darker. Jagged asymmetrical cracks spread through his chest plate, opening to reveal his charred skin beneath. The smoke gave rise to flames, diffusing across the armor, now cracking like an eggshell. Chunks fell away as though links of chain mail, exposing more and more of the burned man underneath. The skin bubbled with the heat of the blaze, popping to reveal amber pus.

War rocked back and screamed, drawing the ire of the lightning, which seared the ground all along the shoreline, striking one black creature after another, their skin rupturing from within and exploding outward with cooked meat and boiling fluids that drove their brethren wild. When War lowered his head again, his massive trunk heaving, the fire took root in the charred remains that had once been Peter Keller. He carved into his own flesh with his claws, but it only served to worsen his plight, opening his fiery core to oxygen and fanning the flames. He dropped to his knees in the melting snow and cursed the heavens with a roar.

Adam seized the opportunity and ran at War, driving the spear through his exposed throat, the momentum bending War's spine backwards at an obscene angle. The lance hit the sand and stuck there, pinning War's head to the ground, his legs beneath him. The flames rose until they stood as tall as War once had, fluids leaking out of his self-inflicted lacerations and sizzling in the pyre that consumed him.

"Come on!" Adam shouted, whirling away from War's body, which continued to thrash, his hands tugging at the staff, but unable to get a firm grip with his useless claws. Phoenix's transferred blood had begun the process of decomposition held at bay for so long, War's fingers stiffening and breaking at the joints.

"I can't…can't…" Missy choked, unable to replenish her air, but Adam scooped her up beneath her arms and limped toward the cave.

Evelyn appeared from the tunnel now that Jill was back in the cavern. As soon as she saw Adam running in her direction, she sprinted to meet him.

"Get her into the cavern!" Adam yelled, passing Missy to her. Evelyn ducked under the younger woman's arm to brace her and started back into the darkened corridor.

"What about you?" Evelyn called.

"I'll be right behind you!"

Adam knelt and grabbed Phoenix around the torso. He lifted the boy from the ground and started down the tunnel backwards. Phoenix's body was limp, so light that it felt as though there was nothing left of him.

"Stay with me," he said, nudging Phoenix's head with his own. The boy's exhalations were so faint that Adam could barely feel them tickling his ear with Phoenix's head lolled onto his shoulder.

Adam looked back to the beach as he shuffled into the shadows, and wished to God he hadn't.

The Swarm descended upon War's dying form, shredding it with practiced ease. Yellow- and black-marbled eyes rose from their feast and latched onto him.

"Jesus," Adam whispered, backing away as fast as he could, despite the stabbing pain in his gut and the burden of Phoenix's weight, as black, lizard-like creatures leapt from what little remained of the horseman, hitting the ground running.

IV

MORMON TEARS

A solitary creature hung back from its scaled kin, staying on the shore as they swarmed en mass onto their former master. It felt the call, same as the others, the combined scent of fresh blood and the promise of death setting its mouth to salivating and tugging at it as though by some invisible cord, but there was another imperative that overrode the first, something that superseded the animalistic feeding compulsion. There was no logic to it. It was now a creature of instinct, though controlled by a more powerful desire than the rest. It wanted to feed, wanted to feel its claws parting pliant flesh, to bury its face in an open maw of blood and organs, to feel the heat draining down its throat and into its starving belly, but more than that, it craved something it couldn't see or hear or taste. Something so powerful that it reverberated inside its bones.

Its crimson dewlap expanded at the sounds of feeding, of gnashing teeth and tearing skin, of fluids spattering the ground, but it resisted the urge and raised its eyes up the steep face of the mountain to the top where so many had plunged to their death. The scar across its eye left a shadow in its vision, but it had long since adapted, even to the constant pain of its split brow and the hole in its cheek that never seemed to heal. It was different and it knew it, though there were no memories to explain why. It simply hungered for something more, something it had come to envision as a blinding light that drew it closer, something that was now so close it felt an overpowering sense of urgency.

It lowered its stare again and weaved through the tall spikes, trampling the fallen minions. Their skin was now loose and sloughing from the rotting flesh beneath, making the footing treacherous enough to curl its claws for traction, tearing them open and filling its path with the white sludge that seeped out. When it reached the stone abruption, it continued upward, sharp claws finding purchase in even the smallest cracks. A third of the way up, it looked back down. The rest of the Swarm had dismembered their master, tasting their first breaths of freedom with the mouthfuls of his blood, leaving only the black remnants of his skeleton arched backwards like a rainbow of death. Lips and claws gleaming, they dashed toward the cave after their prey.

The first pulled up just shy, grappling with its own neck. It opened its shark-like mouth as wide as the hinges would allow and tried to cough, but no air would pass. Its eyes bulged outward and its back arched convulsively. Spreading its claws, it tore out its throat, flames rising from the gash and setting its dewlap ablaze. Three more pounced on it before it could open itself further, savaging it.

Others fell face-first into the snow, floundering before managing to vent the fires inside them through holes in chests and necks of their own design. Those that had gorged themselves were the first to fall, the others either tearing into them or leaping over the carnage, following the scent of fresh human blood. They littered the ground, burning from the inside out at the behest of blood never meant to be consumed. It ate through their scales from within, the master's flesh giving rise to fire burning from their gastric tracts to the outside world.

More and more dropped as it watched, feeling the hunger that would have to wait until the more urgent need was sated.

It scurried up the mountain until it reached the crest and crawled over. One final glance confirmed what its senses already knew. The majority of the others were either already dead or dying, victims of their own undeniable bloodlust.

Their frenetic hissing became high-pitched screams, echoing out of the cave.

It scurried forward on all fours, raising its flattened head every few feet to taste the air on its tongue, separating the myriad tastes, dissecting them one by one until it isolated the one it sought. It was pungent, yet sweet, but still too faint. And if it could taste the object of its desires, then it could be reached. It was only a matter of finding its way through a hundred feet of rock to get it.

Crawling off to the right, the sensation intensified, forming a film on its eager tongue. Its head snapped first one way, then the other, before tilting again to face the sky. It was close now, so close that the taste was driving it mad, working it into an almost mindless whirlwind of hunger. It dug into the snow, clearing it away from the smooth stone beneath, scraping away the layer of ice with its nails.

It caught the scent again, stronger still, savoring it as it trailed down its throat on the massive amounts of saliva secreted into its mouth. Losing conscious control over its appendages, it became a victim of its own instincts, scales peeling away from bloody digits, claws ripping off where they snagged. The smell was all around it, blasting into its face like steam from a vent, stimulating it to hiss its throat raw.

And there it was on the ground in front of him…a wide fissure in the rock where once a pine had sent roots deep into the mountain in search of fresh water. That same tree that had fueled the survivors' fire would prove to be their demise. It looked down into the gap a heartbeat before flattening its head and shoving it within. The stale scents of dust and aged guano rose into its face on the most gentle of currents, but there was air movement nonetheless. And if there was moving air, there had to be a point where it entered. A point where the creature could exit the crevice.

It squeezed its body as thin as its malleable bones would allow and wriggled downward, shimmying in muscular contractions like a snake, the waves passing through its body propelling it into the heart of the mountain. Toward the source of the scent that spurred it on. Toward the blood it could already taste.

Toward the object of the obsession that had followed it even through death and rebirth.

That blood would belong to it again.

It always had.

V

MORMON TEARS

"Hurry!" Adam shouted. Their footsteps still echoed back at him from the tunnel leading into the mountain, while already the sounds of hissing and the scraping of talons on stone were growing louder and louder. He didn't know if they were going to make it in time, expecting any second to be overcome by slashing claws, for Phoenix to be ripped out of his grasp. His back hit the rock wall and he knew he'd found the bend in the passage. Halfway there, but not nearly close enough.

The hissing escalated until it sounded like screams, a noise that caused him to shiver all the way to his soul. A dim light shone around the gentle curve, a subtle aura at first, but before Adam could discern its origin, the answer revealed itself. Dozens of eyes rounded the bend into view, lighting the wall in reflection, shimmering from their smooth scales, highlighting every flexing muscle, snapping jaws and slicing claws leaving tracers against the darkness.

They were gaining too fast. Far too fast.

The creature in the lead fell flat, its momentum causing it to slide along the ground, but the others merely scrambled over it, gaining ground with each furious stride.

"They're right behind us!" Adam screamed, his voice cracking with his rising fear.

The eyes grew closer, shaking like so many flashlights, until the dim glow of the fire in the cavern appeared over Adam's shoulder, casting his shadow onto the ground at their feet. A hand grabbed his jacket from behind, yanking him through the opening into the cavern.

Evelyn was already racing back to the handle of the nail-faced blockade by the time he looked up. Missy was in place to her right, and together they grunted with the strain, pushing the cart forward. It started rolling, slowly at first, but gaining speed as they shoved it forward. Adam watched the doorway until the gap closed and the spikes disappeared into the tunnel. The whole works jerked and both girls slammed forward over the wooden handle when it met with the expected resistance.

Screams filled the air, lancing through the contraption that had impaled them.

Adam slid out from beneath Phoenix, resting the boy's head gently on the ground, and ran to Evelyn's side to help maintain their leverage. It felt like trying to hold a door against the charge of a rhino. It jerked back and forth, the barrier threatening to snap off and leave them exposed, but even with all of the cracking and shuddering, it held. The assault from the opposite side tapered, as did the horrific cries from the other side, until finally the handle stilled in their grasp, the wheels no longer trying to roll in reverse. Light flickered through the cracks between the slats from the burning bodies beyond.

Silence descended upon them, marred only by the distant crackling of the coals in the fire and the occasional dripping of melted snow through the earthen roof.

"Did we…did we get them all?" Evelyn whispered.

"There were so many of them out there," Adam said. "I can't imagine we could have…"

"I can't hear anything out there."

"They could be baiting us, waiting for us to let down our defenses."

They scrutinized the uncomfortable silence, peeling apart the subtle textures to hear even the faintest noise. Every drop of condensation sounded like the thump of a bass drum, their ragged breathing like an untamable wind.

Still they waited.

"What are we supposed to do now?" Jill whispered from his left where she was pulling Phoenix up against the wall with the others.

"I…I don't know, " Adam said, looking to his left at the others. Phoenix was starting to stir, the rise and fall of his chest growing more clearly defined. Mare leaned against the wall beside Ray, staring down at his fractured ankle, biting his lip to keep from moaning, while Ray slipped between states of consciousness, alternately pawing at the crust of blood and scabs on his eyes and letting his head fall slack. Jake crouched beyond, his eyes opened so far it appeared as though he had no lids, tears glimmering on his cheeks.

The morbid realization struck Adam that there were now only eight of them. Eight out of thirteen. That was a little more than half. Five of them had lost their lives so that eight could live. That level of sacrifice was more than he could bear, finally releasing the tears he had held off for so long. Were their lives really worth so much that one had been willing to give his or her life in exchange for merely another single soul?

Adam's hands fell from the handle. He walked to the stash of rocks, pulling the first off the top of the pile and bracing it behind one of the wheels. With the next he braced the other tire. Evelyn and Missy backed away, expecting the cart to come rocketing back toward them as soon as they let go, but when it didn't, they began helping Adam move the stones behind the cart until every last rock was in place and it would have taken an army to shove the blockade back into the cavern.

The lifting and bending had angered the wound in Adam's gut, the fresh seepage running down beneath his waistband and onto his thigh. The sheer pain finally broke through and he fell to his knees, his adrenaline reserves spent. He crawled over to where Phoenix sat beside Mare, his eyes now open, but nary a sound crossing his lips. The boy's face was still hidden beneath a dried mask of blood, through which Adam could hardly see the lacerations.

"Are you all right?" Adam asked, pressing his fingers to the side of the boy's neck to feel his pulse.

"I will be," Phoenix said, forcing a smile.

Adam didn't see Phoenix move his arm, but felt the boy's palm press up against the wound in his abdomen. It was as though someone had run an electric current into the seething maw, a tingling sensation rippling through his body all the way to his fingertips. When Phoenix removed his hand, the pain was gone. Adam brought his own hand away from Phoenix's carotid, the pulse growing stronger with each beat of his heart, and traced his fingertips over his belly. The wound had closed, leaving only the faint impression of a scar. His whole body felt somehow rejuvenated.

"How did you…?" Adam started, his words trailing off. He licked his fingers and smeared away a stretch of blood from Phoenix's forehead. The cuts were gone, leaving only a smooth stretch of unmarred skin.

Phoenix shrugged in response, the inner light returning in his pink eyes.

"I once met someone who could do the same thing," Adam said.

"I know," Phoenix said, his smile dimming. "You'll see him again."

"He's dead."

"True…but now he's so much more."

Phoenix looked into his lap, flexing his fingers before rolling away without another word. His shoulders slumped and his head drooped as he took Mare's ankle between his hands. Mare shrieked, but quickly relaxed as Phoenix moved the bones back into place as though they were made of rubber.

"Thank you," Mare said, bending his toes back and forth. He didn't know what else to say.

Phoenix was already to Ray, his hands trembling as he planted them on Ray's temples.

"I'm sorry," Phoenix whispered, "but I can only take away your pain. I can't replace your eyes."

Ray wrapped his hands over Phoenix's wrists.

"Save your strength. I'll live."

"Thanks to you, we will too," Phoenix said, feeling his life force spread through his hands and into Ray. The scabs crumbled and fell away, the tissue surrounding Ray's eyes sealing closed. The sockets were still gaping black holes, but the ruptured vessels became smooth.

"Thank—" Ray stopped, his heartbeat accelerating. "Did you hear that?"

"I didn't hear anything."

Ray rose and craned his ear to the cavern. It was hardly audible, but there it was.

Click…

Click…

He couldn't find the breath to form words through the knot rising in his throat.

Click…

Click…
"There's someone else in here," he whispered, a split-second before the sound of the first soft hiss.

VI

MORMON TEARS

It lowered its head from the ceiling into the cavern. The light from the fire burned its retinas, but it no longer felt the pain. The obsession it had carried across the afterlife rendered all else irrelevant. It was so close now that it would not be denied. All of the others of its kind were now dead, it was sure. No longer could it taste their vile presence on the air. Only their spilled blood and rotting or burning flesh. It had even survived the master, whose violent passing still festered in its bones like parasites trying to burrow out from the marrow. In an instinctive way, it knew that it should no longer be upon the earth as well, but it was the fervor that had dragged it into this new incarnation that defied even death. It would have what belonged to it.

After a moment of adjusting to the blinding light, it was able to see them at the far end of the cavern, up on a rock ledge by the origin of the stench of his dead brethren. There were eight of them, all full of fresh blood that made its mouth water, but there was one that stood out from the others. He had an aura about him like the sun's rays behind the eclipsing moon. Its heart accelerated until it had no choice but to release the hiss it had managed to hold off since it first saw the light in the room below from the fissure.

It slithered slowly out, flattening itself to the ceiling. They spoke in whispers, yet it could still distinguish their voices from the distance. They were distracted. None of them even looked in its direction. Narrowing its eyes to slits to minimize the glare, it crawled forward. Slowly. Inching along, it watched the ground beneath for the perfect spot to drop. A wash of shadows presented itself, shielded from them by a cluster of stalagmites. When it was content that their attention was diverted, it opened its palms and uncurled its toes, falling rapidly away from the ceiling. Righting itself in midair, it landed on all fours to dampen the sound of the impact.

It craned its head to the ledge above, waiting for any signs that it had been discovered.

Footsteps scuffed on the stone plateau and it held its breath. Voices followed, whispers designed not to be heard from afar.

They knew it was there.

It let out a hiss of frustration and scrabbled around the formation of upside down cones until it reached the base of the ledge, rising until it could compress its chest against the vertical stone. Talons clicking almost imperceptibly, it scaled the rock, urging itself upward without concern for speed, caring only for stealth. It closed its eyes when the voices were directly above it to keep from being seen, and held its breath.

They had heard it. There was no doubt, but they still had no clue where it was. By the tone of their voices and the resultant echoes, it could tell that they were looking deeper into the cavern. It may have lost the element of surprise, but they still couldn't see it right under their noses.

Even as they stood directly above its head, it crept toward them. They would hear it eventually, but not until it was too late.

It could smell its quarry, so close now it could barely restrain itself. It needed the infusion of blood, knowing not why, only that nothing else in the world mattered.

Tensing the muscles in its arms and legs, it was just about to spring up over the edge when the voices startled it, coming from the left where they descended the stone staircase to the cavern floor. One by one they passed, winding around the rock wall until they each passed a paltry couple of feet under its heels. It measured their footfalls, counting five distinct entities now walking across the ground toward the dwelling, trying to be silent as they erroneously thought they had the upper hand.

The one it sought was still above and it knew without a doubt that it could easily slaughter three of them, especially wounded as they were now. One smelled a shade shy of death, though recovering steadily. Another was sticky with perspiration laden with fear. And the third…the third smelled good enough to eat.

It waited until the sounds of footsteps behind it were nearly to the opposite wall of the cavern, every tendon in its body tightening in anticipation. A quiver rippled through its muscular form, emerging from its mouth as a hiss. It heard their gasps of terror and leapt upward, clearing the edge and alighting on its feet. Lowering its head, it extended the cape of scales under its chin, trilling it until it started to flap. It opened its wide mouth, showcasing multiple rows of hooked teeth, spittle spraying from its purple tongue. Flicking its wrists out to either side, its claws snapped open.

The light from its eyes spotlighted them where they stood in front of it, casting their cringing shadows onto the wall behind.

It hissed at them, unable to stand the hunt any longer.

The footsteps pounded across the cavern behind it, but they would never return in time.

Focusing on its prey, it launched itself into the air, preparing to tear its claws through muscle and tissue to free the spurting heat within.

VII

MORMON TEARS

When Ray said he heard something, Phoenix knew exactly what had caused the sound. He had already felt the presence, a presence he knew all too well. It was the source of every misery he had been forced to endure, every waking nightmare. It radiated a sense of impending pain and dread that dripped through his pores and chilled his blood. Even beyond death it was still recognizable. He had known when he slashed the knife across the formerly human face and buried it into its cheek that the encounter wouldn't be their last.

It was the Man, though now he was something else entirely.

Phoenix rose to his feet, swaying. He was utterly exhausted from transferring his life into the others to heal them, the same as he had been after the Man had descended upon him with the Swarm. Only now, the Man was the Swarm, the last remaining of God's army of the damned, his passion, his obsession following him past the grave and into its rebirth. The Man had always told Phoenix that he belonged to him and that he would never allow anyone to take him away, but Phoenix had never truly understood the gravity of that statement until the Man had asphyxiated his own daughter with his blood as punishment for trying to free Phoenix. The fact that his terrible greed and envy had followed him through the netherworld didn't surprise Phoenix any more than the fact that the same unquenchable desires had allowed him to survive the fall of the Swarm to stalk him now. He had always known that it would come to this, the two of them facing each other on the mortal plane with death and God's favor at stake, but Phoenix knew the fate of false prophets. Richard had succumbed to the lure of power, and now Lord only knew what would become of him. The Man was no different. He had lost his flock, his Swarm, in his final play for power as the world was coming to an end, inflicting himself with stigmata by hammer and nails to deceive them.

In a way, Phoenix pitied him. Once upon a time, he had served God in the capacity of a minister, however misguided and zealous his means and motivations. He had brought hope to those who had none and led them into the light. His folly had been allowing himself to absorb their adoration, their worship, as the middle man instead of serving as a conduit to the Almighty. Perhaps Phoenix could find a way to send the Man into the arms of his forgiving God, of appealing to the soul that had once known the glory of the Lord.

The others hurried down the rock stairs toward the source of the lone hiss they had all heard from the shadows beneath, not knowing what they would do if they encountered the creature.

Phoenix allowed a weak smile upon his lips. They would all be safer down there anyway. The Man had come for him and him alone.

Ray still stood to his right, combing the silence beneath the thunder of descending footsteps, while Missy held onto his arm to steady him.

"Why don't you guys go down there with the others?" he said, giving Missy's hand a gentle squeeze. "They might need your help."

"I'm not leaving you," Missy whispered.

"Shhh!" Ray whispered, unable to hear anything.

"Please…" Phoenix whispered into her ear.

She turned to face him and he saw the hurt in her eyes. It made his heart ache to know that his words had inflicted her pain, but versus placing her in physical danger, it was a small price to pay.

"No," she said. "You can hardly stand. Look at you. I'm not about to—"

"Shh!" Ray whispered more insistently. He thought he might have heard—

With a hiss like a ruptured oxygen tank, the black creature leapt up over the edge of the cliff and landed in front of them. Ray stumbled in retreat, tripping over his own feet. Phoenix pushed Missy aside, though not nearly as far as he had hoped.

The creature lowered itself closer to the ground, priming its muscles to strike. Its dewlap snapped open and shook, its long arms stretching to its sides, capped with claws like razors. Phoenix didn't need to see the scar bisecting its brow or the maw in its cheek through which he could see rows of teeth to recognize the thing that had once been the Man. He could see it in the beast's eyes, the same insane flame still burning within. Even when the Man had been mortal, the Man had always looked at him like a starving mongrel eyeing a slab of meat.

"I forgive you," Phoenix whispered. "For all of the pain, for all of the years in darkness, and for the Woman…I forgive you."

It hissed in response, spattering him with saliva and taking a step forward. Its nails clacked on the stone.

Below, the others shouted and raced back to help.

"I know that in your heart you had the most noble of intentions. You gave people the greatest of all gifts. You gave them hope. Look inside yourself, past the hatred and anger—"

It hissed even louder and lunged at him, stopping within inches so that their breath mingled between them. Phoenix could taste the festering meat rising from its gut, but couldn't turn away. He could see the weakness in those glowing eyes. Somewhere, deep inside, his words were getting through to the Man.

"You gave yourself over to a higher power. You can make amends for allowing yourself to become corrupted. You were only human after all."

Something softened behind the amoeboid black splotches on the surface of those golden orbs, but when it melted away, only the rage remained.

It raised both arms to strike him, never stealing its stare from his. He could feel how badly it wanted to tear the skin from his bones, but it hesitated. Maybe he was reaching that last drop of humanity flowing through its pus-like blood. Maybe it—

The creature expelled a tortured hiss, victimized by the emotions brewing inside. It whirled away from him and slashed at the nearest object.

Missy screamed, droplets of her blood patterning the side of Phoenix's face.

Something inside of Phoenix snapped. No more reasoning with it. No more futile attempts at logic. A seething wave of vengeance overwhelmed him.

Missy fell in slow motion, dark fluids arcing from the parallel tears through the front of her jacket. Her eyes sought his before she hit the ground, her face a rictus of pain.

Phoenix turned back to the Man, looking deep into its gecko-like eyes. The rage had vanished as though lashing out had absolved it of the emotion, but Phoenix couldn't see it through his own.

A blinding light blasted from behind his albino eyes, growing out of his pink irises in white hot rays. He grabbed the creature by the shoulders, the light enveloping both of them like a star. Phoenix screamed and the light exploded outward. At the core of the blast was a feeling of hatred that he had never in his life known, changing him in that moment forever.

The searing white aura expanded throughout the cavern, momentarily blinding all of them. Adam and Mare bumped into each other on the stairs, bracing themselves before Jill stumbled into them. Evelyn managed to stop at the base, drawing Jake even tighter to her chest and leaning against the rock wall.

Ray felt the heat and rolled onto his stomach to shield his face.

Phoenix's scream trailed off into a moan, the light returning to him as a though sucked by a great vacuum through his eyes. When his sight returned, he was staring into the black remains of the creature's eyes. Its entire form was now crisp charcoal, which crumbled into a pile at his feet.

Phoenix dropped to his knees and began to cry, his strength all but spent. Never had he even suspected that such power resided inside of him and it scared him. He had used it to kill in cold blood. The Man had turned to him in repentance and he had incinerated him.

Worse still, he didn't regret doing so. He had learned to hate, and nothing would ever be the same again.

Dropping to all fours, he crawled to Missy, collapsing on top of her. He pressed his palms onto the wet gashes on her chest, listening to her sputter and choke on the blood, and forced his life out through his flesh and into her. He gave her everything he had, everything he was, until consciousness fled and darkness drew him into its black embrace.

Now that he had embraced the darkness as well, he feared it might never let him go.

VIII

MORMON TEARS

Adam moved the last of the rocks out from behind the wheels of the cart in the tunnel. They hadn't heard a sound from the other side in a long time, not since Phoenix had killed the lone creature that had circumvented their defenses. The event remained unspoken between them. While it troubled all of them, it was apparent that Phoenix was allowing it to consume him. He had saved all of their lives. Inside that cavern, they had been unprepared to face even a lone member of the Swarm and likely would all have been butchered were it not for Phoenix's intervention. All of them now wore matching sunburns on their faces and any other section of exposed skin, their clothing scorched.

But they were alive.

So many had lost their lives, friends that had been with them since they'd arrived at Mormon Tears, friends whose sacrifices would not be in vain. It was now up to them to not only endure, but to celebrate the gift they had been given. The gift of life, of the future.

Of hope.

Evelyn sidled up to Adam and took hold of the handle between the wheels, waiting for Adam to do the same without a word. Together they drew the contraption back onto the stone ledge, a gust of cold air following it. The only sound was the wind whistling through the corridor, the only scent that of the carnage riding its currents.

Adam took her hand and looked her in the eyes, sharing in her relief and fear. Turning back to the dark tunnel, he led her within, glancing back over his shoulder to see the others waiting nervously to follow. Nodding, they took the first steps forward into the unknown, walking through the deep shadows until the light of the outside world reached into the darkness to welcome them with the sounds of whinnying and crunching.

Snow still blew across the mouth of the cave, though it had already slowed dramatically, the flakes shrinking in size and number. The beach was littered with corpses, the smell overpowering, but if the amphibious winged seahorses on the shoreline had their way, it wouldn't be for long. They moved from one stake to the next, tearing away the reptilian skin of the dead to feast on the meat beneath. They paid no mind to the survivors as they emerged from the mountain and into the open air.

Evelyn looked to either side toward her kelp patches. The pipes had been knocked loose and the plants trampled, but it was a resilient species, and they could always reinstall the heating tubes. She gave Adam's hand a gentle squeeze and leaned into his shoulder, staring out across the lake to the east, where the rising sun stained the clouds a warm pink. There were even patches were the golden rays slanted through the slowly dissipating masses for the first time in what seemed like forever, glimmering on the white caps of the waves in a great section of open water between them and the distant island. Chunks of white floated in it like icebergs in an arctic sea.

They lined up underneath the arch of the cave, side by side, all of them facing a world they would never see the same way again. The terror was still out there, but for now they shared the warmth of the promise of the future like the soft touch of the golden rays reaching down from the heavens to caress their features.

"What are we supposed to do now?" Mare asked, wrapping his arms around Jill and bringing her to him.

"We start over," Adam said. "We honor the memory of those who gave their lives so that we could survive by taking full advantage of the opportunity they've given us."

"Is it over?" Ray asked, wishing he could see the source of the warmth upon his cheeks and the waves splashing against the ice in the distance.

"No," Jake said. He held one of Phoenix's hands while Missy clung to the other. It was clearly visible that something had changed about

Phoenix, his features hardening, his eyes not nearly so round with innocence, roiling with turmoil within. "We still have a lot left to do."

Phoenix released both of their hands and walked out into the snow, his eyes affixed to the eastern horizon. He shivered, not from the cold or its contrast with the sun perforating the clouds, but from the darkness that simultaneously repelled and called to him. It was inside of him now, like a parasite. He wanted to get it out, just reach inside and tear it from within, but he was scared to death of what might happen to him if he loosed it on the outside world again, or worse…what it would do to those he loved.

He turned again to face them, the sun behind him turning him to a black silhouette in their vision, an entity of shadow. Looking from one to the next, he lowered his voice to purvey the gravity of his words and to prepare them for the trials ahead.

"The worst is yet to come."

CHAPTER 10

THE RUINS OF
DENVER,
COLORADO

Richard had given up screaming long ago and succumbed to the intense pain. Consciousness returned in fleeting spurts, but he chased it away in favor of the cold darkness of the unconscious, where the agony was only peripheral, and he didn't have to think about the claws curled around his ankles, so sharp they had carved clear through to the bone, or the snow that continually buried his face, making every breath a struggle. In his mind, he was at home in his den with a snifter of brandy and CNN on the plasma screen, while his body was dragged through countless miles of snow, bouncing off of hidden boulders and skimming over frozen lakes. The only respite came when the creatures that dragged him climbed into the trees to wait out the light of day, leaving him dangling upside down from the branches, never relinquishing their hold. In those moments, when all of the blood in his body rushed to his head, he had no choice but to experience the pain. He wondered how much a man could endure before his body simply shut down, and prayed he would soon reach that point. The pangs of hunger went unheeded, his water requirements met the by the accumulation that fell into his mouth, warming just enough to trickle down his throat.

If he had met with madness before, there was no name for what he now experienced. Rage and hate were beyond the reach of his emotions. Fear was a thing of the past. Now he simply existed, banished to the recesses of his mind, a mind that had shattered like a stained glass window, leaving only the colored shards of a life that no longer meant anything to him upon which to reflect.

When the movement stopped, it took a few minutes to rationalize it. He kept waiting to be yanked upward to dangle inverted, but it never happened. The pressure around his ankles abated and his eyelids slowly parted, even the darkness of night stinging his retinas. He had no idea how long they had been traveling or how far they had come, only that eternities had passed in the interim. The black clouds came into focus above, violet lightning rippling from one to the next, swirling around the top of the black structure behind him. The imposing monolith loomed over him, leaning slightly to the side where the building beside it had fallen to prop it up. All of the windows had been shattered, leaving the exposed framework and girders as though permanently arrested somewhere between creation and demolition, life and death, as he felt right now. There was a shadow in the upper reaches, barely within sight on the top floor. Were it not for the obscene glow of the eyes, he might never have noticed it at all. The darkness and coldness that surrounded him seemed to emanate from the figure. He was frightened to the point that he wished for death, but deep down, he knew that should such a wish be granted, it would only bring him closer to whatever it was that watched him from above.

Why had they dragged him across so many endless miles only to abandon him at the base of this tower? Surely they had butchered all of the others at the hotel. He couldn't fathom the prospect that all of them were somewhere in the black heart of this dead construct. What did they want from him that they had gone to so much effort to procure? Why couldn't they just kill him and be done with it?

Footsteps approached on the fused glass and crusted ice, two sets, their tread so soft it sounded as though they merely floated over the surface. A pair of small, cold hands closed around his left ankle while a larger pair seized his right. Their touch caused exposed nerve endings to sing, racing up his spine and exiting his mouth as a scream. Again he was moving, the jagged earth cutting into his back. Blinking the snowflakes away, he watched the tower as it drew near, growing larger until it eclipsed the sky. They dragged him across the threshold and into the dark lobby, passing the demolished reception desk and uprooted plants in a scattering of the soil that had once housed their now bare roots. His last thought before they dragged him out of the diffuse light and into the absolute darkness was that it looked like a hurricane had blown through. Shattered glass ground beneath him, the waterfall a pile of rubble to his left, the elevator doors standing permanently open, the mirrored walls destroyed.

A foul smell grew stronger with each breath, reminding him of the scent that had bloomed from the fly-covered carcass of one of his grandfather's cattle. Raw meat dissociating from bone, the hide slipping off as whatever infected the intestines gnawed its way out through the rotting flesh. He retched, but was unable to produce anything more substantial than a mouthful of stomach acid.

They turned to the left and he felt his legs lower, his back bending sharply before his shoulder dropped onto something hard, his head ricocheting off of what felt like a boulder. Again and again the process was repeated as though being dragged down a flight of stairs crafted for giants. The repeated blows to the base of his cranium tried to send him into the comfort of unconsciousness, but the fear bound him to his senses.

The descent finally ended and they slid him along on his back, over heaps of rubble and what he was sure had to be corpses, but he couldn't turn his head enough to see. As the uneven floor rose and fell under him, he caught glimpses of the two shapes at the end of his stretched legs in the weak aura of light ahead. One was so small it hardly looked like more than a child, its appendages like twigs. The other was much taller, its contours smooth and polished. As the light beyond them became brighter, it converted them to shadows again. The yellow glow shivered and flickered, cast by flames that came into view as torches on the walls, though rather than burning from lanterns or atop wooden clubs, the fire crackled from human skulls.

Richard tried to scream, but nothing came out. He tried to fight against them, but his arms and legs were unresponsive.

No! his inner voice shouted. *You can't do this to me! Not me! Kill you...I'll kill you all!*

They passed out of the hallway and into a larger room, the walls covered with those skull torches, lending the impression that the whole room was on fire. Tables passed to either side, from atop them the thumping of bodies and hideous guttural sounds unlike anything he had ever heard. There was another sound beneath...a high-pitched whine...vaguely familiar, though he couldn't immediately place it. All he could tell was that it originated from everywhere at once. The ceiling above was slanted, as though the floor above had partially collapsed, invaded by shadows that almost appeared to be moving, writhing like still waters with life forms just beneath the surface.

The hands tightened around his ankles and yanked him into the air, his back folding over the edge of the table. He saw their faces clearly now, one almost skeletal with parchment skin pulled taut over sharp bones, the other appearing to be made of pearl, even his eyes stark white. Their very existence caused him to shake. They were abominations against nature. He had to turn away as they opened his palms and staked them to the table with copper spikes and then did the same to his feet. In that one moment, he was grateful for the lack of sensation, but he would have gladly welcomed the pain in exchange for the loss of sight.

On the table beside him, similarly staked and thrashing against its restraints, was a creature beyond his imagination, the mere sight of it finally freeing the scream from his chest, but it was quickly drowned out by a high-pitched buzzing sound. The walls and ceiling came to life, mosquitoes swarming above him like smoke, descending upon him before he had the chance to close his mouth. Spindly legs crawled over his bare eyes until he closed the lids, pinning them between his lashes, but there was nothing he could do to prevent them from covering his skin. He shook his head, but they still crept into his ears and skittered up his nose.

He screamed against the searing agony of their stingers burning into his flesh, his own cries trailing him into the eternal darkness, along with the image of the monstrosity on the table beside him.

And the understanding of what he would soon become.

II

MORMON TEARS

Jill dropped through the roof of the upper chamber of the pueblo, sitting down on the floor with her legs crossed, across from the skeleton as she had before. She lifted the skull from where it had fallen into its lap and set it atop the bony cervical column. Drawing a deep breath, she took the remainder of the woman's hands into her own and looked into her hollow eyes.

"Thank you," she said, offering a sad smile. "We owe you so much. Everything, in fact."

Vacuous sockets stared back at her through eons of dust.

"Well..." Jill said, not exactly sure what she was supposed to say or do. She had a vague understanding that this woman's people, the noble Goshute, had given themselves to the blizzard hundreds of years prior in preparation for the battle they had narrowly won, offering their souls to whichever of the gods controlled it so that they could help their species persevere without thought as to the personal consequences. They had trusted the decomposed woman's visions enough to build a place for them to live and had then just wandered out into the wicked storm and blowing snow to their deaths.

All for them.

There weren't words to express the kind of gratitude owed for such an enormous sacrifice based on nothing more substantial than the dreams of a girl hardly older than she was. The mere thought that a group of people so long ago could care so much about the perpetuation of future generations was staggering.

"Don't get me wrong," she said, lowering her brow. "We're grateful for everything and all, but I just don't understand. Why would all of you give your lives for us? We were the ones who claimed the land as our own and drove the natives from it. We built the weapons that destroyed the planet and we were the ones hell-bent on using them. Why sacrifice yourselves for future generations who have so little regard for the value of life?"

Silence.

Jill chuckled at herself. She wasn't sure why she had gone there. Had she expected the bones to answer? Perhaps she'd been hoping the woman's spirit would offer a vision to explain everything. There was nothing within the human range of emotion to justify such a gift. Mankind was greedy and self-serving, and as much as she wished it weren't true, deep down, she knew she was too. They all were. Wouldn't the world have truly been a better place had humanity been wiped out? Man was merely a blink of time's eye, and yet they had pillaged the planet of every natural resource, and all but destroyed the atmosphere with industrialization and the landscape of war. Had they the kind of altruism and passion that the Goshute had demonstrated, they would have knelt graciously before the legion of War and done the same to secure the future of species that wouldn't destroy, but rather would rebuild. Wouldn't fight, but colonize. Why should they survive when all man was capable of bringing to the world was death?

The darkness in the skull's sockets drew her in, swallowing her and spitting her out into another time and place entirely. She was standing before a rock wall lit by flames dancing behind her, a blank canvas awaiting the chalk scattered around her feet. She looked down at the colors needing only her inspiration and application, noticing the clothes made from stretched and dried animal skins and the large round belly contained beneath. With great effort she knelt and took a piece of chalk from the cavern floor, struggling to bend with the life inside her. Bringing the chalk to the wall she started to draw, her eyes rolling up inside her head to better see the vision that spawned her art. When she lowered her eyes again, the mural was halfway to completion as though weeks had passed in the interim. Dropping the nub of chalk, her eyes followed it to the ground, where a puddle expanded beneath her.

She saw fires all around her and the faces of natives that she recognized on some instinctive level. Her cries echoed all around her. The source of her pain emerged and was quickly swaddled and rushed away from her, despite her screams and the arms that were not her own reaching for the bundle of fur and the heartbreaking wailing coming from within.

The vision blinked and she was standing in the cave, watching as an old woman with sable hair rushed away from her up the beach to the north, the infant's cries trailing in her wake. She fell to her knees in the sand, pleading with the woman to come back with words Jill couldn't understand. The sand sluiced through her fanned fingers as she crawled toward the lake with the vague notion of continuing to crawl until the salt water filled her lungs and cured her pain, but when she reached the gentle tide, she stared down at her own reflection on the water that lapped at her elbows and thighs. The face she saw was that of the woman whom she had only known as a skeleton, but the eyes...the eyes were her own.

Jill looked away from the image only partly her own and to the distant eastern horizon where the black storm clouds swelled into the stratosphere like dark pillars, through which she could see a single black tower through the passage of time. It radiated a wave of coldness that stung her and she knew she must return to her work. For her. For her child. And for the child of her countless grandchildren who would have to face more than a vision of the tower.

When Jill opened her eyes, she was again in the top room of the pueblo, though the bones were gone. Something squirmed in her grasp and she looked down at the bundle of fur across her legs. A tiny pink face stared back up at her, again through eyes just like her own. The tiny girl's hair was thin and wispy, a shade of blonde so light it was transparent. When she smiled up at Jill, the right side of her mouth curled upward. Just like her father's.

Her consciousness spiraled down into her child's eyes and she emerged into the same room in a place that felt like here and a time that felt like now. She still stared through the generations into the vacant eyes of the woman who had cared enough for her without having met her to give up everything she loved for her.

Will you sacrifice everything for the child? the wind whispered, swirling the dust from the floor.

"Of course," she whispered, tears drawing tracks through the dust on her cheeks.

She looked up through the open hole in the roof in time to see a great white bird leap from the ledge, long wing feathers clapping to gust a smell of dust and age into her face.

She finally understood. There were few things that were eternal, and only one that could be offered willingly. A mother's love for her child could transcend even time, and they had offered their souls to the blizzard so that she would learn that lesson, giving her the only gift that would survive even eternity.

Hope.

III

THE RUINS OF
DENVER,
COLORADO

In the black heart of the monolith, something stirred. Something never meant to exist. An abomination against the Lord and His creation, against even the life that flowed through its veins.

Pestilence opened her mouth, producing a sound like a scream in reverse. The mosquitoes covering its body rose as one to be sucked into the vortex and whisked down her throat. The locusts remained a moment longer, scurrying across its black skin while their seed took root inside of it, formalizing the changes that had twisted its body into something evil, feeding the hatred of the host to give rise to something without pity or remorse. Their red eyes glowed as the locusts sang a final tune with their spindly hind legs. Famine called to them silently and they leapt at his command, merging back into his opaline form.

Death stood behind them in the doorway, fire burning from human skulls to either side of his cloaked head. His eyes glowed beneath, causing his sharp teeth to shine when he spread them into a smile.

Their task was nowhere near complete.

The thing bolted upright on the table, ripping its bloody flesh from the stakes that had held it without knowing the sensation of pain. Rocking its head back, it let slip a roar that made the girders shake in the building's framework, dropping dust onto them all, hovering around them like a fog.

They would not be banished again to the darkness. They were stronger now. Smarter.

The Master that had summoned them

was weak. He could only wage war against them from beneath the pathetic flesh suits of the chosen.

More and more of their experiments tore through their own hands and feet to be free of the tables upon which they had been birthed, grotesque black shadows in the settling dust.

The time had come to usurp His golden throne and replace it with one crafted from the bones of His disciples. Death was supposed to have been the Lord's chosen son. The one to separate the faithful from the sinners and exterminate the species that had strayed from His favor and fallen from His grace.

But in the end, He had aligned Himself with His creations, taking pity upon them, choosing one son over the other.

Death hissed and his blood-red flap unfurled under his chin.

He would kill his brother to spite his Father.

Damn all the rest to hell.

The earth was his. He was God now.

Let them come to him this time.

He would be ready.

His reign of blood had begun.

Turn the Page for an Exclusive
Extract from

God's End
_____

TRAIL OF BLOOD

CHAPTER 1

I

MORMON TEARS

Time passed on the banks of the Great Salt Lake, though the fear never did. Each setting of the sun brought them one day closer to the final confrontation, though none knew precisely when it would come, each rising of that celestial orb stirring the deep-seated terror that today would be that day. Two days had come and gone since the siege at the hands of War and his reptilian army, the Swarm. Two arduous days of watching the horizon for the first signs of movement, of looking over their shoulders to ensure that no one was sneaking up on them from behind. It was the worst possible way to live, though vastly preferable to the alternative. After the first whole day had ended without event, they had begun the process of trying to establish some semblance of normalcy, though it was merely a play they performed for one another.

Adam stood on the white sand with Phoenix, looking to the east as it seemed he always did. The sun had finally called an end to the nuclear winter, the blizzard now a memory marked only by the drifts of snow remaining against the stone face of the mountain where the precious rays never reached them and the spotted chunks of ice floating out on the lake. It wasn't warm by any stretch, but at least the snowflakes no longer fell and the torrential wind had seen fit to leave them be, if only for a while. The sunshine felt divine on their faces, a sensation all had worried they might never experience again.

"So what comes next?" Adam asked. "We know there are still more of them out there…"

"They're waiting for us to come to them this time."

"And what if we never do? The way I see it, they can wait forever."

"Staying here is suicide. I'm sure of that much."

"So how long do we have then?"

"I…don't know," Phoenix said, and that was the truth. He hadn't been able to dream since the battle and the visions had been elusive and incomprehensible. He knew why, of course, but he wasn't willing to admit it yet as it was still tearing him up inside. His silence troubled Adam, he could tell, but the truth would frighten him worse.

Adam walked to the edge of the water, which had now risen several feet, swelling with the melted snow and ice to the point that the barrier they had constructed on the shoreline was now barely visible over the waves a dozen feet out, the new shore only ten feet from the mouth of the cave leading to their subterranean dwelling. Small bones rolled in with the tide before being stolen away like seashells, the last reminder of the Swarm, whose corpses had been dragged out into the deep lake by the giant winged seahorses. The very same creatures they were waiting for now.

He could see them out there in the distance, their coarse, spiny necks cresting the surface like the coils of so many sea serpents, growing incrementally closer, stalking them. The time had come to make their journey into Salt Lake City, but the walk was out of the question. Evelyn's truck was useless without the rear wheels and the gas tank was bone-dry besides. The semi had been consumed by the flames of the barricade they had used to block off the lone point of access from the western side of the mountain and was now buried beneath an enormous pile of charred lumber. They couldn't afford to be gone for several days, not with the future so uncertain, so they had no choice but to count on being able to mount those amphibious steeds. How Phoenix had called to them, summoning them slowly toward the shore, was beyond him, but so little of the world around him made sense anymore that it was simply easier to accept these things and move on.

The beach all around them was still torn asunder from the assault, especially where the ground had opened in widening fissures beneath the red horseman War in his death throes. Sand was only now beginning to slide down into the muddy crevasses that channeled the water during high tide. Originally, they had intended to leave all of the tall spikes that had impaled the invaders leaping down from the top of the cliff, but they had begun to stink to high heaven. They could always replace the poles as the holes still remained where they had been planted, along with the rent earth the creatures had ravaged while trying to rip through their own flesh to free themselves from the pikes. But it was the sections of mounded sand to the south, one beside another, that Adam couldn't bring himself to contemplate. There were six of them in all. Six constant reminders of the debt they now owed and the enormity of the gift they'd been given.

They'd managed to collect Darren's and April's broken and gnawed bones, laying what little remained to rest in the same grave for fear of mixing up the bones. Jill insisted they would have preferred it that way regardless. Lindsay was buried beside them, her body mostly intact as the Swarm had only picked at her on their way to attacking the fresh meat, while Norman was beneath a much smaller mound beside her, his head the only part of him they'd been able to find. Gray's ashes were beneath the ground next to where he had laid his wife Carrie to rest, the tangled vines with their strange red blossoms already beginning to overtake the haphazardly-assembled cross marking her passage. The final grave belonged to the man who had stood up to Richard for them on the island and had been subsequently shot. For his kindness, they had hauled his ashes and burnt bones out of the charcoaled leftovers of the bonfire with Gray's and committed them to what they all now considered to be sacred ground. Here they could be properly mourned, properly thanked. It was a seemingly pathetic gesture, but it was the best they could do for now.

A gentle breeze rose from their right, carrying the smoke from the pit warming the kelp and blowing it over the graves and across the water. What appeared to be a rocky crag broke the choppy surface, parting the gray cloud and gaining height as it moved inland. A spiny mane capped its head and neck, spikes crowned with jagged wire-like filaments. Rather than the smooth contours of the equine it had once been, the taut skin stretched between sharp outcroppings along its neck and into its haunches, sloping down its tapered snout. Its eyes were a puzzle of turquoise and black marble within which Adam could find himself lost. As the strange creature stood at the edge of the lake, its spindly legs shin-deep in saltwater, Adam could only appreciate its unusual beauty, which had been lost during the previous days when the reclusive herd had slipped out of the lake at sunrise and sunset to feast on the bloated bodies of the Swarm, consuming their fill and dragging the scavenged carcasses back to wherever it was they lived under the landlocked sea.

Phoenix approached the steed, allowing it to sniff his open palm. It shook its head and whinnied, but presented its flank for Phoenix to stroke skin that felt like fuzzy flesh drawn snugly over a brittle framework of bone, working his hands toward the tall spines capping its shoulders. He swung up onto the horse's back, gripping the spikes on its neck. It tromped from side to side nervously before adapting to his weight and the gentle touch of the boy's right hand rubbing it behind the erect ears.

"Come on," Phoenix said without looking at Adam. He continued to slide his hand along the side of its neck, tracing the swell of its cheek.

Grabbing one of the bony spines, Adam swung up behind Phoenix, wrapping his arms around the boy and holding on for dear life. The behemoth's wings rose upward like the arms of a praying mantis before extending outward to reach their full length.

As the aura of the dawning sun faded from red to gold, the others emerged from the cave to see them off, shielding their eyes against the blinding glare.

"Be careful!" Evelyn called.

"And then some," Adam said, nearly squeezing Phoenix right through as the horse galloped forward along the tide, its wings billowing. It launched nearly vertically into the air, banking out over the lake. Adam looked back over his shoulder to see them walk out onto the white sand, too nervous even to wave.

There was a part of him that wished he could have stayed behind where it was warm and somewhat comfortable. While they weren't safe in the cavern, at least there was the element of familiarity, which was a far cry better than flying off into the vast unknown.

They needed to go. Either that or face the possibility of having to defend themselves without the benefit of fortified perimeters. That, and as much as he was thankful for the meals of stewed kelp from Evelyn's flourishing colonies that had sustained them through the first two days, he needed to find something a little more substantial.

With one last glance at his friends shrinking in front of the shadowed orifice, he turned to look ahead at the rising sun and their destination somewhere beneath, mouthing a silent prayer that he and Phoenix would return, and that the others would still be alive when they did.

ABOUT THE AUTHOR

Michael McBride lives with his wife and four children in the shadow of the Rocky Mountains, where he shoots people for money. He thanks you for joining him on this journey through the apocalypse and invites you to return for its conclusion in God's End: Trail of Blood. To explore the author's other novels and short fiction or to contact him directly, please visit:

www.mcbridehorror.com.

SPECIAL THANKS

Anna Torborg, Emma Barnes, and Snowbooks; Shane Staley; Dennis Duncan; Greg Gifune; Leigh Haig; Brian Keene; Troy Knutson; Don Koish; David Marty; Dallas Mayr; Elizabeth and Tom Monteleone, and the BBC grunts; Matt Schwartz; Tom Tessier; and my wife and family.